About the Authors

USA Today bestselling, *RITA*®-nominated, and critically-acclaimed author **Caitlin Crews** has written more than 100 books and counting. She has a Masters and Ph.D. in English Literature, thinks everyone should read more category romance, and is always available to discuss her beloved alpha heroes. Just ask. She lives in the Pacific Northwest with her comic book artist husband, is always planning her next trip, and will never, ever, read all the books in her to-be-read pile. Thank goodness.

Pamela Sadadi Yaye has a bachelor's degree in Christian Education and her love for African-American fiction prompted her to pursue a career in writing romance. When she's not working on her latest novel, this busy wife, mother and teacher is watching basketball, cooking or planning her next holiday. Pamela lives in Alberta, Canada with her gorgeous husband and adorable, but mischievous son and daughter.

Joss Wood's passion for putting black letters on a white screen is only matched by her love of books and travelling and her hatred of making school lunches and ironing. Fuelled by coffee and craziness, Joss is a hands-on Mum and, after a career in local economic development and business lobbying, she now writes full time. Surrounded by family, friends and books she lives in Kwa-Zulu Natal, South Africa with her husband and two children.

Hot Winter Nights

CAITLIN CREWS

PAMELA YAYE

JOSS WOOD

MILLS & BOON

First Published in Great Britain 2021
by Mills & Boon, an imprint of HarperCollins*Publishers* Ltd,
1 London Bridge Street, London, SE1 9GF

www.harpercollins.co.uk

HarperCollins*Publishers*
1st Floor, Watermarque Building,
Ringsend Road, Dublin 4, Ireland

HOT WINTER NIGHTS © 2021 Harlequin Books S.A.

Unwrapping the Castelli Secret © 2015 Caitlin Crews
Seduced by the Tycoon at Christmas © 2017 Pamela Sadadi
Hot Christmas Kisses © 2018 Joss Wood

ISBN: 978-0-263-30254-7

MIX
Paper from
responsible sources
FSC™ C007454

This book is produced from independently certified FSC™ paper to ensure responsible forest management.

For more information visit: www.harpercollins.co.uk/green

Printed and bound in Spain
by CPI, Barcelona

UNWRAPPING THE CASTELLI SECRET

CAITLIN CREWS

CHAPTER ONE

RAFAEL CASTELLI WAS entirely too familiar with ghosts.

He'd seen them everywhere in those first dark months following the accident. Every woman with anything resembling strawberry blond hair was his Lily in a certain light. A hint of her scent in a passing crowd, the suggestion of her delicate features across a busy train car, a low, faintly hoarse bit of feminine laughter in a packed restaurant. All Lily for a heart-stopping instant of wild recognition—and hope.

Always that delirious scrap of hope, as desperate as it was doomed.

He'd once chased a woman halfway across London before he'd realized that she wasn't Lily. That she couldn't have been Lily. His stepsister had died in that terrible crash on the rugged California coast north of San Francisco. And despite the fact that her body had never been recovered from the treacherous waters below that rocky cliff, despite the fact no one had ever found any proof that she'd died in the fire that had burned her car to ash, nothing, not tricks of light or three a.m. conspiracy theories or his own despairing heart playing games with him, could change that.

It had been five years. Lily was gone.

He understood, finally, that they weren't ghosts at all, these flashing glimpses of what might have been. They were his bitter, consuming regret mapped onto a hundred strangers, and none of them the woman he wanted.

But this ghost was different.

And the last, Rafael vowed as a deep, black fury surged through him. Five years was long enough to grieve what had never been, thanks to his own selfishness. More than long enough. It was time to move on.

It was a December late afternoon in Charlottesville, Virginia, a picturesque American university town nestled at the foot of the Blue Ridge Mountains, some three hours by car from Washington, DC, and a world away from his native Italy. Rafael had made the trip from the nation's capital by helicopter today, the better to tour the region's vineyards from above with an eye toward expanding the global reach of the Castelli family's historic wine business. As acting CEO—because his ailing father's immense pride did not allow for an official transfer of leadership to Rafael or his younger brother, Luca, while the old man still drew breath, which was as unsurprising as it was irritating—Rafael had taken many such trips in the past few years. Portugal. South Africa. Chile.

This latest trip to the central Virginia wine region was more of the same. The late-afternoon stop in self-consciously charming Charlottesville en route to a later dinner event with one of the local wine associations was the typical excursion to help promote the charm of the area. Rafael had expected it and in truth, the bustle of the holiday season made the entire town feel like an interactive Christmas card.

It was not unpleasant, he'd thought as they'd walked the outdoor mall, though he had never much cared for the holiday frenzy. Carolers were strewn along the pedestrianized street, their voices mingling and competing in the crisp air. Shoppers milled in and out of the brightly lit shops beneath festive lights and around clusters of street vendors hawking their wares, and Rafael's small group had ducked inside one of the cafés for strong local coffee to ward off the cold. And to battle any traces of jet lag, no doubt. Rafael had made his order a triple shot of espresso, *per piacere*.

And then he'd seen *her*.

The woman moved like poetry against the falling dark, the particular rhythm of her stride chiming deep inside him even though he knew better, drowning out the barrage of Christmas carols assaulting him from the café's overloud sound system.

It had been five years, but Rafael knew that walk in an instant. He knew the swing of those hips and the stretch of those legs. That irresistible roll as she strode past the window where he stood. He caught the flash of her cheek, nothing more.

But that *walk*.

This must stop, he ordered himself coldly. *Lily is dead.*

"Are you all right, Mr. Castelli?" the local wine association host asked worriedly from beside him. His brother, Luca, here in his capacity as global marketing director of Castelli Wine, was too busy on his mobile to do more then frown distractedly in Rafael's direction.

"I will be fine," Rafael gritted out. "Excuse me for a moment."

And he stalked out of the café, pushing his way through the milling holiday crowds and into the waning light.

For a moment, he thought he'd lost her, and he knew that was the best possible outcome of this tired old madness— but then he saw her again, moving on the far side of the mall with that gait that recalled Lily like a shout across the busy street, and that dark current of pure rage sparked in him all over again.

It wasn't Lily. It was never Lily. And yet every time this

happened, Rafael raced after the poor stranger who looked a bit too much like his memories and made a goddamned fool of himself.

"This will be the last time you indulge this weakness," he muttered to himself, and then he set out after this latest incarnation of the woman he knew—*he knew*—he'd never see again.

One more time to stamp out the last spark of that nasty little flame of hope that still refused to die. One last time to prove what he already knew: Lily was gone, she was never coming back, and he would never, ever see her equal.

And maybe, just maybe, he wouldn't look for her in all these strangers' faces if he hadn't been such a bastard to her in the first place.

Rafael doubted he'd ever shift the guilt of all he'd done from its usual place, crouched fat and greasy and bristling with malice in the spot where his soul should have been. But tonight, in this charming little town in a part of America he'd never visited before and likely wouldn't visit again, he would lay what he could of his wretched history to rest.

He didn't expect peace. He didn't deserve it. But he was done chasing phantoms.

She will be a stranger. She is always a stranger. And after you confirm that for the hundredth time, you will never doubt it again.

This had to end. He had to end it.

He couldn't see the face of his quarry, only the fine line of her back and the hint of her willowy form as she walked briskly away from him. She was wrapped up against the December chill in a long black coat and a bright scarf, with only hints of honey-colored hair peeking out from beneath the black knit hat she wore tugged low over her ears. Her hands were thrust deep into her pockets. She was weaving her way through the crowds in a manner that suggested she knew exactly where she was going, and she didn't look back.

And the memories rolled through him like waves against the rocks, crashing over him one after the next. Lily, the only woman who'd ever captured him so completely. Lily, whom he'd lost. Lily, his forbidden lover, his secret and dirty passion, whom he'd hidden from the world and then had to mourn as if she was no more than the daughter of his father's fourth wife. As if she had been nothing more to him than that.

He'd hated himself for so long now it was indistinguishable from that grief that never quite left him. That grief that had transformed him—turning him from a too-rich dilettante who'd been content to throw his family money around rather than make any himself into one of the most formidable businessmen in Italy.

That, too, had taken years. It had been another form of penance.

"Inside you is the seed of a far better man," Lily had said to him the last time he'd seen her, after he'd made her come and then made her cry: his specialty. "I know it. But if you keep going the way you're going, you'll kill it off before it ever has a chance to grow."

"You mistake me for someone who *wants* to grow," Rafael had replied with all that confidently lazy indifference he'd had no idea he'd spend the rest of his life hating himself for feeling. "I don't need to be a bloody garden, Lily. I'm happy as I am."

It was one of the last conversations they'd ever had.

His heart was a hard, almost painful drum inside his chest. His breath came like clouds against the deepening night. He tracked her past this novelty shop, that restaurant and a band of singers in period dress singing "Ave Maria" while he drank in *that walk* as if it was a prayer.

As if this time around, after all these years of regret, he could appreciate that it was the last time he'd ever see it.

He followed her as she left the clamor and bright mess of the downtown mall and started down one of the side streets, marveling at her hauntingly familiar silhouette, that figure he could have drawn in his sleep, the sheer perfection of this woman who *was not Lily* yet looked exactly the way he remembered her.

His Lily, stalking off down a foggy San Francisco street, claiming she wanted nothing more than to get the hell away from him and their twisted relationship at last. Back then he'd laughed, so arrogantly certain she'd come back to him the way she always did. The way she'd been coming back to him since the day they'd first crossed that line when she'd been nineteen.

Another tryst in a hall closet, perhaps, with his hand wrapped over her mouth to muffle her cries as they drove each other crazy only feet away from their families. Another stolen night in her bedroom in her mother's stately home in the moneyed hills of Sausalito, tearing each other apart in the stillness of the northern California night, hands in fists and teeth clenched against the pillows. A hotel room here, a stolen moment in the gardening shed of a summer rental there—all so tawdry, now, in his recollection. All so stupid and wasteful. But then, he'd been so certain there would always be *another*.

His mobile vibrated in his pocket; the assistant he'd left back in that café, he assumed, wondering where in the hell Rafael was. Or perhaps even his brother, Luca, irritated by Rafael's absence when there was work to be done. Either way, he ignored it.

The afternoon was falling fast into evening and Rafael was a different man now than the one he'd been five years ago. He had responsibilities these days; he welcomed them. He couldn't simply chase women across cities the way he had in his youth, though back then, of course, he'd done such things for entirely different reasons. Gluttony, not guilt. He was no longer the inveterate womanizer he'd been then, content to enjoy his questionable relationship with his stepsister in private and all his other and varied conquests in the bright glare of the public eye, never caring if that hurt her.

Never caring about much of anything at all, if he was honest, except keeping himself safe from the claws of emotional entanglements.

This is how it must be, cara, he'd told her with all the offhanded certainty of the shallow, pleasure-seeking fool he'd been then. *No one can ever know what happens between us. They wouldn't understand.*

He was no longer the selfish and twisted young man who had taken a certain delight in carrying on his shameful affair right under the noses of their blended families, simply because he could. Because Lily could not resist him.

The truth was, he'd been equally unable to resist her. A terrible reality he'd only understood when it was much too late.

He'd changed since those days, ghosts or no ghosts. But he was still Rafael Castelli. And this was the very last time he intended to wallow in his guilt. It was time to grow up, accept that he could not change his past no matter how he wished it could be otherwise and stop imagining he saw a dead woman around every corner.

There was no bringing Lily back. There was only living with himself, with what he'd done, as best he could.

The woman slowed that mesmerizing walk of hers, pulling her hand from her pocket and pointing a key fob at a nearby car. The alarm beeped as she stepped into the street

and swung around to open the driver's door, and the light
from the street lamp just blooming to life above her caught
her full in the face—

And hit him like a battle-ax to the gut.

There was a buzzing in his head, a dizzy, lurching thing
that almost cut him in half. She jerked against the car door
and left it shut, and he had the dim realization that he'd
barked out some kind of order. Or had it been her name?
She froze where she stood, staring back at him across the
hood of a stout little American wagon that could fit six
or seven Italian cars, the frigid sidewalk, the whole of the
night.

But there was no mistaking who she was.

Lily.

It could be no other. Not with those fine, sculpted cheekbones that perfectly framed her wide, carnal mouth that
he'd tasted a thousand times. Not with that perfect heart-
shaped face that belonged in a painting in the Uffizi. Her
eyes were still that dreamy, sleepy blue that reminded him
of California winters. Her hair poked out from beneath her
knit hat to tumble down over her shoulders, still that rich
summer honey, golds and auburns combined. Her brows
were the same shade, arched slightly to give her the look
of a seventeenth-century Madonna, and she looked as if
she had not aged a single day in five years.

He thought his heart might have dropped from his chest.
He felt it plummet to the ground. He took a breath, then another, expecting her features to rearrange themselves into a
stranger's as he stared. Expecting to jolt awake somewhere
to find this all a dream. Expecting *something*—

He dragged in a deep breath, then let it out. Another.
And it was still *her*.

"Lily," he whispered.

Then he was moving. He closed the distance between

them in a moment, and there was nothing but noise inside him. A great din, pounding at him and tearing at him and ripping him apart, and his hands shook when he reached to take her by the shoulders. She made a startled sort of sound, but he was drinking her in, looking for signs. For evidence, like that faint freckle to the left of her mouth, to mark that dent in her cheek when she smiled.

And his hands knew the shape of her shoulders even beneath that thick coat, slender yet strong. He had the sense of that easy fit he remembered, his body and hers, as if they'd been fashioned as puzzle pieces that interlocked. He recognized the way her head fell back, the way her lips parted.

"What are you doing?"

He saw her lips form the words, read them from her mouth, but he couldn't make sense of them. He only knew that was her voice—*her voice*—the voice he'd never expected to hear again, faintly husky and indisputably Lily's. It was like a sledgehammer through him, inside him. Wrecking him and remaking him at once.

And the scent of her, that indefinable fragrance that was some combination of hand lotion and moisturizer, shampoo and perfume, all rolled together and mixed with the simple truth of her beneath it all. All Lily. His Lily.

She was alive. Or this was a psychotic break. And Rafael didn't give much of a damn which.

He simply hauled her toward him and took her mouth with his.

She tasted the way she always had, like light. Like laughter. Like the deepest, darkest cravings and the heaviest need. He was careful at first, tasting her, testing her, his whole body exulting in this impossibility, this thing he'd dreamed a thousand times only to wake up without her, again and again across whole years.

But then, the way it always had, that electric thing that arced between them shifted, blasted into heat lightning and took him whole. So he merely angled his head for that perfect fit he remembered so well and devoured her.

His lost love. His true love.

Finalmente, he thought, his grasp on the English he'd been fluent in since he was a boy eluding him, as if only Italian could make any sense of this. *At last.*

His hands were in her hair, against her cheeks, when she jerked her mouth from his. Their breath mingled into another cloud between them. Her eyes were that impossible blue that had haunted him for half a decade, the color of the crisp San Francisco sky.

"Where the hell have you been?" he grated out at her, sounding more heavily Italian than he had in years. "What the hell is this?"

"Let go of me."

"What?" He didn't understand.

"You seem very upset," she said, in that voice that was etched into his soul, as much a part of him as his own. Her blue eyes were dark with something that looked like panic, which didn't make any kind of sense. "But I need you to let me go. Right now. I promise I won't call the police."

"The police." He couldn't make any sense of this, and only partly because of that great buzzing still in his head. "Why would you call the police?"

Rafael studied her, that lovely face he'd believed he'd never see again. Not in this life. There was heat on her cheeks now, staining them pink. Her mouth was slick from his. But she wasn't melting against him the way she always had before at his slightest touch, and if he wasn't entirely mistaken, the hands she'd lifted to his chest were pushing at him.

At him.

As if, for the first time in almost as long as he'd known her, she was trying to push him away.

Everything in him rebelled, but he let her go. And he more than half expected her to disappear into the darkness drawing tight around them, or a plume of smoke, but she didn't. She held his gaze for a long, cool moment, and then, very deliberately, she wiped her mouth with one hand.

Rafael couldn't define the thing that seared through him then, too bright and much too hot. He only knew it wasn't the least bit civilized.

"What the hell is going on?" he demanded, in the voice he only ever had to use once with his staff. Never twice.

Lily stiffened, but she was still looking at him strangely. Too strangely.

"Please step back." Her voice was low and intense. "We might appear to be alone here, but I assure you, there are all kinds of people who will hear me scream."

"Scream?" He felt something like ill. Or dull. Or—but there were no words for the devastation inside him. There was nothing but need and fury, grief and despair. And that terrible hope he'd held on to all this time, though he'd known it was unhealthy. He'd known it was a weakness he could ill afford. He'd known it was sentimental and morbid.

He'd considered it the least of his penance. But she was alive.

Lily was alive.

"If you assault me again—"

But the fact she was standing here, on a side street in Charlottesville, Virginia, made about as little sense to him as her apparent death had five years ago. He brushed aside whatever she was saying, scowling down at her as the haze began to recede and the shock of this eased. Slightly.

"How did you survive that accident?" he demanded. "How did you end up here, of all places? Where have you been all this time?" Her words caught up with him and he blinked. "Did you say *assault*?"

He hadn't imagined it. She edged away from him, one hand on the side of the car. Her gaze was dark and troubled, and she certainly hadn't greeted him the way he might have expected Lily would—if, of course, he'd ever allowed himself to imagine that she could really still be alive.

Not a ghost this time. The real, flesh-and-blood Lily, standing before him on a cold, dark street.

Even if she was looking at him as if he was a monster.

"Why," he asked, very softly, "are you looking at me as if you don't know who I am?"

She frowned. "Because I don't."

Rafael laughed, though it was a cracked and battered sort of sound.

"You don't," he repeated, as if he was sounding out the words. "You don't know *me*."

"I'm getting in my car now," she told him, too carefully, as if he was some kind of wild animal or psychotic. "You should know that I have my hand on the panic button on my key chain. If you make another move toward me, I will—"

"Lily, stop this," he ordered her, scowling. Or shaking. Or both.

"My name is not Lily." Her frown deepened. "Did you fall and hit your head? It's very icy and they aren't as good about putting down salt as they—"

"I did not hit my head and you are, in fact, Lily Holloway," he gritted out at her, though he wanted to shout it. He wanted to shout down the world. "Do you imagine I wouldn't recognize you? I've known you since you were sixteen."

"My name is Alison Herbert," she replied, eyeing him as if he'd shouted after all, and perhaps in tongues. As he'd done any of the wild, dark things inside his head, none of which could be classified as remotely civilized. "You look like the kind of man people remember, but I'm afraid I don't."

"Lily—"

She moved back and opened the car door beside her, putting it between them. A barrier. A *deliberate* barrier. "I can call nine-one-one for you. Maybe you're hurt."

"Your name is Lily Holloway." He threw it at her, but she didn't react. She only gazed back at him with her too-blue eyes, and he realized he must have knocked that cap from her head when he'd kissed her so wildly, as her hair gleamed in the streetlight's glow, a strawberry blond tangle. He recognized that, too. That indefinable color, only hers. "You grew up outside San Francisco. Your father died when you were a toddler, and your mother married my father, Gianni Castelli, when you were a teenager."

She shook her head, which was better than that blank stare.

"You're afraid of heights, spiders and the stomach flu. You're allergic to shellfish but you love lobster. You graduated from Berkeley with a degree in English literature after writing an absolutely useless thesis on Anglo-Saxon elegies that will serve you in no way whatsoever in any job market. You have a regrettable tattoo of your namesake flower on your right hip and up along your side that you got as an act of drunken rebellion. You were on a spring break trip to Mexico that year and sampled entirely too much tequila. Do you think I'm making these things up to amuse myself?"

"I think you need help," she said with a certain firmness that didn't match his memories of her at all. "Medical help."

"You lost your virginity when you were nineteen," he

threw at her, everything inside him a pitched and mighty roar. "*To me.* You might not remember it, but I bloody well do. I'm the love of your goddamn life!"

CHAPTER TWO

HE WAS HERE.

Five years later, *he* was here. Rafael. *Right here*.

Standing in front of her and looking at her as if she was a ghost, speaking of *love* as if he knew the meaning of the word.

Lily wanted to die on the spot—and for real this time. That kiss still thudded through her, setting her on fire in ways she'd convinced herself were fantasies, not memories, and certainly not the truth. She wanted to throw herself back in his arms, in that same sick, addicted, utterly heedless way she always had. Always. No matter what had happened or not happened between them. She wanted to disappear into him—

But she wasn't that girl anymore. She had other responsibilities now, far bigger ones. Far more important things to think about than her own dizzy pleasure or this destructively self-centered man who had loomed far too large over too much of her life already.

Rafael Castelli was the demon she carried inside her, the dark, selfish thing she fought against every single day of her life. The emblem of her bad behavior, all her terrible choices, her inability to think of anyone or anything but herself. The hurt she'd caused, the pain she'd meted out, whether intentional or not. Rafael was intimately wrapped up in all of that. He was her incentive to live the new life she'd chosen, so far away from the literal wreck of the old. Her boogeyman. The monster beneath her bed in more ways than one.

She hadn't expected that particular metaphor, that vivid memory she'd used as her guiding compass *away* from the person she'd been back when she'd known him, to bloom into life on a random Thursday evening in December. Right here in Charlottesville, where she'd believed she was safe. She'd finally started to *believe* she really could sink into the life she'd made as Alison Herbert. That she could fully become that other, better, new and improved version of herself and never look back.

"Should I go on?" Rafael asked in a tone of voice she couldn't remember him ever using before. Hard, uncompromising. Very nearly ruthless. It should have scared her, and she told herself it did, but what shuddered through her was far more complicated than that as it pooled hot and deep in her belly. Lower. "I've hardly scratched the surface of the things I know about you. I could write a book."

Lily hadn't meant to pretend she didn't know him. Not exactly. She'd been stunned. Frozen in some mix of horror and delight, and then horror *at* that delight. She'd been walking back to her car after running a few errands, had heard a noise behind her on the darkening street as she'd unlocked the car and there he'd been like a dark angel straight out of her nightmares.

Rafael.

She'd hardly had time to take him in. She'd had that flash of recognition—his lean and muscled form that she'd know anywhere in a sleek and extraordinarily well-cut black coat, his gorgeous face a symphony of male beauty from the thick, dark hair he wore cut closer than she remembered it to that mouth of his that had laughed with so little care and then tempted her beyond measure and tormented her beyond imagining—and that stunned, haunted, wondering look in his searing dark gaze.

And then none of that mattered, because he'd been kissing her.

His mouth on hers, after all this time. His taste, his touch. His heat.

Everything had disappeared. The street. The faint music from the outdoor mall in the air around them. The whole city, state, country.

The past five years, gone in a single blast of heat and hunger that had roared through her, blowing apart every single lie she'd been telling herself all this time. That she'd been infatuated with him and nothing more. That time and distance would erode that mad light between them, dimming it into nothing more than girlish silliness. That there was nothing to fear from this man who had been no more than a spoiled little rich boy who'd refused to give up a favorite toy—

The truth was so hot, so demanding, it burned. It told her things she didn't want to know—proved she was as much an addict as she'd ever been, and worse, as her own mother had always been. Clean for five years and that quickly a junkie again. It had shaken her so deeply, so profoundly, that she didn't know what might have happened next—but then she'd remembered.

With a thud so hard it should have toppled her, though it didn't. She'd yanked her mouth from his, appalled at herself.

Because she'd remembered why she couldn't simply fall into this man the way everything inside her yearned to do. Why she couldn't trust herself around him, not even for an instant. Why she had to make him go away again, no matter what it took.

But he was not looking at her as if he had the slightest intention of doing anything of the sort.

"It would be a work of fiction, then," she managed to say now. "If you wrote a book. Because none of those things ever happened to me."

His face changed, then. That haunted expression dimmed, and something far more considering gleamed gold there in the depths of his dark gaze.

"My apologies," he said softly. She felt how dangerous it would be to believe that tone of voice in the goose bumps that prickled all over her, though she kept herself from shivering in reaction. Barely. "Who did you say you were?"

"I'm not sure I want to share my personal information with some ranting madman on the street."

"I am Rafael Castelli," he said, and the way he said his name lilted through her like a song, lyrical and right. Yet another reason to hate herself. "If you don't know me, as you claim, the pertinent details would be these—I am the eldest son of Gianni Castelli and heir to the ancient Castelli fortune. I am acting CEO of the Castelli Wine Company, renowned the world over for my business acumen. I do not hunt women down in the streets. I do not have to do such things."

"Because rich men are so well-known for their reasonable behavior."

"Because if I was in the habit of accosting strange women in the street, it would have been noted before now," he said dryly. "I suspect countries would think twice before letting me cross their borders."

Lily shifted and tried to look the appropriate mixture of blank and confused. "I really think I should call nine-one-one," she murmured. "You're not making any sense."

"There is no need," he said, sounding more Italian than he had a moment ago, which made everything inside her feel edgy. Jagged. That and the tightness of his lean jaw were the only hints she could see of his anger, but she knew it was there. She could feel it. "I will call them myself. You were reported dead five years ago, Lily. Do you really imagine I will be the only person interested in your resurrection?"

"I have to go."

He reached out a hand and wrapped it over the top of her car door as if he intended to keep her there simply by holding the vehicle itself in place. Her curse was that she believed he probably could.

"There is no way in hell I'm letting you out of my sight."

Lily stared back at him, a war raging inside that she fervently hoped wasn't visible on her face. He had to leave. He *had* to. There was no other option. But this was Rafael. He'd never done a single thing he didn't want to do in as long as she'd known him—even back when he'd seemed far more languid and perpetually unbothered than this man who stood before her now, radiating a kind of authority she really didn't want to investigate any further.

"My name is Alison Herbert," she said again. She tipped her head back to meet his gaze, and then she told him the Alison story in all its particulars—save one crucial detail. "I'm originally from Tennessee. I've never been to California and I didn't go to college. I live on a farm outside of town with my friend and landlady, Pepper, who runs a dog boarding and day care facility. I walk the dogs. I play with them. I clean up after them and live in a little cottage there. I have for years. I don't know anything about wine and to be honest, I prefer a good beer." She lifted a shoulder and then dropped it. "I'm not who you think I am."

"Then you will have no problem submitting to a DNA test, to set my mind at ease."

"Why on earth would the state of your mind be of interest to me?"

"Lily has people who care about her." Rafael's shrug seemed far more lethal than hers, a weapon more than a gesture. "There are legal issues. If you are not the woman I would swear you are, prove it."

"Or," she said, distinctly, "I could reach into my pocket and produce the driver's license that proves I'm exactly who I say I am."

"Licenses can be forged. Blood work is much more honest."

"I'm not taking a DNA test because some crazy man on a street thinks I should," Lily snapped. "Listen. I've been more than nice, considering the fact you grabbed me, terrified me and—"

"Was that terror I tasted on your tongue?" His voice was like silk. It slid over her, through her, demolishing what few defenses she had in an instant. Reminding her again why this man was more dangerous to her than heroin. "I rather thought it was something else."

"Step away from this car," she ordered him. She couldn't let herself react. She couldn't let him see that he got under her skin. "I'm going to get in it and drive away, and you're going to let me."

"Not one of those things is going to happen."

"What do you *want*?" she hurled at him. "I told you I don't know who you are!"

"I want the last five years of my life back!" he thundered, his voice a loud, dark thing in the quiet of the street, bouncing back from the walls of the surrounding buildings and making Lily feel flattened. Punctured. "I want you. I've been chasing your ghost for half a decade."

"I'm not—"

"I went to your funeral." The thunder was a stark thing,

then, and far more painful because of it. It punched through her, leaving her winded. Wobbly. "I stood there and played your stepbrother, nothing more. As if my heart hadn't been ripped from my body and battered apart on the rocks where that car went off the road. I didn't sleep for months, for *years*, imagining you losing control of the wheel and plummeting over—" His fine lips pressed together, hard and grim, as he cut himself off. When he spoke again, his voice was hoarse. "Every time I closed my eyes I pictured you screaming."

She would never know how she stood there and stared back at him, as if he was talking about someone else. *He is*, she told herself fiercely. *The Lily Holloway he knew really did die that day. She's never coming back.*

And the Rafael she'd known had never cared about her—or anything—that much. Who was he kidding? She'd been but one of his many women at the time, and she'd accepted that because what else had she known? She'd learned how to lose herself in awful, narcotic men at her mother's knee.

"I'm sorry," she managed to say. "For everyone involved. That sounds horrific."

"Your mother never recovered."

But Lily didn't want to talk about her mother. Her bright and fragile and largely absent mother, who had shivered at the slightest wind, susceptible to every emotional storm that rolled her way. Her mother, who had self-medicated with ever more dangerous combinations of prescription pills, always under the aegis of this or that quack of a doctor.

"Did you know that she died eighteen months ago?" Rafael continued. "That wouldn't have happened if she'd known her daughter was still alive."

That one would leave deep, deep scars, Lily knew. But

she didn't crack. What she felt about her doomed and careless mother paled in comparison to what she had to keep safe here.

"My mother is in jail," she told him, and she had no idea how she managed to sound so even. "Last I heard she'd found Jesus, for the third time. Maybe this time it'll stick."

"These are all lies." He was too intense. His gaze was too penetrating. She was terribly afraid he could see straight through her, see everything. "What I can't understand is how you imagine you can tell them to my face. You can't really think I'm likely to believe them, can you?"

Lily didn't know what might have happened then. They were at a stalemate and she had no idea how to extricate herself from this—but then she heard voices calling to her from across the street.

Two of Pepper's clients stood there, a married couple who called her Alison and made polite enough conversation while she held herself still, icy with terror, waiting for them to ask after Arlo. But when they did, as they inevitably did because this was the South and people still took manners seriously here, she realized there was no need to panic. The man beside her didn't move a muscle. And why would he? It wasn't as if Rafael knew that name. He couldn't possibly know what it meant.

She was something like giddy with her relief when the couple moved on.

"I hope that clears things up for you," she said.

"Because they called you by this assumed name of yours?" Rafael's voice was mild. "Questions only lead to more questions. You've been living here for some time, clearly. You've made yourself part of this community." His expression was harsh. Something like unforgiving. "You had no intention of ever coming home, did you? You were content to let us mourn your death as if it was real."

He'd let go of her car door, and she slammed it shut then, aware of the way his dark eyes narrowed on her as she did. She ignored him, beeping the alarm on and swinging around again, heading back toward the mall. Where there would be lights and people. More people who knew her. More people to put between them and use as a barrier.

"Where are you going?" he asked, not particularly nicely. "Is this what you do now, Lily? You run away? Where will I find you next time—roaming the streets of Paraguay? Mozambique? Under an entirely different assumed name?"

She kept walking, and he fell into step beside her, which wasn't any kind of help. It made her remember far too many things best left shut away inside her. It made her think about things that could only hurt. He matched his athletic stride to hers, the way he always had. He was so close that if she merely leaned a little bit to the left, she could nudge up against his arm, which was the closest they'd ever come to public displays of affection back in the day.

She felt blinded with grief, then, and with that old, sick need that had taken over so much of her life back then. But she kept her eyes straight ahead and told herself it was the cold weather stinging at her eyes, nothing more.

There had to be a way out of this. There had to be a way to get rid of him. She had to keep Arlo safe. That was the only thing that mattered in the past five years and it was the only thing that she could let matter now.

She felt safer once they reached the crowd on the festive mall. Not that she thought Rafael was likely to abduct her or anything that required so much commitment—but if he'd had any thoughts in that direction, it would be a great deal harder surrounded by so many people.

"Are we shopping?" Rafael's voice was sardonic, managing to slice through the noise, the singing. The barricades she'd been erecting inside her as they'd walked. "This reminds me far more of the lonely little heiress I once knew."

"I thought I'd get something hot to drink and get out of the cold for a moment," she said, refusing to react outwardly to what he'd said. Though she had to blink hard to get the red haze to roll back, and it actually hurt to bite her tongue.

She hadn't been a lonely little heiress. There'd been little enough to inherit, first of all, outside her mother's house. But the poor little rich kid in this scenario had been bored, sybaritic party boy Rafael, beloved of C-list actresses, reality television pseudostars and a host of lingerie models. Those had been the women he'd paraded around with in public. Those had been the women he'd brought home with him, the women he'd taunted Lily with on all those terrible family vacations at Lake Tahoe, letting them drape their cosmetically enhanced bodies all over him and then making her admit her jealousy before he'd ease her pain a little with his clever fingers, that awful mouth of his and the things he could do with a few stolen moments against a locked door.

He was a terrible man, she reminded herself fiercely as they ducked out of the way of a kid on a skateboard. He'd been hideous to her, and worse, she'd let him. There was nothing here to be conflicted about. Everything between them had been twisted and wrong. She loathed who she'd been around him. The lies she'd told, the secrets she'd kept. She'd hated that life she'd been trapped in.

She refused to go back to it. She refused to accept that her only fate was to become her sad mother, one way or another. She refused to let the poison of that life, those people, infect Arlo. *She refused.*

Lily didn't wait to see if Rafael was following her—she knew he was, she could *feel* that he was right on her heels like an agent of doom—she simply marched down the mall until she reached her favorite café, then she tossed open the door and walked in.

Straight into another male body.

She heard an Italian curse that Rafael had taught her when she was a teenager—as pretty to the ear as it was profoundly filthy—and she jerked back, only to look up into another set of those dark Castelli eyes.

Damn it.

Luca, younger than Rafael by three years. The quieter, more solid stepbrother, to her recollection, but then, she'd never seen much besides Rafael. Luca looked as if she'd sucker punched him. Lily felt as if she'd sustained the same blow. It might have been possible to convince only Rafael that she was someone else—or so she'd been desperate to believe the whole walk here. But both Castelli brothers? There was no way.

She was completely and utterly screwed.

"Ah, yes," Rafael said from behind her, that sardonic tone of his wrapping around her, far hotter than the heat of the café or the shock in his brother's gaze. "Luca, you remember our late stepsister, Lily. It turns out she's been alive and well and right here in Virginia this whole time. Hale and hearty, as you can see."

"I'm not Lily," she snapped, though she suspected that was more desperate than strategic, especially with both men scowling at her. But there was only one man's scowl she could feel inside her, like acid. "I'm getting tired of telling you that."

Rafael's gaze was a blast of dark fire as he stepped to the side and then steered her out of the way of oncoming foot traffic, there in the café doorway, with a hand on her arm she couldn't shake off fast enough. But perhaps that was even less strategic, she thought, when his lush mouth quirked slightly—very much as if he knew exactly what his touch did to her, even all these years later.

As if he could feel the lick of that fire as well as she could.

He directed his attention to his brother. "Though, you will note, she does appear to be suffering from a convenient case of amnesia."

Which was not a solution, but was the best answer to her current situation, of course.

And it was how Lily decided, right there on the spot in that crowded little café, that amnesia was exactly what she had. In spades.

CHAPTER THREE

"THIS IS IMPOSSIBLE," was all that Luca said, while Lily pretended she wasn't affected by the shock on his face.

"Behold," Rafael answered him darkly, though that hot, furious gaze of his was on Lily, making her skin feel much too hot beneath her winter layers. "I bring you tidings of comfort and joy. Our own Christmas miracle."

"How?" Luca asked. It was the closest to shaken she'd ever heard him.

It made her feel awful. Hollow. But this was no time to indulge that.

The three of them shifted out of the flow of café traffic, over near the row of stools that sat at the window looking over the mall and all its holiday splendor. The Castelli brothers stood there like a six-foot-and-then-some wall of her past, staring at her with entirely too much emotion and intensity. She tried to look unbothered. Or perhaps slightly concerned, if that—the way a stranger would.

"How did she manage to walk away from that crash?" Luca asked. "How did she disappear for five years without a single trace?"

Lily had no intention of telling either one of them how easy that had been. All she'd needed to do was walk away. And then never, ever revisit her past. Never look back. Never revisit any of the people or places she'd known before. All she'd needed was a good enough reason to pretend that she'd had no history whatsoever—and then six weeks into her impetuous, spur-of-the-moment decision, she'd found she had the best reason of all. But how could she explain that to two Italian men who could trace their lineage back centuries?

Even if she'd wanted to explain. Which she didn't.

You can't, she reminded herself sharply. That was the trouble with the Castelli family. Any exposure to them at all and she stopped doing what she knew she should do and started doing whatever it was they wanted, instead.

"Oddly," Rafael replied, in that same dark tone, still studying her though he was clearly speaking to Luca, "she is claiming that she is a different person and that none of that happened to her."

"She is also standing right here in front of you and can speak for herself," Lily said tartly then. "I'm not claiming anything. Your confusion over my identity is very much your problem, not mine. *You* assaulted *me* on a dark street. I think I'm being remarkably indulgent, given the circumstances."

"You assaulted her?" Luca's dark brows edged up his forehead as he shifted his gaze to his brother. "That doesn't sound much like you."

"Of course not." But Rafael still did not look away from Lily as he said that.

Inside, in the warmth and the light of the café, she could see the hints of gold in those dark eyes of his that had once fascinated her beyond measure. And she could feel his mouth against hers again, a wild bright thing in all that December dark. She told herself what moved in her then was a memory, that was all. Nothing more than a memory.

"I don't think—" She almost said *your brother* but caught herself in the nick of time.

Would a stranger to these men know they were brothers at a glance? She thought the family resemblance was like a shout in a quiet room—unmistakable and obvious. Their imposing height, their strong shoulders, their rangy, rampantly masculine forms and all that absurd muscle that made them look carved to perfection. The thick black hair that, when left to its own devices, flirted with the tendency to curl.

Luca wore his in a haphazard manner he'd already raked back from his brow several times as they stood there. Rafael, by contrast, looked like some kind of lethal monk, with his hair so short and that grim look on his face. But they shared the same mouth, carnal and full, and she knew they even laughed in that same captivating, stunning way—using the whole of their bodies as if giving themselves over to pleasure was why they'd been placed on this earth.

Not that she could imagine this stark, furious, older version of Rafael laughing about anything—and she told herself she felt nothing at that thought. No pang. No sharp thing in the vicinity of her chest. Nothing at all.

She directed her attention toward Luca. "I don't think your friend is well."

"That's a nice touch," Rafael said flatly. "'Friend.' Very convincing. But I am not the one who is in some doubt as to his identity."

"I'm so glad you're here," Lily continued, still looking at Luca, though it was almost as if he appeared in silhouette, with Rafael the dark and brooding sun that was the only thing she could see no matter where she looked. "I'm not sure, but he might need medical attention."

Rafael said something in a sleek torrent of Italian that made Luca blink, then nod once, sharply. Clearly Rafael had issued an order. And it seemed that in this incarnation of the Castelli family, Rafael expected his orders to be followed and, more astonishing by far, they were. Because Luca turned away, toward a man and woman she'd completely failed to notice were sitting on the stools a few feet away watching this interaction with varying degrees of interest, and started talking to them in a manner clearly designed to turn their attention to him.

And off Lily and Rafael.

"I'm going to leave you in your friend's hands now," Lily told Rafael then, in a falsely bright sort of voice that she hoped carried over the shout of the espresso machine and some pop star's whiny rendition of a Christmas carol on the sound system.

Rafael's mouth moved again, another one of those too-hard quirks that felt wired directly to every last nerve in her body. It set them all alight and shivering. "Do you think so?"

"I have a life." She shouldn't have snapped that. It sounded defensive. A true stranger wouldn't be *defensive*, would she? "I have—" She had to be careful. So very careful "—things to do that don't include tending to strange men and their confusion over matters that have nothing to do with me."

"Why did you come here?" he asked, much too quietly, when she could see temper and pain and something far darker in gaze.

Maybe that was why she didn't throw herself out the door. That darkness that she could feel inside her, too. The guilt she couldn't quite shake. But she did deliberately misunderstand him.

"This is my favorite coffee shop in Charlottesville. I was hoping a peppermint mocha might wash away all of that weirdness out in the street, and give you time to sober up."

Amusement lit his dark gaze and it walloped her hard in the gut. So hard she saw stars for a moment.

"Am I drunk?"

"I don't know what you are." She tilted her head slightly. "I don't know *who* you are."

"So you have said."

Lily waved a dismissive hand in the air. "I think this must be a rich-man thing. You think you see someone you know in the street, so you hunt them down and demand that they admit they're that person, despite their insistence—and documented proof—that they're someone else. I'd end up in jail if I tried that—or on a psychiatric ward. But I imagine that's not a concern for someone as wealthy as you are."

"Has my net worth penetrated the shroud of your broken memory?" His voice should have left marks, it was so scathing. "I find that is often the case. It's amazing how many women I've never met can estimate my net worth to the penny."

"You told me you were rich." She used a tone she was quite certain no one had ever used on him before. One that suggested he was extraordinarily dim, though he looked more entertained by that than he did furious. "Not to mention, you're not exactly dressed like a vagrant, are you?"

"When will this performance end?" he asked softly.

"Right now." She straightened. "I'm going home. And I'm not asking you if that's all right with you. I'm informing you. I suggest you get a good night's sleep—maybe then you'll stop seeing things."

"What is amusing about that, Lily, is that tonight is the first time in five years that I haven't seen a ghost when I thought I saw you." He didn't look as if he found that even remotely amusing. She knew she didn't. "You are entirely real and standing right here in front of me, at long last."

She forced a smile. "They say everyone has a twin."

"If I were to open your coat and look beneath your shirt right now, what would I find?" he asked in the same softly menacing way.

"An assault charge," she retorted, her tone brisk. "And a potential jail sentence, God willing."

His mouth shifted into something not quite a smile. "A scarlet lily nestled in a climbing black vine, crawling over your right hip and stretching up your side, perhaps?"

His dark gaze was so intent, so absolutely certain, that it took her breath away. And it was far harder than it should have been to simply stand there. To do nothing. To keep herself from touching her side in wordless acknowledgment, jerking back as if he'd caught her or any of a hundred other little tells that would show him her guilt.

Not that he appeared to be in any doubt about her guilt. Or her identity.

"There are a number of good psychiatrists in the Charlottesville area," she told him when she was certain she could speak without any of that turmoil in her voice. Only the politeness she'd offer any random person she encountered, with a little compassion for someone so obviously nutty. "I'm sure one of them would see you for an emergency session. Your net worth will undoubtedly help with that."

He really smiled then, though it was nothing like the Rafael smiles of old, so bright and carefree he could have lit up the whole of Europe if he'd wanted. This one was hard. Focused. Determined—and still it echoed deep inside her like a touch.

She was so busy telling herself that he didn't affect her and he didn't get to her *at all* that she didn't move out of the way fast enough. She didn't even see the danger until it was too late. His hand was on her too quickly, his fingers brushing over her temple, and Lily didn't know how to react as sensation seared through her.

Would a stranger leap away? Or stand there, frozen in shock and disbelief?

"Get your hand off me right now," she gritted out, going with the frozen option—because that was what she was. Head to toe. She didn't think she could move if she'd wanted to, she was so rooted to the ground in what she told herself was *outrage*. She could feel his touch everywhere. *Everywhere.* Hot and right and perfect. As if all these years later, the merest brush of his fingers was all he had to do to prove that she'd been stumbling around in the cold black-and-white dark without him.

This was heat. *This* was color and light and—

This is dangerous! everything inside her shrieked in belated alarm.

"You got this scar skiing in Tahoe one winter," he murmured, his voice pitched low, as if those were words of love or sex instead of accusation as he traced the tiny mark she'd long since forgotten was there. Up, then down. The effect was narcotic. "You hit a patch of ice and then, shortly after that, a tree. You were lucky you didn't break anything except one ski. You had to walk down the side of the mountain, and you terrified the entire family when you appeared in the chalet, bleeding."

He moved closer, those dark eyes of his intense and moody, focused on that little scar she didn't even see anymore when she looked at herself. And surely the stranger she was pretending to be would have been paralyzed just as she was, then—suspended between the need to run screaming into the street and the desire to stay right where she was. Surely anyone would do the same.

Anyone for whom this man has always been a terrible addiction, a harsh voice inside told her.

But she still didn't move.

"And I had to make the sarcastic remarks of the bored older brother I never was to you," Rafael said gruffly. "Playing it off for our parents. Until later."

Lily blinked. She remembered *later*. He'd used the key she shouldn't have given him to her hotel room and found her in the shower. She could remember it too easily, too well, in too much detail. The steam. The sting of the hot water against her chilled skin. Rafael shouldering his way into the glassed-in little cubicle still fully dressed, his mouth uncharacteristically grim and a harsh light in his beautiful eyes.

Then his mouth had been on hers, and she'd wrapped herself around him, melting into him the way she always had. His hands had slicked over the curve of her hips, that damned tattoo she'd claimed she hated and he'd claimed he loved, until he'd simply dispensed with his wet trousers, picked her up and surged deep inside her with one slick, sure thrust.

"Don't ever scare me like that again," he'd muttered into her hair, and then he'd pounded them both into a wild, screaming oblivion. Then he'd carried her out of the shower, laid her out on the hotel bed and done it all over again. Twice.

She'd found that desperately romantic at the time, but then, she'd been a pathetic twenty-two-year-old under this man's spell that winter. Now, she told herself firmly, it was nothing more than another bad memory wrapped up in too much sex she shouldn't have been having with a man she never, ever should have touched.

"That is a very disturbing story with some deeply troubling family dynamics," she said now, batting his hand away from her face. "But it still doesn't make me this other woman, no matter how many stories you tell to convince yourself otherwise."

"Then you must take a DNA test and prove it."

She rolled her eyes. "Thank you, but I'll pass."

"It wasn't a suggestion."

"It was an order?" She laughed then, and kept it light somehow. She could see Luca looking over, and those people with him, and knew she'd stayed too long. She had to walk away, because a stranger would have done that long ago. "I'm sure you're used to giving lots of orders. But that doesn't have anything to do with me, either." She caught Luca's gaze and forced a tight smile. "He's all yours."

Lily started for the door then, and she expected Rafael to stop her. She expected a hand on her arm, or worse, and she told herself she *absolutely did not* feel anything like a letdown when nothing happened. She threw the door open and then, though she knew better, she couldn't help looking back over her shoulder.

Rafael stood where she'd left him and watched her, dark and beautiful and harsher than she'd ever seen him before. She repressed a shiver and told herself it was the December evening. Not him.

"*Mi appartieni*," he said, soft and fierce at once. And she understood that little scrap of Italian. He'd taught it to her a long time ago. *You belong to me.*

Lily sniffed, the cold night in her hair and slapping at her cheeks.

"I don't speak Spanish," she managed to say, though her voice was rougher than it should have been had she really not been able to tell the difference between Spanish and Italian. "I'm not her."

Once she was gone, swallowed back up by the thick Virginia night, everything inside Rafael went still. Quiet. From that insane buzzing when he'd realized it was really, truly her to a sharp clarity he couldn't recall ever feeling before.

His brother and their wine association host were talking, and his assistant was trying to show him something business related on his mobile screen, but Rafael simply slashed a hand through the air and they all subsided.

"There is a kennel outside of town run by someone called Pepper," he told his aide in rapid-fire Italian. "Find it." He shifted his gaze to Luca. "Call Father's personal doctor and ask him how a person could have walked away from that accident five years ago and what kind of head injuries she might have sustained when she did."

"Do you believe she truly has amnesia?" Luca asked. "It sounds like something out of a soap opera. But it is Lily, certainly."

"There is no doubt about that whatsoever," Rafael agreed. He'd known it was Lily the moment he'd seen her walk past this window. All the rest was mere confirmation of a truth he already knew, and the taste of her in his mouth after much too long.

Luca stared at him for a moment. "Your grief at her death was extreme. I am closer to her in age and I was less affected. You altered the whole of your life afterward, very much as if…"

Rafael only stared back at his younger brother, brows raised in challenge, daring him to finish that sentence. He didn't know what Luca saw on his face, but the younger man only nodded, very wisely checked what looked like a smile and then pulled out his mobile.

It took very little time to get the answers he'd requested, dispatch the wine association woman off to tender their apologies to their would-be dinner companions and set out to find Lily in the car his assistant had waiting for them a block outside the pedestrianized area.

"If she is faking this memory loss," Luca said as he lounged in the back of the sleek vehicle with Rafael, "she might be gone already. Why would she stay? She obviously didn't want to be found."

Rafael kept his gaze out the window as the car slipped through the streets and then out into the fields, barren this time of year and gleaming beneath a pale moon. He didn't think Lily would have moved on yet, with that same gut-deep certainty that told him she was faking this whole thing. She'd been so adamant that she was this other woman, this *Alison*. He thought the stubborn girl he'd known was far more likely to dig in her heels and brave it out than turn and run—

But the truth is, you don't know her at all, a dark little voice inside him whispered harshly. *Because the girl you knew would never have walked away from you.*

"We have a responsibility, as the closest thing Lily has left to any kind of family, to determine that she is not suffering from some kind of post-traumatic stress brought on by the accident," Rafael said. "At the very least."

The words came so easily to him, when deep down, he knew they were excuses. *Lily was alive.* That meant he would do whatever he must to claim her the way he should have done five years ago.

But he didn't want to say that to his brother. Not yet.

It was all for the best, he thought, that Luca did not respond.

The roads were emptier the farther they got from the center of Charlottesville, and the land on either side of the car was beautiful. Stark trees with their empty branches rose over fields still white from the last snow. This was rich, arable land, Rafael knew. Lily had always loved the extensive Castelli vineyards in the northern Sonoma Valley. Perhaps it should not surprise him that she'd found a place to live that was reminiscent. Gnarled vines and plump grapes had been a part of her life since she'd been sixteen and not at all pleased her mother was remarrying.

And even less pleased with him.

He could remember it all so clearly as the car made its way through the frozen Virginia fields. Rafael had been twenty-two. Their parents had gathered them together in the sprawling château that served as the Castelli Wine hub of operation and foremost winery in the States.

And Francine Holloway had been exactly what they'd expected. Beautiful, if fragile and fine featured, with masses of white-blond hair and sky-blue eyes. She'd trembled like a high-strung Thoroughbred and spoken in the kind of soft, high-pitched voice that made a certain sort of man lean in closer. Rafael's father was precisely that type. He'd loved nothing more than wading in and solving the problems of broken, pretty things like Francine—a preference that dated back to Rafael's mother, who had spent many years, before and after the divorce, institutionalized in a high-end facility in Switzerland.

Rafael had expected the teenaged daughter to be much the same as the mother, especially with such a wispy, feminine name. But this Lily was fierce. Laughably so, he'd thought, as she'd sat stiffly on an overwrought settee in the formal sitting room at the château and scowled through the introductions.

"You do not appear to hold our parents' mutual happiness foremost in your heart," he'd teased her after an endless dinner during which his father had delivered the sort of speeches that might have been moving had Francine not been the old man's fourth wife, and had Rafael not heard them all before.

"I don't care about our parents' happiness at all," she'd retorted, without looking at him. That had been different. Most girls her age took one look at him and melted into shallow little puddles at his feet. That hadn't been arrogance on his part. It had been pure, glorious fact— though he'd been, by his own estimation, far too worldly and sophisticated to sample the charms of such young, silly creatures. This one, apparently immune, had sniffed, her gaze trained somewhere far off in the distance through the great windows. "Which is about how much they care about ours, I imagine."

"I'm sure they care," Rafael had said, thinking he might soothe her girlish fears with the wisdom of his years. "You have to give them a chance to get over how perfect they imagine they are for each other so they can pay attention to their lives again."

But Lily had turned to face him, that heart-shaped face of hers still faintly rounded with youth, those impossible eyes scornful. She'd been dressed in a perfectly appropriate sundress that showed nothing untoward at all and yet there had been something about the way she'd worn the masses of her strawberry blond hair tumbling in every direction, or the fact that her shoulders were far too smooth, that had made Rafael wonder what it would be like to touch her—

He'd been horrified.

"I don't need a big brother," she'd told him baldly, compounding his shock at the direction of his own thoughts. "I don't want the unsolicited advice, especially from someone like you."

"Someone like me?"

"Someone who dates people purely to end up on tabloid television shows, which I'm sure keeps you super relevant in the world of the vapid and the rich. Congrats. And I don't need you to fill me in on my mother's ridiculous patterns. I know them all too well, thank you. Your father is the latest in a long line of white knights who never quite manage to save her. It won't last."

She'd turned back to the view, her manner clearly dismissive, but Rafael had not been accustomed to being dismissed. Especially not by teenage girls who were usually much more apt to follow him around and giggle. He hadn't been able to imagine Lily Holloway doing anything of the sort.

"Ah," he'd said, "but I think you'll find it will last."

She'd heaved a sigh but hadn't looked at him again. "My mother's relationships have the shelf life of organic produce. Just FYI."

"But my father is a Castelli." He'd only shrugged when she'd looked back at him then, her nose wrinkled as if he was more than a little distasteful. "We always get what we want, Lily. Always."

Sitting in the back of his car as it turned from the main country road and headed down a smaller, private lane lit with quiet lights shaped like lanterns, Rafael still didn't know why he'd said that. Had he known then? Had he suspected what was to come? Lily had hated him openly and happily for three more years, which had distinguished her from pretty much every other woman on the planet. She'd insulted him, laughed at him, mocked him and dismissed him a thousand times. He'd told himself she was obnoxious. He'd told himself she was jealous.

"She is unbearable," he'd growled at Luca once, when Lily had spent an evening singing pointed old songs at him and his date.

"But your date really is acting her shoe size instead of her age," his brother had replied, with a lazy grin. "Lily's not wrong."

And then had come that fateful New Year's Eve party at the château in Sonoma. Rafael had perhaps had too much of the Castelli champagne. He'd long told himself he was simply drunk and she must have been, too, but he'd had five long years thinking she was dead and gone to admit to himself that he hadn't been anything like drunk. He'd known exactly what he'd been doing when she'd sauntered past him in the upstairs hall of the family wing, in what he'd openly called "hooker shoes" earlier and a dress he'd thought trashily short. Her hair had been tumbling down the way it always had back then, sliding this way and that. The scent of her, a sugared heat, had been maddening.

"If you're looking for *Calliope*," she'd said, and had managed to make his then girlfriend's ridiculous name sound like an insult, "she's probably in the nursery with the other children. Your father hired a babysitting service." She'd smirked at him. "He was obviously expecting you."

Rafael had known that the last thing in the world he should have done was reach over, slide his palm around her neck and yank that smart mouth to his. Of course he'd known. He'd imagined he would kiss her, she would punch him and he would laugh at her and tell her that if she wasn't angling to take Calliope's place, she should keep quiet.

But one touch of her mouth with his, and everything had changed.

Everything.

And you ruined it, he told himself savagely then, as an old farmhouse came into view at the end of the lane. *Because that is what you do.*

The car pulled up in front of the bright old house and was promptly surrounded by a pack of baying dogs. Rafael climbed out of the car as a silver-haired woman charged out of the house and straight toward them in some misguided attempt to corral her charges.

But despite the barking and howling and general din,

Rafael knew it the moment Lily appeared on the step behind the older woman, as if everything else fell quiet. He drank her in. Again. She was no longer wearing her coat and scarf, and he couldn't keep himself from tracing the fine, elegant lines of that willowy body of hers. Her jeans were snug, making his mouth water, and the long-sleeved shirt she wore hugged her breasts and made him realize how hard and hungry he was for her—even in this sea of animals.

And even if she looked horrified to see him.

"This is stalking!" she threw at him from her place on the steps. "You can't hunt me down at my home. You don't have any right!"

Before Rafael could reply, a streaking shape shoved past her and would have hurtled itself down the steps and into the chaos had Lily not reached out and grabbed it.

Not an it. A boy. A small one.

"I told you to stay inside no matter what," Lily told him sharply.

"Arlo is barely five," the older woman said from somewhere off to the side where, Rafael was dimly aware, she'd managed to move all the dogs into a fenced-off pen. But he couldn't look away from Lily. And the boy. "He doesn't get 'no matter what.'"

The little boy looked at the older woman, then angled his head back to look up at Lily, who still held him by the collar of his shirt.

"Sorry, Mama," he said, angelically, and then he grinned up at her.

It was a mischievous grin. It was filled with light and laughter and the expectation that his sins would be forgiven in an instant, simply because he'd wielded it. Rafael knew that smile well. He'd seen a version of it on his brother's face throughout Luca's whole life. He'd seen it in his own mirror a thousand times more.

His heart stopped beating. Then started again with a deafening, terrible kick that should have knocked him to the ground. He couldn't quite understand why it hadn't.

"You don't have the right to be here," Lily said again, her cheeks flushed and her eyes glittering, and Rafael didn't know how he could want her this badly. He'd never understood it. And it was back as if she'd never been gone, a yearning so deep it was like an ache inside him.

But it didn't matter any longer. None of that mattered. The little boy didn't resemble the fair woman he'd called Mama at all. He had Rafael's dark curls and the Castelli dark eyes. He looked like every picture Rafael had ever seen of himself as a child, scattered all over the ancestral Castelli home in northern Italy.

"Are you so certain I don't have the right to be here, *Alison*?" Rafael asked, amazed he could speak when everything inside him was a shout again, long and loud and drowning out the world. "Because unless I am very much mistaken, that appears to be my son."

CHAPTER FOUR

THEY LANDED AT the private Castelli airstrip, high in the far reaches of northern Italy in the shadow of the towering Dolomites, just after dawn the following morning. Daylight was only beginning to stretch out pink and crystalline over the jagged spires and craggy, snowcapped heights of the sharply imposing mountains on either side of the narrow valley. Lily stared out of the window as the plane taxied down the scenic little runway, feeling as if someone had kicked her in the stomach.

She'd never imagined she'd see this place again. For years now she'd told herself she didn't want to see it or anything else the Castellis owned again, including those wine bottles with their distinctive labels in the liquor store—yet there was no mistaking the way her heart leaped as the private jet touched down. There was no denying the fact that this felt a whole lot more like a homecoming than it should. Certainly more than was safe.

Last night had been the second-worst night of her life, all things considered.

She'd known on the long drive home from Charlottesville after she'd left Rafael in that café that he wasn't likely to simply disappear. Not Rafael. He might have been spoiled rotten when she'd known him, a being created entirely out of wealth and privilege and more than happy to exploit both to serve his own ends—but he'd always gotten what he'd wanted. Lily being but one in a long line of things he'd taken because he could.

She'd sped along the dark country roads, hardly seeing the cold winter beauty of this place she'd come to call home. Lost in that kiss again. Lost in *him*. If it had been only her, she would have left then and there. Just kept on driving until she became someone else, somewhere else. She'd done it before. She knew exactly what it took to disappear without a trace.

But she wasn't twenty-three and desperate any longer, and there was Arlo now. Her beautiful, magical little boy. She'd turned it over and over in her head all throughout that drive, but she couldn't see how she could legitimately uproot Arlo and make *him* act like he was in the witness protection program for the rest of his life simply because *she* didn't want to deal with his father.

His father.

It still made her shiver to think of Rafael that way.

She could remember when she'd confirmed she was pregnant as vividly as if it had happened last night out there on those lonely country roads. She'd been dead for six weeks by then. Every day that she'd stayed away from her old life had been easier than the one before, because it was that much harder to go back. Too much time had passed. A day or two's worth of confusion, maybe a couple of weeks—she could have explained that away in the wake of her accident. But six whole weeks without so much as a scratch on her? That indicated intent, she'd thought. They'd know she'd disappeared deliberately.

Lily had looked at the coverage of her car accident from a library computer in Texas once, early on, but that had been a mistake she hadn't repeated. Seeing the people that she'd loved grieving for her loss had made her feel like the lowest kind of worm. A truly despicable human being. How could she walk back into their lives having caused them so much pain? What could she say?

Oh, sorry, everybody, I thought I wanted to make a clean break from all this and making you think I died horribly in that accident seemed like a good idea at the time...

After a few weeks of feeling strangely thick and deeply ill in turns, she'd taken a pregnancy test in a truck stop bathroom near the Missouri-Arkansas border. She could remember every detail of that winter morning. The sound of the big rigs outside. The chill in the air that seemed to have crept deep into her bones in the unheated little stall. The way her stomach had sunk down to the dirty floor and stayed there as she'd stared in an unmitigated horror at the positive test in her hand for what might have been whole years.

There'd been no going back. She'd understood several things with a rush of clarity in that badly lit bathroom in the middle of nowhere. That, despite everything—like the memorial service they'd held for her in Sausalito a few weeks after the accident—she'd believed until that moment that she might go back someday. That she'd pretended it wasn't an option for her while holding it there in reserve, tucked away in the back of her mind.

And that the fact she'd been pregnant with Rafael's child meant that door was forever closed to her.

It had been bad enough that she'd had a relationship with Rafael for all those years, no matter who else he'd been seeing and no matter how badly their families would have reacted to it if they'd known. It had been twisted and it had been wrong, given the fact her mother had insisted on referring to Rafael and Luca as *your big brothers* at every opportunity. How could she bring a baby into that gnarled, sick mess? Not to mention, she'd had no idea how Rafael might behave in the face of real adversity. Would he deny he was the father? Would he order her to terminate the pregnancy?

How had her life come to this? she'd wondered. That she'd felt she had no option but to walk away from everything she knew—only to discover that she'd made a new life with a man she obviously didn't know at all if she had so little idea how he might react or what he might do.

She'd vowed then and there that she would raise this child better than this squalid little beginning in a truck stop bathroom. That she would give her baby a fresh start in a new place where her sick need for Rafael—like her own mother's varied addictions that had marked Lily's own life so deeply—was no longer a factor. Where the child could come first, and not her—the very opposite of how she'd been raised.

And she'd done a good job sticking to all of those vows, she'd thought last night as she'd pulled up in front of the farmhouse. Arlo had come hurtling outside as she'd parked, heedless of the wintry weather the way he always was—as excited and bouncy as the dogs who romped along with him. She'd caught his hot and squirmy little body against hers in a hard hug, and had poured all her regrets and apologies into the way she squeezed him tight until he wriggled free.

Because she'd known it was only a matter of time, and sure enough, they hadn't even started their usual nightly dinner with Pepper when the car had pulled up outside. She'd tried to hold back the inevitable that little bit longer—but there had been no stopping it. On some level, she'd known that since she'd looked up and seen Rafael on the street.

And it had been even worse than she'd imagined.

She'd known that Arlo took after his father, of course, but it had been one thing to know it and another entirely to *see* it in the flesh. It had made her heart flip over in her chest and her eyes prickle with heat…

But then Rafael had turned that frozen, astonished glare on her, his eyes so dark they'd made the deep December night around him seem bright by comparison. And while it hadn't been as terrifying or dramatic as that car crash five years ago, Lily had known that it amounted to the same thing.

One life was over. A new one was beginning—whether she wanted it or not.

It had all been very cut-and-dried. There had been no mistaking the connection between father and son. It was written on both their faces, as obvious as the sun. And though Lily had valiantly stuck to her Alison story, which included a part about a drug dealer boyfriend who'd conveniently died after helping make Arlo, Pepper had been involved in the conversation this time.

Pepper, who'd confirmed that yes, Alison had that exact tattoo that Rafael mentioned, which had made Rafael's mouth curve in a way that had in turn made Lily's heart kick at her. And no, Pepper had said when pressed, she'd never met a single person from Alison's life before Charlottesville. And therefore, no, there was no corroboration to any of the Alison stories at all.

Only what Lily had told her.

"I told you what I know," Lily had said at that point, and she'd worried that the lies were like tattoos she wore on her face. That they were that bright, that indelible. "Everything I know."

Lily had been involved in a serious car accident on the winding California coastal road five years ago, Rafael had said—for Pepper's benefit, presumably—and Luca had confirmed. Her body had never been found. Now they knew why.

"How can you explain the fact that I'm here and don't remember you?" Lily had demanded, as Pepper had stared at her from across the table as if looking for the truth on her face. Or those terrible tattoos Lily was sure she could *feel* stamped across her cheekbones. "This doesn't make any sense."

"I don't know how a woman could go over the side of a cliff on the Sonoma Coast and yet turn up unharmed five years later on the other side of the country, with a memory of a completely different woman's life and a child who is inarguably mine," Rafael had said, a seething fury in his voice and in his eyes though he'd sat at Pepper's table so easily. So calmly. As if he was a friend instead of a foe—but Lily couldn't accuse him of that if she was pretending she didn't know him, could she? Maybe a stranger wouldn't be able to read him as well as she could. "I only know that you are the same woman. That means it happened, whether it makes sense or not."

And the truth was, there had been no need to trot out all the old pictures Rafael apparently kept cached on his mobile and ready to show, because this game had ended the moment Pepper had seen Rafael next to his son.

His son.

"This is a good thing," Pepper had whispered fiercely, hugging Lily as the Castelli brothers had led them away from the only home Arlo had ever known. "Everyone should know who they really are, honey. And that little boy needs his father."

Lily had questioned whether anybody needed Rafael Castelli, especially the child she had no intention of allowing him to corrupt, but she'd known better than to say that out loud. And it had been out of her hands. She'd been utterly outmaneuvered. The only card she could possibly have played was a demand for a blood test as some kind of stalling tactic—but to what end? She already knew what it would say.

And anyway, Rafael had anticipated that move.

"We will take the helicopter back to Washington, DC," he'd told her in that cool way of his, at such odds with her memories of his tempestuousness and that ferocious gleam in his gaze. "Where a suitably discreet doctor is waiting to perform the necessary blood work. We will know the whole biological truth before we land in Italy. If there has been some mistake, I promise you that the Castelli family will see to it that you and your son have a lovely holiday in Italy before we return you back here to your home, safe and sound."

"Wonderful," she'd retorted, baring her teeth in some approximation of a smile. "I've always wanted to see Venice. Before it sinks."

The jet rolled to a stop on the Castelli airfield, jerking her back into the wholly unwelcome present. Arlo was already bouncing up and down in his seat beside her with his usual boundless energy, and she could hardly blame him for taking off at a dead run once the plane's door opened and the cold, crisp mountain air poured in.

She took her time, but there was only so much dawdling she could do before she, too, had to step off the plane and climb down the metal steps. Putting her well and truly back in Italy. The truth of that felt like a blow. And it was even more beautiful here than she remembered it, so stunning it actually hurt—the soaring heights of the Alps dressed up in their winter whites, the blue sky with hints of pink and coral from the exultant dawn still fading away as she watched—and the man who waited for her at the foot of the steps as darkly gorgeous and even more dangerous than the view.

Rafael slid his mobile into his pocket as she stepped onto the solid, frozen ground beside him. Lily refused to look at him, and then despaired of herself if something so small and pointless was her only potential rebellion. *Pathetic.* She could feel her heart in her throat, and for the first time in her entire life, thought it was within the realm of possibility that she might faint.

Don't you dare! she snapped at herself. And not because fainting was a weakness, though it likely was and she didn't want to show any weakness here. But because she knew Rafael would catch her and the very last place she needed to be, ever again, was in his arms.

She kept her gaze trained on Arlo, who was chasing his uncle up and down the otherwise empty runway, kept as it was for the family's use alone. A gleaming black Range Rover waited at a discreet distance, poised to sweep them all down to the grand old house that lounged across several acres at one end of the crystal-blue mountain-rimmed alpine lake the locals called Lago di Lacrime.

Lake of Tears, Lily thought darkly, glaring in the direction where she knew the lake waited, out of sight behind the nearest wall of alpine rock. *How appropriate.*

"I'm afraid the results of the blood tests are in and allow no further room for debate," Rafael told her then, his voice quietly triumphant in a way that made her skin feel shrunken down too tight against her own bones. "You are Lily Holloway. And Arlo is very much our son."

She should feel something big, Lily thought then. Panic. Desperation. Even the polar opposite of that—a pervasive sense of relief, perhaps. Or perhaps of homecoming, after all these years of hiding.

But what she felt, instead, was profoundly sad.

Our son, he'd said, as if they were like other people. As if that was a possibility. As if they hadn't ruined each other, down deep into their cores, so comprehensively that even the past five years hadn't healed it or changed it at all.

Lily didn't think anything ever could.

They stood there together in one of the most gorgeous and remote spots in the world. The thrust of the fierce mountains was exhilarating, the sky bluer by the moment while the crisp wind danced through her hair and moved over her face like a caress, and it was beautiful. It was more than beautiful. And yet all she could see was the dark, twisted past that had brought them here. Her terrible addiction to him and his profound selfishness. Their dirty, tawdry secrets. The awful choices she'd made to escape him, as necessary as they were unforgivable.

This was no new start. It was a prison sentence. And the only thing she knew for sure was that while Rafael was responsible for her son—the single greatest thing in her life and, as far as she could tell, her singular purpose on this earth—Rafael was also the reason she'd had to burn down every bridge and walk away from everything she'd ever loved.

And Arlo was worth that. Arlo was worth anything.

But that didn't mean she had the slightest idea how she would survive proximity to Rafael again now.

"I don't know how to respond to that," she told him, long after the silence between them had grown strained and awkward and possibly revealing, too. That was what made her tell him as much of the truth as she could. "I don't feel like Lily Holloway. I don't know who that is. I certainly don't understand who she was to you."

"Never fear," Rafael said, his voice soft but somehow containing all the might of those mountains looming up above them, solid rock and sheer, dizzying magnitude, and all of that dark heat besides. "I'll teach you."

Rafael had no idea what to do with himself now that he'd brought Lily and her son—*his* son—back to Italy.

It was a novel, distinctly unpleasant sensation.

He heard his brother walk into the cozy, private study he used as his office in the great old house, but he didn't turn away from the window where he stood. He'd been there some time, still gripped in the same tight fist that had held him fast since Virginia. Before him, the pristine alpine lake stretched off into the low afternoon mists that concealed the small, picturesque village that adorned its far end and the tall mountains that thrust up like a fortress behind it, as if to protect it.

And much closer, down in the gardens that were little more than a suggestion beneath packed and frozen earth this time of year, the five-year-old child who was indisputably his own ran in loopy circles around the woman who claimed she could not remember Rafael at all.

He was certain she could. More than certain. He'd seen it in those lovely eyes of hers the way he'd always seen her need. Her surrender. He knew she was lying as sure as he'd known who she was when he'd seen her on the street.

What Rafael didn't know was *why*.

"Are you planning to speak?" he asked Luca with perhaps more aggression than necessary. "Or will you loom there like one of the mountains, silent and disapproving?"

"I can speak, if you like," Luca replied, sounding wholly unaffected by Rafael's tone, much as he always did. "But the stories I have to tell are far less interesting than yours, I think."

Rafael turned then and eyed his little brother. "I thought you were heading down to Rome tonight."

"I am. I imagine you and Lily have a bit more to talk about than she and I do." The sound of a child's excited laughter wafted up from the gardens then, as if on cue, and hung there between them. Luca only smiled. "All of those interesting stories, for example, that you still haven't seen fit to tell me."

They looked at each other across the relatively small room. The fire licked at the grate. The December wind shook the windows, sweeping down from the heights of the mountains and off the surface of the freezing lake. And outside, a little boy was running hard enough to make himself dizzy in the very same spot they'd done so themselves, though in their case, it had been entirely without any parental supervision from the increasingly unwell woman who had never wanted to be a mother in the first place.

Rafael had never intended to have a child of his own. He didn't have the slightest idea what to do now it turned out he had one, without his permission. Without his knowledge, even. Thanks to a woman who had run from him and then concealed that child's very existence from him for all these years.

Deliberately. She had done this *deliberately*.

He didn't know what he felt. Or more precisely, which dark thing he should feel *first*.

"Have you come to ask me something?" Rafael asked after a moment or two dragged by. "Or is this the sort of tactic you use in negotiations, hoping the other party will fall to pieces in the silence?"

Luca laughed, but he didn't deny that. "I would ask you to confirm that you did, in fact, sleep with our sister—"

"Stepsister," Rafael growled. "A crucial distinction, I think you are aware."

"—but that would be for dramatic effect, nothing more." Luca waved a languid hand. "I already know the answer. Unless you have a contorted tale of a petri dish and a turkey baster you'd like to tell me, in which case, I am all ears."

Luca proceeded to drape himself over the nearest chair, lounging there as if this really was a bit of mildly entertaining theater and not Rafael's life. But then, he supposed that for Luca, it was.

Rafael sighed. "Was there a question in there somewhere?"

"Is this why she ran away, then?" Luca's voice was light. Almost carefree, but Rafael didn't quite believe it. He'd seen the shock on Luca's face when she'd walked into that café.

"I couldn't say why she ran away," Rafael replied evenly. Or faked her own death, if he was to call this situation what it truly was. That was what she'd done, after all. Why pretty it up? "And she doesn't appear to have any intention of telling me."

Luca watched him for a moment, as if weighing his words. "It's uncanny, how much that little boy looks like you. Father might well have a heart attack when he sees him. Or lapse further into dementia, never to return, mumbling on about ghosts in the family wing."

"I will be certain to schedule time to worry about that," Rafael assured him, his lips twitching despite himself. "But as I do not expect the old man and his brand-new child bride until much nearer Christmas, I think we can hold off on the family melodrama until then."

"*Buon Natale*, brother," Luca murmured, and then laughed again. "It will be the most joyous Christmas yet, I'm sure. Ghosts and resurrections and a surprise grandson, too. It's nearly biblical."

"I'm glad you find this amusing."

"I wouldn't say this is amusing, exactly," Luca said then, the laughter disappearing. "But what would be the point in beating you up any further? You've been rolling around in the proverbial hair shirt for the last five years and have taken all the pleasure out of needling you, to be honest."

"There was no hair shirt," Rafael said, trying to keep his tone even, because the penance he'd done for a woman who hadn't actually died was not his brother's business. "It was time to grow up. I did."

"Rafael." Luca shifted in his chair, then blew out a breath, shoving back that unruly hair of his. "You were a wreck when you thought she was dead, and for a long time after. Maybe you should take heart that she is not. All the rest is noise that will sort itself out, surely."

Rafael frowned at him. "Of course I'm pleased that she's not dead, Luca."

"But are you happy she's alive?" Luca asked, with that uncanny insight of his that suggested he was something more than the lazy creature he'd spent most of his life pretending he was. At least in public. "It's not quite the same thing, is it?"

"Of course." But Rafael had waited a moment too long to respond, and he knew it. "Of course I'm happy she's alive. What a thing to ask."

His younger brother studied him for a moment. "Is it that she can't remember you?" His mouth curved slightly. "Or anything else, for that matter?"

"I don't believe that she has forgotten a thing," Rafael said quietly, and it took him a moment to recognize the sheer savagery in his voice, to hear the way it sliced through the air between them, harsh and unmistakable. "Not one single thing. She left."

He did not say, *she left me*, and yet that sat there for a moment in the middle of the room as well. Right there in the center of the priceless rug that was older than the two of them and Lily combined. Obvious and terrible, and Rafael thought he couldn't possibly loathe himself more than he did at that moment.

Luca shifted in his chair, his whole body suddenly gripped with a different kind of tension.

"Rafael," he began. "*Mio fratello*—"

"I'm finished discussing this," Rafael gritted out.

"But I am not." Luca shook his head. "This is not the same. Lily is not our mother. There is no comparison between an accident and what happened here."

"You don't actually know that," Rafael said quietly. Too quietly. It revealed too much and even if he hadn't heard that in his own voice as it hung there between them, he saw it in his brother's eyes.

"Raf—"

"No more," Rafael said, cutting his brother off. "Lily and I will come to terms with what she's actually forgotten and what she's found convenient to pretend she's forgotten, I'm sure. That's quite enough ancient history to dredge up. There's no need to drag our mother into this."

For a moment he thought Luca would protest that. He felt himself tense, as if he thought he might fight back if his brother dared—

You need to pull yourself together, he ordered himself. *This is Luca. He's the only person you love who's never betrayed you.*

"Do you have any particular reason to think she's pretending?" Luca asked after a moment, his voice as light and easy as if they'd never strayed into the muddy waters of their mother's sad fate. He even smiled again. "Most women, of course, would hold you like the North Star deep within them, knowing you even if they lost themselves.

Such is the Castelli charm. I know this myself, obviously. But Lily always was different."

Rafael forced himself to smile. To play off the darkness pounding through his veins even then, whispering things he didn't want to hear.

"She was that."

"Her memory will return or it won't," Luca said carefully, watching Rafael much too closely. "And in the meantime, there is the child. My nephew."

"My son," Rafael agreed.

He didn't think he'd said that out loud before. *My son.* He wasn't prepared for that rush inside, that simmering, inarticulate joy, beating back the darkness. He hardly knew what to make of it.

"Indeed." Luca's dark eyes gleamed. "So perhaps what she remembers, or what happened in this ancient history of yours, is unimportant next to that. Or should be."

"Goodbye, Luca," Rafael said softly, and he didn't care what his brother could read in his tone. He didn't care what he revealed, as long as this uncomfortable conversation ended immediately. As long as Luca left him here to fight his way toward his equilibrium again. Rafael was sure it had to be in there somewhere. "I don't expect to see you again until Christmas. What a shame. You'll be missed. By someone, I'm sure."

"Liar," said his irrepressible brother, wholly unconcerned by his dismissal. "You miss me already."

Rafael shook his head, then turned back to the window and ignored the sound of his brother's laughter behind him as Luca took his leave.

Outside, the little boy—*his* little boy—was still running, the hood of his bright blue coat tossed back and his head tipped toward the sky.

Arlo was a miracle. Arlo was impossible. Arlo was a

perfect, wonderful mistake Rafael hadn't known he'd made, and Rafael already thought he was a pure delight.

But he changed nothing.

He only made Rafael's course of action that much more clear.

The ancient Castelli mansion bristled with the kind of supernaturally perfect staff that Lily had forgotten about over the course of these past five years. Impeccably trained, they made her feel as if *she* was gleaming and perfectly presentable at all times. When in fact it was their ability to clean rooms while she was still in them, produce a phalanx of nannies with credentials in hand to watch Arlo whenever she needed a moment and maintain the elegance all around her so expertly that made it feel quite natural that she should find herself living in it again.

It had been different going in the other direction, from these nonchalant everyday luxuries to the challenges of real life without them, but at the time, Lily had viewed all of that as her penance. And her test. If she could manage it, she'd told herself as she'd waited tables in places the old Lily wouldn't have dared enter, she'd earn the right to raise her child herself.

She'd given herself a deadline. If, by her eighth month of pregnancy, she couldn't come up with a better life than the hand-to-mouth, on-the-run existence she'd fashioned for herself, then she would have to tell Rafael about the baby. Or arrange for him to get custody without directly confronting him, maybe. *Something.* No child deserved to struggle along in poverty at all, but certainly not when his mother could make one phone call and whisk him away from a truck stop diner to a place like this. Lily might have left her life the way she had for what had felt like very good reasons, despite the pain she knew she'd caused—but she hoped she wasn't *that* selfish.

Lily had been six months pregnant when Pepper had walked into her diner, headed home after delivering a pair of rescue dogs from a high-kill shelter in Virginia to their loving new home in Missouri. Maybe it wasn't surprising that they'd hit it off instantly—after all, Pepper had a way with strays.

And when she'd hit that eight-month deadline, Lily had been living in the guest cottage on Pepper's land, with a job she quite enjoyed to go along with it. She'd liked her life there and had seen no reason her baby wouldn't, too. Pepper had felt like the long-lost older sister Lily had never had. And then she'd been more like a doting grandmother to Arlo.

Lily didn't regret a single minute of her time in Virginia, and she told herself she didn't regret keeping Arlo's existence from Rafael, either.

But it was shockingly easy to adjust to life in all of that Castelli luxury again, she found, regrets or no. From the stately ballrooms to the gracious salons to the many libraries, large and small, that dotted the rambling old house, every inch of the place was a song of praise to the ancient Castelli name and a celebration of their many centuries of wealth and prominence. She'd made her way to her favorite library tonight, a week after they'd arrived in Italy, while the nannies she'd have said she didn't need tended to Arlo's nightly bath.

This was what they'd been hired to do, she'd been informed the first night they'd come to spirit him away. Which meant Rafael had decreed it—and in this great house, what Rafael decreed was law. That took some getting used to.

"You always loved this room."

Lily jumped at the sound of his voice. It was as if she'd summoned him out of thin air with a single thought, and it took everything she had not to whirl around and face him, the way a guilty person who remembered exactly how much she'd loved this room might do.

"I do like libraries," she said, trying to sound vague. "Doesn't everyone?"

"You like this one because you said it felt like a tree house," Rafael said, and it was only when she heard how calm and even his voice was that she realized she'd been much too close to snapping at him.

Lily heard him move farther into the cozy room, all dark woods and packed bookshelves and the bay window that sat out amid the leafy green treetops in summer. This time of year the bare branches scratched at the glass and made her think about all the ghosts that stood in this room with them, none of whom she wanted to contend with just then.

She turned to find Rafael much closer than she'd expected. He stood there in casual trousers and a sleek sweater that made her palms itch to touch it—*him*—and she told herself the way her heart leaped inside her chest was anxiety. Panic at this awful role she had to play, when she'd never been any good at pretending much of anything.

But the heat that washed over her told a much different story, especially as it settled low and deep and heavy in her belly. And then began to pulse.

It was then that she realized that she hadn't been alone with Rafael since that cold street back in Charlottesville. Not truly alone. Not like this—closed off in a faraway room in a rambling old house where no one could hear them and no one was likely to intervene even if they could.

Lily's heart began to drum against her ribs, so loud that for a moment she was genuinely afraid he could hear it.

"A tree house?" she asked now. She frowned at him,

then out the window and into the darkness, where the December trees were skeletal at best. Someone who had never been here before would certainly not make the summertime connection. It required having whiled away hours in the window seat, surrounded by all of those leaves. "I don't get it."

His dark gaze was intent on hers, as if he was parsing it—*her*—for lies, though he still stood a few feet away, his hands thrust in his pockets. She supposed that was meant to be a safe distance. But this was Rafael. Nothing about him was safe and there was no distance in the world that cut off that electricity that bloomed in the air between them. Even now, as if nothing had happened. As if it was five years ago and no time had passed.

No car accidents. No Arlo. Just this *thing* that had stalked them both for years.

"How have you enjoyed your week here?" Rafael asked. So mildly, as if he had nothing on his mind save the duties of a host and this was a mere holiday for the both of them.

Lily didn't believe that tone of voice at all.

"It's very pretty here," she said, the way a first-time guest might have. "If a bit bleak this time of year. And obviously, the house itself is amazing. But that doesn't make it feel like any less of a prison."

"You are not in prison, Lily."

"That's not—" She cut herself off. "I don't like it when you call me that."

"I can't call you anything else," he said, a dark fire in his voice, his eyes, and it stirred up that dangerous matching blaze inside her. "It sits on my tongue like lead."

She didn't really want to think about his tongue. "If this isn't a prison, when can I leave?"

"Don't."

"I don't know you. I don't know this place. The fact that

you remember this life you think I had doesn't change the fact that *I* don't remember living it. A blood test doesn't change how I feel."

She thought if she kept saying that, over and over again, it might make it true.

"I'm sorry you feel that way," Rafael said, in a remarkably calm tone that was completely at odds with that harsh look on his dark, beautiful face. "But things are complicated. I can't simply let you go and hope you'll be kind enough to stay in touch. You are somewhat more than a mere flight risk."

Lily thought better of showing him her reaction to that. She might not have been truly alone with him since they'd arrived here, but she'd certainly suffered through too many of these sorts of seemingly innocuous barbs that she worried were actually tests. At the various meals they'd taken together with Arlo, because, she'd been informed, hiding away with a tray in her room was not allowed. Every time Rafael encountered her, in fact.

Was she responding as Lily? Or as someone who didn't know who Lily was? Having to worry over every single word she said or expression she let show on her face was like talking through a stone wall, and she was beginning to feel the weight of it inside her, dragging her down.

"And why not?" she asked crisply. "When you know that's what I want?"

"Because," he said softly, "I am a father."

"Arlo doesn't know you from a can of paint," she snapped at him.

"And whose fault is that?"

The silky rejoinder stopped her short. She could feel her temper pounding in her temples, her throat, down in her gut, goading her on. When she knew the very last thing she could be around Rafael was out of control in any way.

Temper would take her down as fast as passion. Faster. At least if she was kissing him, she couldn't run her mouth at the same time.

Lily blinked. Where had *that* come from?

But of course, she knew. She was in a small room, alone with Rafael. Five years ago he would already have been inside her. There would have been no hesitation, no hands thrust into his pockets and that wary distance. He'd once hitched her up on the back of the deep leather sofa to her right and had her biting her own hand within seconds of closing the door behind them.

She went and sat on that same sofa now and saw a gleam of something edgy and very male in his gaze as she did, telling her he was remembering the same thing. She toed off the short boots she wore, pulled her legs in their warm leggings beneath her where she sat and wrapped her arms around her middle and the oversize tunic of a sweater she wore, with the great big cowl neck that was perfect for drafty old European halls like this one.

"So, tell me your theories," she said, with a calm she didn't feel at all.

Rafael stood where she'd left him, over near the wall of books. He didn't cross over and sit down in the chair across from her. He only studied her.

Looking for weaknesses, she thought, and tried to steel herself.

Because she was well aware that Rafael didn't buy her amnesia story for an instant.

"What theory would you prefer to hear?" he asked after a moment. "I have so many."

This angle, staring up at him from below, was unsettling. It was impossible not to be entirely too aware of every hard plane of his perfect chest, or that ridged abdomen of his. It was hard not to lose herself in the stark male lines of his fine, athletic form, much less that ruthlessness he'd always exuded. But where it had been purely sexual five years ago, now it was tempered. Steelier. Harder. More focused and intent. It made him that much more devastating.

And Lily had to find a way to ignore it. All of it. When she'd never managed to do so before.

You're an addict like any other, she told herself now. Like her mother. Hadn't she sat in those meetings from time to time in those first days on the run, pretending it had been something else that had overtaken and ruined her life so totally? *You know how to do this. One excruciating moment at a time.*

Though heroin didn't talk back, she imagined.

"What do you think happened to me?" she asked him then. "If I'm this Lily person, why do I think I'm someone else?"

His dark eyes glittered, and she knew he was biting back the urge to tell her there was no *if* about it. That she was Lily Holloway, whether she liked it or not. She could practically hear him say it—but to his credit, he didn't.

"What did you think when I asked you about your tattoo in that café?" he asked instead. "Didn't you think it was odd that a total stranger could describe it so perfectly when, according to you, we'd never met before?"

"Of course I did. But I thought everything about you was odd."

"That was it? It didn't cross your mind that what I was saying might be true?"

"Not at all." She eyed him, hoping the tension in her arms as she hugged her legs closer into her chest wasn't obvious. "If I walked up to you and said, oh, hello, your name is actually Eugene Marigold and I know you from our days in Wisconsin, would you believe me?"

His eyes gleamed with a hint of golden amusement that danced down the length of her spine, making her shiver deep within. "It would depend on the evidence."

She shrugged. "I'm here to tell you that the evidence doesn't help. I guess I thought you must have seen my tattoo before."

"You often parade around with it showing, do you?"

Lily stilled. She knew that tone. Possessive. And darkly thrilling to her in a way that felt physical, when she knew she should have found it appalling. *The only appalling thing here is you*, she snapped at herself.

"I wear a bathing suit at the lake sometimes, if that's what you mean by 'parading around.'"

"A rather skimpy bathing costume."

"In America we call them bikinis."

He made a sound that wasn't quite a laugh and then he moved toward her, which made her throat go dry in an instant and every part of her body go stiff—but he only dropped down in the chair across from her.

And that suddenly, Lily was tossed back in time. It was the way he lounged there, so surpassingly indolent, as if nothing on earth could ever truly bother him. She remembered that too well. This was the Rafael she'd known. Provocative. Sensual. Even now, with that considering sort of gleam in his gaze that told her he wasn't the least bit relaxed no matter how he happened to be stretched out in that chair, her body reacted to the memory.

More than simply *reacted*. She burst into long, hot, blistering flames. They shuddered through her, one lick after the next, making her want to writhe where she sat. But she didn't dare move. She hardly dared breathe. And she had to hope against hope he thought she was blushing about the mention of bikinis. Or from the crackling fire in the nearby grate. Who was she kidding? He knew exactly why she'd flushed red, and she knew he did, too.

But none of this was about what Rafael knew. It was about what he could prove.

"How did you come up with the name Alison Herbert in the first place?" he asked, much too quietly, after another heavy moment dragged by, leaving furrows of stone deep in her gut. "You had a very specific biography at the ready. Where did it come from?"

Where indeed, Lily thought darkly. The truth—that she'd bought that driver's license off a girl she'd vaguely resembled in a truck stop parking lot with a week's worth of tips, and had helped herself to that same girl's hastily told life story, too—was obviously out of the question. And she had to bite her tongue against the urge to overexplain and overcomplicate, because that could only make this harder.

She shrugged. "I don't really know."

"I think you can do better than that." A crook of his sensual lips when she frowned at him. He propped up his head against the fingers of one hand like some emperor of old and didn't shift his hard gaze from hers for a moment. "Do you remember your childhood as this Alison?"

She'd had a little more than a week to prepare for this particular performance, and had thought of little else in that time. So she scowled at him now, bristling a bit where she sat.

"Of course." He waited when she paused. She made herself breathe in, then out. Count to ten. "I mean… I think I do."

"Ah."

Lily didn't understand how he could steal all the air from the room when she was looking straight at him and could see with her own eyes that he hadn't moved at all.

She frowned harder in his direction, though it didn't seem to help. If anything, she found it harder to breathe.

"I don't see the point in talking about this," she said then. She jerked her gaze away from his, sure he could read entirely too much on her face, and scowled down at the cuff of her sweater as if it contained the answers to these mysteries. She picked at it with her other hand. "Obviously, what I remember or don't remember is irrelevant. You have the blood work."

"I do."

"And that's why we're here." Lily swallowed, then lifted her head again to meet his gaze. This time, she held it. "But what about you?"

"Me?" He looked faintly amused, or as amused as anyone could look with so much thunder in his gaze. "I know exactly who I am."

"But you were my stepbrother," Lily said, and tilted her head slightly to one side, hoping she looked curious rather than challenging. "How did any of this happen?"

She looked fragile and something like otherworldly tonight, Rafael thought, with her thick strawberry blond hair piled high on her head. It only called attention to the delicate elegance of her fine neck, something he realized he hadn't paid enough attention to five years ago. Here, now, he couldn't think of anything else. She was swallowed up in that oversize sweater, which he imagined was the point of it. The bigger and baggier the sweater, the less of her he could see.

He doubted she realized that without the distraction of that lithe, intoxicating body of hers that still drove him mad, he had nothing to do but parse every single expression that crossed her face and every last telling look in her lovely eyes.

Rafael didn't believe for one moment that she couldn't remember him.

And if she didn't remember him as she claimed, then she couldn't remember what had actually happened between them, and he could paint it any way he liked. If she could remember him, well, it was up to her to interrupt and set the record straight, wasn't it?

After all, this was the woman who had failed to tell him he was a father, that he had a son, *for five years*—and had certainly not come clean about it on her own. If he hadn't seen her on that street in Virginia, would she ever have told him about Arlo? He doubted it. He would never have known.

He almost wished she really did have amnesia. For her sake.

Rafael smiled at her then and felt rather more like a wolf than was wise.

"It's really a very sweet story," he said. He was sure he saw her stiffen. "You were an awkward sort of teenager when our parents got together, ungainly and shy. You hardly spoke."

"What?" She coughed when he looked at her, and she managed to look so guileless that he almost doubted that he'd heard that sharpness in her voice then. Almost. "I'm sorry. Did you say *ungainly*?"

"Many teenage girls have those rough patches," he said, as if he was trying to be comforting. "But I think being around Luca and me helped you a bit. Smoothed out the edges."

"Because you were both such excellent brothers to me?" she asked, and wrinkled her nose in that way he'd always liked a little too much. He still did. "That pushes us straight into icky territory, doesn't it?"

Rafael laughed. "Nothing could be farther from the

truth. We more or less ignored you." He waved a languid hand in the air. "Our father is always marrying various women, the more broken the better, and sometimes they come with children we're expected to treat as family for a while. We all know it's temporary. A form of charity, really." He smiled at her, and there was a bit more color on those remarkable cheeks of hers than there had been before. Though that could also have been the cheerful fire that crackled away beside them. "No, I mean that Luca and I dated a wide selection of very elegant, fashionable, socially adept women. You idolized them, of course. It must have been a master class for a girl like you, from such different circumstances."

She returned her attention to the sleeve of her sweater and fiddled with her cuff. "Were our circumstances so different?"

"I'm really talking more about a certain polish that some girls have. They're born with it, I think." He eyed the growing flush on her cheeks, certain it was her temper and not the fire this time, and kept going. "I hope my honesty doesn't upset you. If it helps, I think European women are better at achieving this polish than American women. Perhaps it's cultural."

"How lucky that I had all of the many women you dated to help me overcome my Americanness," she said evenly. He hoped she was remembering the women he'd dated back then, all of them about as polished as mud, and that her even tone was painful for her. But she only flicked a look at him, her blue gaze unreadable. "Is that what happened? These paragons of womanhood made me one of them and you found you had to date me, too?"

He actually grinned at that and saw the reaction in her clear blue eyes before she dropped them again. But the heat he'd seen there licked over him like wildfire, and his voice was huskier than it had been when he continued.

"You wrote me daily poems, confessing your girlish feelings to me. It was adorable."

"Poems," she echoed flatly. "I find that…amazing. Truly. Since I haven't written a word in as long as I can remember."

"We haven't established how long that is, have we?"

"And how long did I attempt to woo you with teenage poetry?" she asked, with a smile that didn't quite reach her eyes. "You must have found the whole thing embarrassing."

"Very," he agreed. "You were so bad at it, you see."

"Were it not for the existence of Arlo, I'd think this story was heading in a very different direction," she said dryly.

"On your eighteenth birthday," he said, as if recalling a favorite old story instead of making it up on the spot, "you stood before me in a white dress, like a wedding gown, and asked me if I would grant you one wish."

"Oh," she breathed. "Like a fairy tale. Did you say I was eighteen or eight?"

"Eighteen." His voice was reproving, and it was hard to keep himself from laughing. "You were quite sheltered, Lily."

"But not by you, because then the fact that we actually did get together would surely be gross." She smiled faintly at him. "I'm guessing."

"You were sheltered by the strict convent school you attended," he lied happily. She'd been nowhere near a convent in all her life, to his recollection. "You entertained some notion of becoming a nun."

He could almost hear the crackle of her temper, like water against hot metal, though she only swallowed. Hard.

"A nun," she repeated, her gaze narrow on his. "I wanted to become a nun."

He smiled with entirely too much satisfaction. "It was cute."

"And yet somehow we produced a child," she prompted him, a touch of acid in her voice, though her expression was impressively impassive. "Despite the fact I was, apparently, an eight-year-old wannabe nun with no greater ambition than to live in a fairy tale. A poetic fairy tale."

"On your eighteenth birthday you asked me for a kiss," he told her, sitting back farther in his chair and enjoying himself. He couldn't remember the last time in the past five years he'd enjoyed himself quite so much, in fact. "'Please, Rafael,' you begged. 'I want to know what it is to be a woman.'"

"Oh, come on. No one says things like that. Not in real life."

He shrugged. "And yet, you did. Or do you remember it differently?"

"I don't remember it at all," she murmured, and he saw that mutinous light in her eyes. His stubborn girl. "Though that sounds a little bit dramatic, if I'm being honest."

"You were a very theatrical teenager, Lily. The despair of your mother and a trial to all your teachers, or so I was told at the time."

She rubbed her hands over her face. "And yet somehow all this drama led to a secret relationship? That strains belief, doesn't it?"

"That was your call," he told her without a single qualm, watching her for a reaction to what might have been the biggest lie of all, but she only stared back at him. "You begged for a kiss, which, of course, I refused."

"I can't say I blame you. I'd question the man who looked at a gawky teenager in a makeshift bridal gown who'd seriously considered taking up the veil and thought, *I want some of that.*"

Rafael had no idea how he kept from laughing. "I told you that I couldn't possibly kiss such an innocent. That you would have to prove yourself a woman if you wanted me to kiss you like one."

"You felt this was the right approach to an obviously confused teenager?" Lily sniffed. "I wonder if a kind word or two might have been a little more helpful. Or the number of a good therapist."

"I thought you would run screaming back into your sheltered little world." He didn't know when he'd slipped from his fantastical story into something a lot like the truth, but he knew he didn't like it. Rafael stretched out his legs before him and eyed her across the accent rug, where she'd once slipped to her knees and taken him in her mouth while his father and her mother had talked loudly in the hallway on the other side of the door. He remembered the heat of her mouth, the sweep of her tongue, as if it had happened yesterday. So did the hardest part of him. "I thought you were all bark and no bite."

"Let me guess," she said softly. "I bit."

"In a manner of speaking." Rafael remembered that kiss on New Year's Eve. He remembered the taste of her flooding him, and the weight of her thick, wild hair against his palms. He remembered the press of her breasts against his chest and the silky-smooth expanse of the sweet skin at the tops of her thighs, where he shouldn't have reached in the first place. "You decided you needed to prove yourself a woman."

"Was there a series of tests?" Lily asked in that same soft voice, yet with something far edgier beneath it. "A gauntlet of fire, one can only hope?"

"Do you really want the details?"

Her gaze was too hot when it met his. She looked away—but it took a moment. "No."

"You insisted we keep it a secret. You demanded I date other women in public so no one would know. You were determined."

"And you, of course, acquiesced."

"Of course. I am nothing if not a gentleman."

There was a long silence, then. There was only the sound of the fire. The far-off noises that all old houses made, the shift and creak of settling. The moody December weather on the other side of the old glass windows.

His own heart, beating a little too hard for a simple conversation like this one.

"Can I be honest with you?" she asked.

"Always."

"I don't think I believe you."

Rafael couldn't keep from smiling then, and stopped trying. "Do you remember another version of events, then?"

"Of course I don't. You know I don't."

He watched her ball her hands into fists, and took that as a victory. "Then my version will have to stand, as told."

"Let's say that all of this is true." She studied him. "Why would you fall in love with me? The person you describe is a disaster at best."

"Love makes us all fools, Lily," he said quietly.

"You as much as admitted you made all of that up," she pointed out. "Or you wouldn't ask me for a different version."

"Tell me which part," he dared her.

She sat up then, so abruptly it made him blink. She stamped her feet back into her boots, one after the next with a certain nearly leashed violence, and then stood up in a rush. Rafael wanted nothing more than to do the same—but stayed where he was, lounging there as if he'd never in his life been more at his ease.

"This is crazy," she muttered, as much to herself as to

him. But then her blue eyes slammed into his. "What kind of person are you, to play games like this?"

"Do you really want to know the truth?" he asked her, and he wasn't at all languid any longer. He couldn't even pretend. He sat up, never shifting his hard gaze from hers.

"I thought that was the point of you bringing me here. All the truth, all the time. Whether I like it or not."

"Because you knew the truth once, Lily," he said, with a harshness that surprised him even as he spoke. He couldn't seem to contain it. "You lived it. And then you sent your car over the side of a cliff and walked away from it. You had a baby, changed your name and hid in a place no one you'd known before would ever think to look for you. Maybe you don't want to know the truth."

Lily shook her head, more as if she was shaking this off than negating what he'd said, and he viewed that as a victory, too.

"Or," he said in the same tone, with that same edge, "you already know the truth and all of this is a game you're playing for reasons of your own. What kind of person would that make you?"

She stiffened as if he'd slapped her.

"I think you're not right in the head," she threw at him as she started for the door. "Why would you tell me a bunch of lies? How could fake stories of a made-up past do anything but make things worse?"

"I wouldn't worry about it," Rafael replied, and even he could hear the danger in his voice. The menace. And it took everything he had to stay where he was. To let her go when that was the last thing he wanted, ever again. "Chances are, you'll forget that, too."

CHAPTER FIVE

THE HISTORIC CASTELLI palazzo was small by Venetian standards, set on the stately Grand Canal in the shadow of far loftier residences once inhabited by the great and noble families of old Venice. But no matter how many times Lily told herself that, no matter how she reminded herself of the offhanded way her former stepfather had referred to this place as *a pile of sentiment and rising tides* as if it was beyond him why anyone would come here, her first sight of it from the water of the Grand Canal made her breath catch in her throat.

Catch, then hold too tight, as if that much beauty in one place might damage her heart within her chest.

She told herself it was the view. The rise of the old stone building from the depths of the canal as if it was floating there, the quality of the pure gold light that beamed out from within and spilled across the water, like a dark dream made real on this cold, breezy evening. It was the view, she assured herself, not the man who stood so tall and brooding and forbiddingly silent beside her in the private water taxi, as if the wind that ruffled at her hair and made her wrap herself even more tightly in her winter coat was yet one more detail that was far beneath his notice.

He looked like a dark prince, she thought then, as if she was channeling the teenaged poet she'd never been. Made of shifting shadows and the graceful lights that moved over the water like songs. He looked otherworldly. More fable than man.

You need to get a grip, she told herself sternly. *Lose control with this man and you lose everything.*

"It is beautiful, is it not?" Rafael's voice was silky, like the falling night in this nearly submerged city of echoes and arches, mysteries and dreams, and there was no reason at all that it should shiver down the length of Lily's spine like that, then pool too hot at its base. "And not yet sunk into the sea."

"It's lovely, of course, as I'm sure you're well aware," she replied, sounding stiff and unfriendly to her own ears. "I'm sure every guidebook printed in the last three hundred years agrees. But I still don't understand why we're here."

"I told you." He shifted his position against the polished hull of the small, sleek boat that cut through the water as efficiently as he seemed to slice deep into her with that dark look he kept trained on her. Lily wished she'd sat down in the sheltered interior, away from him. But she'd wanted to see Venice more than she'd wanted to avoid him, and contending with Rafael was the price of that decision. "It is the Christmas season. I must make my annual appearance at our neighbors' ball or the world as we know it will come to a shuddering halt. My ancestors will rise from their graves in protest and the Castelli name will ring in infamy throughout the ages. Or so my father has informed me in a series of theatrical voice mail messages."

Her hands clenched tight deep inside her pockets against a certain warmth that threaded its way through her chest and would be her downfall, she knew it. "I don't see what any of that has to do with me. Or why I had to leave my son with strangers to accompany you on some family errand."

Rafael's hard mouth moved then, into that little crook

that undid her. "Do you not? You are the mother of my child—who could not be happier where he is, with a veritable army of nannies to tend to his every whim, as I think you are well aware. Where else should you be but at my side, for all the world to see and marvel at your resurrection?"

Lily didn't know what scraped at her more—that he'd called her the mother of his child with such matter-of-fact possessiveness it made her head spin, or that he claimed he wanted her with him, as if that was the most natural thing in the world.

When the Rafael she'd known had refused, point-blank, to ever keep her anything but his own dirty secret.

Of course, she wasn't supposed to remember that. And for a taut moment, she let herself imagine what it might have been like if she truly couldn't remember him. If she could take all of this—him—at face value. If she could believe him this time around.

But that way lay nothing but madness. Heartbreak and betrayal. She tried to shake it off.

"When you say, 'for all the world to see,' I hope you don't mean that whole paparazzi thing." She frowned, and shook her head. "I work in a kennel in Virginia. I don't want strangers looking at me."

She couldn't read that dark gleam in his gaze then, or the way his hard, lean jaw moved as if he was biting something back.

"You can wear a mask if you like, even if it is not yet *Carnevale*," he said, after a moment. "Many do, though perhaps not out of the same misplaced sense of modesty you seem to feel. Given that you are but a kennel worker. From Virginia."

Lily looked sharply at him at that too-dry tone, then away, as the boat reached the palazzo's low dock and the driver leaped out to pull the ropes taut and bring the sleek vessel in close so they could disembark. Though it seemed Rafael's voice was the tighter noose, wrapped like a hand around her throat.

"But make no mistake, Lily. I will always know who you are."

His voice was like a touch, and she hated that traitorous part of her that wished it really was. More than wished it— *longed* for him in all those ways she was afraid to admit, even to herself. Afraid that once she did, it would be the emotional equivalent of hurling herself off the side of a cliff for real this time, and then what would become of her? But of course, she already knew. *Maybe you don't want to know the truth*, he'd accused her the other night, and he was right. She really didn't want to know it. Because she'd already seen exactly where it led. She already knew exactly what loving him made her do.

At the very least, the fallout of those feelings had turned her into someone she despised.

"It's a clear day," Rafael had said on a bright morning this past week, walking into the private salon in the family wing of the old house where Lily and Arlo had become accustomed to having their breakfast.

Lily had glanced up and lost her breath for a moment at the unexpected *hit* of him. That rangy body of his that he'd dressed that morning in the kind of deceptively casual clothing she knew only appeared to be simple and straightforward. The stretch of exquisite luxury wools across his perfect chest, the way those trousers clung to the lean muscles in his thighs. He looked like some kind of infinitely powerful adventurer, some modern-day Italian prince, as likely to leap over one of the looming mountains outside as he was to take to the nearest throne—

Maybe, she'd thought then, *all those ridiculous lies he*

told you about your absurd and overdramatic teenaged behavior weren't so far off the mark.

"Thank you," she'd said, with as little inflection as she could manage, as if maintaining an even tone could repel him. As if anything could have. She'd looked past him toward the floor-to-ceiling windows, where she could see what kind of day it was all by herself, then back. "I appreciate the weather report."

Rafael's mouth had moved in that same curve, not quite a smirk, that had lit her on fire no matter how she'd tried to tell herself that was simply the old house's unwieldy heating, not him at all.

"Your appreciation is overwhelming," he'd murmured, and she didn't understand how he could make that sound like sex. How he could make *anything* sound like sex when he said it in that voice of his.

Arlo, meanwhile, appreciated all things Rafael in a pure and straightforward way that made Lily's heart squeeze too tight in her chest. And something like shame form a thick, oily slick deep in her belly. That morning, Arlo had tossed his arms above his head and started singing at the top of his lungs, completely unaware of all those dangerous undercurrents swirling through the room.

Lily had forced a smile when Rafael raised a querying brow at her.

"That is the hello song," she'd told him with as much dignity as she could muster while sitting next to a five-year-old who was singing and dancing and wriggling madly in his seat. "He learned it in his preschool. They sing it every morning."

"I'm honored," Rafael had said, smiling at his son. A real smile, she'd noted. One of those pure Rafael smiles she remembered from before that could have knocked them straight into spring, it had been so bright.

And Lily had officially hated herself, then. Because the smile he'd used when he'd looked at Arlo had been genuine. It had been beautiful. It was lit with pride and longing and a sweetness she'd have said Rafael Castelli could not—did not—possess. Arlo had catapulted himself off the side of his chair and raced around the table at the sight of it, tossing himself at Rafael's legs to bestow one of his heedless, reckless full-body hugs.

Lily hadn't known whether to smile or cry. Especially when Rafael had looked so stunned for a second. He'd put his hand on his son's head as if it belonged there and then he'd smiled down at the little boy as if Arlo was a burst of pure summer sunshine on such a chilly December morning.

And so she'd ruined it.

"He does that to every man he meets," Lily had heard herself say, ugly and sharp.

The words had hung there in the air of the salon between them. They'd seemed to grow louder with every second, as if they were amplified off the graceful old walls. If she could have reached into the air and plucked them back, thought better of them and kept them to herself, she would have done it.

But there was no repairing the kind of damage she'd always done to this man, and him to her. There was only the living with it.

Rafael's smile had dimmed, then disappeared altogether, and he'd taken his time looking back at her. His gaze had been dark and something much too bleak and furious at once, and it had hurt as much as if he'd thrown something back at her. More, perhaps. Lily kept thinking she couldn't feel any more horrible than she already did, and then sure enough, she found there was a darker, deeper, far worse place.

This is what you do, she'd told herself. *When you're with him, this is who you are.* She'd wanted to say that out loud. To remind him that they'd always ended in the same ugly place—but she couldn't say a word. She'd had to sit and stew in it instead.

"It's clear enough to walk down to the village today," Rafael had said after a long, heavy sort of moment, when she'd thought he could see all the ugliness inside her. When she'd imagined it filled the whole room—the whole sprawling length of the house. Arlo, happily, had seemed completely oblivious, still clinging to his father's legs and chanting something new and bright. "I thought it would be a pleasant family excursion, assuming you're not too busy coming up with further vicious comments to fling at me."

Lily had refused to apologize to him, but still, her throat hurt as if she had more than one apology stacked there. She'd swallowed hard against it. And maybe it would have been different if she hadn't tried to take him out at the knees. Maybe then she might have come up with some way to resist him. But she'd made that glorious smile of his go away because she was a terrible person, and she didn't seem to have any resistance in her just then.

And he'd used the word *family*.

"That sounds lovely," she'd said, her voice hoarse with all the things she couldn't say. The things she didn't want to admit she could feel. The memories she'd been terribly afraid he could see all over her face. "Thank you."

Lily jolted back into the present to find Rafael studying her expression in that way of his that made her forget to breathe. She kept herself from scowling her reaction at him by sheer force of will, and realized only after a long, shuddering beat of her treacherous heart that he was holding out his hand to her. And waiting for her to take it.

She wanted to touch him about as much as she wanted

to fling herself off the side of the boat into the frigid waters of the Grand Canal and swim for it, but she swallowed that down, aware that he was measuring her reaction. That he was clocking exactly how much time it took her to look from that extended hand back up to his face. That, worse, he could probably read every last thought she had as she did it.

Because she was perfectly aware that he knew she could remember him.

He still couldn't *prove* that she could.

"I only want to help you from the boat, Lily," he said softly, the hint of a dark amusement in his voice.

"That is another lie." She hadn't meant to say that. She should have swallowed that down with all the rest of it, she knew that. And maybe to prove how little he bothered her, to herself if nothing else, she slid her hand into his.

It was a mistake. She'd known it would be.

It didn't matter that they both wore gloves to ward off the cold. It didn't matter that she couldn't feel the slide of his skin against her palm or the true heat of his hand. She could feel his strength. She could feel that leashed power of his like a deep, dark ricochet inside her, flooding her with sensation she didn't want, as dangerous as the mysterious Venetian night all around them.

There was no curve at all to that hard mouth of his, then. Rafael's gaze locked to hers.

Heat. Passion. Need.

It slammed into her. It made her feel distorted. Altered. She moved then, jerky and uncertain, as if the world was as rickety beneath her feet as the boat. As the dock that extended out from the palazzo's first-level loggia. As the grand houses of Venice themselves, arrayed around them up and down the canal on their ancient and uncertain ground—some dark with disuse and age, some lit from within like sets of perfect Christmas ornaments made from local Murano glass—and none of them as safe as they were beautiful.

Just like Rafael.

Lily climbed up onto the dock with more alacrity than grace and then dropped his hand as if he'd burned her.

And he didn't have to laugh at her, though she could sense more than hear the deep, dark rumble of it. It was already inside her, where she was still so attuned to him, a part of him. As if they were still connected that way— deeper than sex, like a fire in the blood nothing had ever been able to quench. Not time, not distance. Not betrayal. Not her own supposed death. She began to understand that nothing ever would. That she'd been kidding herself all these long years, imagining it could ever be otherwise.

The palazzo loomed before her, its graceful upper floors gleaming bright against the dark like some kind of bea-con, and Lily assured herself it was nothing more than the cold wind sweeping down the canal from the lagoon in the distance and slapping against her face that made her eyes water.

It's the cold, she assured herself. *It's only the cold.*

But then she felt his hands on her, turning her to face him, and she knew better. She was doomed. They were both doomed. They'd been destined to do nothing but rip each other apart since the moment they'd met and set them-selves on this terrible collision course that destroyed them both. Over and over again.

She could see it in that stern set to his beautiful mouth. That bold fire in his gaze. Worse, she could feel it in the way she simply…melted. Everything inside her turned soft and ran sweet, and she thought she'd never wanted anything more in all her life than the press of that mouth of his against hers again.

Just one more time, she told herself, almost wistfully, as she looked up at him.

But she knew that was the biggest lie of all.

"Don't kiss me," she whispered then, too quick and too revealing. "I don't want you to kiss me again."

Rafael's stern mouth was so close then—*so close*—and that look in his eyes was enough to raze whole cities, and there was no disguising the way it made her tremble, too. She didn't try.

"Speaking of lies," he said, and drew closer still, his arms moving around her to hold her there in a parody of a lover's embrace.

Or perhaps it was no parody, after all.

She braced her hands against his chest, though she couldn't have said if she was pushing him away or, far more worrying, simply holding him there. "It's not a lie just because you don't like it."

He studied her for a moment, and Lily forgot where they were. What continent, what year. What city. There was nothing but that dark gold brilliance in his gaze, the riot deep inside her, and her ever more fragile resistance. He shifted, raising one gloved hand to smooth over her cheek, the leather both a caress and a punishment, as it was not the lick of heat his bare skin would have been.

She imagined he knew that, too.

"Relax," he said, and he sounded far too amused, then. As if she was the only one torn asunder by this. The only one so affected. "I'm not going to kiss you here. It's far too cold."

"You mean public."

There was a dangerous gleam in his eyes then. "I mean cold."

"I don't understand what the temperature has to do with it." She sounded far more cross than was wise. Rafael's mouth curved.

"The next time I kiss you, Lily, I won't be as thrown as I was on the street in Virginia. There will be nothing but our usual chemistry." He shrugged, though the hand against her cheek tightened, and she knew then that he wasn't nearly as unaffected as he seemed. "And you know what happens then."

She did. A thousand images surged through her then, one brighter and more sinfully wicked than the next. A messy, slick tumult of his mouth, his hands. The thrust of his body deep into hers. The taste of his skin beneath her tongue, the hard perfection of him beneath her hands. Salt and steel.

The ache, the fire. The impossible, unconquerable fire.

"No," she gritted out, glaring at him no matter how much emotion she feared was right there in her eyes to make a liar of her. "I don't know what happens."

He dragged his thumb over her bottom lip, his mouth cruel and harsh and no less beguiling, because he knew exactly what it did to her. The thick heat that wound tight and dropped low, nearly making her moan. Nearly.

"Then you'll be in for quite a ride." He looked at her as if he was already inside her. Already setting a lazy, mind-wrecking pace. "It's uncontrollable. It always has been."

Lily jerked her head back, out of his grip, much too aware that he let her. That he could have stopped her, if he chose. His hand dropped from her face and she wanted to slap that deeply male, wholly satisfied look straight off his face. She had to grit her teeth to keep from doing it.

"I don't know what that means," she told him, her voice as frigid as the air around them. As the dark, mysterious waters of the canal behind him. "I feel certain I don't *want* to know what it means."

His dark eyes were hooded as they met hers. He still looked like they were already having sex. As if it was a foregone conclusion. As if this was nothing more than foreplay—and every part of her body burst into jubilant flame at the sight.

"It means I kiss you, then I'm inside you," he told her, in a voice straight out of those wild, feverish dreams she lied and told herself were nightmares. She'd been telling herself that for years. "Always."

"I will take that as a threat," she threw at him and stepped back, as if that tiny wedge of space could make what he said less true. His mouth shifted, and she thought she'd never seen him look more like a wolf than he did then.

And she didn't think she'd ever wanted him more.

"You may take it any way you choose," he told her, all dark intent and certainty. "It is a fact, Lily. As inevitable as the dawn after a long, cold night. And as unavoidable."

Rafael thought she might run.

He set footmen at the door to her bedchamber and found himself rather more grim than he should have been as he considered what pointless attempt she might make to escape him this time. Yet despite his dark imaginings as the hours crept by, no alarm was raised.

And when the clock struck the appointed hour, Lily appeared at the top of the grand stair inside the palazzo like every last one of the fantasies he'd conjured up over the past five years.

He'd planned this well, he'd thought. He'd had the gown shipped in from Milan, had dispatched servants to tend to her hair and her cosmetics. He'd thought he'd prepared himself for the inevitable result.

But it was one thing to imagine Lily, *his Lily*, alive and well and dressed like a member of the scrupulously high-class Venetian society they would mix with tonight. It was something else to see her again with his own eyes.

Rafael had never been so glad of that long staircase that swept down from the upper floor of the palazzo to the main level where he stood.

It gave him time to compose himself. Lily moved like water, grace and beauty in every light step, as she made her way toward him. Her honey-colored hair was piled high on her head, held fast with a series of glittering combs, just as he'd asked. The dress he'd had crafted to her precise measurements cupped her gorgeous breasts and then swept in a wide arc toward the floor, managing to hint at her lithe figure even as it concealed it in yards upon yards of a deep, mellow blue-green that made her seem to glow a pale, festive gold.

He'd never seen anything more beautiful.

And then she stopped at the foot of the stair, this perfect goddess with her heart-shaped and heart-stopping face that made his own battered heart ache within his chest, and scowled at him.

"I want a mask," she said.

Rafael blinked. And tried to wrestle his roaring, possessive reaction into some kind of manageable bounds. It wouldn't do to throw her down on the stairs, to lick his way into her heat and taste the secrets she still hid from him. It wouldn't do to rip that perfect gown into shreds where she stood, the better to worship the curve of her sweet hip and the lily tattoo that he knew danced there, out of sight.

"Why?"

He thought he sounded relatively polite and civilized, all things considered, but her scowl only deepened.

"Do I need a reason? You said people wear them."

"So they do." He couldn't let himself touch her. Not

until he was certain he could keep himself in check. "This is Venice. But I want you to tell me why *you* want one."

Lily tilted up that marvelous chin of hers and he felt it like a bolt of heat lightning, straight into his aching sex. Soon he would be unable to walk entirely, and those stairs would look that much better. He could pull her astride him, taking the cold floor against his back, and he could—

He shook the vivid images away. Somehow.

"I want to pretend to be one of the great Venetian courtesans," she told him sharply, as if she'd read his mind. She eyed him, and Rafael was sure she had. "Isn't that why you brought me here? So I could recreate history?"

"Unless you'd like to recreate our own history right here on the hard marble steps," he said with a quiet savagery, "I suggest you try again."

She looked at him, then away, though that proud chin remained high.

"I don't want to be recognized. I don't particularly enjoy being treated like a ghost from beyond the grave." He watched the elegant line of her lovely neck as she swallowed. "Especially when I can't remember the person they'll think I am."

"I will remember for the both of us."

He didn't know where that pledge came from, as if he was a good man and this was that kind of situation. And then she looked back at him, her blue eyes lit with a kind of warm, wry humor that he thought might be the end of him right there. And she didn't quite smile, but he felt it as if she did. Like a gift.

"That's what I'm afraid of," she said.

And Rafael found he couldn't speak. He summoned the nearest servant with a lift of his finger and was glad of the few moments it took to produce a golden demimask, the perfect foil for her gown. For her lovely face.

She reached out for it, but he anticipated that and ignored her. He stepped closer to her than was entirely wise and fit the mask to her face carefully, something like reverently. He ran his fingers along the edges and smoothed it over the top of her elegant cheekbones, and felt the sweet reward of that catch in her breath and then the shiver of it, just that little bit ragged, against his hands.

"There," he said, and he sounded like a stranger. "Now no one will know who you are but me."

Lily's eyes met his through the mask, and he thought they were troubled. Too dark. Something like lonely.

Or maybe that was him.

"I thought that was the point," she whispered, and her voice was as thick as it was accusing, with that undercurrent of something like grief besides. "I thought that was what you've been at such pains to show me. That no one but you does."

"Or ever will," he agreed, more growl than vow.

And he couldn't do what he wanted to do, not then and there, so he did the next best thing. He took her hand and led her out into the night.

CHAPTER SIX

THEY TOOK A water taxi to the party, which was being held in a stately Renaissance-era palazzo that appeared to genuflect toward the dark waters of the Grand Canal. As they came in toward the dock wreathed in holiday lanterns, Lily tipped her head back to gaze up at three full stories of blazing lights from every finely carved window. Music poured out into the night, folding in on itself against the water and the stone buildings of the city, and elegantly dressed partygoers laughed loud enough to spike the breeze.

And Lily was finding it very, very difficult to breathe. At least she had the mask tonight, she thought. Not only would it conceal her identity from the rest of the world a little while longer, she hoped it might go a long way toward hiding her thoughts from Rafael, too. He read her far too easily.

The thought of what, exactly, he might be reading on her face and in her eyes at any given moment—well. That didn't exactly help her breathe any better. She tried to conceal that, too, as she slipped out of her warm cape and left it in the cabin of the water taxi Rafael had hired for the night, as directed.

Rafael handed her out of the boat when it reached the grand palazzo's guest dock, and Lily was proud of herself when she simply climbed out, as if touching him was nothing to her. Then he took her arm as they walked up the elegant steps toward the festive great hall, its doors flung open to the night as if the cold dared not enter and the dark had best submit to the blaze of so many torches. He was warm beside her, and something like steel, and Lily told herself her awareness of him was a warning, that was all.

Beware. That was what her pulse was trying to tell her as it beat out a frenetic pattern against her neck. *Be careful here. With him.*

Nothing more than a warning.

Inside the open central hall of the magnificent palazzo, it was like a dizzying sort of dream. Like being swept up into a jewel-studded music box and meant to twirl along with all the gorgeous creatures who were already there in all their finery, moving this way and that across the marble floors and beneath the benign majesty of priceless glass chandeliers some two stories above. Rafael excused himself to go and do his duty to their hosts, his neighbors, leaving Lily to find her way to one of the great pillars and stand there, happily anonymous. She braced herself against the stout, cool marble as if it could anchor her to the earth. She didn't know where to look first. A single glance at the scene before her and she felt glutted, overdone on sensation and stimuli.

On this particular Venetian magic.

Lily had certainly attended her share of fancy parties in the past. She'd even gone to a great ball in a Roman villa once, with the entire Castelli family and her own mother in attendance. She'd attended glamorous weddings in stunning locales international and domestic, exclusive charity events that had seemed to compete for the title of Most Over the Top, and had once danced in a brand-new year with most of Manhattan spread out at her feet in a desperately chic four-story penthouse on Central Park West.

But all of that had been a long time ago, and none of it had been Venice.

Tonight, everyone glittered the way the finest diamonds did, unmistakably well cut and intriguingly multifaceted. The women were nothing less than stunning, while each and every man was distractingly debonair. Was it the people or the place itself? Lily couldn't tell. The air itself seemed richer, brighter. There were jovial feathers and the occasional masks, striking black tie and sumptuous couture. Gowns and jewels and sartorial splendor crowded the whole of the expansive first level of the palace, a gracious orchestra played holiday-tinged music from a raised marble dais that seemed to hover as if by magic just above the throng and the sleek marble dance floor in the center of the grand space opened up to the night sky above, yet was surrounded by so many clever little heaters that it was impossible to feel the mid-December chill.

Lily shivered anyway, and she knew it wasn't the temperature. It was the sheer, exultant decadence. This was a sinking city, a nearly forgotten way of life, and yet not a single bright and shining person before her seemed the least bit aware of any of those unpleasant realities as they danced and laughed and pushed back the night.

Something inside her turned over too hard, then ached.

"Come," Rafael said, his mouth against her ear and the steel expanse of his chest at her back, and that ache bloomed instantly into something darker. Thicker. Infinitely more dangerous. "I want to dance."

"There must be hundreds of women here," Lily replied, her eyes on the spectacle before her. It was overwhelming, yes—but he was worse. He was so much worse and infinitely more tempting. "I'm sure one of them would dance with you. If you asked nicely."

His laughter was a dark and silvery thing, light against

her ear and then, deep inside her, a tectonic shift that sent tendrils of need shooting off in all directions, and she couldn't bring herself to jerk away from him the way she knew she should.

"I don't want to dance with them, *cara*. I want to dance with you."

Lily wanted to dance with him in this magical palace more than she could recall wanting anything, ever, which was precisely how she knew she shouldn't do anything of the kind. She pulled her head away from that sweet brush of his mouth against her ear, though it took her much too long and hurt a bit too much to break that connection. When she turned to face him, his gaze was trained on the upper swells of her breasts where they rose above her bodice, where she could feel the goose bumps from his proximity prickling to life. The truth of her reaction to him. Obvious and unmistakable, no matter what she said.

Rafael took a long time raising that dark gold gaze to meet hers, and when he finally did, his expression was a molten, simmering thing that nearly made her moan out loud.

"I don't dance," she told him. Quickly, before she could betray herself by saying nothing at all—by letting him simply sweep her along with him. He stood there, tall and darkly beautiful and wearing black tie as if it had been crafted specifically as an homage to his perfect masculine form, and she wanted to cry. Sob. Scream. Anything to break that rising tension inside her. Anything to break the hold he had on her. Anything but what she felt called to do, down deep in her bones, and in that deep, lush throb between her legs. "I mean, I don't think I know how."

"You do."

"I don't know what good it will do to tell me that, if I can't remember and trip all over your feet and make a terrible scene. I doubt that's the kind of spectacle you want at a party like this."

She only realized how snappish she sounded when he reached over and traced the lower edge of her mask with a single finger. It was pressure, not heat. He wasn't touching her, not really, and there was absolutely no reason whatso-ever that her pulse should speed up like that, or her breath should hitch. Noticeably.

More evidence against her, she knew.

"You don't have to remember, Lily," he said, his gaze much too bright and his voice a low, caressing thing that did everything his finger did and more, winding inside her and making her whole body clench tight and hot and needy. "You only need to follow where I lead."

Rafael didn't wait for her answer, which she supposed was some kind of blessing. Or more likely, it being the two of them, a curse. He simply reached down, took her hand and led her out on to the floor.

And Lily told herself she was blending in with the crowd here, nothing more. That she didn't want to be rec-ognized at all tonight, which meant she also didn't want to draw any attention to herself by causing a scene. It was bad enough that Rafael was so gorgeous and so instantly recognizable—she could see heads turn as he cut through the crowd, something that was so commonplace to him, clearly, that he didn't even seem to notice it as it happened. Lily told herself it was the right thing to do, to go along with him so obediently, so easily. That she was simply mak-ing sure she remained anonymous and unremarkable—just another well-dressed woman in a demimask, one of many here tonight.

But then he turned and took her in his arms, and Lily stopped thinking about anything but him.

Rafael.

His sensual mouth was a grim line, but she could see that searing intensity in his eyes, and it made her tremble deep inside. She had no defense against that hand that wrapped around hers, or the one that settled low on her back, as if she was naked, as if the sleek fall of her dress was no barrier at all. He could have pressed a burning coal to her bare skin and she thought that might have affected her less. She swallowed hard as she slid her own hand into place, over the taut, corded muscles of his sculpted shoulder, and felt the bright hot heat of him blaze into her as if he was a radiator.

Lily felt scalded. Turned pink and raw from even that much fully clothed contact—but all she could seem to do was stare up at him, her lips parting on a ragged breath, his own dark need like a physical presence she could feel as well as her own.

She knew she should have done something—anything—to lighten the moment, to wrench herself away or to conceal how she shook at his touch, at that predatory, possessive look in his dark eyes, but she didn't.

She didn't do a thing. And for a moment they only stood there, staring at each other. Stock-still as the dance wove and swirled around them, as if they were the center of a carousel, and the only thing Lily knew for that moment—that endless eternity—was that they were touching at last. After five long and lonely years, she was in his arms again.

Where you belong, some suicidal part of her whispered. *Where you have always belonged and always will.*

And then Rafael began to move.

Lily felt as if she was floating. She had no sense of him, of her, as separate entities—there was only the glory of the waltz and of his masterful touch, the way they flew across the floor as if they were all alone, the way his gaze wrecked her and remade her with every step. She forgot where she ended and he began. She was too close to him, her hand gripping his hand and her fingers digging deep into his shoulder, and his palm against her back was a revelation.

Around and around they went. And it was like falling. It was like flying.

It was all the poetry she'd never written, step by well-executed step, pooling in the white-hot space that was barely there between them.

And then the song blended into something else, something far more Christmas inspired than sweepingly romantic. Lily blinked as if a spell had been lifted. Rafael slowed, muttering out what sounded like one of his fanciful Italian curses beneath his breath.

"What's the matter?" she asked, but she was too dazed still to worry overmuch. Besides, she felt *everything*. The press of her fine clothes against her heated skin. The warmth of the great room, of his hard, hot hand in the small of her back, flirting with the upper swell of her bottom. The way he held her against him, his strong thigh too close to that wild, wanton place that hungered for him the most.

She was molten and he was steel and she *wanted*. God help her, how she always *wanted* this man, no matter what.

Rafael didn't respond to her halfhearted question, and Lily didn't care. The look on his face was stark, almost pained, and she exulted in it. Because she knew exactly what it was—what had happened to him in the course of that waltz. It was the same thing that always happened, no matter what they did. It was this *thing* of theirs that had destroyed them so many times already it hardly bore tallying up any longer. But here, now, at a fanciful pageant of a Christmas party in the depths of December in this city of light and magic, she couldn't manage to care about all that the way she knew she should.

It was as if that dance was inside them now, insistent and elegant, elemental and demanding.

He made a sound that was more that wolf in him than the genteel and civilized man he was playing tonight, and Lily felt her nipples go hard against the constriction of her dress's bodice and her toes cramp up in her impractical shoes. Then Rafael was moving again, not dancing this time, but striding through the crowd. Pulling her with him as he went, weaving in and out of the dancing couples and then propelling them down a dimly lit corridor off to the side of the main hall, where ancient oil paintings featured dour and scowling men on the ornately paneled walls while smaller doors led off into the bowels of the palace.

"I don't think this is open to the public," Lily said dubiously, looking around with a frown. "I don't think we're supposed to be back here. Do you?"

"I cannot imagine caring about anything less than that," Rafael muttered. And then something else in gruff Italian. "*Mi appartieni.*"

Or that was what she thought he said, it was so fierce and low. *You belong to me.* And then he swung her around so her back was against the nearest wall. She had a glimmering moment to take in the nearly savage look on his dark face, and then his mouth was on hers.

And all hell broke loose.

This wasn't a moment of shocked surprise on the street. This was nothing but need, pure and greedy and entirely, exultantly mutual.

Lily couldn't pretend otherwise. She didn't bother to try.

This was fire. This was passion. Their history and that electric perfection that charged so hot and bright between them, an instant conflagration. Lily burned. She wrapped herself around him, she forgot herself completely and she let him set them both alight.

Rafael kissed the way he did everything. With sheer, uncompromising ruthlessness and devastating skill. He took over her mouth, tasting her again and again, shoving her back into the wall and using it to keep her exactly where he wanted her. He made a low noise as he kissed her, over and over, as if he couldn't get enough. As if it would never be enough.

As if there was no word for *enough* in either one of their languages.

He held her face between his hands, and he angled his head, blasting the kiss straight into another level of sheer, dizzying sensation. Lily felt her knees go weak and her whole body seem to shake, and still she met every thrust of his tongue, tasting him and taking him in her turn, each kiss as drugging and impossible and wildly delirious as the next.

She must have dreamed the taste of him a thousand times since she'd walked away from that life, from him, but the reality was better. *So much better.*

Rafael shifted, his hands moving from her face to test the shape of her breasts through the smooth fabric of her bodice, and she knew from the appreciative noise he made precisely when he found the stiff peaks. But then it was her turn to cry out when he covered them with his palms and pressed into them, rough and greedy and infinitely knowing, making her throw her head back and arch into his touch for more of that delicious pressure.

He followed her mouth with his, as if he was unwilling to lose her taste for even a moment, and she didn't know which one of them strained toward the other. Who moved, who touched. Who took, who gave. It was all a wild, brilliant tangle of sensation. Need and longing and their age-old ability to drive each other mad, like an explosion that kept going off. And off. Without end.

She had to pull away from that hard, clever mouth of his for a moment to breathe, or at least to try. The hall they stood in was still as dark and deserted as before, but the lights and music beckoned just there, just out of reach through that far-off arch, so many people *right there* who could walk in on them at any moment—

The way it had always been. Desire and the risk of discovery, all knotted together and hidden away where only they could see it, feel it, succumb to it.

And then she forgot about their past, about the party and the people and the whole damned world, because his hands were on her long skirt and then beneath it, and he was urging her leg over his hip with those sure, hard hands, his mouth an open fire against her neck.

Lily didn't think. She burned.

She wrapped her arms around his neck and she gripped him with her leg as he reached between them, and then his gaze found hers. Dark and wild. She felt her mouth drop open. She saw his jaw clench tight as he dealt with his trousers. And then his fingers were moving her panties to one side and the thick, blunt head of his hardness was probing her entrance.

She shook. Everywhere. She shook and she shook and she'd forgotten it, this glorious shaking from the inside out. She'd forgotten how visceral this was, how necessary. Like breath.

Only better.

"I told you," he gritted out. "One kiss. That's all it ever takes."

And then he thrust deep inside her. Hard and deep and true.

Perfect and *Rafael*, after all this time.

Lily fell to pieces, shattering into a thousand fragments at that glorious fit, and only then did he move. Each thrust wilder and deeper than the last. The fever of it, the wild and glorious dance, catching her up when she would have come down and winding her tighter and tighter all over again.

As if all of this need was new.

As if they were.

He slid a hand down to her bottom to lift her against him, pulling her higher until she crossed her legs around him and gripped his shoulders, and then he leaned her back against the wall, braced them with his other hand and hammered himself into her.

Lily loved it. She more than loved it. It was coming home, drenched in fire. It was Rafael. It was *them*.

Again. At last.

And when she threw back her head and came apart again, biting her lip to keep from screaming though her throat ached, he groaned out her name against the side of her neck and followed.

Rafael had no idea how long they stood there like that.

His breath came so hard it almost hurt, he rested his forehead against hers while he tried to catch it and he understood that he had not felt this *rightness* in so long he'd begun to think he'd imagined the whole thing. *Her.* The way they moved together, the sheer and blazing poetry of their lovemaking that had been the only thing he'd thought about some years.

If anything, he'd minimized her effect on him. Her power over him. The beauty of this wild flame that still danced so brightly between them.

He was already hardening again inside her, and he moved his hips experimentally, but it was still the same. That desperate heat. That wildness like a thirst, that all these years later he still had no earthly idea how to quench. He still didn't want to do anything but drown in it. In her.

Lily had never been anything but a revelation to him. That hadn't changed.

But she pushed against him. Then again, harder, and he realized she'd gone stiff in his arms.

"Let me down," she said, her voice thick and something like dangerous, edgy and tight.

Rafael angled himself back, little as that appealed, and then helped her lower her legs to the floor. He bit back a satisfied smile when she sagged slightly, then gripped the wall, as if her knees were precarious beneath her.

But he felt his amusement fade when he met her tormented gaze.

"Lily," he began, reaching over to brush her cheek, not entirely surprised that she was trembling uncontrollably. He could feel it like a series of earthquakes, rippling over her, through her. He felt the same in him. "*Cara*, surely—"

"I can't do this again!" she threw at him. She made a sharp sound as if she was in pain, or as if she hadn't meant to speak. Her eyes were much too dark, and he tucked himself back in his trousers as he studied her expression, as she splayed out a hand over her middle as if she ached while her dress fell back into place all around her as if they'd never touched at all. He found he hated it. "I can't *do* this!"

"Lily," he said again, but it was as if she couldn't hear him. As if there was a storm enveloping her where she stood, only a few inches away from him and yet somewhere else entirely.

"Look where we are!" she hissed at him. She slashed a hand in the direction of the party down the hall, her face contorted and moisture leaking down her cheeks from behind the demimask she still wore. "We might as well have put on a show in the center of the dance floor! Anyone could have seen us!"

He made an impatient noise. "No one did."

"You don't know that. You *hope* that. And it's as childish and immature and *irresponsible* now as it was five years ago—except worse, because what happens to Arlo if our sexcapades make the tabloids this time?"

Rafael started to speak, to reassure her again, but then stopped. Froze, more like, into a column of sheer and solid ice where he stood. He felt something like light-headed. As if the great stone palazzo had turned on its end and landed square in the center of his chest.

"What did you say?" He realized he'd asked that in Italian and translated it into clipped English, his pulse like a clanging bell in his temples.

"I can't do this!" she hurled at him, as if he hadn't spoken. "I know exactly where this leads. Me, alone on the side of the road, with no choice but to run away from my entire life. You're heroin and I'm little better than a junkie and everything between us is toxic, Rafael. *It always has been.*"

And then she whirled and threw herself back toward the crowd, not seeming to notice or care that she was still unsteady on her feet. The mad, elegant whirl was still carrying on just on the far side of the nearest archway, bright and loud, and she lurched toward it as if she might fall over in her haste to escape him—as if she wouldn't much care if she did.

While Rafael stood there in the dim hallway, as stunned as if she'd clubbed him over the head. She might as well have.

She remembered. She knew.

It had been one thing to suspect she remembered. It was another to have her confirm it.

He heard a low, inarticulate noise and understood he'd made it. That it had welled up from deep inside him, from that dark place where he'd locked these things away—

Then, feeling blinded somehow by the intensity of what pounded into him in waves, blinded and yet focused and understanding that was as much the force of his temper as anything else, he went after her.

He caught up to her on the steps of the palazzo, outside near the canal. She whirled around before he could take her elbow, as if she'd heard him coming and had known it was him by the sound of his feet against the stone, and she dashed moisture from her cheeks with her hands clenched in fists.

Rafael told himself he didn't care if she cried. That the very least she could do, after what she'd done to him, was shed a few tears.

It took him long moments to recognize that the moisture on her face was not tears at all. It was snow. It fell all around them, soft and silent, disappearing as it met the water of the canal, the dock at their feet, the lovely bridge lit up in the distance. It was possibly the only thing in the world more beautiful than this treacherous liar in front of him, and he couldn't bring himself to care about that, either.

"You lied." He hardly sounded like himself, and he didn't dare reach for her. He didn't trust himself to touch her just then. She had finally admitted the truth. That she had betrayed him so terribly he could hardly make sense of it, and in that moment he was so hollow and so desperate he didn't know what he might do. For the first time in his life, he didn't know himself at all. "You lied all this time. You hid from me, on purpose. You deliberately kept my son from me for *five years*. Then you lied even more when I found you."

He didn't realize, until he heard the echo of his own voice on the water, that he was not exactly speaking softly. Standing on the steps of a Venice palazzo in the snow with a woman long presumed dead, who had been his stepsister when alive, was not exactly discreet.

But she didn't cower. Lily—and she was wholly Lily, *his* Lily, and she had never been anything else, goddamn her—laughed. There was nothing like joy in it. It was a terrible sound, as wretched as he felt, and he thought it must have hurt her. He hated that he cared about that. That her pain mattered to him when his clearly did not register with her at all.

"Which glass house should we throw stones at tonight, Rafael?" she demanded, her voice as awful as that brittle, broken laugh, as his own had been. "This is what we do. This is who we are and who we've always been. We hurt each other. Again and again and again. What does it matter how?"

"You faked your death!" he roared at her, through the snow and the cold and the echo of the music pouring out from inside the grand palace that rose up behind them in all its Christmas finery. Then he checked himself, though it cost him. "How is anything I did to you equivalent?"

"I didn't fake it." She was breathing so hard it was as if she was running, but she was standing still, just as he was. As if they were both frozen together here in this horrid moment of truth. As if there could be no escaping it, no avoiding it, for either one of them. "I simply didn't come forward and correct anybody when they thought the worst. It's not the same thing."

He didn't recognize the harsh, nearly violent feeling that rushed through him then, nearly taking him from his feet. He took a step back, and the world rushed back at him, reminding him again that they were standing outside, in public, in view of most of Venice and half the world, airing laundry so dirty he thought exposure to it could contaminate the whole of Italy.

He had to contain this. He had to lock this down before it consumed him whole. Before he looked behind the stunned fury that worked in him and truly let himself feel what lurked there on the other side—

But that was for another time. Another place. Rafael whistled for his water taxi, and his driver appeared from the shadows so quickly he couldn't help but wonder how much the man had overheard. He couldn't do anything about that, so he took Lily's arm again instead.

He thought the sheer audacity of her betrayal might have dimmed his raging, timeless, insatiable lust for her—but it was the opposite. The moment he touched her, he hungered for her as if he hadn't just had her. It was almost as if he wanted her *more*, knowing what she'd done to him.

You've never been anything but wildly obsessed where she was concerned, he told himself then. *Why should this surprise you?*

"Not here," he bit out at her, and he didn't let himself look at her. He wasn't sure he'd be able to keep himself from snarling at her—or worse, kissing her until all of this ugly truth faded away. "I think we've put on quite enough of a show for one night."

She tried to extricate herself from his grip, then scowled at him when he didn't give her an inch as he pulled her along with him down the stairs, through the swirling snow and toward the dock.

"So near-public sex is fine, but heaven forbid anyone overhear an argument?" Lily demanded. She balked when they approached the boat, digging her heels into the slippery dock surface, but he kept moving and therefore, so did she. It was that or let him drag her, and he wasn't surprised she chose the former. "I'm not going anywhere with you. You must be insane!"

"I am a long way past insane, Lily," Rafael said, and

he saw her eyes go wide at his tone, soft and lethal. He leaned in close, holding her gaze with his, and made no attempt at all to hide his dark, seething fury. "I mourned you. I missed you. My life was little more than mausoleum erected to your memory, and it was all a lie. A lie you told by your purposeful absence for years and then, when I found you completely by accident, you told deliberately, to my face."

He could feel her shake beneath his hand, and he didn't think it was that same heat that had worked in her before, that shimmering need he knew as well as his own. He could see that complicated storm in her blue eyes, in the way her lovely mouth trembled and hinted at her reasons, and he didn't want this. Any of this. He'd spent five years dreaming of her return to him, safe and unharmed and his again, but he'd never spent much time worrying about how that might happen. He wasn't sure he wanted to know.

Maybe there were some doors better left closed.

"Rafael—" she began, with a catch in her voice that would be his undoing, if he let it. He refused to let it. And this wasn't the place, no matter what.

He didn't quite bare his teeth as he cut her off.

"If I were you, I'd get in the goddamned boat."

CHAPTER SEVEN

THE BOAT RIDE back across the canal was tense and silent. The snow fell around them like the kind of holiday blessing neither one of them deserved, muffling out the sounds of the old city and transforming it, making it that much more serene. But far worse than that, Lily thought darkly as she wrapped her warm cape tightly around her bare shoulders and glared out at the world become a literal snow globe, the ride across the water was entirely too brief.

She'd revealed herself at last. Lily had no idea what that meant, only that it was done and there was no taking it back.

Much too soon, Rafael led her from the boat and into the waiting loggia level of his family's palazzo, his temper a living thing that walked beside them, between them, thicker than the Venice night all around them and stronger than the hand wrapped around her arm. It didn't occur to her to defy him. She didn't imagine it would do her any good.

And if she was honest with herself, Lily knew that as much as she'd tried to avoid this moment of unfortunate truth, a far deeper part of her was glad. Not that she'd succumbed to that destructive passion again, the way she always did like the addict she was—but that there would be no more lies.

She told herself that was a good thing, as she handed

off her cape to the waiting servant and shivered—though not because she was cold. It was time for honesty, however ugly. It was past time.

Rafael strode through the collection of rooms on the second level, more commonly rented out for things like art exhibits these days than for giving parties like the one they'd just left, then up the stairs she'd come down what seemed like a lifetime ago to the private family living suites above. He kept that seemingly polite hand anchored in the small of her back, guiding her where he wanted her to go, and somehow she didn't quite dare disobey him. Not when she sensed he was holding on the pretense of civility by the skin of his teeth, if that. When a glance at his set, hard face made her think of wild and untamed things, uncontrollable passions, and challenges she hoped she was too wise these days to take.

She hoped.

He ushered her into the vast common room in the center of the bedroom suites that rambled over the upper floor, commanding views of lovely, snowy Venice in all directions. Then he left her standing there in the center of all that opulent art and ancient craft, from the frescoes that adorned the walls to the stunning sweep of paintings to the elegance of the furnishings themselves. An excessive example of the Castelli wealth—and its power—in a single overwarm room, with the brooding fury of Rafael at its center. She watched him stride over to the carved wood cabinet that served as a bar in the corner and pour himself something rich and dark into a heavy-looking tumbler. He tossed it back, then poured himself another, and only then did he turn to face her.

Only then did Lily fully comprehend that she'd simply stood there where he'd left her, like a windup doll waiting to be played with again. Or as if she was awaiting his judgment. As if she deserved his condemnation—but she shied away from that thought almost as soon as it formed.

Rafael was not the victim here. Neither was she. Or they both were, perhaps, and of the same wild passion.

And she told herself that the fact she was still standing there had nothing to do with that glimpse of something like hurt she thought she'd seen on his face when he'd come after her on the steps of the palazzo across the canal. So dark and tormented, and she knew she'd put that there. She knew she'd done that to him, no matter who was the victim here.

Lily had left him, and in the worst way imaginable. That was undeniable. Why should she care if knowing what she'd done hurt him? Hadn't she already hurt him—and everyone else she knew? What could one more hurt matter, set against all the rest?

But she found she was pressing the heel of her hand against her chest, as if that might make it—*her*—feel less hollow.

"Take off that mask," he rasped at her, and the great room they stood in felt closer. Tighter all around her, as if he could control the walls themselves with that terrible voice. "It's time to face each other, after all this time. Don't you think?"

And the truth was, Lily had forgotten she wore the mask at all. Just as she'd forgotten how cold it had been outside until now, when the heat wrapped around her and made her chilled skin seem obvious. Almost painful. She thought there was some shade of meaning in that, as if even the weather was conspiring with Rafael, forcing her to feel all the things she'd vowed she'd never feel again.

But it was time for the truth. For honesty, however brutal.

She pulled the mask from her face and cast it down on the nearest settee that sat with its high back facing her, and she told herself there was no reason whatsoever she should feel vulnerable, suddenly, without it. How had it protected her? The truth was, it hadn't. She could still feel his possession like a pulsing brand between her legs, hot and wild.

He hadn't touched her mask. He'd taken her instead.

And she'd let him. She'd more than *let* him—she'd encouraged him.

Neither one of them had caused this mad thing between them, she knew that. They were both its victim. They were both equally lost in it. They always had been.

"Now," Rafael said, when she looked at him again, still in that voice far darker than the snowy December night at the windows. "Explain."

"You already know what happened."

"No." He looked something more than simply angry. Something more, too, than *hurt*, and she felt that like a fluttering unease deep in her belly. "I know that you died, supposedly. And I know that I then saw you years later on a street in a funny little corner of America. I have drawn conclusions about what must have happened between those two events while you were busy playing identity games, but no. I do not know what happened." She saw his hand tighten around his glass. She felt it as if it had tightened around her, instead. "I certainly don't know *why*."

Lily had spent five years trying to answer these questions to her own satisfaction—but it was something else to answer to *him*. To Rafael, who was the reason behind all of the terrible decisions she'd made in her life, one way or another. She swallowed, found her throat dry and tucked her arms beneath her chest as if that could bolster her against him. Or against this story she'd never wanted to tell.

She still didn't.

"Maybe it's better to let these things lie," she suggested, shocked that her voice sounded so small. She cleared her throat, tried to stand taller. "Please remember that I didn't want to be found."

"Believe me, I remember." His voice was a lash. He swirled the liquid in his glass, his dark eyes on her, and she had the distinct impression he could see all the fine hairs on the back of her neck and along her arms stand up. "And you are stalling."

"What does it matter why?" She fought to sound calm, no matter what she might feel inside. "What can knowing *why* do except make things worse?"

"You let me think you were dead," he hurled at her, and she realized as he did how much he'd been holding back before, out there on the canal. He wasn't restraining himself now, and it took everything she had to keep from flinching away from all that rough emotion. "You let the whole world think you were dead. What kind of person would visit her own death on the people who loved her?"

"You didn't love me," she threw back at him before she had time to temper that. He stiffened, but it was said. There was no taking it back. And besides, it was true. This was about truth. "You were obsessed. You were addicted, maybe. To the secrecy. To the twistedness. To the sheer delight in all the sneaking around and the excitement of all that passion. I know. I was there. But love? No."

"You've done enough, I think, without lecturing me on how I felt."

"I know what you felt," she retorted. "I felt what you felt."

"Evidently not," he gritted out. "Or you would not have sent a car over the side of a cliff and walked away from the wreckage, leaving me to imagine your horrible, painful death forever. You did not feel what I felt, Lily. I rather doubt you feel anything at all."

That stung, but she stood tall and took it. She waited

until her heart felt less painful in her chest as it beat. Until she could speak without that betraying thickness clogging up her throat.

"I felt too much," she told him. "Too much of everything. Too much to bear."

His lips pressed flat, and his gaze was a dark condemnation far worse than anything he could have said. "You'll forgive me if I am unconvinced. Your actions speak their own truth, Lily."

"And what of yours?"

"*I loved you.*" He didn't shout that, either, not quite, and yet Lily thought it rattled the walls, made the whole palazzo shake on its uncertain foundation. "I have never been whole since."

"I think you've fallen in love with a ghost," she told him, her voice shaking slightly. "In retrospect." He made a rough noise, but she ignored it and kept going. "You had five years to make your lost Lily up in your head. Was she virtuous and pure? Did you love her so desperately no living woman can compare? Was her loss a blow from which you've never quite recovered?" She shrugged when he scowled at her. "She sounds like a paragon. But that's not me, Rafael. And that was certainly not you."

"I loved you," he gritted out again, and though he was quieter this time, she still felt it slam through her. "You can't make that go away because it isn't convenient for you."

"I remember exactly how you loved me, Rafael," she told him in the same sort of voice, holding herself tightly in check, as if that might keep her safe from all these truths filling the room. "I remember all the women you slept with while you claimed we had to remain a secret. You said you had to maintain your cover. You laughed when it upset me. Tell me, did you love me this much while you were inside them?"

And for a moment Lily didn't know which was worse—the possibility that he wouldn't answer her...or that he would.

"If this is your version of an explanation, it's terrible," he snarled at her after a long beat, and then he tossed back the contents of his glass in a single smooth motion. He slapped the tumbler down on the cabinet behind him with a loud *crack* that made Lily jump. "I'm not the liar in this room."

"On the contrary," she replied, hoping there was none of that jumpiness in her voice. "There are two liars in this room. You're not the story you've been telling yourself, Rafael."

"Is this the real Lily talking now or this ghost I made up in my head?" he asked, his dark gaze glittering with fury. "I'm finding it difficult to keep track."

She shook her head at him. "Liars are all we've ever been, starting that first night when you took my virginity on a pile of coats in the guest room of your father's château and then strolled back into the party to kiss your girlfriend at midnight as if it had never happened." Lily laughed softly at his expression, not sure where the will to do so came from, when he looked so fierce. "I'm sorry, had you prettied that up in your imagination? Made it all wine and roses and no cheating or sneaking around? Well, that wasn't us. And I'm as bad as you are, make no mistake, because I knew perfectly well you had a girlfriend and I didn't try to stop it."

He stared at her, all outraged male and dark ruthlessness besides, and she watched as that sank in. As it moved through him. And she'd imagined this moment so many times. She'd envisioned bludgeoning him with the truth and that changing everything, somehow.

But instead she felt worse. Incalculably worse.

"We were terrible people," she said then, with an urgency that made her voice shake slightly.

"We must have been," he said as he moved toward her, a kind of bleakness in his voice she'd never heard before. "Look at where we are."

"Maybe," she told him, her voice low, "you should have let us both forget."

He shook his head, an expression she'd never seen before moving over his dark face.

"But that's the problem, isn't it? Neither one of us has forgotten a thing."

That felt like a dig. Lily stiffened. "That doesn't mean we have to wallow in the past."

"Is that what you think this is?" Rafael asked. He shrugged, an edgy movement that did nothing to mask that thunderous, broken thing in his gaze. "Maybe so. But I'm not going to apologize for how I mourned you, Lily. How I coped with your loss. You walked away. You knew what you were doing. I didn't have that choice."

"Your choices came before that," she retorted, stung and hurt and furious at the both of them, that all of this could still hurt like this after so much time had passed. After so much had changed. "And you chose secrets. Lies. Other women."

"I won't deny that I was a selfish man, Lily," he bit out, his gaze like fire, and she didn't know when he'd ventured so close to her. "I can't. I regret it every day. But we had no commitment. I may not have treated you as well as I should have, but I didn't betray you."

She pulled in a breath, amazed at the burst of white-hot pain that caused when there was nothing fresh or new in this. Nothing but an old wound, a dull blade.

And the same familiar hand to wield it.

"Of course you didn't." She wished she could hate him.

She truly did. Surely that would be better. Simpler. "Oh, and along those lines, I never concealed Arlo from you. Technically. Had I seen you, I would have told you."

That shimmered in the air between them, like anguish.

If she could die from this, Lily thought, she would have already. Years ago. God knew, she'd come close.

Rafael said something harsh in Italian, vicious and low. He hauled her to him with a wholly inelegant hand around her neck, sending her sprawling into his hard chest. Then he stopped talking and took her mouth with his.

And this time, there was no party nearby. No parents who might be horrified at what their stepprogeny were about. No one to walk in on them. No one to hear.

This time, Rafael took his time.

He kissed her like this really was love. Like she'd been wrong all along. His mouth was condemnation and caress at once, taking her over and drawing her near, and Lily lost herself the way she always did.

Heedless. Hungry. Needy and desperate and entirely his.

Just as it had always been.

Rafael shrugged his way out of his coat, letting it drop to the thick carpet beneath them, and still he kissed her. He sank his hands deep into her hair, scattering the combs that held it in place until the heavy mass of it tumbled down around them and the sparkling accessories rained out across the floor, and still he stroked her tongue with his, deeper and more intense, as if nothing in the world could ever matter as much as the delirious friction of his mouth against hers.

Lily traced the planes of his chest, unable to control herself and not certain she wanted to try. She dug her fingers into the gaps between his buttons and pulled, gratified when the buttons burst free and exposed the smooth, hard planes of his sculpted chest. And then she succumbed to that same old need and ran her palms against his hot, smooth skin like red-hot steel with its dusting of dark hair. She was aware of his scent, soap and Rafael, his devil's mouth teasing hers to endless wickedness, and the truth of her own mounting desire for this man she shouldn't want like a near-painful ache low in her belly.

She wrenched her mouth from his and they both panted as they stared at each other, all the twisted wrongness of their connection, all the lies they'd told and the things they'd done, like a thick mist between them, blurring the edges of things.

He said something despairing in Italian that hurt to hear, and she didn't even understand the words. Lily didn't know what to do. It was easier to hurl old, embittered words at him. It was easier to try to hate him.

It was so very easy to hate herself, lecture herself on the importance of abstinence, call herself an addict. But heroin didn't feel pain in return. Heroin didn't *hurt*.

It was infinitely harder to tilt her head closer and to press her lips into the hollow between his pectoral muscles, like the apology she didn't dare utter. That she was afraid to admit she wanted to speak out loud at all.

Rafael sighed, or perhaps it was a groan, and tore the rest of his shirt off without her having to ask. And then he stood there, bared to the waist, even more perfect than he'd been all these years inside her head.

She couldn't read the look on his face then, nor define what rose in her in response. What tore at her and threatened to rip her apart, and it was all there in the dark gold of his eyes. In the constriction in her chest, making her wonder if she'd ever really breathe again.

"Turn around," he ordered her. She froze, but he only stared back at her implacably, his eyes too dark and too bright. "Do not make me repeat myself."

She obeyed without quite meaning to, turning so her back was to him and she faced the scrolled height of the nearby settee.

"Rafael—" she began, but cut herself off on a sharp intake of breath when he came up hard behind her, that mighty chest of his pressed into her back, making her feel dizzy with need.

That endless, delirious, life-altering need.

"These are your choices, Lily." His mouth was close enough to that sensitive place just behind her ear that she could feel the tickle of it, a sharp, impossible electricity that seemed to bolt straight through her to linger in her core. She was surrounded by him, sex and scent and strength, and she didn't know what she felt. Who she was anymore, when she was with him. What the hell she was doing. But she also couldn't seem to stop. "You can walk away right now, go to sleep, dream of all the ways we've wronged each other so we can tear bigger chunks from each other in the morning. I won't blame you if you do."

She felt as if she couldn't breathe, but that was her, she understood, making that rough sound. That harsh breathing a little too close to outright panting.

"Or…?" she asked, in a voice that hardly sounded like hers.

But it was. She knew it was.

So did Rafael.

And he was hard and hot and perfect behind her. "Or you can bend over that settee and hold on tight."

Rafael expected her to bolt. To take a breath and then hurl herself away from him. Run screaming from him. Maybe some part of him wanted her to do exactly that.

Maybe he didn't know which one of them he was trying to scare.

He heard the deep, shuddering breath she took. He braced himself for her to walk away. Told himself that he would let her. That he had no other choice.

"And…" She shifted from one foot to the other. "And what happens if I do that?"

He didn't pretend he didn't know which *that* she meant. Triumph lashed at him, more potent than the whiskey he'd tossed back, and he smiled. Hard.

His hand smoothed down the length of her side, all that silken heat and the tattoo he knew waited for him beneath her dress. She bucked slightly against him, then went too still, as if she couldn't control herself any better than he could.

And he found that made all the difference. It clarified things.

It didn't matter how messy this was. What they'd lost. How they'd lied.

It didn't make her any less his.

Nothing could.

"Bend over, Lily," he ordered her, as gruff as he was certain, and he was animal enough to enjoy the trembling reaction he could see her fight to repress when he said it. "Now."

CHAPTER EIGHT

LILY STEPPED AWAY from him, and Rafael found he hardly breathed as she stood there for a moment, as if she hadn't quite made up her mind. Not quite yet. She shifted her weight again and he heard the faint rustle of her skirt like a shout before she twisted around to look over her shoulder at him.

Her eyes were so blue. Like that fathomless California sky. He'd thought he'd never see them again, that marvelous color. He'd had to content himself with memory. He'd had to settle for lesser blues, minor marvels.

He wasn't going to settle again.

Rafael had a thousand things he wanted to say to her, but none of that mattered when what they boiled down to was the same thing: she was his. No matter the distance, the years. The hurts lodged and the lies told. What she thought of him, them, the past, the future they'd have to work out now that there was Arlo to consider. That was all noise.

Lily was the sweet, deep quiet at the center of all of that. *She was his.*

He saw her breathe in, then let it out. He saw her decision flash in her gorgeous eyes, a resolve that lifted her chin again and made every part of him clench tight in anticipation and a spark of something much too close to fear—

She turned away from him again and took another step, then bent herself forward, gripping the back of the settee the way he'd told her to do.

Lust and need and a deep kick of pure triumph punched into him then. So hard it hollowed him out. He wanted her so badly in that moment that if he touched her, he imagined he'd simply implode. And that wouldn't do at all.

So instead, he made her wait.

He went back over to the bar and poured himself another drink. He took his time with it, watching her intently.

"Do not move," he ordered her, more silk than reprimand, when he saw her shift as if she meant to straighten. "It is your turn to wait, Lily. I waited for five years with no hope that you would ever return. You've waited five seconds so far and you know exactly where I am. You can suffer the unknown a little while longer, don't you think?"

"I didn't know you were into torture," she retorted, and he could see her defiance in the way she braced herself against the ornate little settee, too fussy to be a couch. The way she tilted her head to one side, sending all that heavy, slippery strawberry blond hair of hers cascading over one shoulder. "Is that a new hobby?"

"You have no idea," he murmured.

"You could simply kiss me like a normal person," she pointed out, almost chattily, as if she wasn't standing there in a remarkably provocative position, awaiting his pleasure. "Or is that too pedestrian for a Castelli heir in a Venetian palazzo?"

"Ogni volta che ti bacio dimentico dove sono." Every time I kiss you I forget where I am. He hadn't meant to say that.

But the truth was, he didn't simply want this woman. He admired her. He craved her sharp tongue as much as he wanted to feel the wet heat of it against his skin. He had never managed to reconcile himself to the loss of her. He had been made a different man entirely by her loss—and he didn't know, now, how to pull those different pieces of himself together into one again. If that was even possible.

He set his drink back down untouched and roamed back toward her, eyeing the picture she made as she waited there with the dress the color of the sea all around her and her exquisite form within it like some kind of mythical creature, too perfect to be believed. Yet this was Venice, after all. It was easier to believe all things were possible in a city that should not exist, propped up like so many dreams nailed fast to alder trees and left in the sea for centuries.

But Lily was here again, wasn't she? She lived, as his brother had pointed out to him. She had not died in that car accident. This was not a dream, despite the many, many times he'd had dreams just like it. Rafael could call this—*her*—a miracle if he chose, and he told himself he would worry later over the vicious little details that had made it all possible.

Much later.

He leaned over her, into her, caging her where she stood with his hands on either side of hers. She shuddered in that deep, luxuriant way that seemed to roll all the way through her and then into him, and when he bent to press his mouth to the nape of her neck, they both sighed.

She was so warm, so delicately fragrant. He could smell that particular scent that was only hers, a sultry blend of her skin and her sex, and layered over that the hints of bathing products and stylist's tools, cosmetics and the faint touch of something not quite slate that made him think of the snow outside.

And the skin beneath his lips was so soft. So very soft. She shivered, and he wanted to inhale her. All of her.

"La tua pelle e' come seta," Rafael murmured, right

there against that sensitive spot at her nape, knowing full well she couldn't understand him. Enjoying that fact, if he was honest. *Your skin is like silk.*

"Why can't I turn around?" Her voice was little more than a breath.

He smiled against her skin. "Because this way, there can only be honesty between us. No harsh words to confuse the issue. No lies or make-believe memories. You will either respond to me or you won't."

"You don't seem worried that I won't," she said, almost ruefully.

He grazed her lightly with his teeth and heard the sharp little noise she made in response, music to him the way it always had been, and he leaned in closer and indulged himself.

"No," he said against her soft, warm skin, "I'm not."

Rafael laid a trail of fire down the length of her neck, then across the delicate ridges of her finely wrought shoulder blades. He explored one with his mouth, his hands, then the other. He kept her caged there by his much larger body, drinking in every little sweet and helpless sound she made—far more intoxicating than any whiskey.

And only when he'd relearned every sweet inch of her upper back did he pull back. She was shuddering again, her head low between her shoulders, breathing as hard as if she'd been running.

"You might want to brace yourself, *cara*," he told her, making no attempt to hide the sheer male satisfaction in his voice. "I'm only getting started."

He heard a hitch in her breath and it took him a moment to realize it was a laugh. Low, husky. Infinitely sensual. It wrapped around him and pierced his bones, shaking through him like a quiet little tsunami.

"Promises, promises," she taunted him softly.

She was lethal. Rafael would do well to remember that.

He reached out then and found the hidden zipper closure of her dress, unhooking it and then beginning to pull it down, exposing the long line of her spine and the acres of her soft skin. His mouth watered, but still he unzipped her, letting the dress fall from her mouthwatering curves to foam around her feet, effectively caging her there in yards and yards of fabric so soft to the touch that the only thing that could possibly be softer was her.

She was like a feast spread before him, and he let himself breathe her in, exposed at last to his view. His own personal miracle. He took in the wavy tangle of her strawberry blond hair, the elegance of her lovely back and the scrap of scarlet he'd shoved out of his way at the party that was, from this angle, a mere hint of fabric circling her hips and then disappearing between the high, proud curves of her bottom. Then he took his time on the way back up, lingering on that tattoo he'd believed he'd never see again, that tattoo that had proved she was who he knew her to be at a glance, that tattoo that marked her *his Lily* forever.

He touched her there, tracing the winding black lines that curled this way and that, the tendrils reaching down almost to the top of her thong panties at the bottom and then nearly to what would have been her bra line, had she been wearing one, at the top. Then he worked his fingers over the delicate lily blossom some stranger had lovingly drawn into her skin, the arched petals and the sweet bud within, as if he was painting her with his possession.

"Rafael…" Her voice cracked on his name, and he smiled at the raw need in it. "Please."

"Please, what?" he asked. "I've hardly begun. And I think this tattoo is yet another lie you've told."

She shook her head, lifting herself up but still, he noticed, maintaining her position. Staying where he'd put her, and he didn't know what made him want her more, her obedience or her need. Both.

"A tattoo is the opposite of a lie," she said, still in that breathy, needy way of hers that was messing with his resolve. "It's ink on skin and unchangeable."

"And if you hated it as much as you claimed you did," he murmured as he leaned in closer, then sank down so he could set his mouth against the center bud of that pretty red blossom, "you would have had it removed by now."

He heard her shudder out another breath that was edging toward a sob, and he continued to taste that delicate flower while he let his hands wander, smoothing their way over her hips and then testing the sweet curves of her bottom. And only when he could feel her shake did he tease his way into the hidden hollow beneath, where she was molten and hot and more than ready for him.

Rafael knew her body better than his own. He knew her taste, her shape. He knew exactly how to touch her to drive her slowly, slowly insane. And if it killed him too, well—resurrections were going around. He was certain he'd survive, somehow, if only to find her again. He stroked his way into her heat, tracing her folds and the center of her need until she was surging back to meet him.

"Tell me something," he said darkly, moving as he spoke from the sweet tattoo to the sweep of her spine, relearning that perfect curve, that tempting shape. "How many men did Alison have in those five years?"

He could feel her stiffen at that, but he had two fingers deep inside her, and there was only one truth that had ever mattered between them. It didn't matter what he said to her, or what lies she told. It didn't matter how furious she was with him or what she'd done. What he'd done with all those other women, for that matter, or how much he regretted every one of them. He could feel her, molten and sweet, clenching tight around him even so.

This was the only truth. This heat. This need. This was who they were.

"You're a hypocrite," she panted out, sounding as desperate as she did furious, and yet her hips moved in wild abandon, meeting every stroke. "You must know that."

"I have never claimed otherwise," he said, his voice rough. "Especially not to you. But that doesn't answer my question, does it?"

"What does it matter?" she demanded, and then she let out a small cry when he changed his angle and drove deeper within her. Harder.

"How many?"

He felt her shudder beneath him, and he stopped pretending he was anything but an animal where this woman was concerned. Or that he'd ever been anything else. Or would ever be anything else. Five years apart, thinking she was dead, hadn't changed this. Nothing could.

"Tell me," he gritted out at her.

"None, Rafael," she cried out as he pressed hard against the center of her hunger with one hand and stroked deep with the other. "There has never been anyone but you."

And there never will be, he thought, feeling something clawed and fierce inside him, fighting its way out through his rib cage.

"For that," he said, moving up higher and setting his mouth against her ear, exulting in the way she bucked and writhed beneath him, "you get a reward."

Then he twisted his hand and hit her in precisely the right spot, and held her as she broke apart.

And he was only getting started.

* * *

Lily hardly registered it when he lifted her, sweeping her out of the dress that was now crumpled on the floor and up into his arms. But she did feel the change in temperature when he strode through the doors of the great room and out into the hall, holding her high against his bare chest.

She should have been cold, she knew, but what she felt instead was something like cherished, in nothing but her thong with her hair trailing over his arm. *Safe*, a small voice inside her whispered. The way it always had when she was with this man—the very last man who could ever be considered even remotely safe.

But Lily hooked her arms around his neck and didn't ask herself any questions.

Rafael shouldered his way through another set of doors, and Lily only had a moment to take in a sitting room lit by cheerful little lamps made of colorful glass before he'd walked straight through it and into a majestic bedroom set high above the Grand Canal. She saw the glittering lights of the old buildings outside and the snow that fell all around, and then the world narrowed down to the canopied four-poster bed that dominated the richly patterned room. Paintings framed in gold graced the solemn red walls, there was a dancing fire in the massive fireplace on the far wall, and there was Rafael in the center of everything.

He set her down at the side of the great bed, his expression unreadable. Her hair hung around her in a great mess, and she was naked while he still wore the bottom half of his dark suit. Lily thought that any one of those things should have bothered her, but they didn't.

She could sense all the things she *ought* to have felt dancing all around her, just out of sight. As if, were she to turn her head fast enough, she'd see them there, waiting to pounce. But she didn't turn her head. She couldn't seem to tear her gaze away from Rafael's.

"You remember me," he said then, after what felt like a very long while.

It could have been an accusation—but it wasn't. He lifted his hand and held it out and she matched it with hers, laying it against his in that small space between them, so they were palm to palm.

"Yes," she said softly, aware that it sounded like a vow in the quiet of the vast room. "I remember you. I remember this."

It was easier to remember the wild highs and the dark lows, she knew. All the sex and the lies, the betrayals and the fights. But that hadn't been the sum total of what had passed between them. The truth was, Lily didn't like to remember the other part. It still hurt too much.

But that didn't seem to matter now, in a fairy tale of a bedchamber in this magical city, while the snow kept falling and the fire danced, and he was right there in front of her and far more beautiful than she'd let herself remember.

She'd been nineteen that New Year's Eve. She'd taunted him and he'd taken her and then they'd walked back into their lives and pretended nothing had happened. He'd played the attentive boyfriend to whatever silly girlfriend he'd had then. She'd pretended to be as disgusted with him and the entire Castelli family as she always had been.

Then the holiday had passed, and it had been time for her to head back to Berkeley, to carry on with her sophomore year of college. He'd caught up to her in the grand front foyer of the château as she'd headed out toward her car with her bags. His girlfriend had been laughing it up in the next room with the rest of their families. They could have been discovered at any moment.

Rafael hadn't spoken. He'd hardly looked at her since New Year's Eve. But he'd held out his hand like this, and she'd met it. And it had felt a lot like crying, that heaviness within, that constriction and that ache, all bound up in such a simple touch. But they'd stood like that for what had felt like a very long time.

Now, all these years later, Lily understood it better. This was their connection in its least destructive form. This touch. This *thing*. It still arced between them, tying them together, rendering all the rest of what they were unimportant beside it.

"I thought I'd lost you," he said quietly, so quietly she almost thought she'd imagined it. But then his dark eyes met hers and held. "I thought you were gone forever."

The sheer brutality of what she'd done hit her, then. She'd understood she'd hurt him, yes. She'd hurt a lot of people. She'd told herself she'd accepted that, and that Arlo was worth it. But she'd never thought about *this*. The warmth of his flesh against hers. This connection of theirs that defied all thought, all reason, all efforts to squash it. What would she have done if she'd thought he'd died? How could she possibly have lived with that?

Her throat was too tight to speak. She didn't try. Instead, she leaned forward and pressed a kiss in the center of his chest. She felt his breath rush out, but she didn't stop. She pushed him back against the bed, aware that he let her move him like that, that she couldn't have shifted his powerful frame if he hadn't allowed it.

She still couldn't speak. But that didn't mean she couldn't apologize in her way.

Lily poured her sorrow and her regret all over him, making it into heat. He leaned back on his hands and she crawled over him, pressing kisses down the strong column of his throat, over that strong, hard pulse that she knew beat for her, then lower, to celebrate the sheer masculine perfection of his chest. She let her hair slip this way and that as she slid down the length of him, tasting him and celebrating him, pouring herself over him like sunlight until she unbuckled his trousers, pulled them down, then shoved them out of her way.

She paused then, flicking a look at him as she took his hard length in her hands. His gaze was black with need, his face set in stark and glorious lines of pure hunger, and apology merged with simple desire as she bent and sucked him deep into her mouth.

Rafael groaned. Or maybe that was her name.

Lily sank down between his legs, reveling in him. The taste of his hardness, salt and man. Satin poured over steel, and he trembled faintly the more she played with him, the deeper she took him.

He sank his hands in her hair and held her there as she taunted him with her tongue then took him deep yet again. He murmured Italian phrases that sounded like prayers but were, she knew, words of sex and need. Encouragement and stark male approval.

"Enough."

His voice was so gruff she hardly recognized it, but she understood it when he pulled her from him and lifted her against him, rolling them back and onto the wide bed. For a moment she thought he would simply take over, but he rolled once more, settling her there on top of him so he nudged up against her slick folds.

His gaze was like fire, or maybe the fire was in her. Maybe this was all fire.

She reached between them and took him in her hand. She felt his swift intake of breath, or perhaps it was a curse, and then they both groaned when she shifted and took him deep inside her.

Naked, she thought, as if the word was an incantation. Or a prayer.

They were both naked. This wasn't a coatroom, an alcove outside a dance or any of the other semipublic places they'd done this over the years. This was no illicit hotel room when they'd both claimed to be somewhere else. No one was looking for them and even if they were, it wouldn't matter if they were found.

This was simply them, skin to skin, at last.

And then Lily began to move.

That same fire burned high, but this was a sweeter blaze. The pace she set was lazy. Dangerous. Rafael lay beneath her, his hands at her hips, his gaze locked to hers.

Perfect, Lily thought. *He has always been perfect.*

And then she rode them both right off the side of the earth, and into bliss.

CHAPTER NINE

LILY WOKE TO find herself all alone in that great bed, the sheets a tangle below her and the canopy like a filmy tent high above.

For a moment, she couldn't remember where she was.

It came back to her slowly at first, then with a great rush. That quick plane ride down from the remote lake in the Dolomites yesterday afternoon, then the boat that had whisked them through the eerie, echoing wonder of the Venice canals, past winding, narrow byways and under more than one distractingly elegant bridge. After which she'd spent hours getting ready for a ball she hadn't wanted to attend in the first place, surrounded by servants like some kind of latter-day queen, finding herself less and less averse to the night ahead the more she liked the way they made her look in the beveled mirror in front her.

There was the most unpalatable truth of all: that she really was that vain.

But it had been worth it when she'd seen that stunned, famished look on Rafael's face as she'd made her way down the long stair to his side. It had all been worth it.

Looking back, Lily thought she could trace all the rest of her questionable decisions last night to that moment. The long walk down, her gaze fastened to his, while he looked at her as if she was the answer to a very fervent prayer.

She sat up slowly now, the long night evident in the small tugs and pulls all over her body, unable to regret a single one of them. She imagined that would come. But in the meantime, she rolled from the bed and drew the coverlet around her as she stood. The fire was low in the grate, while the thin light of dawn made the air seem blue. Rafael was nowhere to be found and when she cocked her head to listen intently, she couldn't hear him in the bath suite either. Outside, last night's snow dusted all the boats moored along the edges of the canal and the tops of the grand palazzos opposite, making a particularly Venetian Christmas card out of the already lovely view.

Lily placed her hand against the glass the same way she'd placed it against Rafael's hand the night before, felt that deep ache in her heart, and understood entirely too many things at once.

She was in love with him. Of course she was. She had always been in love with him, and it was as wretched a thing now as it had been when she'd been nineteen.

Because nothing had changed. Not really.

They were the same people they had always been and now the past five years were between them. And Arlo. And all the sex in the world, no matter how good, couldn't change what she'd done or who Rafael was or any of the many, many reasons they could never, ever work.

At heart he was his father, who married and remarried at the drop of a hat and believed himself deeply in love without ever having to prove it for too long. And she was entirely too much like her own mother, who had disappeared into the things she loved, whether they were prescription drugs or men—until it had killed her. So selfish. So destructive.

Running away in the way she had might not have been a particularly mature choice, or even a good one. Lily understood that. The pain she'd caused was incalculable. One night in Venice couldn't change that. Maybe nothing could.

She was no less selfish. No less destructive. But at least she was aware of it; she accepted the truth about her behavior, however unpleasant. Like everything else, she thought then, there was nothing to do but live with it. One way or another.

She squared her shoulders and dropped her chilled hand back down from the window, feeling scraped raw inside. Lily decided that was hunger. She couldn't remember the last time she'd eaten something. She pushed her way out of the bedroom into the sitting room she'd glimpsed so haphazardly last night, sure there must be something to eat somewhere in a palace so grand.

But she stopped short when she entered the sitting room. The fire in here was blazing, and there was an impressive selection of breakfast foods laid out along the side table as she'd expected, but what caught her attention was Rafael.

He stood by the windows, looking out on what she assumed was the same view she'd left behind in the other room. She thought that was the sum total of who they were. Forever separated, forever lost to each other in pursuit of the same end. A wave of melancholy threatened to take her from her feet then, surprising her with its strength.

She shoved it back down and blinked that heat in her eyes away.

"It's pretty out there," she said, inanely, and it was worse because her throat was so raw. She coughed and pulled the coverlet tighter around her, cold despite the warmth of the room. "Though very raw, I think. With all that snow."

It had something to do with the way Rafael stood there, so remote, wearing nothing but low-slung trousers that showed off that powerful body of his. It was the set of his broad shoulders, or that sense that he wasn't really there at all. That he saw something other than the snow and the canal, and the light of a winter morning turning the sky to liquid gold.

"My mother was mad," he said without turning around, as if he was wholly impervious to the cold on the other side of that window. Or in his own voice. "That is not the preferred term, I know. There were so many diagnoses, so many suppositions. But in the end, mad is what she was, no matter how they tried to sanitize it."

All it had taken was an internet connection to find the few articles about Gianni Castelli's doomed first marriage, so this was not precisely news to Lily. She'd read everything she could in a fury when she'd been sixteen and less than pleased about her mother's new fiancé. But she couldn't remember Rafael ever discussing his family history before. Not ever, in all the time she'd known him. That he was choosing to do so now, unprompted, made her heart beat hard and low in her chest.

"That is the excuse that was always trotted out in those years before she was taken away," he said after a moment, when Lily didn't respond. "That she was sick. Unwell. That she wasn't responsible for her actions." He shifted then, turning to look at her, though that wasn't an improvement. That darkly gorgeous face of his was shuttered. Hard. Her heart kicked that much harder against her ribs. "As it turns out, it's not much of an excuse when it's your mother they're talking about."

"What did she do?" Lily didn't know how she dared to speak. She realized she'd stopped dead a step from the door, and forced herself to move again. She walked farther into the deceptively cheery room and perched on the edge of the nearest chaise, as if she couldn't feel the terrible tension in the air.

"Nothing," Rafael said softly, his dark eyes bleak on hers. "She did absolutely nothing."

Lily swallowed, hard. "I don't know what that means."

His mouth shifted into something not at all a smile. "It means she did nothing, Lily. When we fell. When we ran to her. When we jockeyed for her attention, when we ignored her. It was all the same. She acted as if she was alone. Perhaps, in her mind, she was."

"I'm sorry." Lily didn't know why he was telling her this story, and she couldn't read any clues on his face. "That can't have been easy."

"Eventually she was whisked away to a hospital in Switzerland," he continued in the same distant tone. "At first we visited her there. I think my father must have believed that she could be fixed, you see. He's always liked to put broken things back together. But my mother could not be repaired, no matter how many drugs or therapies or exciting new regimens they tried. Eventually, they all gave up." He thrust his hands in his pockets, and though he didn't look away from her, Lily wasn't sure he saw her, either. "My father divorced her, claiming that was best for everyone, though it seemed it was really only best for him. The hospital started talking about her comfort and safety rather than her progress, and told us it was better if we stayed away."

Lily didn't know what she meant to say. What she could say. Only that she wanted to help him, heal him somehow, and couldn't. "I'm so sorry."

His mouth moved into a harsh curve. "I was thirteen the last time I saw her. I'd taken the train from my boarding school, filled with all the requisite drama and purpose of a young man on a mission. I had long since determined that my father was to blame for her decline, and that if I could see her alone, I could know the truth. I wanted to *rescue* her."

Lily stared back at him, stricken. The fire popped and crackled beside her, but Rafael didn't appear to hear it. And she couldn't seem to read a single thing on that hard face of his.

"Rafael," she said in a low voice. "You don't have to tell me any of this."

"But I do," he replied. He studied her for a moment, then continued. "The hospital wouldn't let me see her, only observe her from afar. My memories of her were of her rages, her tears. The way she would go blank in the middle of crowded rooms. Yet the woman I saw, alone in her little room, was at peace." He laughed, a hollow sound. "She was *happy* there, locked up in that place. Far happier than she had ever been outside it."

Lily studied him for a moment. "What did you do?"

He shrugged in that supremely Italian way. "What could I do? I was thirteen and she wasn't in need of rescuing. I left her there. Three years later, she was dead. They say she accidentally overdosed on pills she should not have been hoarding. I doubt very much it was an accident. But by then, I had discovered women."

Lily stiffened where she sat, and a harsh sort of light gleamed in his dark eyes, as if he could track her every movement. "I don't understand why you're sharing these things with me."

"I had no intention of becoming my father," Rafael told her quietly. "I had no interest in becoming some kind of relationship mechanic, forever tinkering around beneath the hood of another broken thing. I liked a laugh. I liked sex. I wanted nothing but a good time and when it turned heavy, the way it inevitably did? I was gone. I never wanted to feel that urge to rescue anyone, not ever again. I wanted no complications, no trouble." His gaze was hard on hers, bright and hot. "And then came you."

"You shouldn't have kissed me," she threw at him, as if this was a fight they were having instead of a quiet conversation in a cheerfully cozy room on a snowy December morning.

"No," he murmured, and she might have said it first, but she found she greatly disliked his ready agreement. "I shouldn't have touched you. I had no idea what I was unleashing." She thought he tensed where he stood. Maybe that was how he seemed to crowd out all the air in the room. "And I hated it. I hated you."

She couldn't breathe. "You hated me," she repeated, flatly, as if that would make it hurt less.

"I thought if I could pretend it hadn't happened, it would go away. But it kept happening." That dark, ruthless gaze of his tore her up. It made her shake. But he didn't stop. "I thought if I could contain it, control it, diminish it or dilute it, I could conquer it. Keep it hidden. Choke the life out of it before it swallowed me whole."

"I didn't ask you to tell me any of this," she said then, feeling off balance. Something like dizzy, as if she was propped there on the edge of a cliff instead of an overstuffed chaise. "I wish you would stop."

"But then you went over the side of a cliff you shouldn't have been near, in a car you shouldn't have been driving, going much too fast," he said, his voice hoarse, and she could see from that look in his eyes that he had no intention of stopping. "I knew perfectly well that if you'd been upset, the way they claimed you must have been to drive like that, it was my fault. They said it was an accident, that you'd lost control and skidded, but I wondered. Was it really an accident? Or had I made your life so bloody miserable that your only chance at any kind of happiness was to escape me the only way you could? Just like she did."

She was shaking outright then. "Rafael—"

"Except here you are," he said softly, and she wished he would move. She wished he would *do something* more than simply stand there like some kind of creature of stone, breaking her heart more with every word. "And you still make my breath catch when you enter a room. And I've long since understood that it was never hate I felt for you, but that I was too immature or too afraid to understand the enormity of it any other way. And you have my child, this perfect and beautiful son I thought I didn't want until I met him." He shook his head slightly, as if the reality of Arlo still overwhelmed him. "And I don't hate you, Lily. I want you in ways I've never wanted any other woman. I can't imagine that changing if it hasn't yet. But you're right."

His gaze was so bright, so hard, it hurt. And she'd been turned to stone herself.

"I don't love you," Rafael said. "If I can love anything at all, if I'm capable of such a thing, I love that ghost."

Lily was dimly surprised that she was still in one piece after that. That the building hadn't sunk into the water all around them. That there was still a sun to peek in the windows on this cold, ruined day. That she hadn't simply turned to a column of ash and blown off into nothingness in the next breath.

And he wasn't finished.

"I will always love that ghost," he said, very distinctly, so there could be no mistake. So she could not misunderstand. "She's in my head, my heart, as selfish and as worthless as I might be. Yet it's the flesh and blood woman I can't forgive, Lily. If I'm honest with you, I don't know that I ever will." His smile then was a razor, sad and lethal at once. "But don't worry. I doubt I'll forgive myself."

Rafael watched her take that in, a kaleidoscope of emotion moving over her expressive face, and told himself it wasn't a lie. Not quite. It was the truth—*a* truth. It was just that there was a greater truth he had no intention of sharing with her.

Because he couldn't trust her, no matter the temptation to do exactly that. He knew her better than any other person alive, and he knew her not at all, and he'd understood over the course of that long, blisteringly hot night that he thought was branded into his very flesh that this was exactly the kind of heaviness he'd spent his life avoiding. For good reason.

There were other words for all those weighty things that rolled over him, pressing down on him like some kind of pitiless vise. He wasn't afraid of them any longer. But he'd succumbed to his vulnerabilities last night. He wouldn't do it again. There was Arlo to consider now.

And Rafael would be damned if he would ruin his son's life the way his parents had so cavalierly wrecked his, by betting on *feelings* when it was the practical application of reason and strength that got things done. He'd spent the past five years proving exactly that in his business affairs. He could do no less for his only child.

He wouldn't live his life for the ghost he hadn't saved. He couldn't.

"We are going to have to decide what story we wish to tell," he said coolly, when it looked as if Lily had wrestled her reactions under control. She was wrapped up in that gold thing she must have pulled from his bed, her hair a glorious halo of strawberry blond all around her and falling over her shoulders, and he felt like a saint for maintaining his distance when it was the last thing he wanted to do. But it was necessary. No matter that her blue eyes looked slicked with hurt and it caused him physical pain to know he'd done that to her. Again. "Whatever the version, I have no intention of hiding the fact that I'm Arlo's father. From the world or from him. You need to come to terms with that."

She blinked, and then she rose somewhat stiffly to her feet, and he couldn't tell if that was a remnant of the night they'd shared or if it was an emotional response to the things he'd told her. Or both.

"What do you mean?" she asked, and the gaze she fixed on him was blue and cool, no hint of any hurt or wetness. He was tempted to think he'd imagined it. "I'm in Italy, aren't I? If I hadn't come to terms with it, I imagine I'd still be back home in Virginia, knee-deep in dogs."

"You are in Italy, yes," Rafael said quietly. "Hidden away in a house off in the mountains where no one has seen you or him except a handful of villagers who would never question the family. And then masked in public here, so no one could recognize you. You can't have it both ways for too much longer, I'm afraid."

Lily yanked her gaze from his and moved over to the side table, where she poured herself a cup of coffee with a hand that looked perfectly steady—and a good man, he was aware, would not *want* to see this woman, the mother of his child, so upset she shook. He understood that once again, he'd proved he could never be anything like *good*. Especially not where Lily was involved.

"I don't know why you think a certain reticence is trying to have it both ways," she said after a moment. She glanced at him over her shoulder, looking as though she belonged in the paintings that graced the walls, draped in gold and her own wavy hair. "What story do you think we ought to tell, Rafael? The one you just bludgeoned me with?"

He acknowledged the truth in that with a shrug. "You can't imagine that you can rise from the dead unremarked, can you?"

"I don't see why not," she said, blowing on her coffee and then taking a sip before she turned to face him again. "It's not anybody's business."

"Perhaps not. But the media attention will be unavoidable." He sounded impatient even by his own reckoning, but that coverlet was sliding down her upper arm, now, coming perilously close to shifting just far enough to expose the rosy tip of her breast. He needed to focus. "You died tragically and very young. That you are alive and well and in possession of the heir to the Castelli fortune will make it all that much more irresistible."

She'd become that stranger again, cool and unreadable—or maybe she, too, had grown up in these intervening years. Become less raw, less emotional. Or at least less likely to show her every thought on her face. It was his own curse that he should feel that like a loss. Like one more thing to grieve.

"It sounds like you already know what they'll say," she said mildly. It was her turn to shrug. "Why can't we let them say it?"

"The real story here isn't your unexpected resurrection, as exciting as that might be," he replied after a moment, after he'd had to force himself to look away from her almost-yet-not-quite-revealed breast. "It's the question of what happened five years ago."

"And here I thought rising from the dead would be sufficient," she said, cool and dry, though he did not mistake that edge beneath it. "The media really is voracious these days."

"It depends on the story. Did you deliberately hide yourself away all this time? Or did you hit your head and forget who you were?" He kept his gaze trained on hers. "The former leads to all manner of unpleasant inquiries about why you might have felt it necessary to do such an irrevocable thing and who might have been responsible. The latter, meanwhile, is a special interest story that will no doubt capture the public's interest for a while, as these things do, but will then fade away."

"So to be clear, we're not talking about the truth right now, despite how many times you've called me a liar in the past two weeks." She raised a challenging brow. "We're talking about manipulating the media for your own murky ends."

"No, Lily." His tone was harsh. He made no attempt to soften it. "We're talking about Arlo."

She looked shocked by that. "What does this have to do with Arlo?"

"He will eventually be able to read all about this," Rafael pointed out. "Assuming someone doesn't share the whole of it with him on a playground, as children are wont to do. It will be part of the very public story that he and anyone else can access at will. I'd prefer that story not be about his mother thinking so little of his father that she pretended to kill herself and then hid herself away for half a decade. What good could possibly come of his knowing that?"

Something glittered in that too-blue gaze of hers. "I'm not going to lie to him. I can't believe you'd really think I would."

"Please spare me the moral outrage. You've already lied to him. You've lied to everyone you've ever met, before and after that accident. At least this time, the lie would be in his best interests."

"You're assuming a lot," she said in a clipped tone, that glitter in her gaze even more hectic and a dark thing in her voice besides. "You barely know him. And one night with me after five years hardly gives you the right to make any kind of decision about what's in his best interests."

"I'm not assuming anything," Rafael said, soft and harsh, giving absolutely no quarter. "Arlo is my son. You either hid him away from me deliberately, in which case any court in the land is likely to award me custody in the face of such a contemptible parental act—or you didn't know what you were doing until I found you, which suggests a brain injury that hardly sets you up as mother of the year. I'd think long and hard about that, if I were you. I don't want to treat you like a business rival and take you down by any available means necessary. But if I have to, I will."

She eyed him as if she'd never seen him before and didn't much like what she saw now.

"Is that what last night was about?" There was no particular inflection in her voice, though he could see all manner of shadows in her gaze as she set her coffee back down on the nearby side table with a bit too much precision. "Trying to sneak your way beneath my defenses so you could better knock me flat today?"

"Lily." He said her name the way he heard it in his head, delicate and light, that same song that had been torturing him for all these years. "I have no reason whatsoever to think anything I did could reach you. Ever."

He saw her hands shake then, very slightly, before she clenched them into the fabric slipping and sliding around her. And it made him feel worse, not better. Hollow.

"So the fact it sounds a lot like you're threatening me is what, then?" she asked, her voice crisp, as if he'd imagined that small, telling tremor. "My overactive imagination? A remnant of that convent school poet you made up for your own amusement?"

"I wasn't threatening you. I'm merely pointing out the realities of the situation we find ourselves in."

"A man standing half-naked in a Venetian palazzo passed down through his family line for centuries maybe shouldn't set himself up as the last word on reality," she retorted. "It makes you sound silly." She lifted a hand when he started to respond to that. "I understand that your feelings are hurt, Rafael. That sex only made it all that much more raw, and maybe that much worse."

"You have no idea." He hadn't meant to say that. But he had, and so he thought he might as well keep going. "I want you, Lily. I can't deny that. It doesn't go anywhere, no matter how many times I lose myself in you. But that doesn't change what we did to each other. How we behaved and what came of it. As you said yourself last night."

"Neither does using my son—*our son*—as a weapon." She held his gaze. "What does that make you?"

"Determined," he retorted, a little more temper in his voice than he liked. As if he still had absolutely no control over himself where she was concerned. "I lost five years of his life. I won't lose a moment more."

"I haven't denied you access to him," she said stiffly. "I won't. We can work something out, I'm sure. People who can't manage to spend three seconds in a room together without drawing blood can do it. So can we."

"You're not understanding me." He waited for her to focus on him again. "There will be no split custody, no separate homes. He stays with me."

Lily's mouth actually dropped open. "You must have lost your mind."

"That leaves you with a very few options, I'm afraid, and I'm sorry for that," he said, and there was a part of him that hated that she'd gone pale, that this clearly surprised and hurt her. But not enough to stop. "You can stay with him, with me. But that will require we make this official—and while I won't pretend I'll manage to keep my hands off you, I can't promise I'll ever give you more than sex. I can't imagine I'll ever trust you." He shrugged as if that was of no matter to him. "Alternatively, you can go back to your life in Virginia or come up with a new one if you prefer, and you can call yourself any name you like until the end of time. But if you choose that option, you'll do so alone."

She didn't move, though he had the impression she swayed on her feet, and he wished this was different. He wished he could gather her in his arms, make her smile. Make all of this all right. But the saddest truth of all was that he didn't know how. Theirs was the high drama, the angst and the deeply thrust knife of betrayal. He didn't know how to make her smile. He only knew how to bring out the worst in her—and how to make her cry.

He'd done nothing but that, over and over again.

She's not the only one who needs forgiving, a tiny voice inside him suggested then, like a chill through his body. *There are monsters enough in both of you, more than enough to go around.*

But he didn't know how to stop this. How to fix it. How to save either one of them.

"I'm not leaving Arlo with you," she said, very precisely, as if she was worried she might scream if she didn't choose each word that carefully. "That will never happen, Rafael."

"My son will have my name, Lily," he warned her, yielding to his temper rather than that other voice that whispered things he didn't want to hear. "One way or another. You can be a part of this family or not, as you choose. But you're running out of time to decide."

"Running out of time?" She stared at him as if he'd

grown a monster's misshapen head as he stood there, and he wouldn't have been particularly surprised if he had. "Arlo didn't know you existed two weeks ago. You thought I was dead. You can't make these kind of ultimatums and expect me to take you seriously."

"Here's the thing, *cara*," he murmured, feeling that familiar kick of ruthlessness move in him, spreading out and taking over everything. It felt a lot like peace. He crossed his arms over his chest and told himself she was the enemy, like all the rivals he'd decimated in his years as acting CEO of the family business. He assured himself she was his to conquer as he chose. And more, that she'd earned it. "I'm sorry that this is hard for you. I feel for you, I do. But it won't change a thing."

Though it might have changed things if that glitter in her gaze had spilled over into tears. It might have reminded him that he could be merciful. That he really had loved her all along. But this was Lily, stubborn to the bitter end. She blinked, then again, and then those blue eyes were clear and hard as they met his. She tipped up that chin and she looked at him almost regally, as if there was nothing he could do to touch her, not really.

The same way she'd looked at him in that hallway when she was nineteen.

And he had the same riotous urge now as he had then: to prove that he damn well could. That he could do a great deal more than *touch* her. That he could mess her up but good.

He told himself that this time, at least, it was far healthier than it had been then, because it wasn't about either one of them. It was about their son.

Which was why he kept his distance. The way he hadn't done then.

And so what if it was killing him? That was the price. He assured himself Arlo was worth paying it.

"You have until Christmas," Rafael told her matter-of-factly. "Then you will either marry me or you'll get the hell out of my life, for good this time. And his."

CHAPTER TEN

"HAVE YOU DECIDED what you'll do?" Rafael asked her the first morning after their somewhat subdued return from Venice later that frigid morning, smiling at her in that mocking way of his over the breakfast table. "The Dolomites themselves await your answer, I'm sure. As do I."

It was the feigned politeness, Lily thought, that made her want to fling the nearest plate of sausages at his head, if not at the mountains themselves. As if he was truly interested in her answer instead of merely needling her for his own amusement.

"Go to hell," she mouthed over Arlo's head, and only just managed to restrain herself from an inappropriate hand gesture to match.

But that only made his smile deepen.

It didn't help that Lily didn't know what she was going to do. There was no way she could ever leave Arlo, of course. Surely that went without saying. The very idea made her stomach cramp up in protest. But how could she marry Rafael? Especially when the kind of marriage he'd mentioned in Venice was a far cry indeed from the sort she'd imagined when she'd been young and silly and still thought things between them might work out one day.

Well, this was *one day*, and this was not at all what she'd call worked out, was it? This was, she was certain, pretty much the exact opposite of that.

"Perhaps we should make a list of pros and cons," he suggested on another afternoon even closer to Christmas, coming to stand beside her. She was on the warm and cozy side of the glass doors overlooking the garden, where Arlo and two of his nannies were building a legion of snowmen in what little gloomy light there was left at the tail end of the year. "Maybe a spreadsheet would help?"

Again, that courteous tone, as if she was deciding on nothing more pressing than which one of his wines she might choose to complement her dinner. It set her teeth on edge.

"Is this a game to you?" Lily asked him then, amazed that she could keep her voice so even when she wanted to take a swing at him. When she thought she might have, had that not involved touching him—which she knew better than to do, thank you. That way led only to madness and tears. Hers. "This isn't only my life we're talking about, you know. I get that you don't care about that. But it's Arlo's life, too, whom you do claim to care about, and you're messing with everything he holds dear."

She didn't expect him to touch her—much less reach over and take her chin in his hard hand, forcing her to look deep into his dark, dark eyes. Lily had to fight back that sweet, deep shudder that would have told him a thousand truths she didn't want him to know, and all of them things she'd already showed him in detail in that bed in Venice.

"We both made the choices that led us here," Rafael said softly, his hard fingers like a brand, blistering hot and something like delicious at once, damn him. "I can't help it if you don't like the way I'm handling the fallout, Lily. Do you have a better solution?"

"Anything would be a better solution!" she threw at him.

He dropped his hand, though he didn't step back for another jolting beat or two. That was her heart, she understood, not the world itself, though it was hard to tell the difference. She couldn't look at him—she couldn't bear it—so she directed her gaze out through the glass again instead, where the best thing they'd ever done together rolled a ball of snow that was bigger than he was across the snowy garden.

This is about Arlo, she reminded herself. *This is all about Arlo. Everything else that happens is secondary.*

"Name one, then," Rafael said, dark and too close. Daring her, she thought. Or begging her—but no. That wasn't Rafael. He didn't beg. "Name a better solution."

She shot him a look, then looked back toward their son. Their beautiful son, whom she'd loved hard and deep and forever since the moment she'd known he existed. Right there in that truck stop bathroom. She'd been terrified, certainly. And so alone. But she'd had Arlo and she'd loved him, long before she'd met him.

"You can think whatever you like," Lily said, low and fierce. "But none of the choices I made were easy. Not one of them. They all left scars."

"None of that changes where we are, does it?" he asked, his own voice quiet, and yet it still tore through her. "Our scars are of our own making, Lily. Each and every one of them. I find I can't forgive that, either."

Lily didn't answer him. And the next time she glanced over, he'd gone.

She told herself that was just as well.

And maybe it wasn't entirely surprising that the nightmares came back that night. And the next. And the night after that, too.

The screech of brakes, the sickening spin. That horrifying, stomach-dropping, chilling understanding that she wouldn't—*couldn't*—correct it. Then the impact that had thrown her from the car and left her sprawling, or so she'd pieced together afterward. She'd found herself face-down in the dirt, completely disoriented, scraped and raw in only a few places while around her, the northern California night had been quiet. A little bit foggy around the edges. Pretty, even, especially with the sea foaming over the rocks down below.

It hadn't been until the car had burst into flames some ways down the cliff that she'd realized what had happened. How close she'd come to death. How narrowly she'd escaped it, completely by accident.

Lily sat up too fast in her bed—again. This was, what? The fourth night in a row? Her heart was pounding so hard she thought it might punch a hole in her chest. The same way it had felt that night five years ago, when she'd finally comprehended what had happened. She'd almost forgotten the terror, all these years later. The insane *what if*s that had galloped through her head. The smell of brake fluid and burned rubber and that thick, choking smoke from the fire so real in her nose she took a few deep breaths before she understood it was a memory.

It had already happened. It wasn't happening now.

"It's only a dream," she whispered. "It isn't real."

Though the shadow that detached itself from the darkness near her doorway then was. It moved, it made her jaw drop—and then it was Rafael.

"What are you doing?" she gasped when she could speak, though she'd huddled up in a tiny ball against the ornate headboard. "You scared me!"

"That is going around," Rafael murmured.

He looked rumpled and irritable and something else she couldn't identify when he came to a stop beside her bed. She stared at him, the sight of his gorgeous body in nothing but a very low-riding pair of athletic trousers as soothing, oddly, as it was thrilling in the usual way. And his bare feet against the old carpet struck her as some kind of benediction.

"Rafael?" she asked, before that fire in her took over and made her do or say something she knew she'd regret. "What's the matter? What are you doing here?"

"You screamed," he said gruffly.

She swallowed, and took the time to uncurl her hands so they were no longer balled into fists. She felt cold, even under all of her blankets. And because she couldn't make sense of that—of his presence here. Had he come running?

"Oh," she said.

"Lily." There was none of that sharp politeness in his voice then. None of that mockery. And she couldn't see so much as a trace of either one on his face when he moved to the bedside table and snapped on the light. "Don't you think it's time you told me what happened that night?"

"That night?" she echoed, though she knew. Of course she knew. It was still reverberating in her head, still oozing around in the corners of the room. She frowned at him instead, because that was easier. "How did you hear me, anyway?"

"I have a gift," Rafael said, sounding dry and grumpy at once, which Lily realized was comforting, somehow. Though that made no sense. "I can hear two things with perfect clarity anywhere I go. The screams of terrified women, and irritating evasiveness at three twenty-seven in the morning."

He didn't reach for her, as she'd half expected. He leaned against the side of the bed, crossed his arms while he fixed that dark gaze of his on her, and waited.

And this was the story Lily had never told another living soul.

Maybe, she thought now, because he was the only person on earth who might understand what had happened and what she'd done—and she wasn't even sure about that. Not any longer.

"Are you sure you want me to tell you?" she asked him. "You've really been enjoying vilifying me. I'd hate to ruin that for you."

His dark eyes grew sterner and his jaw tightened, but he didn't say a word. He only waited—as if he could stand there all night, no matter what she threw at him.

Lily sighed and shoved her hair back from her face, moving to sit cross-legged there at the head of the bed. And then she'd run out of ways to stall. And he was so dark and so beautiful, and he was so wrapped up inside her that she felt him when she breathed in, and she'd never managed to get him out of her head or her heart. Not then. Certainly not now.

And she still didn't know what that made her. What that meant.

But it was the middle of the night. And the only light in the world seemed to fall in that tiny little circle from the side of her bed. She told herself it was the only confessional she'd be likely to get. And she took it.

Maybe all of this—from the moment he'd seen her on the street in Charlottesville all the way across the world to that night in Venice—had been leading them straight here. Maybe this had been the destination all along.

"You remember that last fight we had." She looked at him, then down at her hands, threading them together in her lap. It had been a long time ago, that fight. "In San Francisco that Thursday."

His sensual mouth flattened into a stern line. "I remember."

"It was the usual thing. I cried, you laughed. There

was that other woman you'd been in all the papers with. You dared me to leave you. I told you that this time I really would." Lily frowned at her fingers as she lifted one shoulder, then dropped it. "I didn't believe a word I said. Neither did you. We must have had that exact same fight a thousand times by then."

"More," Rafael agreed in that same too-dark voice, and she thought that was self-loathing she heard in his voice then. She recognized it. She'd heard it enough times in her own voice during those years.

"That weekend I went up to the château. It was a pretty night, I was bored and I was mad at you, so I helped myself to one of the overly fast cars in that absurd garage of your father's, and I took it for a drive." She lifted her head and looked at him. "I drove back down into the city. I wanted to see you."

She had the notion he was holding his breath. She pushed on.

"You weren't answering your phone, but I had a key to your house in Pacific Heights. I let myself in." She let out a sound that even she knew wasn't a laugh, but there was no helping it. This story was like an avalanche. Once it started, it rolled on and on until it wrecked everything. No wonder she'd never told it before. "I think I knew what was happening long before I made it to your bedroom. I don't remember hearing any sounds, but I must have—"

He swore. Deep and rich and inventively Italian.

"—because when I made it to your bedroom and looked inside, I wasn't as surprised as I should have been. If I hadn't had some warning, I mean. If I'd been surprised, I would have done something more than simply stand there, don't you think? Made a noise. Cried. Screamed. *Something.*" She shook her head. "But I didn't."

"I don't know if it makes it better or worse," Rafael said

after a moment, as if it hurt him. As if he was speaking with someone else's voice, some stranger's voice that hadn't worked in years. "But I don't even remember her name."

Lily remembered far too much. She'd stared at the figures on the bed, willing them to not make sense, the way such things always failed to make sense in books. To be some kind of hectic blur—that would have been a blessing.

But she could see both of them, with perfect and horrifying clarity. She could still see both of them, burned forever into her brain.

Rafael had been deep inside a stunning brunette, and both of them had been breathing hard, getting closer and closer to a big finish. Lily had felt almost clinical for a moment, looking at them, because she'd known exactly what it felt like when Rafael did precisely what he'd been doing to that woman, and yet she'd been seeing it from a completely different angle...

The clinical thing hadn't lasted. It had fallen away, hard, and when it had gone Lily had felt sick.

"No," she said now. "I don't think that helps."

"Why didn't you say something?" he asked, his voice rough. "Then. As you stood there."

She eyed him. "Like what?"

He didn't answer that. Because what could she have said? What was there to say in such situations? Lily turned her attention back to her hands. She forced them to open, then clenched them again.

"It was one thing to know that you had other women. I always knew that. You didn't exactly make a secret of it. You even brought them home with you. But it was different to *see*."

She stopped to take a breath, and thought he almost said something—but he didn't. She hadn't asked him for forgiveness, Lily reminded herself. Maybe he wouldn't ask for

any, either. Maybe there was no point bothering to apologize when wounds ran this deep. What was an apology
between them, after all of this, but a pat little Band-Aid
slapped over an amputated leg? What good would one do
either one of them now?

What good does any of this do? some voice inside
her demanded, but she couldn't stop now. She knew she
couldn't.

"I didn't know what to do, so I turned around and I left,"
she told him. "As quietly as I'd come in. I walked out and
stood there in front of your house. It was like an out-of-
body experience. I kept thinking that at any moment, I'd
start sobbing. That I would cry so hard and so long that
it would rip me in half." She looked at him then. "But I
didn't. I stood there a long time, but it never happened. So
I got in the car again and I drove."

"Where were you going?" Rafael hardly sounded like
himself, but Lily couldn't let herself worry about that. Not
now. "To find your friends?"

"My friends hated you," she said and watched him blink
as he took that in. "Oh, they didn't actually know it was
you, but the secret man who always hurt me? They'd hated
him for years. Openly. Any mention of you and it was all
tough love and yelling. I didn't bother calling any of them.
I knew what they'd say."

She shifted position, pulling her knees up beneath her
chin. Rafael didn't move, standing there so still and so cold
that Lily almost thought he'd turned himself into a statue.

"I just drove," she said. "Out of San Francisco and then
out to the coast. I didn't have a plan. I wasn't sobbing or
screaming or anything. I felt numb, really. But I knew what
I was doing." She found his gaze in the dimly lit room, and
imagined hers was no less tortured than his was. "I wasn't
trying to hurt myself. You should know that."

"Then how did it happen?"

Lily shrugged. "I was going too fast in a too-powerful car. I took a turn and there was a rock in the middle of the road. I swerved, and then I couldn't correct it. I was skidding and there was nothing I could do about it."

She heard the brakes again, could hear her own swift curse so loud in the car's interior, and she remembered that stunned moment when she'd realized she really wasn't going to make it, she really wasn't going to save herself—

Lily shook it off and blew out a breath. "Then the car crashed. I don't remember that part. Only that I knew I was going to die." She swallowed, determined not to surrender to the emotion she could feel knocking around inside her. "But then I didn't. I was lying on the ground, not dead. I still don't know how."

"They think you went through the windshield," Rafael said, clipped and low. "That was the theory. From what was left of the car."

"Oh." She tried to picture it, but it made her feel dizzy again. Dizzy and fragile and entirely too breakable. "I guess that makes sense. I kind of came to on the shoulder, facedown in the dirt."

"You weren't hurt?"

He sounded so tense, she almost asked him if he was all right, but caught herself.

"I was shaken up," she told him. "I had some scrapes and was bleeding a little bit. The wind was knocked out of me. The bruises took a few days to really fully form and then a long time to fade." She hugged her knees closer to her. "But I was fine. Alarmingly fine, I thought, when the car blew up."

"Alarmingly?"

"I thought I was dead," she said simply. He went still

again. "It didn't make sense that I was...*fine*. The car was..."

"I know," he said harshly, his face in stark lines. "I saw it. It was mangled beyond recognition."

"How could anyone survive that?" Lily asked. "But then, when I tried to stand up, I got sick. And I figured dead people didn't throw up. I was pretty shaky." She braced herself for this next part and couldn't bring herself to look at him. She plucked at the blanket over her lap instead. "And then all I could think about was that I wanted you. I needed you."

She heard the sharp sound he made, but couldn't let herself analyze it or slow down. "I'd passed that town not far back, so I decided to walk back there and find a phone. I thought if I heard your voice, it would all be okay." Lily could still feel the heavy air that night, salt and wet, as the fog rolled in. She'd had dirt and blood in her mouth, and it had hurt a little bit to walk. But she'd kept going. "By the time I made it into town, the fire trucks were heading out. I don't know why I didn't flag them down. I think I was worried about the fact it was your father's car? And I didn't have permission to drive it. The whole walk to town, I kept thinking about how many hundreds of thousands of dollars I'd owe him and how I'd ever pay him back with a stupid degree in Anglo-Saxon elegies. It was on a loop in my head. I don't think I was thinking straight."

Rafael muttered something in Italian then, ragged and something like savage. But Lily kept going.

"I made it to a gas station and found a pay phone. Maybe the last working pay phone in California. And I picked it up to call you." She mimed picking up the phone, and she didn't know where that lump in her throat came from. That great pressure in her chest. She looked at him. She dropped her hand. "But what would have been the point?"

"Lily," he said, as if her name hurt him. He rubbed a hand over his jaw. But he didn't argue.

"Nothing was going to change," she said, almost as if he'd argued after all. He sat down hard on the end of the bed, then. His too-dark eyes were a torment, his mouth twisted, but she didn't look away. "It was this moment of awful clarity. You were in bed with that woman, but she could have been any woman and it could have been any given night. It didn't matter. It had been years and it was still the same. It wasn't going to change. *We* weren't going to change. And it was killing me, Rafael. It was *killing* me."

They sat there, separated by the length of the mattress and all of their history, for so long that if the sun had come up outside her windows Lily wouldn't have been at all surprised. But it was still dark when Rafael shifted position again. It was still dark when he cleared his throat.

And it told Lily everything she needed to know about how little she'd changed in all this time that she would have given absolutely anything to know what he was thinking then. She didn't even have the strength to call herself pathetic. It was simply that same old madness, all these years later. It was all the proof she needed that nothing was different. Herself least of all.

"What did you do then?" he asked.

"I told a nice Canadian couple at the gas station that my abusive boyfriend had left me there after a fight. They were so nice, they drove me all the way to Portland, Oregon, to get me away from him. When they kept going toward Vancouver, they left me at the bus station with cash and a ticket for my aunt's place in Texas."

"You don't have an aunt in Texas." His gaze moved over her face. "You don't have an aunt."

"No," she agreed. "But that was no reason not to go to Texas. So that was what I did. And then it was a week later, and everyone thought I was dead. No one even looked for me. So I decided I might as well stay dead."

"But you were pregnant."

She nodded. "Yes, though I didn't know that then."

"If you had?"

She wanted to lie to him, but didn't. "I don't know."

Rafael nodded once. Harshly, as if it hurt him. "And when you discovered that you were pregnant, it didn't occur to you a woman on the run, presumed dead, might not be the best parental figure for a child?"

"Of course it did," she said, frowning at him. "If I couldn't provide for him myself, I wasn't going to keep him. I had it all planned out."

"Adoption?" he asked, almost indifferently, though she didn't quite believe that tone of voice.

"No," she said. "You, Rafael. Of course, you. I figured I'd leave him on your doorstep or something. It seemed like a miracle that women hadn't already done that a hundred times, when I thought about it."

He absorbed that for a moment.

"But in no version of this story were you planning to come back," he said, when the silence began to feel much too thick between them. "Is that what I'm hearing?"

Lily hadn't expected that. She tried to read that closed-off look on his face, or the oddly stiff way he sat there at the foot of the bed. But either she'd lost her ability to see through him, or he was doing a far better job of hiding himself. She felt both possibilities as a loss.

"No, Rafael," she said quietly. "I wasn't coming back. Why would I?"

He met her gaze then, and she caught her breath. He looked haunted. Wrecked. She didn't understand why that made everything inside her seem to shatter like so much glass.

Lily wanted to go to him. She wanted to hold him, touch him—anything to make that terrible look on his face go away. Anything to make it better.

But she didn't move. She didn't dare.

"I can't think why you would," Rafael said into the dark, into what was left of the night. Straight into that heart of hers that Lily thought should have been healed by now, but was, she understood, still broken. "Not one single reason."

CHAPTER ELEVEN

RAFAEL FINALLY EMERGED from his offices on Christmas Eve, long after the sun went down and entirely lacking in anything approximating seasonal good cheer.

It had been years and it was still the same, Lily had said. *It wasn't going to change.* We *weren't going to change.*

He hadn't been able to get it out of his head since she'd said it. Tonight it was even worse. It had echoed inside his head, louder and louder, merging into some kind of ringing sound until he thought it might actually drive him mad. He'd been in his office, furiously working on projects no one would glance at until well into the new year, and he'd thought for a moment that he'd finally tipped over the edge into that madness that had so beguiled his own mother.

It had taken him long moments to realize that was not Lily's voice, but the sound of actual bells. Sleigh bells, if he was not mistaken, which had been curious enough to send him from his office and through the halls of the old house in search of the source.

He found his staff engaged in decking the old house even farther than they had already, despite the fact he'd informed them that his father and new bride would be in the Bahamas and Luca had decided to attend a house party abroad. And the decorating was being performed with significantly more enthusiasm than he recalled from previous years, which Rafael had no doubt had everything to do with the overexcited five-year-old who was all but turning somersaults in the grand front hall.

Rafael stood there, apart from the bustle down below. He leaned on the railing from the floor above and looked down at servants he'd never seen smile in all his life beaming at his son.

His son.

Arlo, who was like sunlight. Arlo, who emanated sheer joy like a homing beacon.

Arlo, whose mother had hated Rafael—or had despaired of him, and Rafael couldn't say he'd been able to discern the difference—so much that she'd gone to tremendous, all but unimaginable lengths to get the hell away from him. She'd walked away from a horrific car crash. She'd hitchhiked out of state. She'd found herself pregnant and penniless, and even then her plans had centered around what might be best for the baby, but never, not once, had she considered returning to Rafael.

And he couldn't argue about a single point in that story she'd finally told him. He'd been in that bed, with that nameless, faceless woman, not that he'd imagined for a moment that Lily might have seen him. He'd been the man Lily had described in every regard—the one who'd laughed at her, cheated on her though he'd claimed they had no formal commitment, and he had always, always assumed she'd come back to him.

How had he convinced himself that if she'd lived, she'd have been his? When he'd done everything in his power back then to make sure they would never, ever be together?

Lily had decided that she'd rather let everyone she knew think she was dead than play those terrible games any longer, and Rafael couldn't blame her. It was time he told her that, he thought then, watching his son laugh and jump up and down on the floor below. He had no business making ultimatums when the truth was, he was the one who ought to—

"How nice of you to emerge from your cave at last." Rafael turned slowly at the sound of that bone-dry voice. Lily stood in the gallery that functioned as a kind of upper-story foyer in this part of the house, her arms crossed over her chest and a scowl on her face. "The self-flagellation cave, presumably. I was beginning to think we'd have to break you out with dynamite. I was leaning toward throwing some at your head."

Rafael blinked. "I beg your pardon?"

Her scowl deepened, and he couldn't help but feel that like any other woman's sexiest come-hither glance. It slid along his spine and pooled in his groin, licking him with the sweet flame of it. She was wearing nothing but a pair of loose trousers and a soft, dark sweater, with all of her hair piled up on the top of her head, and still, he wanted her. Deeply. Utterly. Desperately.

The more she scowled at him, the more he wanted her. And the more he hated himself for it.

"Arlo thinks you've been sick," Lily told him, sounding unaccountably furious. "Because guess what, Rafael? When you're a parent, you don't get to flounce off whenever you feel like it and lie about like an opera heroine until you feel like coming back. You're a father all of the time, not just when it's convenient."

He'd spent more than forty-eight hours wrestling with his guilt, his shame and all the self-loathing that went with it, and it turned out two seconds in Lily's company was all it took to slice right through it. He tilted his head to one side and narrowed his gaze as he looked at her.

"Am I Arlo's parent, Lily?" he asked coolly. "Because I

was under the impression that, blood tests aside, you had no intention of telling that boy who his father is."

"I could have told him the entire history of the Castelli family over the past two days," she fired back at him. "A hundred times over. And you wouldn't know either way, because you've been locked up in your office feeling sorry for yourself."

"I wasn't feeling sorry for myself," he grated at her. "I was feeling sorry for you. For having put you through this in the first place."

That came out a little too rough and shimmered there between them, entirely too honest. Bald and naked in the shadows of the gallery where they stood.

"Well," she said, her voice a little less sharp than it had been a moment before. "There's no need to retrace those steps. I did that for years. It doesn't actually help."

"Lily…" But he didn't know how to say what needed to be said.

Her eyes were too bright suddenly, and that scowl of hers seemed fiercer and more precarious at once. "And you know what else doesn't help? You demanding the truth and then running away when you get it, leaving me to deal with it. Again."

"I am every last thing you accused me of being," he said then. "More. There's no pretending otherwise."

"That's very noble, of course," she threw at him. "But that doesn't change the fact that we have a son, and he doesn't care if you've just discovered that the great and epic love story you've been holding onto for all these years is a sham."

"Don't." He didn't mean to growl that at her. "Don't say that."

Her eyes were still too bright and much too dark at once. "Come on, Rafael," she said quietly, though there was that edgy thing in her voice, and the way she held herself, like broken glass that would never fit together again. "You know better. This was nothing more than sex and secrecy. Two kids playing games with dangerous and unforeseen consequences, nothing more."

"You don't believe that." He shook his head when she started to speak. "If you did, you never would have run away. You certainly wouldn't have raised Arlo on your own. 'Two kids playing games' isn't a good enough reason for a deception of that magnitude, Lily, and you know it."

She looked brittle in the mellow light, but that didn't make her any less beautiful.

"I don't want to marry you," she told him, and there was something in her voice then that pierced straight through him, as if she'd broken apart where she stood. But she hadn't. He could see she stood proud and tall, the way she always had. Maybe he was the one who was broken. "And I'm not leaving Arlo here with you and going off somewhere. I would tell you what I think you can do with your ultimatum, but you've already spent days brooding in his office. God knows what it would do to you if I really let loose."

He studied her for a moment, while Arlo's high-pitched voice, nearly a soprano tonight with all his excitement, echoed all around them. And this was wrong. He felt that, deep inside. This was all wrong. But he shoved his hands in his pockets instead of touching her the way he wanted to do.

He told himself that was what a good man would do. And once—just once—he would be the good man for her he'd never been when it counted.

"Consider the plane at your disposal," he told her, and he thought he saw her shoulders sag, slightly, as if she'd wanted—but that was wishful thinking, and a second later, he was sure he'd imagined it. "It can take you wherever you want to go. I won't fight you for custody. As you said before, all kinds of people figure out visitation. I'm sure we will, too."

"I'm sure we will." Lily's voice was hollow. "How civilized, Rafael. I wouldn't have thought we had it in us."

And this time when she walked away from him, Rafael let her go.

Lily tried to sleep.

Arlo was so fired up about Christmas that he'd inevitably had a complete and total meltdown and ended up sprawled out on her bed in an exhausted heap of five-year-old tears. Lily had soothed him as best she could when the issue was too much sugar and the sheer injustice of it *still* not being Christmas morning until he'd finally fallen asleep. She'd crawled into bed beside him, flipped open a book and told herself that this was perfect. That this was the life she'd had for the past five years and it was the life she wanted. Her little boy and the little life they led together, somewhere far away from here. From Rafael. Books and dogs and absolute and total freedom. What could be better?

But she hadn't been able to make any sense at all out of the words on the page before her, no matter how many times she reread the sentences. Eventually she'd given up. She'd cuddled Arlo's flushed little-boy body next to hers and she'd shut her eyes tight, confident that she would drift off into sleep immediately.

Instead, she lay awake, glaring at the ceiling of this old house, growing more and more furious by the minute. And the more she tried to keep herself from tossing and turning, the worse it got.

It was after midnight when she finally gave up. She

climbed out of the bed, taking care to tuck Arlo back in. She shoved her feet into her warm slippers and she wrapped a long sweater around her like a robe, and she found herself out in the dark, cold hallway before she could think better of it.

She made her way down the main stairs, where the Christmas decorations looked stately and quiet in the dimness. She stood there for a moment, at the foot of the stairs, but then whatever demon had spurred her out of bed kept her going. She found herself at the doors to the main library before she could talk herself out of it.

The room was a showpiece. The jewel of the house, she'd heard Rafael's father say once. It was a huge library filled with floor-to-ceiling shelves accessed with the kind of rolling stairs and ladders that made Lily giddy with a book lover's joy, though this was the kind of library that featured books that were better looked at than read. This time of year, that hardly mattered, as the huge Christmas tree dominated the far end of the room, where there was normally a larger sitting area done up in pompous leather chairs and blocky masculine accessories.

And tonight, Rafael stood at the fireplace, one arm braced on the mantel above it, his face toward the flames.

Lily stood there in the doorway for a moment, letting that great, yawning thing that was all her many and complicated feelings for this man take her over. It washed through her, buffeting her like a riptide, turning her over and over and over until she could hardly see straight.

Until she focused on Rafael, that was, and he was all she could see.

Maybe, she thought, it had always been that way for a reason. Maybe she wasn't sick or twisted. Maybe they'd simply been too young to handle what had been there between them from the very start.

Maybe.

She was so damned tired of all these *maybe*s.

"You did it again," she said, and her voice sounded reedy and strange in the vastness of this formal, stuffy room. By the fire, Rafael didn't move. It made her think he'd known she was there, and something curled up deep inside her at the thought. "You ran away. Right there in plain sight. You used to do it with other women. Tonight you did it with your supposed self-loathing and your noble gestures no one asked you to make. But it was still running away, wasn't it?"

"I suppose we could have a competition to see who gets farther," he replied after a moment, but at least his voice was dark and low again. Not that strained, polite voice he'd been using earlier tonight. At least here and now he sounded like *Rafael* again. He looked at her then, without straightening. "Have you packed, then? Or are you planning to walk back to Virginia as you are?"

The unfairness of that felt like another great wave crashing over her head, and the smart move would have been to turn around and leave—but she didn't. Instead, Lily took another step into the room.

"What would it matter if I did or didn't?" she demanded. "You don't care either way."

"I care." His voice was a lash across the firelit room. "Believe whatever you must, but know that. *I care.*"

He straightened then, and it took her a moment to truly appreciate how disreputable he looked at the moment. Gone were the tailored suits, the casually elegant daywear. This version of Rafael seemed a good deal more… raw. His shirt was open, potentially misbuttoned. She didn't think he'd shaved recently. And that look in his dark gaze…burned.

Lily still didn't leave. She studied him for a moment

while too many emotions battled it out inside her. Too many to count. Too many to name.

"You've convinced yourself that this is all some great love story, haven't you?" she demanded. "It wasn't."

"No?" he asked, and he roamed toward her then, that stark, dangerous expression on her face thrilling her in a way she told herself she didn't understand. But her body did, the way it always did. It flushed hot, then melted. Everywhere. "It should have been."

"Things are only epic to you when you've lost them, Rafael, have you noticed that?" She didn't know what made her more furious—him, or her body's response to him, which had only intensified. If anything, that night in Venice had made it worse. "This can only be a love story if I leave you. That's what you want."

"I love you." It was harsh and flat, and they both stared at each other as it hung there between them, dancing like an errant spark from the fire on the old rug, then disappearing. She thought he would take it back, but instead, he breathed deep and held her gaze. "I should have told you then. I should have told you every day since I found you again. I should have told you tonight. I love you, Lily."

Lily stared back at him, stunned. Scraped through and emptied out. But then another wave hit, this one harder than the ones before, and she laughed. It was an ugly sound. She heard the harshness of it echo back to her, but she couldn't stop. She couldn't make it stop, not even when Rafael drew closer and stood there above her.

"Stop," he said, and he made it worse with that look on his face, something like gentle, and the way his hard mouth softened. It nearly did her in. She jabbed at her eyes with hands that had turned into fists without her noticing. "You don't need to do this."

"Love doesn't *do* anything, Rafael," she threw at him

then. "It doesn't save anyone. It can't change anything. It's an excuse. A catchall. In the end, it's meaningless. And, at its worst, destructive."

He reached over and slid his hand around the side of her neck, holding his palm there. Over her pulse, she realized. As if he was checking in with her heart—and that, too, made everything inside her seem to lurch and then slide. She was finding it hard to stay on her feet.

But she couldn't look away from him, either.

"You're talking about what people do with love, or in its name," he said. "But that's people. Love is bigger and better than all those things."

Lily shook her head. "How would you know? My mother's shining example? Or maybe your father's?"

She wanted to jerk her head away from him, knock his hand off her. But she didn't, and she couldn't have said why. Only that it was connected to that trembling knot inside her that seemed to get harder and bigger the more it shook.

"They're people," Rafael said. "Flawed and limited, like anyone."

"My mother spent her life chasing the next high. Men. Drugs. Whatever. Your father gets married for sport. You call those flaws? I'd call it something more like pathological."

"Are you and I any better?" Rafael asked, and he couldn't know, she thought, how much the heat of his hand warmed her. How much she wanted to simply topple into it and let him hold her there forever… He couldn't possibly know that, could he?

"That's my point." Her voice was little more than a whisper. "I told you the truth and you wanted nothing to do with me. I told you I'd take your child away from you again and you'd let me do it. You and I are *worse* than our parents, Rafael. We're much, much worse."

He shifted then, bringing his other hand up to hold her on the other side and tipping her face toward his.

"No," he said, in his uncompromising way. So certain. So ruthlessly *sure*. "We are not."

But she was warming to her theme, to that knotted thing inside her, as if it might choke her if she didn't get all of this out.

"And what I don't understand is what it's all for," she threw at him. "What's the point? The things you did or I did, then or now. The things anyone does. What is there to show for any of it?"

"You," Rafael said. "Me. Arlo." He shrugged in that way of his, Italian and uncompromisingly male, his dark eyes fixed to hers. "This is what love is. This is what *life* is. Complicated. Brutal. Glorious." His hands tightened and he drew her closer, until they stood in what was nearly a kiss. Nearly. "Ours, Lily. This is *ours*."

"Rafael…"

"I will put you on that plane myself," he gritted out. "If that's what you want. If you really want to put this— *me*—behind you."

And she opened her mouth to tell him that was exactly what she wanted, but didn't. She couldn't, somehow. It all whirled around inside her. All the fear, the pain. The running and the hiding across all these years. The lies, then and now. Had she cut herself off from her life because of Rafael? Or had Rafael been the last strike in a life spent coming a distant second to whatever her mother was losing herself in that month?

Maybe, just maybe, it was all the same running away.

And maybe it was finally time she stopped.

She'd never stopped loving this man. She'd simply never learned how to do it without losing everything in the process. Her life. *Herself.*

"And if I don't?" she dared to ask, if softly. "If I don't want that?"

Rafael studied her face for a long, long time. So long that Lily forgot everything except the stark male beauty of his face. So long that she forgot herself, too, all those dark things that crowded their past, and smiled up at him with every last bit of that shaking, knotted thing inside her that she was very much afraid was hope.

And it was worth everything, she thought, to see that answering curve take over his face, transforming him before her eyes from that grim, hard man to the Rafael she'd loved before she'd known she shouldn't. The Rafael who had been so beautiful to a sixteen-year-old girl that she hadn't dared to look at him directly.

As if she'd known even then that once she did, she'd never look away.

"I want to make you smile, Lily. I want to make you happy." His mouth brushed hers, a smile to a smile, and made her shiver deep inside. "But I don't have the slightest idea how to do that."

So she wrapped her arms around his neck and she pulled him close, resting her forehead against his.

"Love me," she said, all of that emotion making her voice thick and her knees feel weak in turn. "I think that's a good start."

"I always have," he told her, his words resonating like a vow. "I always will."

She breathed in deep, then breathed out all the dark and the pain, the hurt and the fury. She let it go, like snow into the water of those dark Venice canals.

"Rafael," she whispered, "I've been in love with you all my life. I wouldn't know how to go about stopping. I never have. I don't think I ever will."

"I'll make sure of it," he promised her.

And Lily didn't know if he kissed her or she kissed him, only that they came together and this time, she felt that knotted thing open up, hope like light inside her and inside him, flooding them both. Love. Life. Complicated and wonderful—and for the first time in her life, she truly believed she could have all of those things. With him. Finally, with him.

Rafael lifted her up into his arms and carried her across the room. Then he laid her down beneath the sparkling lights of the first Christmas tree that was truly theirs, on the very first day of the rest of their lives, and started working on forever.

Kiss by perfect kiss.

CHAPTER TWELVE

THE FOLLOWING YEAR Arlo was his parents' only attendant in their Christmas wedding, there in the chapel in the woods near the grand old house by the lake, in the shadow of those towering Italian mountains that felt like eternity.

"I have something to tell you," Rafael had told his son that first Christmas morning together, after the little boy had lost himself in a frenzy of gifts and wrapping paper and subsided to playing with his current favorite video game. That day.

"Is it about cake?" Arlo had asked without setting the game aside. "I like cake. Yellow cake, but chocolate is okay."

"No," Rafael had said, wondering how it had been possible to feel that awkward and yet that *right* at the same time. "I wanted to tell you that I'm your father."

Lily had been sitting there on the couch, pretending not to listen. She'd been doing it loudly.

Arlo had seemed preoccupied with his game. Then he'd asked, "Forever?" after considering the matter.

"Yes," Rafael had told him solemnly. "Forever. That's how it works."

"Cool," Arlo had said, and that had been that.

His mother had been a different matter.

Rafael gazed at her now as she took one of Arlo's hands

and he took the other. They smiled at each other as they walked toward the priest who waited for them at the small altar.

"Marry me because you want to," he'd said as Christmas gave way into the brand-new year. They were still together. They were filled with that half hope, half certainty that their complicated past meant they'd already weathered the worst storms anyone could. "Not because I told you to."

"Because your son must have your name?" she'd replied lightly, with that teasing glint in her blue eyes but, he thought, something more serious beneath it.

"My son *will* have my name," Rafael had assured her, every inch of him the powerful head of his family's fortune. And the man who loved them both. "It is only a question of when."

But it turned out Lily thought there was some ground to cover first.

There was the issue of her resurrection, first and foremost. For Arlo's sake, they decided to say she'd had amnesia all these years. That running into Rafael on the street had jolted her back to herself.

"And in a way," Lily told him one night as they lay tangled together in his house in San Francisco, "that's even true."

"It's the kinder story to tell," Rafael had agreed, smoothing a hand down the length of her lovely back. "For all of us."

She'd fielded questions from all sides, and not all of it the media. Her old friends, who'd mourned her death and now wanted nothing but to bask in her return. All the various parts of the life she'd left behind and found so different now that she'd come back to it. She'd discovered her time running Pepper's kennels gave her rather more managerial skills than she'd imagined they might, and when a position came up at the Castelli Wine corporate office in Sonoma, she took it. She'd visited her mother's grave and told Rafael that she found some comfort in knowing that the woman was finally at peace.

But it was dealing with his family that she was the most worried about, he knew.

It helped, Rafael thought, that they'd already had a son. There was no hoping the family would get used to the idea—there was a little boy who didn't care whom his grandparents had been married to before his birth.

And after the initial shock, Gianni Castelli had shrugged in a rueful way of his that reminded Rafael of when his father had been a younger man. The child bride—Corinna—had been having a loud conversation on her mobile phone out in the abundant sunshine that danced through the cypress trees at the Sonoma Valley château, and Gianni had gazed at her fondly before turning his gaze back to his son.

"Love levels every one of us, one way or another," he said. "It helps if you don't brace yourself against the fall. You're more likely to break something that way. Better by far to let gravity do what it will. It will anyway."

Luca, of course, had merely laughed. Then clapped Rafael on the back, hard. Then laughed again, but that time, Rafael had laughed with him.

Lily reconnected with Pepper under her real name, and even tracked down the sweet Canadian couple who had spirited her out of California that fateful night, finally able to pay them back for their kindness to her.

And then, on an autumn day in the south of France where they'd flown for a wine show, she'd finally agreed to marry him.

"I don't know what took you so long," Rafael said gruffly.

"Because," she said fiercely, stopping dead in the mid-

dle of a bustling market in Nice to look up at him solemnly,
"I wanted to be sure this time."

He'd been unable to keep himself from touching her. He
hadn't tried. "That I wouldn't run away?"

"That *I* wouldn't," she said softly, and she smiled up at
him, her strawberry blond hair like a halo in the fine French
light. "And I won't, Rafael. Not ever again."

And so at last they stood there in the small chapel and
recited their vows, to each other and for their son. When
they were finally husband and wife, they walked back to
the house while Arlo ran on ahead, pressing their shoulders
together the way they had long ago. Inside, the rest of the
family waited to join in the celebration and tip it straight
into Christmas, but first, Rafael stopped her at the door
before she would have gone in.

It was cold, but when he held out his hand, palm facing
her, she met it with hers.

This was who they were. This heat. This connection.
It had defied their scandalous beginnings, the possibility
of death and far too many lies. It had endured when they
didn't trust each other at all, and while they'd taught each
other how to smile.

"All the rest of our days," Rafael said. "*Mi appartieni.*"

"And you belong to me," Lily agreed, the glimmer of
tears in her gorgeous blue eyes. "Forever."

And then he took her hand in his, his wife at last, and
led them safely home.

* * * * *

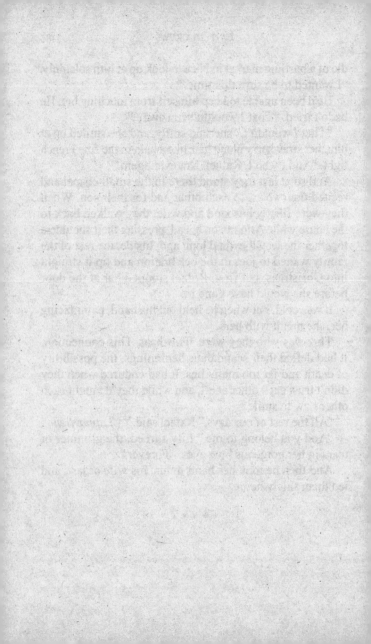

SEDUCED BY THE TYCOON AT CHRISTMAS

PAMELA YAYE

"We don't meet people by accident. They are meant to cross our path for a reason."

—Rubyanne from Read, Love and Learn

Chapter 1

"Forget it. No way," Romeo Morretti snapped, struggling to control his temper. Scowling though his publicist couldn't see him through the phone, he turned off the stereo system inside his yellow Lamborghini Veneno and took a deep breath. Every morning as he drove to work, Giuseppe Del Piero called to discuss social events in and around Milan. But for the first time in eight years Romeo wished he'd let the call go to voice mail. "I'd sooner run through the city center naked singing 'Ave Maria' than appear on that pathetic gossip show."

"But you love the spotlight," Giuseppe argued. "Always have, always will."

"In light of everything that's happened in recent weeks I think it's best I lie low," he said, rubbing his tired eyes. Working fourteen-hour days, seven days a week, was starting to take its toll on him. Romeo loved his company, Morretti Finance and Investments, and wanted it to achieve even greater success. Hence, he was working around the clock. "I need to focus on my clients, instead of wasting my time doing magazine interviews and TV shows."

"Don't be ridiculous. The press love you, and they're obsessed with your fabulous, jet-setting lifestyle. You're the Italian version of James Bond minus the Secret Service thing. If you shy away from the public now it could hurt your bottom line."

"Life is about more than just money."

Giuseppe scoffed, as if he'd never heard anything more outrageous in his life. "Tell that to my three teenage daughters. The more moolah I give them, the more they want."

Romeo stopped at the intersection and stared out the window. His gaze landed on the corner newsstand, zeroing in on the headline splashed across the front of *Celebrity Patella*. He gripped the steering wheel so hard his veins throbbed.

Scanning the glossy magazine cover, he read the large, bold title—The Morretti Family, Sex, Lies and Secrets Exposed!—and gritted his teeth. For the umpteenth time, he wondered where he'd gone wrong, and cursed the day he'd met Lizabeth Larsen. He'd become acquainted with the lingerie model at a beach in Portugal and it had been lust at first sight.

How could Lizabeth do this to me? Doesn't she have a heart? Romeo couldn't wrap his head around what she'd done. They'd been broken up for over a year, and he hadn't seen or heard from her in months, so why now? Why was she trying to ruin him? She'd given a tell-all interview to the trashy gossip magazine, and now the entire city was buzzing about the salacious story. Lizabeth had shared intimate details about their sex life and had also bad-mouthed his family. Thankfully, his brothers and cousins lived in the States and would probably never see the issue. Romeo, on the other hand, couldn't go anywhere in Milan without people staring at him.

He swallowed hard, but the lump in his throat grew. The negative things Lizabeth had said about his family played in his mind. To his shock, she'd discussed his nephew's fatal pool accident at his brother Emilio's estate, the embezzlement accusations against his cousin Nicco, and his cousin Rafael's baby-mama drama in Washington years earlier. But what hurt Romeo more than anything were the lies she'd told about his deceased mother. He only hoped his grandparents, who lived in a small coastal fishing town, didn't hear about Lizabeth's interview.

"You have to do the show," Giuseppe insisted, raising his voice.

His enthusiasm was palpable, but Romeo didn't share in his publicist's excitement. "I don't have to do shit. It's my decision, not yours, so tell your producer friend at the TV station that I'm not interested in doing a sit-down interview tomorrow. Or any day for that matter."

"Lizabeth made explosive claims about you, and I hear she's planning to publish a tell-all book about your on-again, off-again relationship later as well."

Reeling from the news, Romeo spoke through clenched teeth. "Good for her."

"Want some advice?"

No, he thought, raking a hand through his thick brown hair. *I want you to quit badgering me, and cancel all of my public appearances for the rest of the week. I need a break. I'm feeling run down, and I don't want to end up in the hospital again.* Romeo shuddered to think what would have happened if Giuseppe hadn't found him in his home office that fateful day in August, and pressed his eyes shut to clear his mind. His hospital stay last year had been a huge wake-up call, and Romeo wasn't going to let anyone or anything stand in the way of his health or his happiness. If that meant keeping a low profile, so be it.

"Go on Lifestyle TV, tell your side of the story, then give Lizabeth a million-dollar cash settlement to make her disappear once and for all…"

His eyes wide, he started down at his cell phone, unable to believe what he was hearing. Romeo didn't need this shit. Not today. Every day brought new headaches and problems, and yesterday was no exception. As he was leaving his office for the day, he'd received a phone call from his executive team, and their conversation had left a bitter taste in his mouth. One of his favorite clients, Julio Mario Domínguez, had publicly humiliated Romeo's staff at a business conference in Venice, and his repeated attempts to contact the billionaire businessman had been unsuccessful. The Colombian native was one of his wealthiest and most influential clients, and even though Romeo wanted to keep the entrepreneur happy, he had to stick up for his staff.

"Trust me. I know what I'm doing. It's the only answer. If you don't give her a cash settlement, she'll crucify you and your family in the media."

"A cash settlement? For what? Being mean and vindictive? No way. It's not going to happen." It was only seven o'clock in the morning, but his day was going from bad to worse. Talking to Giuseppe, a jovial character with a boisterous laugh, usually put Romeo in a good mood. Not today. His publicist wanted him to go on TV and dish the dirt about his family, and if that wasn't bad enough, he wanted him to pay Lizabeth off. Hell. To. The. No.

The light turned green, and Romeo stepped on the gas pedal, speeding down the street as if he were on a racetrack. He couldn't believe this was happening—again. Not after everything he'd done for Lizabeth over the years. During their tumultuous, drama-filled relationship, he'd showered her with designer clothes, Cartier jewelry, luxury cars and world-class trips, and how did she replay him? By dragging his name through the mud. Through friends, he'd learned of her bitter quest for revenge, and if Romeo didn't respect her ailing father he'd sue her. "I've given Lizabeth enough money to last a lifetime. I'm not giving her another dime."

An awkward silence infected the phone line. Romeo knew Giuseppe was upset, but he had to do what was right for him, not his publicist. A clean, refreshing scent wafted through the open window, and Romeo took a deep breath. The sun was shining, and the sky was a radiant shade of blue, but the balmy November temperature wasn't enough to brighten his mood. He was so angry about Lizabeth's interview his entire body was tense, and he decided a mid-day workout was in order. At lunch, instead of going to his favorite restaurant with his executive team, he'd use the speed bag in the office gym. Then he'd have a Cuban cigar. He hadn't smoked since he was discharged from the hospital last year, but he was having the day from hell, and a stogie was the perfect antidote for his stress.

"You're the boss," Giuseppe said. "Like you always say, there's no such thing as bad press. We'll find a way to spin the story to your advantage, and you'll come out on top."

I was wrong. There is *such a thing as bad press*, Romeo thought with a heavy heart. This was a nightmare. He'd never been more humiliated in his life, and he hated the cruel, spiteful things his ex-fiancée had said about the people he loved most. Thinking about the lies Lizabeth had told the magazine about him, Romeo decided to call Markos later for legal advice.

A smile curled the corners of his lips. Two weeks ago, he'd traveled to Los Angeles to be the best man at his brother's wedding. It still blew his mind that Markos had tied the knot. Years ago, Markos was a workaholic, determined to be the most successful attorney in the state of California, but program director for a non-profit organization, Tatiyana Washington had captured his heart, and now they were husband and wife.

Giuseppe yapped on and on about creative and innovative ways to increase Romeo's online presence, but Romeo's mind wandered. A year ago, the buzz about his company had reached an all-time high. Thanks to his team, his carefully cultivated image had not only added to his insane popularity in Italy, it attracted women like a sale sign in a boutique window. In the hopes of meeting him, socialites and heiresses had flocked to his office in droves, and once there, he had convinced them to invest with his company. A favorite of gossip bloggers, there was a time when Romeo enjoyed the spotlight. The more brazen he was, the more the public seemed to love him, especially the opposite sex.

Slowing down to allow a jaywalker to cross the street, he reflected on the highs and lows of his life in Milan. He'd done it all—partied too hard, drunk too much and spent money recklessly—but after his hospital stay he'd turned over a new leaf. Quit drinking, smoking cigars and eating like a college frat boy. At thirty-two, hooking up with a different woman every night of the week had lost its appeal, and although he had a life most men would kill for, Romeo felt empty inside, lonely now that his closest friends had wives and children. One by one, his brothers and cousins had found love, and they were all ridiculously happy. Romeo wondered if he was missing out on something. Everyone around him was moving forward, and he was stuck in neutral. For months, he'd been playing it safe, doing everything right and following his doctor's orders, but Christmas was right around the corner and he wanted to enjoy the holidays without stressing out about his health. Or his bitter ex-fiancée.

"Handle it, Giuseppe. I don't want this story hanging over my head during the holidays. Make it go away, *now*."

"*Nessun problema.* Leave everything to me. I know just what to do."

"You better," he said in a stern voice. "Or you're fired."

Giuseppe chuckled. "You wouldn't survive a day without me, and you know it."

A grin overwhelmed his mouth. It was true. Giuseppe wasn't just his publicist, he was also a confidante and a trusted friend. If not for Giuseppe, Romeo wouldn't be alive. "Are you on your way to the office or are you having breakfast with Bellisa again?"

"Bellisa *is* my breakfast," he said with a throaty laugh. "I'll give you a ring in the afternoon, but promise me you'll give some thought to what I said about Lizabeth."

"There's nothing to think about." Switching lanes, Romeo punched the gas. "I'm not giving her a damn thing."

"A million euros is chump change to you."

"Dammit, Giuseppe, it's not about the money."

Making a right turn, Romeo heard something hit the passenger-side door and slammed on the brakes. Frowning, he peered in the rearview mirror. His heart stopped. His cell phone fell from his hands and dropped to his feet. Fearing the worst, Romeo took off his seat belt, threw open his car door and ran around the trunk.

Romeo surveyed the scene. A purple mountain bike lay in a tangled heap on the road along with the contents of a handbag. A woman of Caribbean descent with caramel-brown skin, delicate facial features and waist-length black braids sat on the sidewalk, shaking uncontrollably. Filled with concern, he moved toward her, speaking in a quiet tone of voice.

"Miss, are you okay? Are you hurt?"

Romeo tried to help her to her feet, but she pushed his hands away. Standing, she straightened her short sleeveless dress and brushed the dirt off the hem. Watching her every move, he admired everything about her—her almond-shaped eyes, the beauty mark above her lips, the diamond hoop earrings that grazed her shoulders and her womanly physique. He guessed she was in her early twenties, around the same age as his kid sister, Francesca, and suspected she was an exchange student.

Glaring at him, it was obvious she was pissed, and Romeo didn't blame her. He should have been paying attention to the road instead of arguing with Giuseppe about his ex. He'd messed up, and now because of his mistake the cyclist was staring at him with tears in her eyes.

Romeo swallowed hard. Feeling like a specimen under a microspore, his throat dried, and sweat drenched his suit jacket. If looks could kill, he'd be dead, and the coroner would be notifying his next of kin. For the first time in Romeo's life he was tongue-tied, in such a state of shock he couldn't speak. And not just because he'd accidentally struck a cyclist with his car; he was transfixed by the woman's natural beauty. There weren't a lot of people of color in Milan, and she was such a knockout that Romeo couldn't stop staring at her. Her full, sensuous lips and her Lord-have-mercy curves were captivating, instantly seizing his attention.

Romeo was intrigued by her, wanted to know her story. Where was she from? And most importantly, was she single? The woman was off-the-charts hot, and if they'd met under different circumstances he definitely would have asked her out. But since Romeo didn't want her to think he was an insensitive jerk, he quit lusting and wore an apologetic smile. "Miss, I feel horrible about what happened."

Drawn to her, he stepped forward, eager to make amends for what he'd done. Romeo felt like an ass. Guilt-ridden, he opened his mouth to apologize again, but her strident voice filled the air.

"Are you blind?" she shouted. "You could have killed me with your stupid sports car!"

A crowd of curious onlookers had gathered around them, and Romeo wished everyone—except the dark-skinned beauty with the American accent—would disappear. Well-traveled, with vacation homes and real estate properties all across the United States, he guessed she was visiting from New York and wondered how long she'd be in Milan.

The woman gestured to the road, an incredulous expression on her flawless oval face. "I had the right of way, but you turned *right* into me. What's wrong with you? You couldn't wait ten seconds for me to cross the street?"

"Miss, I'm sorry. I didn't see you—"

"Of course you didn't see me," she shot back. "You were too busy on your cell phone."

"You're right," Romeo conceded. "I should have been paying more attention to the road."

"Jerk," she mumbled, shaking her head in disgust. "You should lose your license."

Gasps and whispers ripped through the well-dressed Milanese crowd. A camera flashed in Romeo's face, then another one, and he knew it was just a matter of time before everyone in the city knew about his morning traffic accident. *Great*, he thought, shoving his hands into the pockets of his black, suit pants. *That's all I need. More bad press.*

Horns blared, and pedestrians complained as they maneuvered their way around the accident scene. An irate driver in a gleaming white Porsche stuck his head out the window and yelled in Italian about the traffic jam.

Romeo's car was blocking the intersection, but the street was so narrow that there was nowhere for him to move it. "The accident was my fault, and I take full responsibility for it," he said, hoping to defuse the situation. "I'll pay to replace your bike, your dress and all of the contents in your purse as well—"

"How benevolent of you, Mr. Morretti, but I don't want anything from you."

His mouth fell open, and seconds passed before he spoke. "You know who I am?"

"Of course I know who you are. I haven't been living under a rock the last two years."

"You live here? In Milan?" Romeo asked. "Where?"

A bearded man holding a leather satchel made his way through the crowd. "My name is Lucan Bianchi and I'm an emergency room doctor at Milan General Hospital," he explained, addressing the cyclist. "Is it okay if I check you out while we wait for the paramedics to arrive?"

Nodding, the woman allowed the doctor to lead her over to a wooden bench under a cluster of lush green trees, and she took seat. To Romeo's relief, most of the spectators put their cell phones away and moved on. He heard sirens in the distance, knew the police were on their way to the scene and considered calling Giuseppe back. This was bad. Worse than the stories about him in the tabloids. He'd screwed up and needed his public relations director to work his magic again.

Romeo shook his head. No. He'd handle it. He'd take responsibility for his actions and would deal with the consequences, whatever they may be. But a chilling thought came to mind, and a shudder ripped through his body. What if there was footage of his accident? If the police brought charges against him, would his reputation suffer? Would his billionaire clients take their investments elsewhere? His pulse drummed in his ears, deafening him. Romeo could see the headlines now: Woman Struck by Morretti Millionaire! Wealthy Businessman Charged with Careless Driving! Jail Time for Bad-Boy Tycoon!

"Zoe, where are you visiting from?"

The sound of the doctor's voice interrupted Romeo's thoughts. Eager to learn more about the cyclist, he listened closely to the conversation she was having with the physician. It was a challenge, but Romeo blocked out all the noises on the busy street and committed everything about her to memory. Her name was Zoe Smith; she'd lived in Milan for two years and was the PR director for the fashion house Casa Di Moda. He'd never heard of the company before, but made a mental note to Google it when he returned to his car.

Trying to appear casual, he moved closer to the bench and listened in. Romeo was used to meeting beautiful females and had no shortage of admirers, but this was the first—and only—time in his life a woman had left him flustered, desperate to be in her presence. He couldn't take his eyes off of her and wished he could trade places with the doctor. The physician had the pleasure of touching her, and as Romeo stared at the dark-skinned beauty, all he could think about was kissing her. Undressing her. Making love to her at his villa. And he would. But first, Romeo had to save his neck.

Chapter 2

Zoe Smith stood on the corner of the traffic-congested road, watching the female paramedics fawn all over Romeo Morretti, and rolled her eyes. They were flirting with him, acting as if they were socializing at a cocktail party rather than at the scene of a traffic accident. Their behavior was annoying her. They were flipping their hair, batting their eyelashes, laughing outrageously every five seconds. Why were they showering him with attention? Why weren't they assessing her—the victim? Wasn't that their job? To help her?

Romeo caught her staring at him, and her heart stopped. Zoe wanted to look away, but his gaze held her in its seductive grip. Even though she was a mature, thirty-two-year-old woman, she couldn't muster the strength to break free. The media—and every female in the city—loved the brazen playboy, and although she'd seen numerous pictures of him in the tabloids, Zoe still gave him the once-over. Dressed in a tailored suit, it was easy for her to see why socialites, actresses and pop stars threw themselves at him on a daily basis. He was eye candy. The kind of man women fantasized about, men idolized and children adored. Romeo was twenty feet away from her, but he still made her breathless. Light-headed. It was more than just his ridiculous sex appeal and his dark, soulful features; his calm, cool demeanor drew her in. He was trouble though, no doubt about it. Thoughts she had no business having about Romeo filled her mind, and she couldn't escape them.

Giving her head a shake, Zoe tore her gaze away from his handsome face. She hadn't traveled all the way to Milan to get played by a cocky bachelor with a reputation with the ladies. She'd read the stories in the tabloids, and now that she'd met Romeo Morretti for herself, Zoe knew the gossip was true. According to published reports, he was used to getting his way in the boardroom *and* the bedroom, but she wasn't going to give him the time of day. She was actively searching for Mr. Right, not a bad-boy businessman who reeked of arrogance.

Zoe glanced at her wristwatch, saw that it was eight thirty and felt a rush of panic. The staff meeting started in thirty minutes, and since she didn't want to miss Aurora's announcement, she had to hurry. Her office was only ten minutes away, and once the police finished their investigation, she'd be on her way. Her colleagues at Casa Di Moda were convinced they were receiving Christmas bonuses today, and the news was music to her ears.

For the first time that morning, Zoe smiled. Drowning in debt, she planned to use the money to pay off her bills and buy a plane ticket to New York so she could spend the holidays with her family. Milan was expensive, and it was impossible for her to save money when she had to network every night of the week. Not that Zoe was complaining. She attended red-carpet events, charity galas and award shows, and mingled with the most important people in the fashion industry. In two short years, she'd developed strong relationships with magazine editors, beauty bloggers and supermodels, and her boss was thrilled with the progress she'd made. Best of all, she loved the energy and environment at Casa Di Moda, and hoped to work at the up-and-coming fashion house for many years to come.

"Ms. Smith, would you like to add anything else to your statement?"

Surfacing from her thoughts, Zoe shook her head and faced the police officer with the heavy accent and wiry black hair. "What happens now?" she asked. "Are you going to charge Mr. Morretti with distracted driving?"

The officer closed his notebook and tucked it into his front pocket. "No."

"Why not? He was yapping on his cell phone and driving recklessly when the accident occurred. If that isn't the definition of distracted driving, I don't know what is."

"Witnesses said Mr. Morretti had the right of way when you slammed into his car."

"Yeah, right. And I was an astronaut in a past life," she quipped.

The officer frowned. "Why would the witnesses lie? Furthermore, I interviewed everyone in the café across the street and the staff said the same thing. *You* crossed illegally."

Stumped, Zoe closed her mouth. *Am I at fault? Did I cause the accident?* She tried to remember what happened, to visualize the scene in her mind's eye, but her brain was foggy. Last night, she'd stayed up late working on the December events calendar, and Zoe was so tired, she'd dozed off at the kitchen table while reading the morning newspaper.

Her gaze landed on her mountain bike, lying in pieces on the cobblestoned road, and her shoulders sagged. Milan was flat, with no hills or valleys, and biking around the city was not only fun and economical, it was a great way for her to learn her way around. It had been a gift from her colleague, Jiovanni Costa, and Zoe had fond memories of them cycling through the countryside, talking, laughing and cracking jokes. The associate designer was the brother she'd never had, and if not for his friendship she never would've survived her first month in Milan.

"Am I free to go?" Zoe asked, addressing the police officers.

"You should go to the hospital to get checked out," the emergency room doctor advised, pushing his rimless eyeglasses up the bridge of his nose. "I think it's for the best."

The police officer with the crooked teeth nodded his head. "I agree."

Zoe was annoyed, but she didn't argue with the three men crowded around her on the wooden bench. It wasn't their fault Romeo Morretti had ruined her morning commute, and although she was tired of the doctor pressuring her to go to the hospital, she hid her frustration. "Thanks, but no thanks," Zoe said, rising to her feet. Pain coursed through her right ankle, but she ignored the discomfort. "I'm good."

Worry lines wrinkled the doctor's forehead. "But you're favoring your right side."

He was right; she was. Dodging his gaze, Zoe stared down at her wedge sandals. Her shin was sore and her legs ached, but since it was nothing a warm bath and a glass of Chianti couldn't cure, Zoe dismissed his concerns with a wave of her hand. "I'm fine. I don't need to go the hospital. I need to go to work, and if I don't leave now, I'll be late."

The men shared a worried look, and Zoe wondered if the police had the authority to take her to the hospital against her will. Anxious to get to the office, she crouched down on the road, grabbed her broken handbag and stuffed her personal items back inside. Her cell phone and her tablet were both cracked, and her makeup case was caked in mud. Pausing to look at the family pictures that had fallen out of her journal, her vision blurred. As she'd collided with Romeo Morretti's car, images of her parents and her younger sister had flashed before her eyes. If her cell phone weren't broken, she'd call them right now just to hear their voices. It was hard being away from her close-knit Trinidadian family, but Zoe loved living and working in Milan and wanted to help make Casa Di Moda a household name.

Standing, Zoe glanced around for a taxi stand. Spotting one across the street in front of a bakery, she swung her purse over her shoulder and gingerly approached the intersection. If she hurried, she could make it to the staff meeting on time, and her boss would never know she'd been an hour late for work. Zoe still couldn't wrap her mind around what had happened. Her bike was destroyed, but she was alive and well, and that was all that mattered.

"Hey! Wait! Where are you going?" the police officer said, raising his voice. "You can't leave your bike on the road all day. Someone could get hurt."

Zoe frowned. What did he expect her to do? Carry it on her back to work? His tone was sharp, implying that his patience was limited. To smooth things over, she apologized for the inconvenience and thanked the officers in Italian for their help.

Everyone on the sidewalk—including Romeo Morretti—gawked at her. No doubt, they were shocked she spoke Italian. Everyone was. Two years ago, while traveling through Europe, she'd fallen in love with Milan, and after a chance meeting with up-and-coming fashion designer Aurora Bordellio at a networking event, she'd landed the public relations director position at Casa Di Moda. Thrilled to be living and working in her favorite city in the world, she'd devoted herself to learning the language, culture and history. Taking night classes at the local university and attending community events were the wisest things she'd ever done. When locals heard her speaking Italian, they instantly warmed up to her and went out of their way to help her.

The light changed, and pedestrians flooded the street. Taking her time, despite all of the people rushing past her, Zoe slowly crossed the intersection. High-rise buildings crowded the skyline, but she could still make out the top of the golden-painted statue on the Duomo and admired its beauty. Described by locals as the Italian Manhattan, Milan was a fast-paced city packed with entrepreneurs, university students, attractive women in the latest designer fashions, and wide-eyed tourists toting cameras and backpacks.

Zoe was tired and her ankle ached, but the sounds and aromas around her were invigorating. Milan had it all— historical buildings and monuments, breathtaking architecture, outstanding restaurants, and a vibrant nightlife—and every day, Zoe found something new to love about the city. Her work visa expired in the new year, and although she missed her friends and family back home, she teared up at the thought of leaving Milan.

"Where are you going?"

Zoe glanced over her shoulder and saw Romeo Morretti standing directly behind her, and gulped. *What does he want?* Her eyes zeroed in on him, taking in every aspect of his six-foot-three frame. He had a full head of curly brown hair and skin that looked smooth to the touch, and his lips were so thick and juicy, thoughts of kissing him overwhelmed her mind. He smelled of shampoo and aftershave; the strong, masculine scent tickled her nose. His piercing gaze and his boyish smile were a lethal combination. Zoe feared if she didn't move, her knees would buckle, and she'd fall headfirst into his arms. Desperate to put some distance between them, she increased her pace, speed walking toward the taxi stand even though her ankle was killing her.

"Zoe, please, wait. Don't run off. I can drive you wherever you need to go."

Her feet slowed. Not because of his generous, unexpected offer, but because of the way he said her name. With tenderness and warmth, as if they were lovers and he was pleading for forgiveness. Deleting the thought from her mind, Zoe knew it was important to keep her guard up and wisely took cover behind the green taxi stand. Her mouth was dry, and her stomach was twisted in knots, but she managed to sound calm. "No, thank you."

"Why not?"

"I've seen you drive, and I don't want to end up in the emergency ward."

The light in his eyes dimmed, and Zoe felt guilty for insulting him. She remembered what the police officers had told her about the accident. According to witnesses, she was to blame, so she had no right to insult Romeo Morretti. Still, he made her nervous, uncomfortable. She wished he'd return to his fancy sports car and leave her alone.

"Where are you going?"

"Work," she said, trying to conceal her frustration. Hot and thirsty, all Zoe could think about was drinking a tall, cold glass of ice water, and hoped Jiovanni had remembered to bring snacks to the staff meeting. "I'm late, and if I don't hustle, my boss will kill me."

"Work? In your condition?" His eyebrows slanted in a frown. "You should go home and rest. I'm sure your boss will understand."

"Has anyone ever told you that you're a pest?"

Romeo gave a hearty chuckle. "No, never."

Damn, even his laugh is sexy, Zoe thought as she wiped her damp palms along the sides of her dress. It wasn't every day she met a man of Romeo Morretti's calibre—someone suave, charming and dapper—and being in his presence had an odd effect on her. Every time their eyes met she felt short of breath, as if she were going to have an asthma attack—but she didn't have asthma. Licking her lips, she searched the street for a cab.

"Zoe, what's the number for Casa Di Moda? I'll call on your behalf."

A shiver tickled her spine. Hearing her name come out of his broad, sensuous mouth warmed her all over. Seconds passed before she could speak, and when Zoe finally reunited with her voice, it sounded foreign to her ears. *What's the matter with me? Why am I acting skittish?* For some strange reason, Romeo made her heart race. Zoe wanted him gone, far away from her, before she embarrassed herself.

"No thanks, I'm good. Don't bother."

"I should have known you worked in the fashion industry," he said, his gaze sliding down her physique. "You're stunning, and you have a great sense of style, not to mention a unique, eye-catching look."

Zoe didn't respond, searched the streets once again for a taxicab. Romeo was buttering her up, trying to sweet-talk her because he felt guilty about the accident, but it wasn't going to work. Immune to his charms, she gave him her back.

Undeterred, Romeo stepped forward, moved in so close, Zoe could smell his minty-fresh breath. Her mind went blank and her senses spun. They were standing side by side now, shoulder to shoulder, and for the second time in minutes, Zoe inhaled sharply.

"You speak Italian very well," Romeo said, his tone filled with awe. "How did you learn the language?"

Doesn't he have somewhere to be? His office? A meeting? On his private jet with a bevy of supermodels? Zoe told herself to be nice and forced a smile on her lips. "I took Italian in high school and throughout university, so I had a good handle on the language before I moved to Milan."

Annoyed that her favorite pair of sunglasses had been destroyed in the accident, she shielded her eyes from the sun with her hands. The sky was a brilliant shade of blue, the breeze was warm, and a delicious scent wafted out of the bakery, eliciting groans from her stomach. Zoe thought of going inside the shop to grab a bite to eat, but decided against it. She was pressed for time, and she feared Romeo Morretti would follow her inside if she did. The last thing she wanted was to be alone with him in a cozy, intimate setting. He made her jittery, and there was no telling what would happen if he touched her again.

"I feel horrible about the accident, and I want to make it up to you."

Zoe didn't answer, hoping that if she stayed quiet, he'd take the hint and go away.

"I'd like to take you out for dinner tonight at Dolce Vita Milan," he said.

His broad smile revealed straight, blinding white teeth and dimples in each cheek. He was a pretty boy who was used to getting his way, and although he wasn't her type,

Zoe had to admit that Romeo was one fine-looking man. A handful, too, according to her favorite blog. Every week, there was a story about him hooking up with an Italian actress or model. Zoe didn't doubt it. He had a devilish expression on his face, as if he was cooking up mischief, and Zoe suspected this was his MO—flash a wink and a smile, then pour on the charm. She made up her mind not to be his next victim. Dubbed *Diavolo Sexy* by the local press, which meant sexy devil in Italian, Romeo could have any woman he wanted, and Zoe didn't doubt that he had.

"Put your number in my phone," he instructed, taking his cell out of his back pocket and offering it to her. "I'll call you this afternoon so we can hook up."

Zoe narrowed her eyes. Hook up? After five minutes of conversation? Boy, bye!

Disgust must have shown on her face, because Romeo wore an apologetic smile and brushed his fingertips against her forearm.

"What is it, *bellissima*? You look upset. Did I say something wrong?"

Beautiful? Overcome by his close proximity, Zoe dodged his sexy, steely stare. *Romeo thinks I'm beautiful?* Goose bumps flooded her skin. Feeling out of sorts, as if a shy, flustered teenager had suddenly inhabited her body, her mouth dried and her heart beat in triple time. "You don't have to buy me dinner. It was an accident, and since the police said I'm to blame, you don't owe me anything."

"I'd still like to take you out tonight. I love being in the presence of smart, accomplished women. I think we'll have a great time together at Dolce Vita Milan."

Swallowing hard, Zoe fingered the gold pendant at her neck. "Thanks, but no thanks," she said, still convinced he was up to something. "We're strangers, and—"

"That's why I want us to have dinner. We'll have a nice

meal, a bottle of your favorite wine, and get to know each other better. Doesn't that sound like fun, Zoe?"

Romeo licked his lips with such finesse her skin tingled. It was a struggle, but Zoe maintained her composure, didn't wither under the intensity of his dark, smoldering gaze.

"I can't. I have a work function to attend."

"I understand. No problem. We can have dinner tomorrow night. Same time and place."

Zoe shook her head. "I have plans with friends."

"Cancel them." Glancing around, he lowered his face to hers and spoke in a quiet voice. "We need to get our stories straight about the accident. I don't want any surprises."

His words didn't register. "I don't understand."

"I think you do, but we can discuss the details tomorrow night at dinner."

A taxicab stopped at the curb, and Zoe sighed in relief. "I have to go."

"Not so fast." Romeo put his hand on the passenger side door, thwarting her escape. "You still haven't given me your cell number. How am I supposed to finalize our plans if I don't know how to reach you?"

Zoe couldn't believe his nerve. *Who does he think he is? My man?* The time for being nice was over. It was time to make herself crystal clear. "We're not having dinner tomorrow night or any other night. Now if you'll excuse me, I have to go."

He looked shell-shocked, like a survivor stumbling off a shipwrecked boat. Zoe suspected a woman had never told him no before. Proud of herself for not falling victim to his charms, she gestured to the door and smiled her thanks when he reluctantly opened it.

"Zoe, please, reconsider meeting with me. I know we can work something out."

"There's nothing to reconsider."

To her surprise, Romeo reached into his pocket, took out his wallet and handed the driver several dollar bills. Lowering his head through the open window, his cologne engulfing the compact car, he spoke to the driver in Italian.

His words made her heart smile. *Take this beautiful woman anywhere she wants to go.* Zoe couldn't deny it, the man had a way with words. Romeo straightened to his full height, and watching him made her pulse race. He waved at her, but Zoe dropped her gaze to her lap. Since Zoe didn't want to encourage Romeo's advances, she told the taxi driver to step on it.

Chapter 3

On the outside, Casa Di Moda headquarters in the Milan city center was nothing special, but Zoe called the two-story property her second home. Housed in a brown brick building, with the name of the fashion house written on the windows in fine script, the decor was clean and simple.

Breezing through the front door, Zoe smiled and waved at her colleagues. The interior had bright colors, scrumptious chairs and couches, and vintage mirrors throughout the main floor. Oversize photographs of ad campaigns and fashion shows beautified the walls, and as Zoe entered the reception area, the tranquil atmosphere calmed her nerves. Despite the pain in her ankle, she moved with confidence.

The December program she'd created for Casa Di Moda was packed with creative holiday events, and Zoe was confident her boss would love it, especially the Men of Milan calendar. The idea had come to her days earlier after a loud, spirited conversation with her girlfriends on

FaceChat, and Zoe couldn't wait to pitch it at the morning staff meeting.

Reaching the conference room door, she smoothed her hands over her braids and the front of her dress. It had been one hell of a morning, but her day was about to get better. Excitement coursed through her veins. Cha-ching! Zoe had big plans for her bonus. After she paid her bills and bought her plane ticket to New York, she'd donate the rest of the money to her favorite charity. Last year, she'd organized a Christmas toy drive at the office, and it had been a success. This year, Zoe planned to do more.

For some strange reason, an image of Romeo Morretti popped into her mind, derailing her thoughts. She'd done nothing wrong, so why did she feel guilty about turning down his dinner invitation? Zoe had a bad feeling about him, just knew that he was as cocky as the tabloids said he was, so why did she regret not giving him her cell phone number? Had she made a mistake? During the taxicab ride, she'd read several articles about him on her tablet, and each story was more shocking than the one before. Born into one of the richest families in the country, Romeo had been educated in the finest schools and lived a life most people could only dream of. He owned real estate properties, premier restaurants, spas and fitness centers. Eight years after opening his company, Morretti Finance and Investments, his personal net worth had tripled. Not that Zoe was impressed by his staggering wealth. The most interesting thing she'd read about the brilliant businessman had nothing to do with his flamboyant lifestyle and celebrity friends. Every year, he donated millions of dollars to charity and even fed the homeless. *Maybe he's more than just a bad-boy bachelor*, she'd thought, staring at the images taken of him at local hospitals and orphanages. Maybe he has a heart.

Zoe shook her head to clear her mind. It didn't matter what she thought. She didn't have time to daydream about a man she'd never see again. She was late, and since every second counted, she gripped the door handle, turned it and peeked inside the conference room.

The blinds were drawn, allowing sunlight to fill the room, and decorative vases overflowing with peach and orange roses sweetened the air. Decorated in white with floor-to-ceiling windows, leather armchairs and contemporary art, the conference room was spacious and attractive. Fruit and pastry trays were on the table, and Zoe's mouth watered in anticipation.

Sighing in relief, Zoe eased open the door. Thankfully, Aurora had her back to the door and was furiously writing notes on the Smart Board. Her husband, Davide, was staring down at his iPad. With his clean-cut looks and salt-and-pepper hair, the executive vice president often joked about feeling old. But he had a youthful air, and everyone on staff loved him.

"Come here," Jiovanni mouthed. "I saved you a seat. Hurry up."

Hoping to go unnoticed, Zoe tiptoed across the room. The moment she sat down in the empty chair beside Jiovanni, Aurora called her name.

"Zoe, how nice of you to join us," she said, glancing over shoulder. "I hope my weekly staff meeting isn't interrupting your very busy schedule."

Her cheeks warmed and her stomach churned. Embarrassed that her boss was taking her to task in front of her colleagues, Zoe wore an apologetic smile. "Sorry I'm late Aurora, but I was in a—"

The designer spun around, startling her, and Zoe broke off speaking.

"Save it for someone who cares. We have work to do, and lots of it."

Feeling her mouth drop open, she stared at her boss with wide eyes. Aurora never raised her voice, let alone yelled at her, so Zoe was shocked by her tone. The designer wasn't just her boss, she was also a good friend, and her stinging retort hurt her feelings.

Aurora fussed with her multicolored scarf. Petite, with a brown pixie cut, olive skin and a slender frame, she had perfect posture and impeccable manners. "Zoe, I'm sorry I yelled at you." Sniffing, she dabbed her eyes with the back of her hand. "The last few weeks have been a nightmare…"

Her voice faltered, and she couldn't finish her thought.

Zoe straightened in her chair, tried to make sense of what was going on with her boss. Was Aurora having a mental breakdown? she wondered, scrutinizing the designer's appearance. Dark lines rimmed her eyes, but her black A-line dress complemented her shape, and the leopard-print heels she wore elongated her legs. Were the late nights, and early mornings, finally getting to her? Was she so overwhelmed with stress and fatigue she couldn't function?

Rising from his leather chair at the head of the table, Davide stood behind his wife and placed his hands on her shoulders. "Casa Di Moda is in trouble, and we need your help."

"What are you saying?" a graphic designer asked. "Is the company broke?"

Davide spoke in a solemn tone of voice. "No, but if we don't turn things around in the next three months, we'll have no choice but to file for bankruptcy."

The room was so quiet, Zoe could hear her heart beating inside her chest. Was this a joke? A trick? She wondered if the powerhouse couple were pulling her leg, and studied their faces for clues. They looked serious, sounded serious, too, but Casa Di Moda couldn't be in financial trouble. The line was popular; celebrities wore their designs to award shows, movie premieres and industry events. They'd recently landed a multiyear contract with an international film company to design costumes.

"That's impossible," Jiovanni argued, his short black curls flopping around his face. "We signed several deals this year, and high-end boutiques in Montreal, Dubai and Paris are chomping at the bit to carry our gowns as well."

Jiovanni had a fun-loving personality, an outrageous sense of humor and an infectious laugh. He loved fine wine, Italian rap music, and had a different woman on his arm every week. He liked to joke about marrying her one day, but he was the big brother Zoe never had, and she'd never ruin their friendship by getting involved romantically with him.

"The film company backed out of the deal weeks ago, but we didn't know how to tell you." Davide wore a sad smile. "You worked hard on the presentation, and we didn't want to disappoint you, especially after everything you've done over the years to help the line succeed."

"How could this happen? We've given our blood, sweat and tears to this company for years, and now we have nothing to show for it," grumbled the creative director.

"Casa Di Moda isn't the only company feeling the pinch," Aurora said. "People aren't splurging on designer labels like they used to, and according to official figures, clothing, shoes and jewelry fell another eighteen percent over the last nine months."

"Households are under increasing pressure as they wrestle with rising living costs," Davide added. "There's a lot of fear and uncertainty in the world right now. Consumers are being very conservative with their money, even the rich and famous."

Staff members grumbled and complained, bombarding Aurora and Davide with questions and concerns. Zoe couldn't speak. This couldn't be happening. Not to Aurora and Davide. They had big hearts, and she admired their tireless work ethic. Married for over a decade, the couple had no children, but referred to Casa Di Moda as their baby and treated everyone at the company like family. It was hard to listen to her colleagues bash them, but every time Zoe tried to come to the couple's defense, someone interrupted her.

"Everyone, please settle down. I'm still the boss, and I won't tolerate this kind of behavior at my company. If you can't be respectful, I'll have to ask you to leave."

Silence fell across the room as Aurora spoke, but tension and anger polluted the air.

"It will be business as usual around here during the holidays, but Davide and I will be away from the office a fair bit, so we'll need all of you to hold the fort while we're aggressively seeking new investors who'll help us take Casa Di Moda to the next level."

An associate designer raised her hand. "Are you planning to file for bankruptcy in the new year? Should we be looking for other jobs?"

Aurora stared down at the beige carpet, as if the answer to the question were written there. "I don't know," she said in a quiet tone of voice.

"Let's not dwell on the negative." Davide wore a broad smile. "Tonight's the premiere of *Amore in Tuscany*, and we expect to see all of you at Anteo spazioCinema. You can't get in the theater without your VIP pass, so guard it with your life."

For weeks, Zoe had been looking forward to the movie

premiere, but Aurora and Davide's announcement had soured her mood. Casa Di Moda collaborated with several European directors to design movie sets and costumes, and the success of the film could mean more business for the company. Since Zoe wanted to see the fashion house succeed, she'd post about the event again on her social media pages once she got to her office.

"One last thing," Aurora said, raising an index finger in the air. "If you have any ideas on how to help us turn things around and increase sales, please don't hesitate to share them with us. Speak up. We want to hear from you."

"I know a surefire way to boost sales and increase our popularity as well."

Everyone in the room cranked their heads in Zoe's direction but she wasn't at all intimidated. She had this. Knew what she was talking about. Had the numbers to support her argument. And she was excited to share her knowledge with her colleagues.

"You do?" Interest sparked in Davide's eyes.

"Well, don't keep us in the dark." Aurora spoke in a loud, animated voice. "What is it? What's your brilliant idea for saving Casa Di Moda?"

"Create a plus-size line for curvy women."

A scowl darkened Davide's face, and the smile slid off Aurora's thin pink lips.

"I don't design clothes for big girls," she spat. "And I never will."

"Why not?" Zoe pressed, curious why her boss had shot down her idea. "According to published reports, the average woman in the United Kingdom is a size fourteen, and I think it's high time we tap into that underserved and unappreciated market."

"We will not. I style women from size zero to size eight, and that's it."

"But women don't stop at size eight," Zoe argued. "We come in all shapes and sizes. As a woman with curves, I know firsthand how stressful it is to find attractive designer clothes in Milan. And from what I hear on social media, it's an issue all across Europe."

Aurora inspected her French manicure. "That's not my problem."

Zoe took a moment to collect her thoughts. Having had this conversation with Jiovanni numerous times before, she stared at her best friend for help, but he dodged her gaze. Undeterred, Zoe returned her attention to her boss, forgetting about everyone else in the room and speaking from the heart. "Aurora, you make the most beautiful clothes, and I'd kill to wear your designs but I can't because you don't make them in my size. Why not create clothes for everyone? Why not share your talent with the world?"

"Because if I do I'll never be taken seriously again as a designer. I'll be shunned by the entire fashion community. At this stage in my career that's a risk I can't afford to take."

"You're a designer, and no one can ever take that away from you."

"We could call the line, Chic and Curvy," proposed an intern with colored braces.

"I love it!" Zoe said, unable to hide her excitement. The expression on Aurora's face said *back off,* but she had to speak her mind. Wouldn't be able to live with herself if she kept her feelings bottled up inside. Buying clothes had been an issue ever since she'd moved to Milan. If not for Jiovanni making dresses for her to wear to industry events, she'd be stuck ordering clothes online from the States.

"You have a God-given talent," Zoe continued. "And it's time you share your gift with the world, namely curvy beauties like me. Hey, voluptuous women love fashion, too!"

Her joke fell flat, and for the second time in minutes, an awkward silence filled the air. Needing help, Zoe stared around the table at her colleagues, but everyone avoided her gaze. Undeterred, she flipped open her journal and reviewed her notes.

"I think the Men of Milan calendar promotion would tie in well with the launch of a plus-size line," she explained, continuing her pitch.

Aurora perked up. "A Men of Milan calendar? Sounds dreamy! Tell me more."

"Everyone who buys a Casa Di Moda gown during the Christmas holidays will receive a free calendar. People love getting free things, and I think this holiday promotion will be a hit."

"I love it," Aurora praised. "I think we should go all out. Let's hire male models to serve champagne and pose for pictures with customers as well."

Zoe tapped her pen on her notebook. "Christmas is several weeks away, but I'm going to get started on the Men of Milan today. We need to create buzz about our fabulous new holiday collection, and I think this is the best way to do it."

"Who do you have in mind for the calendar?" Davide asked, cocking an eyebrow. "Money is tight right now, so you'll have a very small budget for this project."

"No problem. Women love to see men in uniform, right, ladies?"

For the first time since the meeting started, her colleagues smiled and nodded.

"I'm going to hire some local models and dress them up as firefighters, paramedics, police officers and doctors.

I'm still working on the logistics, but I should have every-thing finished early next week."

"I want the proposal tomorrow," Aurora said.

Zoe gulped and her pen fell from her hands. *Twenty-four hours? Is Aurora out of her mind? That's not enough time to pull everything together!*

A cell phone rang, filling the air with a popular Italian pop song.

Smiling sheepishly, Davide took his cell out of his pocket, switched it off and put it on the table. "Great work, Zoe. I can tell everyone in here is really excited about this holiday promotion, and I'm pumped about it, too. Well done."

Thrilled that she had her bosses' support, Zoe jotted down ideas as they came to her. "How long will it take for the plus-size line to be ready?" she asked. "I think it would be cool if we had some women posing in Casa Di Moda gowns draped all over the models, don't you?"

Anger flashed in Aurora's eyes, and she spoke through clenched teeth. "We're not doing the plus-size line. Just the calendar. Got it?"

Worried she'd lose her temper if Aurora yelled at her again, Zoe picked up her glass and sipped her water. The self-made woman struck the fear of God in people, but Zoe wasn't going to let anyone disrespect her. "I'm disap-pointed that you won't consider my suggestion, but you're the boss, and I respect your decision," she said with a shrug. "If you don't want to expand the line and increase sales, there's nothing I can do."

Aurora seemed to shrink right before Zoe's eyes. With her head down and her shoulders hunched, she looked fragile and scared. Turning her face toward the windows, she gazed at the sky and fiddled with her wedding ring.

For all her wealth and success, she was stubborn and in-secure, and Zoe had never pitied anyone more.

"As you all know, the Christmas Wonderland Ball will be held on December 20, and I don't have to tell you how important this event is for Casa Di Moda. Everyone who's anyone will be there, and it's a great networking opportunity for us all."

"How many tables will we have this year?" asked the human resources director, straightening in her chair. "Is everyone on staff invited?"

Aurora and Davide shared a troubled look, and Zoe knew the couple was about to share more bad news with the staff. Every year, famous names from fashion, film, politics, business and the world of sports attended the black-tie event, which raised millions of dollars for the local children's hospital in Milan. It had the most expensive and coveted tickets of the year, and Zoe was looking forward to attending her first Christmas Wonderland Ball.

"I wish everyone could go, but the cost of the ball has dramatically increased this year to 100,000 euros a table. Only the executive team can go," Aurora explained.

"That's all for today, everyone." Davide opened the door. "Back to work."

Staff members filed out of the room wearing long faces, and Zoe couldn't recall ever feeling so low. She wanted to stay behind to speak to Aurora privately, but decided against it. Now wasn't the right time. Filled with sympathy, Zoe watched the couple embrace. It was bad enough Casa Di Moda was struggling financially, and since she didn't want to make things worse for Aurora and Davide by arguing with them about expanding the line, Zoe grabbed her things and hurried through the open door.

Needing a moment to catch her breath, Zoe ducked inside the ladies' room and locked herself in a stall. *If I'm a valuable member of the team why won't Aurora and Davide take my ideas seriously? And why did Aurora roll her eyes when I pressed her for details about the plus-size line? Does she want to save Casa Di Moda from bankruptcy or not?*

Zoe used the bathroom, then washed her hands. Deep down, she feared things were going to get worse at Casa Di Moda in the coming weeks, and wondered what that would mean for her future. *Will I have a job after the holidays? Will I be forced to leave Milan for good?*

As Zoe studied her reflection in the mirror, her mind flashed back to her conversation with Romeo Morretti that morning. A thought came to mind. He was a businessman with deep pockets who owned an investment company. Someone with billionaire friends and clients. Maybe if she reached out to him he could help Casa Di Moda— Zoe shook her head, told herself it was a bad idea. No good could come out of calling Romeo Morretti. From what she'd read about him, he was an opportunist who preyed on vulnerable people. Since Zoe didn't like playing with fire, she pushed the thought from her mind. Yanking open the door, she marched down the hallway toward her office, determined to finish her paperwork before the six o'clock movie premiere.

Chapter 4

"I come bearing gifts," Jiovanni announced, poking his head inside the door of Zoe's office on Thursday afternoon. Wearing a broad grin, his eyes alight with mischief, he strolled inside the room clutching a wine bottle in one hand and a garment bag in the other. "After that staff meeting from hell this morning, I figured you could use a pick-me-up, so I brought you a snack."

Hard at work at her desk, Zoe glanced up from the field sales report she was reading and put down her yellow highlighter. "When did Chianti become an afternoon snack?"

"When Aurora announced that Casa Di Moda was floundering and had the nerve to ask *us* to save it." His smile disappeared, and a frown crimped his lips. "I almost fell off my chair when she said profits were down eighteen percent from last year. Of course they're down! What does she expect? She's controlling as hell and stifling everyone's creativity."

All afternoon, Zoe had been holed up in her office, blogging, tweeting and posting about the premiere of *Amore in Tuscany* at Anteo spazioCinema. The response to her online messages on the Casa Di Moda social media pages was so overwhelming, Zoe knew the event was going to be a success. Celebrities would be in attendance, on hand to mingle with fans and pose for pictures. Zoe was pleased her hard work was paying off. She'd been promoting the event for weeks, and was confident her industry friends would come through for her in a big way at the premiere. In a good mood, she didn't want to rehash what had happened at the staff meeting, but it was obvious Jiovanni needed to vent. She set aside her report and gave him her full attention, even though she had a million things to do before calling it quits for the day.

"I'm so angry, I could punch something." Jiovanni put the wine bottle on the mahogany end table and chucked the garment bag on one of the velvet chairs. "My opinions and ideas aren't valued here, and it's frustrating."

Zoe wore a sympathetic smile. "I hear you, J, and I know how you feel."

"This goes down on record as being one of the worst days of my life," Jiovanni confessed, plopping down on the edge of the desk, his shoulders hunched in defeat. "And it's Aurora and Davide's fault. If they respected their staff, instead of treating us like a bunch of dumb schmucks fresh out of fashion school, Casa Di Moda wouldn't be in this mess."

"Don't hold back," she joked, hoping to make her best friend laugh. "Tell me how you really feel."

Hanging his head, he rubbed at his eyes. "For the last nine years, I've given everything to Casa Di Moda, and now I have nothing to show for it."

Filled with compassion, Zoe rose to her feet and came

around her desk. "Don't say things like that." To comfort him, she rubbed his back. "All isn't lost. We'll help Aurora turn things around, and this time next year, Casa Di Moda will be more popular than ever."

"How? How can we make a difference when Aurora is stubborn, and closed-minded?" His voice was resigned, and his expression was grim. "I want answers, Zoe. Tell me how we fix things. How do we save this company and our careers?"

Stumped, Zoe didn't know what to say in response. Seconds passed, but nothing came to mind. Her thoughts returned to the staff meeting, and Zoe mentally reviewed everything that was said and done inside the conference room.

"I thought so. You don't know what to do, either."

"You're right, I don't, but I'm not giving up. I'm committed to Casa Di Moda, and I want to see it succeed."

Jiovanni spoke through clenched teeth. "And I don't?"

Silence descended on the room.

"What happened this morning?" Zoe asked, still bothered by his lack of support at the staff meeting. Educated and well-read, Jiovanni had an opinion about everything, so his silence during the discussion had bothered her. "Why did you leave me hanging? Why didn't you say anything when I lobbied for a plus-size line to be added to the holiday collection?"

"Because I knew Aurora would never go for it. You don't think I've tried to talk to her about expanding the woman's line a million times before? Well, I have, and the last time I submitted a detailed proposal, she tossed it in the trash." Jiovanni dusted his hands, as if they were covered in sand, and fervently shook his head. "Zoe, I don't know about you or anyone else on this sinking ship, but I'm done."

Zoe raised an eyebrow. "What are you saying?"

"That it's time I branched out and did my own thing in the fashion world."

"But you don't have enough money saved up yet to rent a space," she reminded him, recalling the conversation they had weeks earlier about his long-term goals.

"I know, but I'm sick of twiddling my thumbs. I'm just as talented as Aurora, and if I work my ass off, Designs by Jiovanni will be a household name in no time."

"I believe in you, J. You can do anything you put your mind to."

Seizing Zoe's hand, Jiovanni pulled her into his arms and held her close to his chest. He danced around the room, expertly dodging the furniture, then lifted her up in the air. "Jiovanni, stop!" she yelled, scared he'd lose his footing and drop her on the carpet. She'd taken two Asprin at lunch, and her ankle wasn't hurting her anymore, but she didn't want to do anything to aggravate it. "What are you doing? This isn't *Milan Dance Championship* and you're not a professional dancer, so put me down right *now*."

"What do you mean, what am I doing?" he repeated, flashing a toothy smile. "I'm dancing with the most beautiful woman in Milan, and it's the best feeling in the world."

Zoe sighed in relief when her feet touched the ground. She swatted his shoulder. "Don't do that again. I almost had a heart attack when you picked me up, and I'm only thirty-two!"

"Quit playing. You know you loved it." Lowering his face to hers, he kissed her forehead. "I love holding you in my arms, Zoe. You know that."

His fingers grazed her forearm. He was too close for comfort, moving nearer to her, and Zoe feared he was going to do something crazy like kiss her. That would ruin everything. They were friends and nothing more.

She didn't want a romantic relationship with Jiovanni. Not today, not ever. Feeling trapped, she ducked under his arms and slid behind one of the chairs.

Her computer pinged, informing her that she had a new email message, and Zoe returned to her desk. These days Jiovanni was more flirtatious than ever, and she wondered if it had anything to do with his longtime girlfriend dumping him weeks earlier. To cheer him up she'd brought him home-cooked meals, wine and an armload of action movies.

"You and I make a great couple."

His gaze bore down on her, and a lascivious grin spread across his mouth.

"Everyone thinks so, even my nonna, and she's never liked any of my girlfriends."

To lighten the mood, Zoe cracked a joke.

"I'd never dream of arguing with your dear, sweet nonna," she said, making her eyes wide. "But the next time you want to re-create something you saw on your favorite dance show, find another partner, because I prefer having my feet on the ground, not suspended in midair."

Jiovanni stuck out his tongue and Zoe laughed. She could never stay mad at him; he made life fun, and she enjoyed his company so much they spent most of their free time together, much to his nonna's delight.

"You know what they say about male fashion designers, don't you?"

Zoe wore a blank expression on her face. "No. What?"

"They're the world's best lovers."

"According to who? You and the womanizers in your bad-boy posse?"

"My posse? Can't say I've ever heard that expression before," he said with a hearty laugh. "You kill me, you know that? I just love your sass and wit."

"Good, so you won't mind when I ask you to leave."

"So, that's how it is? I bring you wine, and you show your appreciation by kicking me out. That's cold. What's up with that? I thought you were my girl?"

"I am, but you have to go. You're distracting me, and I have tons of work to do." Zoe accessed her email account from her computer and read her newest message. "I have to finish planning the Men of Milan calendar, but we'll meet up later at the premiere. I'll save you a seat."

"No, don't. I have plans tonight, and they don't involve Casa Di Moda."

"You're not going to the movie? Why not? Aurora's expecting everyone to be there."

"She doesn't run my life, and there's no way in hell I'm canceling my date."

"But the after-party's at Milano Cocktail Bar, your favorite spot in the city."

"Like I said, I have other plans." Jiovanni took his cell phone out of his pocket and swiped his finger across the screen. "I met a woman last night at the Blue Note jazz bar, and I'm taking her to the new French restaurant in the Bicocca."

As Zoe listened to Jiovanni boast about his flavor of the week, her gaze fell across the web page on her computer, and she clicked it. An image of Romeo Morretti filled her screen. At lunch, as she'd sat at her desk eating the steak panini she'd ordered from a nearby deli, she'd read several articles about him, and even watched a documentary about his family. The Morretti family was an accomplished, successful bunch who donated their time, money and resources to worthy causes. But it seemed the more money Romeo made, the more ostentatious he was. Sure, he gave generously to charity organizations, but former employees painted him in a bad light.

And they weren't the only ones.

The interview his ex-fiancée had given to the tabloids was so outrageous, Zoe had abandoned her lunch and soaked up every juicy word. There were thousands of pictures of him online with his billionaire clients, supermodel dates and equally attractive family members. To her surprise, Romeo traveled more than a flight attendant. He was in Spain when his brother Emilio won his fifth Formula One championship, on hand when his cousin Demetri smashed another baseball record in the Windy City, at the opening of Dolce Vita Dubai to support his cousin Nicco, and the dutiful best man at his brother Markos's glamorous, over-the-top wedding in LA.

Zoe wet her lips with her tongue. Staring at the images of Romeo, she decided the photographs didn't do him justice. They failed to capture his energy, his zest for life. Truth be told, she was intrigued by him. He was such a force, so charismatic, she couldn't get him out of her mind. No surprise. Like every other woman in the city, she was attracted to his dashing good looks. Not that it mattered. Nothing would come of it. They didn't travel in the same social circles, and Zoe had a better chance of winning *Milan Idol* than making a love connection with one of the richest men in the country.

"Before I go, I want you to check out these outfits I designed specifically for you." Jiovanni grabbed the garment bag off the chair, unzipped it and marched around the desk. His confidence was evident in his broad I'm-the-man grin. "*Mi amore*, prepare to be blown away…"

Finding clothes that fit her hourglass figure in local stores was impossible, but Zoe could always count on Jiovanni to hook her up. Raised by a single mother and three older sisters, he understood women and appreciated the female body. From the moment Aurora had introduced them they'd clicked, and when his mother died unexpectedly last summer they'd grown even closer. He'd said she was his rock, the only person he trusted explicitly. His words had touched her heart. They'd never be lovers, but they'd be friends for life.

"What do you think? Did I hit it out of the park, or completely miss the mark?"

Zoe admired the outfits. Each one was impressive, and she couldn't decide which one she liked best—the beaded dress with the plunging neckline; the one-shoulder gown with the frilly red bow, or the navy pantsuit with the floral-print design along the waist. Overcome with emotion, Zoe gave him a hug and a kiss on the cheek. "Thanks, Jiovanni. I love all of them, and I'm honored to wear your amazing designs."

Dropping into a chair, he clasped his hands behind his head and crossed his legs at the ankles. "Prove it. Try them on, *mi amore*. Go ahead. Give me a show."

"With pleasure." Zoe grabbed the garment bag, draped it over her forearm and entered the bathroom. Much to Jiovanni's delight, she modeled each outfit, but when she sashayed out of the bathroom in the navy pantsuit, he cheered.

"That's it," he said, jumping to his feet. "*That's* what you should wear tonight."

"Are you sure it's not too sexy?" Zoe adjusted her cleavage.

"You have a great body and beautiful décolletage, so flaunt it." Jiovanni wore a proud smile. "I love to see you in my clothes. You make them come alive."

To complete her look, Zoe opened the closet and searched through her wooden jewelry box for the right accessories. Zoe often went straight from work to industry functions, and had everything she needed at her disposal.

Taking Jiovanni's advice, she selected teardrop earrings and a rhinestone necklace and bracelet. As she did her hair and makeup, he snapped pictures of her with his cell phone. With billions of people on social media every day, Zoe knew how important it was to give fans an intimate, behind-the-scenes look at Casa Di Moda and encouraged him to upload the images immediately.

"You look incredible," Jiovanni praised. "All eyes will be on you at the premiere."

Putting on her stilettos, Zoe admired her appearance in the full-length mirror beside the bookshelf. She felt so-phisticated in her chic ensemble, and Zoe was so anxious to hit the red carpet at Anteo spazioCinema, she decided to call it a day. The premiere didn't start for another three hours, but she wanted to get there early to live-stream in-terviews with the cast. As publicity director it was her job to promote Casa Di Moda, and she couldn't pass up the opportunity to rub shoulders with A-list celebrities, en-tertainment reporters and TV personalities.

Her desk phone buzzed, and the receptionist's voice filled the office.

"Hi, Zoe, sorry to bother you, but I need you at recep-tion. You have a visitor."

Jiovanni rose to his feet. "Duty calls, huh?"

"Hopefully it's the blogger I spoke to yesterday," Zoe said, logging off her computer. "I want her to do a piece on Casa Di Moda and invited her to come by today for a tour."

Zoe grabbed her purse, turned off the lights and waved goodbye to Jiovanni. Hustling toward the reception area, she mentally rehearsed what she was going to say to the popular fashion blogger. Zoe hoped the online article would help boost sales, because just the thought of losing the best job she'd ever had made sadness fill her heart.

Chapter 5

The Casa Di Moda reception area was noisier than a train station, and the scent of coffee and expensive perfume wafted through the air. Telephones buzzed and staff members chatted in the hallway. Deliverymen shuffled in and out, carrying oversize boxes and packages.

As Zoe reached the entrance, she noticed a gift bag, a flower bouquet on top of the U-shaped desk and a mountain bike with a gigantic red bow propped against the far wall.

"Great, you're here," the receptionist said brightly, gesturing to the items with a nod of her head. "These things are for you. Do you want me to help you carry them to your office?"

"They are? But I didn't order anything online. Where did they come from?"

A slim man with a thick mustache appeared at Zoe's side and bowed in greeting. "Ms. Smith, these gifts are from Mr. Romeo Morretti. His sincere hope is that everything is to your liking."

Stunned, all Zoe could do was nod in response. Peeking inside the bag, she pushed aside the tissue paper. Her eyes wide with disbelief, she admired each item—the crocodile leather, Chanel handbag with the shiny diamond clasp, the floral-print dress almost identical to the one she was wearing that morning, and a Samsung cell phone and tablet. *Why would Romeo do this? I caused the accident, not him, so why did he buy me thousands of dollars' worth of gifts?* Her head was spinning as she struggled to understand what the gentleman was saying.

"Mr. Morretti wishes to extend his deepest apologies for the incident that happened this morning, and hopes that you will accept these presents as a sign of his deep remorse."

"What incident?"

Aurora appeared at the reception desk with Davide at her side. The couple wore designer outfits and sidled up beside her, asking a million questions.

"What's this about?" Aurora asked, flinging her cashmere shawl over her slender shoulders. "What happened between you and Romeo Morretti this morning?"

Zoe hadn't planned to tell anyone about her ill-fated run-in with the business tycoon, not even her family. Images of her parents, Reuben and Collette Smith, and younger sister, Shelby, popped into her mind. Her mom and dad were happily retired from their jobs, and her twenty-six-year-old sister was a graduate student. During the staff meeting, Aurora had made it clear there wasn't enough money for a Christmas bonus. Without it, Zoe wouldn't be able to go home for the holidays and didn't know how she was going to break the news to her family.

As Aurora questioned her about Romeo Morretti, Zoe's

thoughts wandered. In September, she'd returned home to celebrate her parents' thirty-fifth wedding anniversary, but three days after arriving in Long Island she'd wanted to cut her one-month vacation short. Had actually considered returning to Milan to attend Fashion Week instead. Zoe couldn't go anywhere without her ex-boyfriend, Khalil Tisdale, nipping at her heels. Worse still, her mother adored him and his parents, and invited them over for dinner every evening. It didn't matter how many times she told Khalil that they were over, he wouldn't let her be. He was a successful orthodontist with a thriving medical practice. But he called her several times a day, showed up at her parents' house unannounced and wrote her love letters. They were over, and nothing he said or did would ever change that; still he pursued her relentlessly.

Fond memories filled her heart when she thought about her first love. Zoe was proud of Khalil and everything he'd accomplished, but she had no desire to rekindle their romance. All her life, she'd longed to travel abroad and experience different cultures and she'd refused to let anyone—not even her college sweetheart—stand in the way of her dreams.

"Earth to Zoe." Aurora waved her bejeweled hands in the air. "Tell us what's going on. We're dying to know about your run-in with Romeo Morretti."

Feeling trapped, she reluctantly told the couple about the accident, but left out the part about Romeo's dinner invitation. The less they knew about her interaction with the financier, the better. Aurora was obsessed with the rich and famous, and Zoe didn't want her boss to get the wrong idea about her and Romeo. "Thankfully, I wasn't hurt," she said with a sad smile. "My bike was totaled, but that was the worst of it."

Aurora gasped. "Good God, Zoe, how terrible! Why didn't you say anything?"

"It sounds worse than it was. I'm fine."

"Grazie a Dio!" she exclaimed. "I can't believe you were in a car accident this morning, but still came to work. You should have gone to the hospital to get checked out."

Zoe shook her head. "No way. I'm a New Yorker. I'm strong and resilient."

"Thank God you're okay. I don't know what we'd do if anything ever happened to you," Davide said in a solemn tone of voice. "You're an important part of the Casa Di Moda family. We don't want to lose you."

"I second that." Nodding, Aurora gave Zoe a one-arm hug. "You're the hardest-working employee we have, you've established a strong online presence for the company, and you've made the brand cool among millennials. We're fortunate to have you on board, Zoe."

Zoe was embarrassed by the couple's effusive praise and wished they'd stop showering her with compliments. The receptionist was listening in, and she was afraid the loquacious single mom would gossip to the rest of the staff about what Aurora and Davide had said. That would be a disaster. Jiovanni and the other associate designers were already upset, and Zoe didn't want them to feel worse.

"Now, back to you and Romeo Morretti." Aurora linked arms with Zoe and dropped her voice to a whisper. "What's he like? Does he smell good? What was he wearing this morning? Armani or Kenneth Cole?"

"I-I-I don't know," she stammered. "We only talked for a few minutes."

"Ms. Smith, Mr. Morretti wanted you to have this."

The gentleman reached into his jacket pocket, took out an envelope and offered it to Zoe, but Aurora plucked it out of her hand.

"I'll read it to you. You've had a stressful day, and I don't want anything to upset you."

Before Zoe could protest, Aurora ripped the envelope, took out the card and shrieked in a high-pitched voice in Italian about Zoe being rich.

I'm rich? What is she talking about? Zoe thought, bewildered by her boss's odd behavior.

Aurora was gesturing wildly with her hands, speaking so fast in Italian Zoe didn't understand a word she was saying. "What is it? Why are you screaming? What does the card say?"

Everyone in the reception area was watching them, and the gentleman's face was red.

"You struck pay dirt! Literally. Romeo Morretti just financed your future!"

What? Perplexed, she shook her head. Prying the envelope out of her boss's hands, Zoe realized the piece of paper she'd been waving around was a bank draft, and stared at the check. Zoe choked on her tongue. Rubbing her eyes, she counted the number of zeroes—twice—to make sure she hadn't made a mistake. A hundred thousand euros? What for?

"I have to return this. I can't keep it." Zoe glanced around, searching the reception area for Romeo Morretti's employee, but he was gone. Unsure of where Morretti Investments was, Zoe asked the receptionist to find the address online and waited patiently for her to locate it.

Drumming her fingernails on the desk, Zoe imagined what would happen when she saw Romeo again. Would she be calm and composed this time, or a tongue-tied fool? It was hard not to get flustered when he stared at her. His gaze was unnerving and intense, and his boyish smile could melt the ice around any woman's heart.

"Keep the gifts and the check. You earned it."

Earned it? It was an accident, not a setup! Again, Zoe was bewildered by Aurora's words. Surely she didn't mean it. Furthermore, what kind of person would Zoe be if she took the money? She wouldn't be able to live with herself if she did; guilt would eat her alive.

"Romeo Morretti struck you with his car, and you deserve to be adequately compensated," Aurora continued in a haughty tone of voice. "To be honest, a hundred thousand euros isn't enough money for your terrible pain and suffering."

Zoe frowned. *What pain and suffering? I'm fine!*

"I second that," Davide agreed. "Call Romeo Morretti and demand ten million euros."

"No way! That's crazy. I could never do that."

"If he refuses to pay, take him to court." Dollar signs flashed in Aurora's hazel eyes, and a smirk curled her lips. "You'll definitely win, and when you do, you can use your settlement money to invest in Casa Di Moda. It's a win-win for everyone!"

In businessman mode, Davide confided in Zoe about his meeting with bank officials yesterday, and the stress he was under to find new investors. Listening to him, Zoe was convinced that Aurora was making a mistake about the plus-size line. If they launched the line, and it did well, investors would come running. It wasn't the time or the place to broach the subject, but she decided to speak to her boss again tomorrow in private.

"Rosannah, can you do me a favor and put these things in my office before you leave?"

"No problem," the receptionist said with a curt nod. "I'll do it now."

"Thanks. I better get going or I'll be late for the premiere." Anxious to leave, Zoe took the piece of paper the receptionist gave to her and waved goodbye. "I'll see you guys later."

Aurora slid in front of her, blocking her path to the door, a defiant expression on her face. Looking chic in her backless ivory gown, she'd accessorized the dress with diamond jewelry, satin pumps and a chain-link purse. "Don't be silly. We'll drive you to Morretti Finance and Investments. It's the least we can do. You've had a very rough day."

"No, thank you. I don't want to inconvenience you. I'll just take a cab."

Davide took his car keys out of his pants pocket. "It's no trouble at all."

"We're taking you, and that's final." Aurora linked arms with Zoe. "I've always wanted to meet Romeo Morretti, and this is my big chance."

"You have?" Making her eyes wide, she faked a look of surprise. "Why?"

"Isn't it obvious? He's a smart, influential businessman with friends in high places, and we could use someone like him in our corner."

A cold chill stabbed Zoe's body. *Oh, no*, she thought, panic rising inside her chest.

They're going to ask Romeo for a loan, or worse, beg him to introduce them to his billionaire clients. Either way, Zoe was screwed, and as the couple hustled her out the front door, she couldn't help feeling like the sacrificial lamb.

Chapter 6

The offices of Morretti Finance and Investments was in a prestigious neighborhood in Milan on a tree-lined street teeming with fancy restaurants, supermarkets, art galleries and boutiques. Exiting Davide and Aurora's SUV, Zoe noticed there were beautiful cars, people and buildings everywhere. The sun was low, the traffic was light, and the sidewalks were overrun with millennials in search of the perfect place to eat, drink and party.

"Give my regards to Mr. Morretti!" Aurora shouted out the passenger-side window, cupping her hands around her mouth. "Convince him to invest in Casa Di Moda!"

Zoe nodded, but she had no intention of fulfilling her boss's request. In a stroke of good luck, the couple had forgotten their press passes for the movie premiere at the office, and since they had to return to the fashion house to get them, they couldn't accompany Zoe inside Morretti Finance and Investments. "Bye. Thanks for the ride. See you soon."

"Remember what I said." Aurora fervently nodded her head. "I'm counting on you."

Waving, Zoe escaped inside. On the drive over, Aurora had talked nonstop about her problems with the associate designers. As Zoe sat quietly in the backseat, she'd learned some valuable information about the fashion house. Information that made her body tense and her pulse race. Jiovanni was right. Casa Di Moda was on the brink of financial ruin, and if Aurora and Davide didn't change for the better, the fashion house wouldn't survive the next quarter.

Zoe entered the reception area and took in her elegant surroundings. Designer furniture, gleaming wood floors, sultry lighting and a granite bar filled the space. It looked more like a gentleman's club than an office, and the tantalizing aroma in the air made Zoe's mouth water. The office was quieter than the public library, and the receptionist was standing at attention at the glass desk, her bright smile showcasing every tooth.

Seeing photographs of Romeo with socialites and famous Italian actresses hanging on the ivory walls, Zoe wondered if everything she'd read about him online was true. Did he have a roving eye? Had he cheated on his ex-fiancée repeatedly? Was he deathly afraid of commitment?

Zoe cleared her mind. It didn't matter what Romeo did in his personal life; it was none of her business. Furthermore, she hadn't come to his office to have a heart-to-heart conversation with him about his past. She'd come to return the check, and once she did she was leaving.

Nervous anticipation coursed through Zoe's body as she approached the front desk. Deep down, she was excited to see Romeo again. Odd considering how they'd met, but the articles she'd read about him had piqued her interest. Of course she was curious about him. Everyone in the country was; she was no different. He was a gorgeous specimen of a man who was as successful as he was charming. Although Zoe had no intention of telling him about the problems at Casa Di Moda, she sensed he was exactly what the fashion house needed. An investor who was tough and tenacious, who wasn't afraid to take risks or shake things up. To please her boss, she'd get Romeo's card and pass it along. But that was it. She was the PR director at Casa Di Moda, not the CEO, and it wasn't her job to find investors.

"Hello. I'm Zoe Smith, and I'm here to see Mr. Morretti," she said in a confident voice.

The brunette consulted her leather-bound book. "Is he expecting you?"

"No, but I have something important to return to him, and it can't wait."

"I'm sorry, Miss, but Mr. Morretti is in a web conference and he can't be disturbed."

Zoe was disappointed, but she nodded her head in understanding. Opening her purse, she took out the envelope that had been delivered to her office and wrote a short note on the back. "Can you see to it that Mr. Morretti gets this letter—"

Hearing someone call her name, she broke off speaking and glanced over her shoulder. The pen fell from her hands. Zoe spotted Romeo standing in the corridor and swallowed a moan. *Holy hotness! Diavolo Sexy indeed!* For a moment she couldn't speak, could only stare at him. Romeo wore a suit like it was nobody's business. He looked more like an Armani model than a world-renowned financier. He had salon-ready hair, a cool, laid-back vibe and a killer bod. What more could a girl want?

Butterflies swarmed her stomach, but his smile instantly put her at ease. Zoe was determined to keep her wits about her, wasn't going to get flustered or tongue-tied in his presence like she had that morning at the taxi stand. His citrus cologne washed over, flooding her body with lust. Instead of crashing through the emergency exit and flagging down a taxi, Zoe walked toward him. Ignoring her sweaty palms and wobbly legs, she moved through the reception area with poise and grace.

"This is a pleasant surprise. Welcome to Morretti Investments, Zoe." Lowering his head, he took her hands in his and kissed her on each cheek. "You look sensational, even more beautiful than you did this morning. Where are you going all dressed up?"

"To a movie premiere, and I'm pressed for time, so I'll make this brief."

"Did you receive the gifts I had delivered to your office this afternoon?"

His enthusiasm was contagious, his tone endearing, and his sincerity touched her heart. Maybe she was wrong. Maybe he wasn't as bad as the tabloids made him out to be. If he was a jerk, like the gossip magazines claimed, he wouldn't have bought her presents—presents she didn't deserve. "Yes, and to be honest, I was stunned when I saw them."

"Do you like the bike?" he asked, touching her forearm. "It's the Mercedes-Benz of mountain bikes. The manager at the sporting goods store assured me you'd love it. Do you?"

"Yes, thanks. I'm sure I'll get plenty of use out of it." Zoe handed him the envelope. "I came here to thank you for the gifts and to return the check. I can't accept it."

His smile disappeared. "Please keep it. It's my way of making amends for this morning."

"You don't need to. I caused the accident, not you."

"The media aren't going to see it that way. They're going to blame me. Since I don't need any more bad press, I'd really appreciate if you cashed the check *and* kept quiet."

His words were a slap to the face, a powerful blow

she hadn't seen coming. The check was a bribe. Hush money. His way of buying her silence. "This is crazy," she said aloud. "Is that how you deal with your problems? By throwing money at them?"

"Yes, as a matter of fact it is." Sadness flashed in his eyes. "Unfortunately, I've learned over the years that most people are driven by the almighty dollar, so I decided to cut you a check and have it delivered to your office instead of waiting to hear from your attorney."

Shocked by his words, Zoe shot him an angry look. "I can't be bought."

"So, you're *not* selling your story to the highest bidder? Why not? Everyone else does."

"I'm not everyone else."

"Do us both a favor and cash the check. I'll sleep better if you do."

"I don't want your money," she snapped, feeling her temperature rise.

"Famous last words…"

"You don't believe me?" To prove it, Zoe tucked her purse under her arm, raised the envelope in the air, and ripped it in half. Wearing a cheeky smile, she dumped the pieces into his palm, then flipped her braids over her shoulders. Speaking in Italian, she said, "Bye, Romeo. Have a nice life!"

Eager to leave him in her dust, she spun around and marched toward the glass door.

Romeo captured Zoe's arm, stopping her in her tracks, and she glared at him.

"Maybe I misjudged you—"

"Damn right you did. I don't want your money."

His face softened. "I'm sorry. Do you forgive me?"

Romeo pretended to wipe an imaginary tear from his eye, and Zoe giggled.

"You have the best laugh. It's warm, loud and lively," he said, caressing her arm.

His cologne washed over her, and her temperature spiked. *What's the matter with me? Why am I acting like I've never been in the company of a man before? And why the hell am I making googly eyes at him? Damn, I'm worse than those female paramedics!*

"Where is the movie premiere?" Romeo asked.

"Anteo spazioCinema."

Glancing outside the window overlooking the sidewalk, he cocked an eyebrow. "Where's your date? Isn't he waiting for you outside?"

"I don't have a date."

A grin dimpled his cheek. "You do now."

"No thanks. I don't need one. My colleagues will be at the movie premiere, and they're flying solo, too. We'll keep each other company."

"I look forward to meeting them."

"No offense, Romeo, but you have a lot of relationship drama, and I don't want any of your girlfriends hunting me down for hanging out with you."

"Everything you read in the tabloids isn't true," he countered.

"True, but if you were *my* brother, I'd sit you down and set you straight about women."

"And if I were your man?"

"As if you could be so lucky!" Zoe quipped. "Keep dreaming, Morretti!"

Romeo chuckled long and hard, and the sound of his hearty laugh made her smile.

"You didn't answer my question," he pointed out, stepping forward, a mischievous expression on his face. "If I were lucky enough to be your man, what would you do with me?"

Lock you in my bedroom and throw away the key!

Noise filled the air, drawing Zoe's attention across the room, and she peered over his shoulder. Attractive women in designer dresses and impeccably groomed men strode through the reception area. Romeo greeted them as if they were family members, rather than his employees. "I should go," she said, noting the time on the contemporary clock hanging on the wall. "The premiere doesn't start for a couple more hours, but I want to get there early."

"Zoe, I'd be honored to be your date tonight."

The matter decided, Romeo asked the receptionist to retrieve his briefcase from his office, and as he waited for her to return he showed Zoe his favorite photographs in the reception area. He told her personal stories about his celebrity friends, his family members. Zoe could tell by the warmth in his voice that he was proud of his successful cousins and siblings.

"I brought your coat and cell phone as well, Mr. Morretti."

Taking the items from his receptionist, he nodded and smiled. *"Grazie."*

Needing some fresh air, Zoe ordered her legs to move and marched out the front door. The breeze carried a heady scent and cooled her overheated body. She searched the street for a taxi, but didn't see any on the road. She suddenly feared she wouldn't be able to shake Romeo.

"This is going to be fun. I haven't been to a movie in years."

"The premiere of *Amore in Tuscany* is by invitation only," Zoe blurted out.

"Don't worry. The director is a personal friend of mine. He'll be thrilled to see me."

"Are you always this confident?"

Romeo winked. "I have every reason to be. I know everyone in this town."

"But you don't have a VIP pass," she pointed out. "You'll be turned away."

"No way. It's not going to happen. I have friends in high places."

"Is that supposed to impress me?"

"No. I'm just stating a fact. Furthermore, you strike me as the kind of woman who cares more about a man's heart than who he knows. Is that a fair assessment?"

Distracted by his closeness, she couldn't think straight, and like a balloon in the sky, her thoughts wandered. To regain control, Zoe took a deep breath and clasped her hands in front of her. Good. Now she couldn't rip his suit from his body and have her way with him. It was an outrageous thought, one that caused her mouth to dry and her sex to tingle.

"Right this way, Zoe. My Lamborghini is parked around the corner."

Zoe didn't move. She'd never brought a date with her to a work function, and wondered what her colleagues would think if she showed up at the theater with the bad-boy businessman. Though she knew what her boss would do. Aurora would take one look at Romeo, in his tailored designer suit and diamond watch, and break out in song. Arriving to the premiere with Romeo would definitely put her on Aurora's good side, but Zoe had mixed feelings about taking him up on his offer. On one hand, she was excited about spending the rest of the night with him, but she was worried about attracting unwanted attention. The media would be out in full force tonight, and Zoe shuddered to think what bloggers would write about her. They made an unlikely pair, and she could almost see the headlines now: Italian Heartthrob Arrives at Movie Premiere with American! Romeo Morretti Romances Plus-Sized PR Director! Opposites Attract in Milan!

"Zoe, what's wrong?" he asked, a note of concern in his voice. "Why are you stalling?"

"Because I'd rather go to the premiere alone."

"Why? What do you have against financiers? We need love, too, you know!"

A giggle tickled her throat. "You're ridiculous, you know that?"

"Please don't deny me the joy of escorting you to the premiere. I promise to be on my best behavior, and I won't give you any trouble whatsoever." He clasped his hands together, as if in prayer, and spoke in Italian.

Please, beautiful? You won't regret it. His voice was full of warmth, and his expression was sincere. "Fine, you can come, but no monkey business. Understood?"

"You have my word. I'll be a perfect gentleman."

Romeo squeezed her forearm, and her mouth dried.

"We should go," Zoe said, wishing her sultry, throaty voice didn't betray her need. "The theater's across town, and I don't want to be late for the premiere."

"As you wish, bellissima. And don't worry. I'll have you there in no time."

It took supreme effort, but Zoe fell in step beside him, matching him stride for stride. Romeo was, without a doubt, the sexiest man she'd ever met. And when he wet his lips with his tongue, Zoe moaned inwardly. Her palms were slick with sweat, and she was so nervous about being alone with him in his sports car, she was quivering. She'd been on numerous blind dates since moving to Milan, but none of the men she'd met excited her. They were all successful, clean-cut guys who were exactly her type. But there'd been no chemistry. No magic. No fireworks. No sparks. When Romeo placed a hand on her lower back, electricity shot through her veins. Zoe then knew she was in trouble.

Chapter 7

Romeo stood with Zoe and her colleagues at the wrap-around bar inside Milano Cocktail Bar listening to Aurora and Davide Bordellio entertain the group with titillating stories about last year's Christmas Wonderland Ball. He quickly decided he liked the couple. They finished each other's sentences, and were down-to-earth. The couple were friendly and sociable, and when they welcomed him to the "Casa Di Moda family," Romeo chuckled. "I had to practically beg Zoe to let me tag along, but I'm glad she eventually relented," he said with a grin. "Everyone's real laid-back, and I'm having fun."

Nodding, Zoe gestured around the room with her hands. "Everyone is. The dance floor's packed, guests are chatting and snapping selfies, and the line at the dessert table is out the door."

Romeo raised his glass to his mouth and tasted its contents, but his gaze never left Zoe's face. In her navy jumpsuit and studded pumps, her look was the perfect blend of sophisticated and sexy. Her outfit flattered her fine womanly shape, and her red-painted lips were a turn-on. Romeo noticed heads turn as Zoe swayed to the beat of the music playing in the lounge, and he stepped forward. He wanted to be as close to her as possible, and wanted everyone else in the lounge to know she was taken. Thoughts of kissing her ruled his mind, but Romeo didn't act on his impulses. He didn't want to blow his chance with her. If he came on too strong, she'd show him the door.

"This is one of the best lounges I've ever been to," Zoe said, swiveling her hips like a dancer in Rihanna's latest video. "DJ Bella is amazing. I love this set!"

Romeo swallowed hard. It was hard to focus, impossible not to stare when Zoe was moving her body in such an erotic way. She danced with such confidence that he couldn't take his eyes off of her or concentrate on what she was saying.

"I heard DJ Bella will be at the Christmas Wonderland Ball along with Andrea Bocelli and Il Divo," said one of Zoe's male colleagues. "It's going to be the party of the year."

Zoe's face lit up. "I'd do anything to see Il Divo perform live. I'm their biggest fan!"

Romeo finished his appetizers, then handed the empty plate to a server. A cut above the rest, Milano Cocktail Bar was the most popular restaurant-lounge in the city, and the Hollywood-theme decor was a hit among the crowd. There was a red carpet, shiny helium balloons, life-size cutouts of the characters in *Amore in Tuscany,* and film tape hanging from the ceiling. Romeo thought the movie was a predictable romance with a weak plot, but Zoe loved it. She had gushed about her favorite parts of the film as they'd driven from the theater to the lounge. The entire restaurant had been rented out for the after-party, and the space was packed with celebrities, business executives and entertainment reporters.

Aurora touched Romeo's forearm. "You should come to Casa Di Moda for a private tour. Davide and I are incredibly proud of our business and everything we've accomplished over the last nine years. We'd be honored to have you visit the fashion house."

Romeo considered her words. Mentally reviewing his schedule, he realized he had several meetings and a business lunch on Monday, but decided to juggle his schedule to accommodate Aurora's request. Not because he wanted a behind-the-scenes look at the fashion house, but because he wanted to see Zoe again. "I'm free on Monday at ten o'clock," Romeo said, consulting the calendar on his cell phone. "Would that work for you?"

Aurora bobbed her head. "I'll make it work."

"Great. After the tour we'll have lunch at the Four Seasons. My treat."

Everyone at the bar cheered except Zoe, and Romeo frowned. Bothered by her lackluster response, he studied the expression on her face. Why wasn't she excited? The Four Seasons restaurant, La Veranda, was a magnet for professionals, and Romeo was confident Zoe and her colleagues would love the eclectic menu and quiet ambience. "I hope you're the one giving me the tour," he whispered in her ear. "Because you're my favorite of the Casa Di Moda staff."

"I have meetings all morning, so I won't be back at the office until late."

Romeo kept his feelings in check. Played it cool. Pretended not to care even though he was disappointed. His emotions must have showed on his face, though, because Zoe smiled sympathetically and patted his forearm.

"Don't worry. You'll have a great time at Casa Di Moda. Aurora and Davide are awesome. They can answer any questions you have about the business."

Romeo nodded, but he wasn't going to Casa Di Moda on Monday if Zoe wasn't there. Bent on seeing her, he made up his mind to visit the fashion house in the afternoon, making a mental note to adjust his schedule. Listening to Zoe and her colleagues talk about their plans for the rest of the weekend, Romeo realized it was going to be hard to get close to her. To romance her. She had a busy social life, and everyone wanted to spend time with her. He was anxious to get Zoe away from her colleagues—especially the male associate designer who was staring at her cleavage—but before he could ask her to dance, she spoke to her friend.

"Let's check out the dessert table," Zoe proposed, linking arms with a graphic designer with frizzy hair and red eyeglasses. "I'm craving something sweet."

Look no further, Romeo thought, hiding a grin. *I can satisfy your sweet tooth and more.*

Applause and whistles filled the lounge, and Romeo glanced over his shoulder to see what the commotion was. He didn't recognize the scantily dressed women posing for pictures on the mezzanine, but Zoe did, and cheered as the trio sashayed into the lounge.

"The cast of *Guilty Pleasurers* just walked in, and they're wearing the outfits I sent them from Casa Di Moda's holiday line," Zoe explained.

Romeo had never heard of the show, but he wanted to know more about her, so he listened closely to everything she said about the program. It sounded silly, like one of the ridiculous shows his sister, Francesca, enjoyed watching, but he kept his thoughts to himself. Romeo was a news junkie, and wouldn't be caught dead watching reality TV.

But learning more about Zoe's interests and hobbies was the first step to achieving his goal, so he didn't judge.

"I'm going to snap some pictures of the cast, ask them to record a personal message for Casa Di Moda fans, then upload the images on our social media pages. Wish me luck!"

You don't need luck, Romeo thought, his gaze trailing her through the room. *You're likable and gregarious.* He watched Zoe and several of her female colleagues saunter through the lounge, chatting and laughing with guests, and hoped she'd be back soon. Romeo wanted to dance with her, liked the idea of being alone with her, holding her in his arms, even if it was only for a couple minutes— "Zoe likes assertive, take-charge guys, so quit playing it safe."

The sound of Aurora's voice broke into his thoughts. Cranking his head to the right, he noticed the fashion designer staring at him and pretended he didn't know what she was talking about. "Excuse me?"

"Don't play coy. You want her. Just admit it."

"Is it that obvious?" he asked with a sheepish smile.

"Yes, but don't feel bad. Zoe's a magnet who attracts male attention wherever she goes."

"You're her boss and mentor, but it sounds like you're also good friends."

"We are. I was one of the first people Zoe met when she arrived in Milan, and we instantly hit it off," she said, speaking with a broad smile on her face. "Despite our age difference, we have a lot in common and I value Zoe's opinion. She's wise beyond her years."

Romeo soaked up every word that came out of the fashion designer's mouth, committed every piece of information she shared to memory. "Does she have a boyfriend?" he asked, watching Zoe move around the lounge. She gave out hugs and kisses as if they were going out of style, but he enjoyed seeing her in action. Zoe was a force, so engaging and appealing she turned heads all around the room. "Is she dating anyone special right now?"

"No, but she has plenty of male admirers."

"Figures. Beautiful women always do."

"Zoe's more than just a pretty face, though…"

Tell me something I don't know— Romeo gripped his glass so hard the veins in his hands throbbed. What the hell? There were lots of celebrities in the restaurant, but Romeo was shocked to see the goalkeeper for his favorite football team talking to Zoe. Or rather, flirting with her. The footballer was whispering in her ear, as if they were a couple sharing a private joke. Loved worldwide, the athlete had championship medals and more fans than Beckham. *What does he want with Zoe? Is that the kind of guy she likes? Athletes with tattoos and piercings?*

"She's talented and smart. We'll miss her dearly if she leaves."

His ears perked up. "She's leaving? When? Why? Where is she going?"

Glancing around, Aurora shielded her mouth with her hand and spoke in a quiet tone of voice. "Zoe's here on a work visa, and if I can't find new investors by the end of the year, I'll have to close Casa Di Moda for good. She'll have to leave Milan immediately."

"How many investors do you need?"

"As many as I can get, but…"

Romeo didn't hear a word Aurora said. His eyes tracked Zoe around the room. He saw the goalkeeper take the bubbly PR director in his arms and dance cheek to cheek with her. She was smiling and laughing. Romeo didn't like it one bit. Wanted to break up their cozy slow dance. His eyes narrowed. The footballer was stroking her shoulders and hips, but Romeo forced himself to stay put. Not to react. He wasn't the jealous type and never chased women down, but

Zoe made him act out of character. He wanted to protect her, to take care of her, and hated seeing her with another man. They'd known each other for less than twenty-four hours, so why was he acting like a jealous ex? Why did he want to rip her out of the goalkeeper's arms and hustle her back into his sports car?

"Romeo, if you ever need advice about how to woo Zoe, just give me a ring."

Aurora reached into her purse, took out a business card and stuffed it into his pocket.

"Call anytime. I'm just a phone call away."

"Thank you, Aurora. That's very kind of you."

Davide joined the conversation, echoing his wife's sentiments, and Romeo nodded politely. They needed investors and wanted to talk shop. But getting Zoe away from the touchy-feely goalkeeper was his focus, not saving a fashion house from financial ruin. Though he did like the idea of doing something nice for Zoe since she wouldn't accept his check, and considered investing on her behalf.

Wearing a wry smile, Romeo shook his head. He still couldn't believe she'd ripped up his check and thrown it in his face. He was used to women asking him for money and expensive gifts, not returning them. He respected Zoe for being a person of integrity and character. Not to mention fine as hell. She was a stunner, and like Cristal and Cuban cigars, impossible to resist.

Romeo felt his eyes bulge out of his head and a cold chill stab his flesh. *When it rains, it pours,* he thought, shaking his head. *Damn. What is Lizabeth doing here? Who invited her?* Had she discovered his whereabouts by perusing his social media pages? The more Romeo thought about it, the more he was convinced that Lizabeth had come to the after-party to make trouble.

Hours earlier, he'd asked Zoe to take a picture with him, and she'd declined.

"You don't strike me as the selfie type," she'd said, a what-are-you-up-to expression on her face. "So why do you want to take one with me?"

"Because I want to commemorate our first date." Grinning, he'd draped an arm around her waist and held her close to his side. "One day you're going to thank me."

Using his cell, he'd snapped the photograph and uploaded it to his FaceChat account, with the caption, "Zoe Smith, the Gold Standard of Beauty." Within minutes, hundreds of people had commented on his post, including several of Lizabeth's friends. Is that why she was at the party? To find out who Zoe was? He wouldn't put it past her. When they were dating, she used to snoop through his things and would cause a scene whenever he spoke to someone of the opposite sex. Lizabeth had been the one to call off their engagement, but she was bent on making his life miserable. He feared her sole purpose in coming to the party was to embarrass him.

Lizabeth waved, but Romeo ignored her. Her sheer dress had a plunging neckline and high slits and left nothing to the imagination. It was a wardrobe malfunction waiting to happen, and Romeo didn't want to be around when disaster struck. Because of Lizabeth's obsession with being famous, he was endless fodder for gossip columns, and Romeo was sick of it. In the modeling world, Lizabeth had quite the reputation, and he regretted ever helping her launch her career.

Romeo exited the lounge and strode through the restaurant. Out of the corner of his eye, he saw Zoe dancing with her colleagues and sighed in relief. The goalkeeper was at the bar, flirting with the female bartenders, and Romeo hoped the star athlete stayed there—and far away from

Zoe—for the rest of the night. Impressed by her knowledge of Italian history, world events and pop culture, Romeo wanted to know more about her. He hoped he could convince her to join him for a drink at his favorite bar when the after-party ended.

Also hoping to avoid his ex, Romeo entered the men's room and used the facilities. He washed his hands and stared at his reflection in the mirror. Faint circles lined his eyes, but he looked handsome in his Armani suit and navy tie, like a man who had everything. But it was a facade. The only people he could truly trust were his family, and he had very few real friends.

Exiting the bathroom, Romeo checked his cell phone for missed calls, and noticed he had a new text message from his brother. With three university degrees, and an implausibly high IQ, it was no surprise to anyone in the Morretti family that Enrique's media company, Icon Productions, had made the Forbes list for the fifth consecutive year.

Romeo read the message, and a frown wrinkled his brow. Enrique wanted to meet up tonight for drinks at Hollywood nightclub. He decided he would speak to Zoe before he responded to his brother's message. Happily engaged to his live-in fiancée, Enrique spent all of his free time with the talented art director. Romeo was lucky if he saw him once a month.

"What did you think of my interview in *Celebrity Patella* yesterday?"

Romeo kept his eyes on his cell phone, didn't bother to look at his ex and her minions. "I don't have the time to read tabloids. I have clients to meet, deals to close and millions to make."

"Whatever. Just have my money by Monday or the deal's off."

Confused, he glanced up from his cell. "There is no deal."

"Of course there is. Giuseppe called this morning and made me one hell of an offer." A smirk curled her lips. "He said if I scrap my tell-all book and sign a confidentiality agreement, you'll give me five million dollars *cash*."

Romeo cursed under his breath. He was angry that his publicist had struck a deal with Lizabeth behind his back, but wore a blank expression on his face. Didn't react when she gloated about the seven-figure deal. Romeo didn't want to hear any more. He'd heard enough. He wanted to return to the bar to hang out with Zoe, not argue with his ex-fiancée about money, but he couldn't resist setting her straight. "I'm not giving you another dime. Not today. Not ever."

Her face fell, and she stumbled over her words. "B-B-But, Giuseppe promised me—"

"I don't give a damn what Giuseppe said. There is no deal. And the next time you lie about me or my family, I'll sue you and your modeling agency."

Lizabeth bit her bottom lip. "You wouldn't."

"Think I'm bluffing? Try me."

Romeo returned her stare. Lizabeth was trying to take advantage of him, trying to bully him into giving her millions of dollars, but he wasn't going to let her win. After they broke up, she'd threatened to sue him, arguing she deserved to be financially compensated for the years they'd lived together at his palatial villa in Tuscany. Thankfully the judge had tossed out her case. At his sister's urging, he'd agreed to let Lizabeth keep the sports cars he'd bought her, and the ten-carat diamond ring he'd proposed with on her birthday.

"How can you treat me like this after everything we've been through? After everything I've done for you?" Lizabeth asked, shouting her words.

"You did me a favor calling off our engagement. I only wish you'd done it sooner…"

Romeo's gaze landed on Zoe, and he broke off speaking. Spotting the PR director moving through the lounge, he lost his train of thought. Couldn't focus on anything but the scintillating beauty.

"I called off our engagement because you cared more about your family and your stupid company than you did about me," Lizabeth complained. "What did you expect me to do? Sit around and wait for you to finally come to your senses?"

Romeo tuned her out, instead focusing his attention on Zoe. Tired of arguing with his ex, he marched through the lobby, determined to reach her before someone else whisked her away. "Zoe, where are you going?"

Her smile was so radiant and bright, his anger abated and a grin curved his mouth.

Taking her hand in his own, he gave it a light squeeze. "You're not going anywhere, Ms. Smith. You still owe me a dance."

"It's late, Romeo, and I'm beat. Maybe next time, okay?"

He didn't want her to leave and tried to persuade her to stay. "I'll drive you home."

Zoe yawned. "No, thanks. Lorenz lives near me, and we want to discuss work on the drive home."

She released his hand, and disappointment coursed through his body.

"I have to go," she said, raising her cell phone in the air. "Lorenz just texted me. He's waiting out front—he's anxious to leave."

Out of his peripheral vision, he saw Lizabeth headed his way and narrowed his eyes. There was no way in hell he was letting his ex anywhere near Zoe, and shielded the PR director with his body. Lizabeth was toxic, and he couldn't stand to be around her.

"Gold standard of beauty my ass." Cocking her head to the right, she glared at Zoe like a schoolyard bully looking for trouble. "You're pretty, but you're no Tyra Banks."

"Good, because I'm Zoe Smith. I wouldn't want to be anyone but me. I'm fabulous."

Romeo smiled. Not because Zoe had put Lizabeth in her place, but because of how damn good she looked doing it. Her head was high, her shoulders were pinned back, and she reeked of confidence. Zoe was in control, had the upper hand, and Romeo was impressed with how she carried herself. He stared at her with open admiration.

"Lizabeth, I'm the PR director for Casa Di Moda and I'm always on the lookout for captivating personalities to work with us." Zoe opened her purse, took out a glossy pink card and handed it to Lizabeth. "Call me."

A grin crept across Lizabeth's mouth as she read the information on the business card.

"I'd love to hire you for one of our upcoming fashion shows," Zoe said with a bright smile. "So give me a ring."

"We can talk now. Let's have a cocktail."

"I wish I could, but my ride is waiting for me outside."

Lizabeth tossed her silky brown locks over her shoulders. "Then I'll walk you to your car. You can tell me more about Casa Di Moda, because I'm *totally* intrigued."

"Sounds good." Zoe smiled and waved. "Bye, Romeo! Enjoy the rest of your night."

Panic ballooned inside his chest. He had to do something. Had to stop Zoe from leaving with Lizabeth. He didn't want his ex to poison Zoe's mind toward him, and feared what would happen if the two women were alone.

Romeo stepped forward, but Lizabeth slid in front of him, blocking his view of Zoe. Dumbfounded, he watched

Zoe leave the restaurant lounge with his ex-fiancée. Chatting a mile a minute, the women breezed through the door, oblivious to the wide-eyed expression on his face.

Raking a hand through his hair, Romeo cursed under his breath in Italian. He'd blown it with Zoe again. How was that possible? He was a Morretti. He never struck out with women, never failed to achieve his goal, regardless of what it was. But it had happened twice in one day.

Romeo fixed his tie and leveled a hand over his jacket. He had to redeem himself. Had to prove to Zoe that he was a good man. His confidence returned, and a grin crept across his lips. He'd seduce her, no doubt about it. Even if it meant pouring on the charm.

Chapter 8

The soccer ball sailed in the air at Parco Sempione and dropped onto the freshly cut grass, just inches away from where Romeo was standing. Moving quickly, he sprang into action. Dodging approaching defenders, he ran toward the net, bent on scoring another goal for his team. Filled with adrenaline, sweat coursing down his face, he carefully dribbled the soccer ball. Winded, Romeo scanned the field for Enrique, but he couldn't find his brother anywhere.

His heart was beating out of control, roaring in his eardrums, but Romeo ran harder, faster. At his yearly physical last month, his doctors had warned him about overexerting himself, encouraging him to take up golf, but football was his first love, and that would never change.

Using fancy footwork, he raced up the field, twisting and turning to avoid the burly midfielder with the death stare. Romeo kicked the ball with supreme force. Holding his breath, he watched it fly through the goalie's hands, hit the back of the net and fall to the ground.

Filled with pride, Romeo threw his hands in the air. Cheers erupted around him as his teammates celebrated his second goal of the game. Once a month, regardless of the temperature, Romeo and his friends played football at Parco Sempione. It was Milan's version of Central Park, and there was so much to see and do he often spent the entire day there. Nature lovers were cycling, jogging, playing Frisbee and flying handmade kites. It was noisy and crowded, and children were running in every direction. Romeo couldn't have asked for a better day.

"What a goal!" Enrique shouted, jumping onto his back. "You were amazing, bro!"

"Thanks, man. I learned from the best."

Grinning, he plucked at the front of his blue Manchester United jersey. "You're right. I *did* teach you everything I know about the game."

"I was talking about Immanuel."

A scowl curled his lips. "I should have known. You always liked him better."

"That's not true, but Sharpshooter looked out for me a lot when we were kids. I'm very grateful," Romeo explained. His brother, Immanuel, was a security specialist, who provided protection to high-powered people. "I was a wimp. If not for Immanuel, bullies would have kicked my ass up and down the school yard every day."

"And look at you now. You're one of the most successful businessmen in the country, a bona fide ladies' man and a hell of a football player, too." Enrique ruffled Romeo's dark brown hair. "Let's go grab a cold one. You've earned it."

Jogging across the field toward the picnic tables their teammates were eating at, Romeo heard laughter and the

distant sound of a guitar. He saw couples kissing and cud-
dling under maple trees and college students playing coed
rugby. A female with curly hair waved at him, but Romeo
dodged her gaze. She was attractive, sure, but she had
nothing on Zoe. The PR director was a knockout, desirable
in every way. He needed to see her again. It had been five
days since he'd gone for a private tour of Casa Di Moda,
and although they texted each other every day, it wasn't
enough. Did Lizabeth fill her mind with lies? Is that why
Zoe was keeping him at arm's length?

His week had been a disaster. He'd had a heated argument with Giuseppe for making an unauthorized deal with
Lizabeth behind his back; the local newspaper had done a
write-up about his car accident; and yesterday he'd arrived
at the office to find reporters camped outside Morretti Finance and Investments. They shouted his name, snapped
pictures of him every time he left the building and filmed
his every move. It was annoying, frustrating as hell for
his staff and clients, but there was nothing Romeo could
do about it. What had frustrated him more than anything
was that he'd made zero progress with Zoe since the after-
party at Milano Cocktail Bar.

What am I doing wrong? he thought, wiping his damp
face with the sleeve of his football jersey. *What do I have
to do to get through to Zoe? To make her see that I'm an
upstanding guy?* He couldn't shake the feeling that Lizabeth had screwed him over. She took pleasure in hurting
him, seemed to get off on making him suffer. He'd known
from the very beginning that the Norwegian model was
spoiled and high-strung. After years of her diva-like behavior, he'd had enough. Initially, he'd been shocked when
she'd called off their engagement, but deep down he'd been
relieved. Dating Lizabeth had been mentally, physically

and emotionally draining. Romeo would rather be celibate for the rest of his life than take his ex back.

For the second time in minutes, an image of Zoe filled his mind, and his thoughts returned to yesterday. He'd called Casa Di Moda to ask her out and ended up talking to Aurora instead. He'd been bummed to find out Zoe was in Florence for a photo shoot, but he enjoyed shooting the breeze with her boss. Eager to help, the fashion designer promised to talk to Zoe on his behalf and encouraged him to visit Casa Di Moda whenever he was in the neighborhood.

Romeo had to see Zoe. She was all he could think about, and he wanted to spend time with her. To stay connected to her, he followed her on social media, and seeing the pictures she'd posted that morning made Romeo desire her more than ever.

"I'm glad you talked me into coming down here today," Enrique said, opening the cooler. "I've had a hell of a week, and playing football with the guys is the ultimate stress reliever."

Starving after their marathon game, Romeo headed straight for the barbecue pit. The savory aroma in the air caused his stomach to grumble. Grabbing a metal serving spoon and a paper plate, Romeo filled it with the mouthwatering foods his friends had grilled for lunch.

Romeo sat down at a picnic table to eat. Everything was hot, seasoned to perfection, and he savored each and every bite. Pressed for time, he hadn't had anything for breakfast that morning, so he thoroughly enjoyed his first meal of the day. His friends cracked jokes and teased each other, and their hearty laughter created a lighthearted mood in the picnic area.

Enrique took the seat across from him. He was clutching his cell phone, and Romeo noticed his brother's eyes darken and wondered if he was having business trouble again. A rival entertainment company had lured away his best employee weeks earlier, and Enrique was still picking up the pieces of the executive's sudden departure.

"What's wrong? You look like you're about to blow a gasket."

"It's Isabelle..." Trailing off, he rubbed a hand along the back of his neck. "Lately, she's been pulling away from me, and I don't know why."

"Have you tried talking to her?"

"Yeah, but we end up fighting about it, then she storms out," he explained. "Last night, we got into it again, and Isabelle went to her parents' place to cool off. I've texted her several times to find out when she'll be home, but she hasn't responded."

"Man, quit sweating her. She'll come around, and if she doesn't you can always find someone else. I like Isabelle, but she's not the only beautiful woman in the world."

"I don't want anyone else. I want Isabelle. She's it for me, bro."

"Such devotion," Romeo drawled. "You need to ease up. You're trying too hard. You don't want her to think you can't live without her—"

"I can't. Isabelle is the best thing that's ever happened to me. I won't lose her."

"Damn, bro, you're gushing like a water fountain," Romeo teased, wiping his fingers with a napkin. "You're worse than Markos and Tatiyana, and they're newlyweds!"

"You don't understand, because you haven't met Mrs. Right yet, but when you do, you'll move heaven and earth to make her happy." Shrugging his shoulder, Enrique wore a sheepish smile. "I used to think Emilio and Immanuel were suckers for settling down and getting married. Now I can't wait to make Isabelle my bride. What can I say? The love bug bit me in the ass, and there isn't a damn thing I can do about it!"

Chuckling, Enrique put his cell down on the wooden table and picked up his fork.

"Are you still going to the Christmas and Cocktails event at the Armani Hotel Milano or have you changed your mind?" Romeo asked, reaching for his water bottle.

"I don't know. I was supposed to go with Isabelle…"

"Don't sweat it, bro. I'll go with you. I love networking with smart, talented people."

"With curves, right?"

"Absolutely. The curvier the better."

Laughing, the brothers bumped bottles, then guzzled down their drinks.

"How are you feeling? Any chest pains, muscle spasms or dizzy spells as of late?"

"No. I'm the picture of health. Doctor said so himself at my physical last month."

Romeo stared at the field, but he wasn't watching the coed rugby game. He was thinking about Zoe. What else was new? It wasn't every day he met a woman who piqued his interest. Just the thought of the vivacious PR director made an erection rise inside his Nike shorts.

His cell phone rang, and he glanced down at the screen. Raising an eyebrow, he cocked his head to the right, surprised to see Aurora Bordellio's name pop up on his phone. Why was the fashion designer calling him? Hope surged inside his heart. Was she with Zoe? Curious, he pressed the accept button and put his cell to his ear. "Hello, Mrs. Bordellio. How are you?"

"Romeo, why are you being so formal? Please, call me Aurora."

"Sure," he said, anxious to find out what she wanted. "What can I do for you?"

"My husband and I are hosting a dinner party tonight, and we'd love if you could join us. I apologize for the short notice. We've been insanely busy the last few days."

"Thank you for the invitation, but I have plans with my brother tonight—"

"Bring him with you!" Aurora offered, interrupting him. "Zoe's really looking forward to seeing you tonight. Don't tell her I told you this, but she has a *huge* crush on you."

His jaw dropped, but he asked the question circling his mind. "She does?"

"Yes, of course. Isn't it obvious? Zoe couldn't take her eyes off of you at the after-party."

Really? Romeo thought, scratching his head. *Then why is she playing hard to get?*

"Zoe's the perfect woman for you," she continued in a haughty tone of voice, as if she had the answers to all of life's mysteries. "She's sincere and loyal, and one of the most selfless women I know. Not to mention she's a total bombshell."

Romeo stared down at his cell. Aurora was laying it on thick, trying to convince him to pursue Zoe, even though he was already interested in her—luckily, he was amused, not annoyed. He liked Aurora and Davide, and appreciated her unexpected dinner invitation. "What time is dinner?"

Aurora hollered like a game show contestant who'd won the grand prize. "Seven o'clock," she chirped. "I'll text you our home address in the next few minutes."

"Sounds good. What should I bring for dinner?"

"Nothing but that charming smile of yours. Ciao, Romeo. *A presto!*"

Ending the call, Romeo told his brother about their plans for the evening. "After the Christmas and Cocktails event we're going to a dinner party at Davide and Aurora Bordellio's apartment."

Frowning, Enrique scratched at his square chin. "Who's that?"

Romeo hesitated, considered his options. If he told Enrique about his traffic accident, he'd ream him out for being distracted behind the wheel. Romeo wasn't in the mood for one of his brother's lectures. Still, he had to tell him something, and decided to come clean to his brother about the accident, Zoe's unexpected arrival at his office hours later, the *Amore in Tuscany* movie premiere, and the disastrous after-party at Milano Cocktail Bar starring Lizabeth.

"All of that happened in one day?" Enrique asked, an awestruck expression on his face.

"Crazy, right?"

"Yeah, man, it is. And Zoe sounds like a spitfire. I can't believe she ripped up a check for a hundred thousand euros, then threw it in your face. I'd take it, and I'm your brother!"

Romeo picked up his cell, punched in his password and accessed the pictures on his phone. Pleased with the photographs he'd taken with Zoe at the after-party, he showed them to his brother. He then pulled up her FaceChat page and read some of her previous posts.

Enrique whistled, and Romeo's chest puffed up with pride.

"Gorgeous, right?" Romeo said, scrolling through the photographs. "What a beauty."

Peering at the cell phone screen, Enrique tapped it with an index finger. "According to Zoe's timeline, she won a cycling competition in June, hiked the Alps with one of her colleagues and is organizing a Christmas toy drive for a Milan orphanage. That's impressive."

"I told you Zoe's the total package. She's everything a man could want, and more."

"Then what are you waiting for? Why haven't you wooed her with your wit and charm?"

Romeo blew out a deep breath. "Because she won't give me the time of day."

"Sucks to be you, huh?"

"Tell me about it. I still feel guilty about the accident, and tried to make amends by giving Zoe gifts and money, but she refused. She accused me of trying to buy her silence, and when I saw her at the fashion house on Monday afternoon, she was ice cold—"

"I don't blame her. You think the worst of people, especially women. The older you get, the more pessimistic you are about life."

"Do you blame me? Every woman I've ever dated has screwed me."

"Quit looking over your shoulder at the past," he admonished in a somber tone of voice. "Learn from the mistakes you made in your previous relationships, then move on. If you don't, you'll never have the love you deserve."

"You need to stop watching Telemundo novelas." Romeo couldn't keep a straight face and chuckled. "They're making you soft and dramatic as hell!"

Enrique chucked his empty beer can at Romeo, but he caught it with one hand, shot it toward the garbage and flashed a toothy grin when it dropped into the oversize bin.

"What are you going to do about Zoe? Come correct or give up?"

"Give up? Man, please." Romeo raised a hand to his mouth, blew on his fingernails, then rubbed them on the sleeve of his orange jersey. "Ambitious is my middle name."

"Cool, so you have a plan? Something big in the works to impress her?"

"Of course. I'm going to have flowers and Godiva chocolate delivered to her office tomorrow. When she calls to thank me I'll convince her to have dinner with me."

Enrique scoffed. "No offense, bro, but you send flowers and candy to everyone."

"Since you fancy yourself a love doctor, what do you propose I do?"

"Think outside the box. Do something different. Plan a date with her interests in mind," he advised. "What does Zoe like? What does she do on her days off? Who's her favorite band?"

Good question, Romeo thought, drumming his fingers on the picnic table. Reflecting on the conversation they'd had at Milano Cocktail Bar, he remembered how excited she'd been discussing her plans for the holidays.

Romeo coughed into his fist. Christmas was hard for him. Had been ever since his nephew Lucca had died. He couldn't look at a gingerbread house without remembering all the times he'd built one with his adorable five-year-old nephew. Romeo wanted to create new memories with Zoe.

Thinking about the holidays and all the fun events in and around the city, an idea took shape in his mind. *Why didn't I think of this sooner?* He'd plan a romantic date for Zoe, and soon she'd be singing his praises. "Thanks, bro. I know just what to do."

"Good. I'll send you my bill." Chuckling, Enrique picked up his cell, swiped his finger across the screen, then sighed in relief. "Thank God. Isabelle finally texted me back."

"We should get going," Romeo said, glancing at his smartwatch. "Christmas and Cocktails starts at five o'clock, which gives us thirty minutes to get ready, so let's bounce."

Enrique stood, grabbed his backpack and slung it over his shoulder. "Count me out."

"Why the sudden change of heart?" Romeo asked, rising to his feet.

"I need to bring my baby back home where she belongs. Isabelle's going to Dolce Vita Milan to celebrate a colleague's birthday. She'll be leaving the celebrity hotspot at the end of the night on *my* arm. There's no ifs, ands or buts about it."

Romeo clapped him on the shoulder. "What are you waiting for, bro? Go get your girl!"

Chapter 9

"Zoe, come here," Aurora called from inside her cozy, wallpapered kitchen. Dipping a serving spoon into the metal pot on the stainless steel stove, she stirred the home-made stew with gusto. "I need you to try this and tell me what you think it's missing."

Zoe glanced up from the CDs she was holding in her hands and stared at Aurora. *Why me?* she thought, her stomach churning in protest. *I hate tortellini stew.* Standing in front of the entertainment unit, riffling through Davide's enormous music collection, Zoe decided to temporarily put her search for a Christmas CD on hold and put the discs on the glass coffee table. "Sure, Aurora, no problem. I'll be right there."

Careful not to bump into anything, Zoe exited the living room. In walking distance of Casa Di Moda, the three-bedroom apartment had high ceilings and oversize windows that offered stunning views of the city center. Small but luxurious, it was packed with antique furniture, wooden sculptures and leafy plants. There were photographs everywhere—on the pale pink walls, on the bookshelves, along the kitchen countertops—and there were so many cushions on the couches, Zoe didn't know where to sit down.

The apartment reflected Casa Di Moda's exuberant prints and colors, and seeing the fashion house logo painted above the fireplace reminded Zoe of all the paperwork waiting for her on her office desk. Tomorrow, after her trip to the market with Jiovanni, she'd stop at the fashion house and finalize the details for the Men of Milan calendar. Zoe wanted everything to be perfect for the Christmas promotion and was pumped about the upcoming photo shoot.

"It smells delicious," Zoe lied, taking the spoon into her mouth and tasting the thick brown liquid. "It needs oregano if you have it."

Chuckling, Davide nodded his head in agreement. "I told her the exact same thing five minutes ago, but she didn't believe me. It's *my* mother's recipe. Go figure!"

"Silenzo!" Aurora yelled, swatting her husband's shoulder. *"So cosa sto facendo!"*

"If you know what you're doing then why does the tortellini taste like medicine?"

Aurora slapped his shoulder, and Davide gave a hearty laugh.

"You know you love me," he joked, wrapping his arms around his wife's trim waist.

"Not as much as you love yourself!"

Laughing, they snuggled against each other. Their display of affection made Zoe wish she had someone special in her life. Or at the very least, someone to hang out with on her days off. Zoe hugged her hands to her chest. It had been so long since she'd been intimate with a man she longed to be kissed and caressed.

Yeah, by Romeo Morretti! shouted her inner voice.

Swallowing hard, she cleared all thoughts of the bad-boy businessman from her mind. It didn't work. The more she tried to bury them, the stronger they were. Like on Monday. Romeo arrived at the office for a private tour, and when she'd bumped into him in the hallway, he'd surprised her with a hug and a kiss on each cheek. It was hard, but she'd kept her distance. Thankfully, she'd spoken to Lizabeth at the after-party and knew what his shtick was. How he got off on seducing women. Deep down, Zoe was flattered by his attention, but she wasn't going to waste her time with a man who'd never commit to her.

"Do you want me to set the table?" Zoe asked.

Davide shook his head. "I got it. You're in charge of the music, remember?"

"We're glad you're here," Aurora said. "It's going to be an amazing night. I can feel it."

Zoe spotted an empty wine bottle beside the toaster and suspected her boss was tipsy. She'd called to invite her over for dinner that afternoon, so Zoe could bring her up to speed about the Casa Di Moda photo shoot in Florence yesterday, and since Jiovanni was busy with his new lady love, Alessandra Esposito, she'd gladly accepted. Spending another Saturday night alone was depressing, and Zoe would rather hang out with her boss than watch TV or journal about her week.

Or so she'd thought.

From the moment Zoe arrived at the apartment the couple had been grilling her about her love life. She'd quickly changed the subject, had chatted excitedly about the overwhelming online response to the pictures she'd posted on Casa Di Moda's website from the Florence photoshoot. Soon the couple was helping her brainstorm ideas for the holiday campaign.

The doorbell rang, and Aurora hopped around the

kitchen like a rabbit in a meadow. "Honey, hurry, it's seven o'clock. Set the table, light some candles and select the wine!" Aurora shrieked. "Zoe, would you be a dear and answer the door? As you can see our hands are full, and I don't want to keep our guest waiting."

Zoe didn't know what the fuss was about, didn't understand why Aurora and Davide were suddenly speaking to each other in hushed tones. She'd had dinner at the Bordellio house before, and although Aurora complained about her mother-in-law being impossible to please, Zoe liked the retired college professor. She loved hearing her hilarious stories about former students. "Not a problem at all."

Not wanting the elderly woman to wait, Zoe rushed into the foyer and opened the front door. Her mouth opened, then closed, and her knees wobbled under her striped sweaterdress. Zoe knew she was staring at Romeo, but she couldn't help it. Couldn't take her eyes off him.

"Good evening, Zoe. It's great to see you again."

The sound of his voice jolted Zoe back to the present. "What are you doing here?" she blurted out.

"I'm here for Davide and Aurora's dinner party, of course."

"What dinner party? I'm the only one here."

Romeo licked his lips, and desire rippled across Zoe's clammy skin.

"Great, so I won't have to compete with anyone else for your attention," he said, his deep brown eyes dark with mischief. "I can have you all to myself tonight. How wonderful."

Flabbergasted, Zoe couldn't think of anything to say in response and fidgeted with her hands. It was either that or use them to caress his broad chest. God help her. Dark and brooding, with a smoldering gaze, she couldn't help checking him out.

Narrowing her eyes, she noticed the unique style and fit of his tan sports coat. It was one of Casa Di Moda's bestsellers, and that morning Zoe had mentioned it on the fashion house's social media pages. Stylishly dressed, he'd paired it with a ribbed flex-collar shirt, slim-fit pants and leather shoes. One look turned her on, but she had to keep her head, knew she couldn't fall victim to his piercing gaze. Like all of the women in his past, she was nothing more than a challenge to him. She deserved more than a one-night stand with a bad-boy bachelor.

"How do you do it?"

Blinking, Zoe wore a blank expression on her face. "Do what?"

"Manage to look more beautiful every time I see you." Leaning forward, he kissed her on each cheek, then took her hand in his. "I'm glad you're here, Zoe. I've missed you."

"Missed me? You don't even know me."

"Not yet, but I'm working on it. In my defense, you're not making it easy for me."

Romeo winked at her. He looked pleased with himself, and the expression on his face made a giggle tickle her throat. Damn him! He was suave and flirtatious, and knew how to make her laugh. His boyish smile and his scent aroused her body.

Soft music filled the apartment, creating a romantic mood. The air smelled of spices and freshly baked garlic bread. Zoe wondered what else Aurora and Davide were cooking up. She loved them, but she didn't appreciate them tricking her.

"Romeo, you made it. Welcome to our humble abode."

Davide appeared in the foyer, grinning from ear to ear.

"Thanks for having me. It's great to be here," he said politely.

"Come in. Aurora's just finishing up in the kitchen. She'll join us shortly."

"This is for you and your lovely wife."

For the first time, Zoe noticed Romeo was holding a gift

bag. Davide opened it and nodded in appreciation at the bottle of Cristal. Listening to the men make small talk, questions rose in Zoe's mind. Was Romeo the only guest? Had they invited other potential investors? Was she expected to help the couple close the deal? There was only one way to find out.

Excusing herself, Zoe marched down the hall, intent on speaking to Aurora before dinner. She spotted Aurora standing in front of the sink and sprang into action. Gripping her shoulders, she steered her into the walk-in pantry and closed the door.

"What are you doing? I have to take the vegetables off the stove or they'll be soggy."

"Dinner can wait," she said, folding her arms across her chest. "You lied to me."

Making her eyes wide, Aurora wore an innocent smile. "No I didn't."

"Why didn't you tell me you invited Romeo to dinner?"

"Because if I told you he was coming tonight you wouldn't have shown up and I need you. You're my good-luck charm."

"Why is he here? Is this a business dinner? Have you invited other potential investors?"

"We don't need anyone else," Aurora said. "Romeo can single-handedly save Casa Di Moda, so be nice to him tonight, okay? Flirt with him, laugh at his jokes and quit playing hard to get. Guys hate that, especially wealthy men."

Zoe didn't speak for a long moment. She couldn't. Didn't know how to react to her boss's statement, and feared if she spoke, she'd lose her temper. Was Aurora drunk? High on seasoning salt and garlic? *She's crazy if she thinks I'm going to sleep with Romeo to save Casa Di Moda from bankruptcy. As if. I'm a public relations director, not a whore.*

"Italian men like bold, assertive women. Don't be afraid to make the first move," Aurora advised. "He's quite the catch, Zoe…"

I know, she thought sourly. *How can I forget? You keep reminding me!*

"Invite Romeo back to your place at the end of the night, toast your newfound friendship with an expensive bottle of wine and do what comes naturally. I would!"

"Are you suggesting I sleep with Romeo Morretti to save Casa Di Moda?"

Aurora scoffed, wore a skeptical expression on her heart-shaped face. "As if you don't want to. He's hot, successful and ridiculously rich. What more could you want in a man?"

What more indeed? Biting her bottom lip, Zoe dodged her boss's gaze.

"Exactly. That's what I thought. You want him, so stop fighting your attraction."

"I've never had a one-night stand—"

"Who says it has to be just one night?" Aurora asked, raising an eyebrow. "You have the entire weekend to explore the mysterious wonders of Romeo Morretti."

"I can't. That's not me. Sex without love is meaningless."

"Says who? I sowed my wild oats before I married Davide, and I'm glad I did. How are you supposed to know what you like sexually if you don't date a variety of men? Hooking up with Romeo Morretti is a once-in-a-lifetime opportunity. Don't blow it."

"Don't blow it?" Zoe repeated. "If you want Romeo to invest in Casa Di Moda so bad, then *you* sleep with him."

"He doesn't want me. He wants you."

Opening her mouth, she realized she didn't know what to say, and closed it.

"You have to help us," Aurora begged, clasping her hands together. "Romeo's not only insanely popular, he also has billionaire friends with deep pockets. If he throws his support behind Casa Di Moda, we'll finally make it to the top."

Hearing voices in the kitchen, Zoe pressed a finger to

her mouth to silence her boss. She didn't want Davide or Romeo to overhear them, or worse, figure out they were hiding in the pantry and come looking for them. How embarrassing, she thought, expelling a deep breath.

Zoe looked down at her outfit and scrunched up her nose. Her dress was cute, just not snazzy enough to have dinner with the sexiest man on the planet. If she'd known Romeo was coming, she would have done her hair and makeup and worn something fancy.

Hoping the coast was clear, Zoe cracked open the door and peered out to the kitchen. Thankfully, Romeo and Davide were in the living room, watching football on the flat-screen TV mounted above the fireplace. "The coast is clear."

"Let's go. It's time to wow our millionaire guest," Aurora whispered, tiptoeing out of the pantry. "Remember what I said. Be warm and friendly and flirt like crazy."

Zoe didn't know whether to laugh or to cry.

"Romeo, how nice for you to join us for dinner. You're looking well…"

Standing, Romeo greeted Aurora, but his gaze was glued to Zoe's face. The Casa Di Moda logo was visible on the pocket of his dress shirt, confirming her initial thought. Romeo was trying to impress her, and she liked seeing him in her favorite designer label.

God help her. He was across the room, but her attraction to him was so strong her body trembled at the sight of him. Zoe pulled herself together. Refused to crumble under pressure. She could do this. It didn't matter that Romeo was all man, all muscle. Zoe had a job to do, and although she disagreed with Aurora's strategy, she was going to help her boss save Casa Di Moda—even though it meant befriending a man who made her weak in the knees.

Chapter 10

Romeo picked up his glass, noticed Zoe watching him from across the dining room table and met her gaze. He read the question in her eyes and smiled to reassure her he didn't bite. That he'd never do anything to embarrass her in front of her boss. Arriving at the Bordellio apartment an hour earlier, he'd discovered Zoe didn't know he'd been invited to dinner, so he'd made small talk with Davide and given her some space.

Sitting back comfortably in his chair, he sipped his drink and savored the sweet, fruity taste. Romeo wished he had something stronger to drink than orange iced tea, but his doctor wanted him to limit his alcohol intake, and he didn't want to do anything to jeopardize his health.

"Would anyone like more chicken cacciatore?" Aurora asked, gesturing to the round ceramic bowl beside the bottle of Cristal he'd brought for the couple as a gift. "Don't be shy. There's a lot more food in the kitchen, so eat up."

Before Romeo could decline, Aurora scooped more pasta onto his plate, and enough sautéed vegetables to feed a family of five. *"Godere!"*

Romeo gulped. His stomach groaned in protest at the thought of eating more food, but he smiled at his eager-to-please host. Italian women took cooking very seriously, and since he didn't want to offend the fashion designer he said, "Thank you, Aurora."

Pride shimmered in her eyes, but she gave a dismissive wave of her hand, as if whipping up a seven-course meal on her day off was no big deal. "It's my pleasure. I love cooking. If I weren't a fashion designer, I'd probably own an Italian restaurant."

Romeo nodded. That explained the extravagant meal and romantic ambience in the dining room. The lights were low, classical music was playing on the stereo system, and rose petals bordered the swan-themed centerpiece. Scented candles perfumed the air with a floral fragrance. Romeo wondered if Aurora was a serial matchmaker who got a kick out of setting people up. Or had she invited him over tonight to persuade him to invest in Casa Di Moda? Romeo was used to people wanting things from him—loans they had no intention of repaying, managerial positions within his company even though they weren't qualified, a meeting with one of his brothers or cousins—but he hoped for Zoe's sake that Aurora wasn't using her as bait.

His brother's words came back to him, filling him with guilt. *You think the worst of people, and the older you get, the more pessimistic you are about life and relationships.* Enrique was right, but it wasn't his fault. Friends and lovers had burned him too many times to count. After everything Lizabeth had put him through, he'd shut himself off to the world. Had stopped giving interviews to the media.

Quit attending social functions and events. Kept the opposite sex at arm's length.

Then why are you sweating Zoe Smith? his inner voice broke into his thoughts. *Why are you pursuing a woman who doesn't want to date you?*

Romeo sighed. It was a good question. One he didn't have an answer to, but wished he did. Her natural beauty had caught his eye. It was what drew him to her that fateful morning. But after attending the movie premiere with her and the after-party, Romeo knew Zoe was more than just a pretty face with God-given curves. Women with a sense of humor who weren't afraid to laugh at themselves always impressed him. He enjoyed the PR director's killer wit. These days, everyone was sensitive about everything, but Zoe wasn't afraid to speak her mind. It was a turn-on, what made him want to be around her, even though she was playing hard to get.

Again, his inner voice mocked him. *Who says she's playing?*

Romeo picked up his fork and forced himself to finish the food. The chicken was dry, the vegetables were overcooked, but he acted as if it were the best meal he'd ever had. It was a small price to pay for spending the night with the object of his affection. Zoe was quiet, only gave one-word responses to his questions, but Romeo wasn't discouraged. He had two concert tickets in his wallet, and Zoe was going to jump for joy when she found out he was taking her to see her favorite group in December.

"Zoe, tell me more about your day trip to Florence."

"Yes," Davide agreed. "Fill us in on the photo shoot in my beloved hometown."

Clearing her throat, she fiddled with her napkin and shifted nervously in her chair.

To put her at ease, Romeo touched her hand, giving it

a light squeeze. Electricity singed his skin. Feeling her soft flesh against his caused his mouth to dry and desire to shoot through his veins. "Was the weather nice, or was it gray and rainy as usual?"

Lines wrinkled her forehead. "How did you know I was in Florence yesterday?"

"Social media, of course."

Freeing her hand from his grasp, Zoe picked up her glass and took a long drink.

"By the way, your post about the Duomo was spot-on. You're right. The city should do something about the pigeons and those sleazy scam artists loitering outside the Duomo cathedral. They're rude and aggressive, and they drive tourists away."

Her face brightened. "I agree. It's a terrible situation. Those scam artists give Milan a bad name. Something *has* to be done about them."

"If you ever decide to run for city council, you have my vote!"

Zoe giggled. Romeo knew if he kept her talking and laughing about the things she was passionate about they'd be friends—and lovers—in no time.

"Florence was lovely." Her shoulders visibly relaxed, her tone filled with excitement. "The weather was warm and sunny, the crew was fantastic, and we had so much fun sightseeing, Jiovanni promised we'd go back next month for the tree-lighting ceremony."

Romeo almost fell off his chair. Zoe had a man? Since when? As he spoke, he tried to maintain his cool, but he heard the bass in his voice and wanted to kick himself for sounding jealous. "Jiovanni? Who's that? Your boyfriend?"

Aurora burst out laughing, and even though Zoe glared at her, she didn't stop giggling.

"He's not her boyfriend. He's an associate designer at Casa Di Moda," Aurora said.

Romeo sighed in relief, thanking his lucky stars that Zoe wasn't spoken for.

"Zoe's interested in someone else, and it isn't her BFF Jiovanni. He's a successful businessman who knows how to treat a woman. Isn't that right, Zoe?"

Eyes narrowed, lips pursed, Zoe gripped her fork in her hands. If looks could kill Aurora would be slumped over her plate, dead. But the designer was so busy chatting a mile a minute she didn't notice the murderous expression on Zoe's face.

Recognizing the tension in the air, Davide wisely changed the subject. He made everyone around the table chuckle when he poked fun at himself for eating so much food one of the buttons popped off his dress shirt. As they ate dinner, the mood lightened and conversation flowed. They discussed their plans for the holidays, their favorite traditions and Christmas events in Milan. Two glasses of Cristal helped Zoe loosen up, and by the time the group retired to the living room, she was in great spirits. She spoke Italian well, even knew slang and cultural jokes. The sound of her voice speaking his native tongue with such confidence and eloquence was a turn-on. A deep thinker who loved to discuss and debate current events, he was completely and utterly captivated by her.

"Have you had an opportunity to review the business proposal I gave you on Monday?" Davide asked, setting his mug down on the coffee table. "I know it's only been a few days since you visited Casa Di Moda, but I'd love to know your initial thoughts on the proposal."

Romeo wiped his mouth with a silk napkin. "Thanks again for having me. It was great to have a behind-the-scenes look at a successful fashion house. I learned a lot about the day-to-day operations of your company. I read your business proposal, and although it was concise and well-written, I'm not prepared to invest in Casa Di Moda at this time."

Davide nodded, and Aurora hung her head.

"We understand. Thanks for taking the time to read the proposal. We appreciate it."

"Davide, all isn't lost." To lighten the mood, Romeo spoke in a jovial tone of voice. "I mentioned the proposal to my sister, Francesca, yesterday and she expressed interest in the line. However, she was disappointed in the size chart—"

"Oh," Aurora said, interrupting him. "Why would your sister be disappointed in our size chart?"

"Francesca isn't a size two. She's a tall, voluptuous woman who has trouble finding designer clothes that fit her shape. If you want her to consider investing in Casa Di Moda, you'll have to revise your size chart."

Aurora's face paled. Her mouth was open so wide Romeo could see her molars.

"Casa Di Moda makes beautiful, fashionable clothes for *all* women," Zoe explained, leaning forward in her armchair, her smile as captivating as her sultry voice. "Our Christmas ad campaign features models of all colors, shapes and sizes, but what we're most excited about this holiday season is unveiling our new Chic and Curvy line."

Davide coughed into his fist, then an awkward silence descended over the room.

What was *that* about? The couple was fidgeting and shifting around on the love seat, but Zoe looked pumped up, as if she were bursting with good news. Frowning, Romeo tried to recall what he'd read in the proposal Davide had given him days earlier. Swamped all week at the office, he'd reviewed so many documents and contracts that facts and statistics were swimming around in his head. "Really? I didn't know Casa Di Moda was in the process of expanding its line. That wasn't mentioned in the proposal."

Aurora and Davide stared at each other, their expressions glum.

"Why don't I send over some sample dresses for your sister to check out?" Zoe proposed, flipping her braids over her shoulders. "If Francesca loves them, which I *know* she will, we can set up a meeting to discuss investment possibilities. How does that sound?"

"Zoe, that would be great," he said with a broad smile. "How generous of you."

Aurora shot to her feet as if the couch were on fire. Zoe offered to help her clear the table, but the fashion designer wouldn't hear of it. "No, no, be a good guest and visit with Romeo while Davide and I prepare dessert."

Leaving the room, the couple smiled politely, but Romeo could tell by their demeanor that they were upset. Were they angry about Zoe's offer? Did they have a problem with the PR director giving away free samples of their clothes? Was Zoe in trouble? He suspected Casa Di Moda wasn't the big, happy family they wanted him to believe it was, but decided not to share his suspicions with his sister. If he did, it would sour her opinion of the fashion house, and possibly even Zoe, and Romeo couldn't risk that happening. Zoe was warming up to him, he could feel it, sensed it in her cheeky grin and easy laugh, and he didn't want to do anything to rock the boat. Not when she'd finally let down her guard.

Pleased to have Zoe to himself, he draped an arm around the back of the couch. "When I tell Francesca about your offer she's going to be your new BFF. My sister loves free clothes."

"Every girl does. Buying a woman a fabulous dress is the quickest way to win her heart."

Romeo made his eyes wide. "Really? Francesca told me it was diamonds!"

"Not for me. Expensive jewelry isn't my thing—"

"What about concert tickets? Would that win you over?"

"It depends." Zoe plucked a piece of cheese off the silver tray and chewed it. "I'd be totally stoked to see Adele, Mariah, or Il Divo. They're an outstanding group, and I'm their biggest fan."

"Ask and ye shall receive." Romeo reached into this pocket and took out the tickets. "I hope you don't have plans on December thirteenth, because it's Il Divo night."

Zoe plucked the tickets out of his hand and studied them as if she were committing the details to memory. "This can't be real. I must be dreaming."

Amused by her reaction, Romeo studied her, his smile growing by the second.

"T-T-These are front-row seats," she stammered. "One ticket is two thousand euros. I don't have that kind of money. It would take me months to pay you back."

"Zoe, we're going on a date. It won't cost you anything."

Worry lines wrinkled her smooth brow.

"I don't know if you've noticed, but I'm very good at what I do, and I make a decent living at Morretti Finance and Investments."

Dodging his gaze, she dropped the tickets on the table and shook her head.

"Don't frown." Angling his body, he moved closer to her on the couch. "When you do, the light in your eyes fades, and your smile loses its warmth."

"I can't go with you to the concert. It's not a good idea."

"Why not? I think you're dope, and I want to date you—"

A smirk curled her lips, distracting him, and Romeo trailed off speaking.

"Dope?" she repeated, the humor evident in her tone of voice. "What is it, 1995? Where's your boom box, your white Adidas kicks and your gold chains?"

Romeo gave a hearty chuckle. He didn't mind her poking fun at him, could feel the tension in the air recede as they chatted and laughed together. The instrumental version of the song "This Christmas" was playing on the stereo system, and Zoe sang the words as she gazed out the windows. Lights twinkled in the distance, showering the night sky with brilliant colors. The music added to the peaceful ambience.

"Why do you keep turning me down? I'm starting to think you don't like me, but what's not to like?" he joked, playfully popping his shirt collar. "I'm a good old-fashioned Italian boy who's chivalrous, ambitious and passionate about life—"

"Yes, I've heard. You *certainly* get around."

Her words gave him pause. Now he understood why Zoe was keeping him at a distance, and decided to put her fears to rest. He didn't talk about his past relationship with anyone except his family, but he felt compelled to open up to Zoe. Didn't want her to think he was a lying dog who mistreated women. He wanted her to know the truth about his past, come what may.

"Have I been a Boy Scout? No. Have I dated more than one woman at a time? Yes. Would I settle down and quit playing the field if I met the right woman? Absolutely." Romeo raised an index finger in the air. "One date. That's all I'm asking. Come on, Zoe. Don't make me beg."

"Why me?" she asked, folding her arms across her chest. "There are tons of women who'd kill to go to the Il Divo concert with you, so why are you sweating me?"

"Sweating you? Is that what you think I'm doing?"

"If the shoe fits…" she said, her voice fading into silence.

Romeo glanced over his shoulder. He heard cupboards slam, high heels smacking against the hardwood floors and strident voices coming from the kitchen. The Bordellios were angry about something, but what?

"Don't take this the wrong way, but we're all wrong for each other. I'm ready to settle down and start a family, and you're busy playing the field."

Her words bothered him, made him regret his partying, boozing ways in the past. But he didn't interrupt, listening as she spoke from the heart.

"Furthermore, Lizabeth told me you're trying to work things out, and I don't want to come between you. I'm not a home-wrecker, and I don't want to be labeled one."

"She said *what*?"

"That you're still madly in love and committed to each other."

Romeo scoffed. *The only thing Lizabeth is committed to is my checkbook!*

He gritted his teeth. His pulse was racing, his heart beating so fast he feared he needed immediate medical attention. It took supreme effort, but Romeo took a deep breath and spoke in a calm voice. "That's not true. None of it is. We broke up over a year ago, and I've moved on with my life." He added, "I wish she'd do the same."

Hope sparked in her big brown eyes. "So, you're not getting back together?"

"Absolutely not. We're through, and there's nothing she could say or do to change my mind."

"Why would Lizabeth lie to me?"

"Because she knows I'm interested in you."

"Romeo, quit saying that. You know nothing about me."

"Of course I do. You're an avid cyclist who loves swimming, traveling, journaling and pop music," he said, proud of himself for taking the time to check out her social media pages when he'd returned home from the park that afternoon. "You're a self-proclaimed shopaholic who's always on the lookout for a unique find and a great bargain."

"You did your homework. I'm impressed."

Zoe wore a pensive expression on her face. He suspected she was contemplating whether or not to go with him to the Il Divo concert. This was a first. He'd met women from all walks of life, from executives to heiresses and international pop stars, but he'd never had to work so hard to convince someone to go on a date with him.

"Over the summer, you were linked to several celebrities in the tabloids. You expect me to believe you're not hooking up with any of them?"

His eyebrows shot up. Romeo wasn't used to being asked point-blank questions about his relationship status. He was taken aback by Zoe's boldness and disappointed by her skepticism. Why didn't she believe him? What did he have to do to prove that he wasn't the heartless Casanova the media made him out to be?

"I'm going to be honest, Romeo. I like you, and I want to get to know you better, but not if you're stringing other women along or playing the field."

"I'm not, so please don't judge me by my past mistakes. Accept me for who I am today, a sincere, trustworthy man who's so damn sexy you can't stop staring at me."

Zoe giggled, and the sound of her loud, high-pitched laugh made Romeo so happy he did the unthinkable… He crushed his lips to her mouth.

Chapter 11

Romeo devoured Zoe's moist, plump lips. Consumed with desire, he savored the taste of her sweet mouth. Flavored with hints of wine and spices, her lips were delicious. Addictive. Stronger than any drug, and Romeo was hooked. He kissed her slowly, softly, with such tender loving care she moaned inside his mouth. As if she were starving and he was dinner. *Have it your way!* he thought, inhaling her fragrant scent. *I'm all in, and eager to please!*

Lost in the moment, he stroked her cheeks, her neck, her shoulders, took great pleasure in caressing her smooth flesh. Her scent consumed him, gave him a rush. He'd never desired a woman more, and could think of nothing better than holding Zoe in his arms for the rest of the night. It took every ounce of self-control he had not to slide his hands under her fitted dress.

"That was nice," he whispered, nibbling on her bottom lip. "Hashtag, best kiss ever."

Her face lit up, and a girlish smile warmed her lips. "You're right. That was some kiss."

Romeo brushed his nose against her cheek, and she purred in his ear. That was all the encouragement he needed. Closing his eyes, he pressed his mouth against hers again. This time, her shoulders didn't stiffen. She touched his cheek with her palm and gently stroked his skin. Romeo wanted to cheer. To pump his fist in the air. She was warming up to him, and that was reason to celebrate. And they would at the Il Divo concert. Thoughts and ideas crowded his mind, but Romeo pushed them aside. In that moment all that mattered was pleasing Zoe, and he needed to focus on the task at hand.

Her tongue tickled his, sending shivers careening down his spine. He caressed her cheek with his thumb, enjoyed the feel of her skin. Romeo hadn't planned on making a move, and never imagined their first kiss would be in her boss's living room, but he had no regrets.

"What are you doing?" she murmured against his mouth.

"Living in the moment."

Romeo reached out and touched her hair, slowly sliding a braid between his fingers.

"I haven't been able to stop thinking about you since the day we met," he confessed, brushing his mouth against hers. "Since nothing would make me happier than taking you to the Il Divo concert, give me an early Christmas present and agree to be my date."

"How can I refuse when you asked me so nicely? *Several* times."

Romeo had nothing to lose and craved the taste of her lips again, so he kissed her passionately with everything he had. To his surprise, Zoe, draped her arms around his neck and pressed her body flat against his. Panting, she explored his mouth, searching, teasing, turning him out with each flick of her tongue. Falling victim to the lust of his flesh, he slipped a hand under her dress and caressed her thighs. Romeo knew he was crossing the line, but he couldn't stop stroking her warm skin. "The Il Divo concert is going to be epic," he whispered.

"Epic, huh? Tell me more."

"And ruin the surprise? *Non c'è modo.*"

"No way?" Her lips flared into a pout. "Keep talking like that, Mr. Man, and you'll be going to the Il Divo concert *alone.*"

"You're bluffing. You're so excited about the concert, I bet it's all you can think about."

A grin curled her lips as she spoke to him in Italian.

Romeo liked hearing Zoe speak Italian. Her low, sultry voice was his undoing. His Kryptonite. What pushed him over the edge. He couldn't resist. Couldn't stop himself from kissing her over and over again, until he couldn't catch his breath and had to come up for air. "You have incredible eyes and the most amazing lips."

"Is that right? And how many women have you used that line on?"

"Just once. I wanted homemade ciabatta, and my nonna refused, so I told her she was the most beautiful woman to ever walk the face of the earth. It worked like a charm."

Romeo heard his cell phone buzzing from inside his back pocket but ignored it, focusing his attention on Zoe and nothing else. To make her laugh, he joked, "You're all that and a bag of chips…and a Kit Kat!"

Zoe cracked up. "You must have been a nineties rapper in another life, because you have the lingo down pat."

"It's not my fault. My older brothers used to love American hip-hop when I was a kid. It was all they listened to," he explained, as fond memories came to mind. "We used to have rap battles every day, so I can spit rhymes with the best of them."

Something crashed to the floor in the kitchen, and Romeo glanced over his shoulder. Zoe said, "I'm going to check on Aurora and Davide."

"Oh, no you're not." Romeo seized Zoe's hand, forcing her to sit back down on the couch, and entwined his fingers with hers. "You're not going anywhere. You're kicking it with me."

Romeo took his cell out of his pocket, punched in his password and noticed he had several new text messages from Giuseppe and his COO, Simona Vitti. His publicist wanted to meet with him on Monday morning to discuss various social events happening during the holiday season. Romeo was looking forward to touching base with him. He wanted to spend the Christmas holidays with Zoe and was eager to show her off to his friends and family.

Reading the text from Simona caused a frown to curl his lips.

Call me back tonight. It doesn't matter how late. We need to talk about the deal with Milan Breweries Limited. I have some concerns, and I need to discuss them with you.

Beads of sweat formed on his forehead. Was the million-dollar deal in jeopardy? Were there legal issues? Did the rest of his executive team have reservations, too, or just Simona? Romeo wanted to return her call, but decided to wait until he left the Bordellio apartment. Zoe was opening to him, and he didn't want to ruin the mood by talking on the phone with his staff. He composed a message to Simona, promising to call her in an hour, then hit the send button.

"You're a popular guy," Zoe said, her eyebrows raised in a questioning slant.

"I'm sorry. It's work. This will only take a minute."

"Romeo, relax. I'm joking. Take as long as you need."

As Romeo responded to his text messages, he enjoyed listening to Zoe sing along with the Andrea Bocelli CD playing on the stereo system. Her voice was strong and clear, full of emotion. As she belted out the lyrics to "I'll Be Home for Christmas," he realized she was a woman of many talents. Finished, he handed Zoe his cell and draped an arm around her waist. "Enter your birthdate on my calendar, because I go all out for women who smell like heaven, sing like angels and look like centerfolds."

"Are you *sure* you're an investment banker and not in show business?"

"If that's your way of telling me I'm the bomb, I agree. I am. Just ask my nonna!"

Zoe pressed her lips together, and Romeo could tell she was trying not to laugh.

"I bet you were a handful in elementary school," she said, with a knowing smile. "You probably had girls fighting over you and pledging their undying love on the playground."

"I didn't, but my brothers did. I was a scrawny kid who had no friends and no game."

Zoe wore a thoughtful expression on her face. "I know how you feel. I was socially awkward, too, and being the tallest person in my class made me an easy target for bullies. If not for my best friend, I never would have survived."

They sat in silence for several moments, listening to the music.

"I like this. Us hanging out. We should do it more often." Watching her type her contact information into his cell, Romeo wished her hands were on him instead of his phone. "Let's have dinner tomorrow night. Pick a time and place and I'm there."

"Sorry, Romeo, but I have plans with Jiovanni."

"Are you free on Monday for *aperitivo*? We can have drinks at Bar Basso at seven o'clock." *Aperitivo* was a way of life in Milan, much like happy hour, it was an excuse for friends, colleagues and business associates to socialize and drink.

"I'll check my planner and get back to you."

Romeo nodded as if it was all good, but a plan was taking shape in his mind. If he didn't hear from her tomorrow he'd drop by Casa Di Moda on Monday and take her out for lunch.

"All done," Zoe said, handing over his cell phone. "Here you go."

When he took it from her, their fingers touched and all Romeo could think about was kissing her again.

Zoe started to speak, but it was Aurora's voice that filled the air.

"How wonderful! I *knew* you two would hit it off. You're a perfect match…"

I couldn't agree more. I've never been this enamored with a woman.

"I brought dessert." Entering the living room holding a silver tray, Aurora wore a bright smile.

"Nothing for me, thanks." Romeo discreetly glanced at his watch. "I had a great time tonight, but I should get going. I have a full day ahead of me tomorrow, and several important meetings."

"But it's Sunday," Zoe pointed out. "You need a day off just like everyone else."

No, he argued, his gaze glued to her lips. *I need to have you back in my arms so we can finish where we left off.*

"You're a man, Romeo, not a machine," she continued.

"I can relax when I retire. Until then, I have clients to impress, deals to close and money to make. It's a tough job, but somebody's gotta do it. I'm glad it's me." Standing, he offered Zoe his right hand. "I'll take you home."

"No, thank you. I'd like to speak to Aurora privately, so I'll call a cab when I'm ready to go."

Romeo was disappointed, but he nodded his head in understanding. Thanking the couple for their hospitality, he shook hands with Davide and kissed Aurora on the cheek.

"Don't be a stranger," Aurora said in a stern voice, though her eyes were smiling. "Next time you come over for dinner, bring your sister. We'd love to meet her."

In the foyer, Davide retrieved Romeo's coat from the closet and handed it to him.

Putting it on, he noticed Zoe standing beside the bookshelf. She waved, and for the second time in minutes, Romeo lost the battle with his flesh. He marched toward her and took her in his arms. Wanting to prove how he felt about her—even though the Bordellios were looking on— he kissed her soft, sweet mouth. Romeo wanted to pick up where they'd left off on the couch, but he felt the tension in her upper body and didn't want to upset her. Scared he was going to lose control, he whispered, *"Buona notte, bellissima,"* against her mouth, then turned and strode out the door.

Chapter 12

Thick gray clouds floated across the December sky, and the air smelled of rain, but there was nowhere else Zoe would rather be than biking through the streets of Milan with Jiovanni. The gloomy weather didn't detract from the beauty of her surroundings, and feeling the wind against her face had a calming effect on her. Every Sunday after morning Mass at the basilica Santa Maria delle Grazie, they'd bike to a nearby bistro to have brunch, then peruse the local flea markets. They'd shopped at booths selling seasonal crafts and traditional winter food and chatted with the vendors about their unique Christmas wares. It was the official start of the holiday season, and the towering cypress trees decorated in colored lights made the city look festive.

"Fifty years ago the rich were 'forced' to shop abroad in cities like Paris and London, but not anymore," Jiovanni explained, gripping the handlebars of his orange all-terrain bike. "I love fashion, but I liked it better when Milan had more green space and fewer boutiques…"

Listening with rapt attention, Zoe soaked up every word he said. Thanks to Jiovanni, she'd not only learned her way around Milan in a few short weeks, she'd also discovered interesting facts about Italy's most fashionable and sophisticated city. He pointed out ancient ruins, educated her about the significance of the architecture and offered valuable insights about living in the bustling metropolitan city. There was more to Milan than just fine cuisine and haute couture, and Zoe enjoyed Jiovanni's stories about the "good old days."

Pumping her brakes, Zoe swerved to avoid hitting a toddler who'd broken away from his family and darted in front of her bike. Milanese locals strolled about, hustling up and down the cobblestoned streets, laughing, snapping selfies and eating gelato.

Admiring the skyscrapers, the modern buildings and the attractive couples streaming in and out of restaurants and bars, Zoe soaked up the atmosphere of the city, the sounds of life and happiness swirling around her.

In the distance, Zoe spotted a wedding party posing for pictures in front of the Duomo and smiled. She loved weddings, and she couldn't take her eyes off the glowing couple hugging in front of the cathedral. They kissed for the cameras, and the sight warmed her heart. *Soon it will be* my *turn*, she thought. *I'll meet Mr. Right, he'll sweep me off my feet, and we'll spend the rest of our lives loving each other.*

An image of Romeo filled her thoughts. The memory of their first kiss burned bright in her mind. Played over and over again. That wasn't the worst of it. Feeling tipsy and flirtatious after several glasses of wine, she'd agreed to be his date for the Il Divo concert, but now she had second thoughts. Should she cancel? Should she go, but keep her distance?

Keep your distance? As if! responded her inner voice. *You were all over Romeo last night!*

Thinking about their impromptu make-out session in Aurora and Davide's living room caused goose bumps to break out. Romeo was unlike anyone she'd ever met, and being with him gave her a rush. They came from two different worlds, but she was curious about Romeo and his large, close-knit family. To her surprise, there was nothing cocky about him. They'd had so much fun at Aurora and Davide's apartment, Zoe was confident they'd have a good time at the Il Divo concert.

Slowing down so their bikes were side by side, Jiovanni led her through the crowded streets, around pedestrians weighed down with glitzy shopping bags and the luxury cars idling in front of stores. He suggested activities for them to do, but Zoe didn't feel like heading across town to Jiovanni's favorite museum. They'd been outside for hours, and just the thought of biking for another ninety minutes made her legs weak.

"*Evasione* is playing at Cinema Centrale at three o'clock." Jiovanni consulted his gold wristwatch. "That gives us an hour to get there. We better hurry, or we won't get seats."

"Or we could stop and have a snack at Goloso di Dolci," she proposed, her mouth watering at the thought of a sweet treat. "I'd love a cup of coffee and some gelato."

Jiovanni pointed across the street at the popular café on the corner. Famous for its unique flavors, fresh ingredients and generous servings, the ice cream shop was beloved by locals. "Count me out. There's a line around the block to get in."

"Okay. No worries," she said with a smile and a wave. "I'll see you tomorrow at work."

"All right, all right, quit twisting my arm. I'm coming."

Zoe smirked. "Of course you are. You love Goloso di Dolci more than I do!"

Stopping at the intersection, they got off their bikes, locked them to a lamppost swathed in garland, and jogged across the street. Joining the slow-moving line, Zoe took out her cell and checked her email. Her parents wanted her to call home, Shelby had sent dozens of pictures of her new Long Island apartment, and Aurora ranted about the full-figured line.

Get over it already! she thought, rolling her eyes. Zoe didn't understand why Aurora was being difficult. Last night, after Romeo left, Davide had thanked her profusely for pitching the Chic and Curvy line and assured her they'd vigorously promote it. He even agreed to a photo shoot in Naples next Friday, so why was Aurora being negative?

"I heard about the stunt you pulled last night at Aurora and Davide's apartment," Jiovanni said with a knowing smile. "You have huge cojones."

Stunned, Zoe glanced up from her cell phone, her mouth agape. Aurora had sworn her to secrecy about the dinner party, and even though she was dying to tell Jiovanni about Romeo and their magical first kiss, she'd respected her boss's wishes.

"I know a lot of gutsy women, but you're in a league of your own. You said you were going to do everything in your power to help Casa Di Moda succeed, and you meant it." Jiovanni saluted. "All hail the queen."

Zoe didn't laugh. "Who told you about the dinner party?"

"Lady Aurora, of course. She called me during lunch

while I was in the men's room and cursed me out for fill-ing your head with outrageous ideas."

"Why didn't you say anything when you returned to the table?"

"Because you were flirting with the owner and I didn't want to ruin the mood!"

Zoe stuck out her tongue. "I was not flirting. You're just jealous because he comped my lunch."

"Guilty as charged. I hate seeing you with other men. You're my future wife, remember?" Jiovanni gave her a one-arm hug. "I'm proud of you, Zoe. What you did took guts. Aurora should be thanking you for saving Casa Di Moda instead of bad-mouthing you."

Her ears perked up, and she cranked her head in Jiovan-ni's direction. *Bad-mouthing me? What did Aurora say?* She opened her mouth to ask, but told herself it didn't mat-ter. Zoe knew she'd done the right thing and was confident one day Aurora would realize it, too. In the meantime, she'd call in favors from her friends at various fashion magazines and work her connections. It was up to her to get the word out about the Chic and Curvy line, and she would. One post at a time. Going forward, the brand would be front and center on the social media pages. For her sake and for Casa Di Moda—she hoped the line was a smashing success.

"I know Aurora's your shero, and you think she's the best thing since platform sneakers were invented, but she has a history of using people, so be smart. Don't let her diminutive stature fool you. She's a she-devil in couture!"

"Then why are you working for her?"

His face paled, and his lips curled into a sneer. "Soon, Designs by Jiovanni, will take the fashion world by storm, and the years I wasted at Casa Di Moda will be a distant memory."

Bothered by his comments, Zoe held her tongue. All week he'd been in a funk, but whenever she tried to talk to him about his negative attitude, he'd brushed her off. Their colleagues were tired of his endless bitching and complaining about management, too. Aurora could be stubborn at times, but she was also thoughtful and generous, and Zoe wanted to see the fashion house succeed. It was a challenging time for the company, but she wanted to be part of the solution, not the problem.

"I told you this was a bad idea," Jiovanni grumbled. "We should go somewhere else."

The line wasn't moving, and the café was packed with wall-to-wall customers, but Zoe wasn't going anywhere until she had something to eat from her favorite café.

"You're shivering." Leaning over, Jiovanni wrapped her up in his arms and rubbed her shoulders. "Go inside and grab us a table."

"But you don't know what I want to order."

"Of course I do. You want an iced caramel latte with three sugars, two scoops of pistachio gelato, and one scoop of hazelnut gelato."

Beaming, Zoe rested a hand on her chest. "A man after my own heart."

"And don't you forget it."

Twenty minutes later, Jiovanni sat down at the corner table Zoe had found beside the window. Carrying a tray of food, he complained in Italian about the clerk who'd screwed up his order. To appease him, Zoe opened her neon-pink backpack, took out enough money to cover the entire bill and stuffed it into his shirt pocket. "Thanks, Jiovanni. It's on me."

"Great, now I have enough money to wine and dine Alessandra."

"That's the woman you met at the jazz bar, right? How are things going with her?"

"Wonderful. She's going to help me raise money to launch my fashion label."

"How? I thought she was a hotel manager at a fancy downtown hotel."

"She is, and she promised to provide me with intimate details about the rich."

"I'm confused." Zoe furrowed her brow. "Why do you need to know the whereabouts of hotel guests? How is that going to help you raise money for your fashion label?"

Jiovanni raised his cell in the air. "I'm now a paparazzo," he announced. "I'm going to take compromising photographs of celebrities. If they don't agree to buy them back from me, I'll sell them to the tabloids. I call it a win-win business deal."

"No, Jiovanni, it's called blackmail."

Zoe was so disappointed in him she didn't want to hear any more about his get-rich scheme. But she felt compelled to tell Jiovanni he was playing with fire. She warned him about the dangers of blackmailing rich people. Instead of addressing her concerns, he changed the subject. Blindsided by his question about Romeo, she stared down at her cup of gelato.

"Aurora said you and Romeo hit it off last night," he said, raising his coffee mug to his lips. "Is that true, or wishful thinking on her part?"

Heat warmed her skin. *We did more than just hit it off,* Zoe thought. *We kissed, and it was the most amazing ninety seconds of my life!*

The truth must have shown on her face, because his shoulders drooped. He made a noise in his throat, then coughed like a smoker on his deathbed.

"The media doesn't call Romeo the Sexy Devil for nothing."

Zoe wasn't one to kiss and tell, but she was excited about Romeo and wanted to tell Jiovanni about their incredible night. Before she could, he spoke in a somber tone of voice.

"Stay away from him," Jiovanni warned. "He's trouble with a capital T."

"You sound like Shelby. We talked this morning. She said I should play hard to get and make Romeo jump through hoops if he wants to be with me, but that's not me. I like him a lot, and I want to get to know him better, so that's what I'm going to do."

"Why would you want Romeo Morretti when you have me?"

"That's just nasty," she joked. "We could never date. You're like a brother to me—"

"Quit saying that," he snapped, raising his voice. "We're not family."

"We might as well be. You're a true friend, Jiovanni. I value your opinion, but you're wrong about Romeo. He's not the selfish womanizer the tabloids make him out to be."

"Yes, he is. He has a checkered past and a horrible track record with women. Don't believe me? Google him—you'll see that I'm right."

"Thanks for your concern, J, but I'm a smart cookie. I know what I'm doing."

"Do you? No disrespect, Zoe, but you're an easy target. I'm worried you'll get hurt."

An easy target? What is that *supposed to mean?*

"By your own admission, you've only had one serious relationship, so you have no idea how men operate. They can be ruthless, especially guys like Romeo Morretti."

"Don't worry about me. I can handle him."

And by handle, *you mean kiss him until you're breathless, right?* asked her inner voice.

"Fine, suit yourself, but don't come crying to me when he breaks your heart."

Worried she was going to lose her temper, Zoe admired the Christmas decorations inside the café. Giant paper ornaments hung from the ceiling, chairs were tied with red ribbons, and snowflakes were stuck to the window. Spotting a black sports car—that looked like something out of a James Bond movie—pull up to the curb, she noticed everyone on the street stop what they were doing to stare at the new arrival.

Jiovanni whistled. "Wow, what a beauty."

"You've seen one overpriced luxury car, you've seen them all."

"Did you know that the Alfa Romeo Disco Volante is one of the most coveted Italian sports cars in the world?" he asked, an awestruck expression on his face. "They only make a handful of them a year, and only the richest of the rich can afford the million-dollar price tag."

"What a waste of money. It's just a car—"

Jiovanni pressed a finger to her lips, and a giggle fell from Zoe's mouth.

"Woman, hush your mouth. It's not just a car. It's a work of art. Show some respect."

They laughed, and the tension hovering about their table disappeared.

The driver's-side door opened, and a dark-haired man in aviator sunglasses emerged. Zoe did a double take. Then another. *Romeo!* Goose bumps rippled across her skin as she watched her dreamy, brown-eyed crush march around the hood of the car. Opening the other door, Romeo helped his passenger to her feet and draped an arm around her shoulder. Zoe's stomach clenched. Surely her eyes were deceiving her. Blinking rapidly, Zoe struggled to focus her gaze.

Zoe leaned forward in her seat, couldn't take her eyes off Romeo and his date. With their creamy olive skin, dark hair and model-perfect features, they made a striking couple. As they headed toward the café, the crowd parted like the Red Sea. The brunette was fashionably dressed in a white fringe sweater, skinny jeans and beige heels, and Zoe suspected she was in the entertainment business. Watching them, she realized Romeo had lied to her about being single. Zoe wanted to run outside and confront him, but she forced herself to remain in her seat.

"I told you, Romeo Morretti isn't worth your time," Jiovanni said, a sympathetic expression on his face. "Do you want to leave?"

Picking up her spoon, she resumed eating her gelato. "No. Of course not."

"Just ignore him. Pretend he's not here."

Zoe scoffed. Romeo wasn't the kind of man a woman could ignore, but she was determined to try. Wanting to be a good friend, she turned away from the window, listening as Jiovanni chatted about his plans for New Year's Eve. Out of the corner of her eye, she saw the owner of the café sprint through the open door and greet Romeo and his date. Leading the couple inside the shop, he ushered them to the front of the line and filled their orders.

"Entitled bastard," Jiovanni grumbled. "Romeo gets preferential treatment everywhere he goes in Milan, and it's unfair. He's no better than anyone else. He should have to wait in line like the rest of us."

"Oh, stop, you use your looks to get preferential treatment all the time—"

The sound of Romeo's voice filled the air, and Zoe trailed off speaking.

"I was just talking about you, and here you are. *Che meravigliosa coincidenza.*"

Zoe froze. Her eyes were wide, her spoon was suspended in midair, and the walls of her throat were so thick she couldn't swallow. *What a wonderful coincidence? You're happy to see me? Really?* she thought, feeling as if she were having an out-of-body experience. "Romeo, what are you doing here?" she asked. "I thought you had to work today."

"I do, but Francesca dropped by the office and insisted I take her out for lunch," he explained. "She's my favorite sister, so of course I agreed."

Relief flooded Zoe's body. "That's so sweet of you, Romeo."

"Boy, please," Francesca said, swatting her brother's shoulder. "You're not fooling anyone with that good-boy act. I'm your *only* sister."

The siblings laughed, and watching them together made Zoe miss her sister.

Introductions were made, and everyone shook hands.

"So, *you're* Zoe," Francesca said, cocking an eyebrow. "Very interesting."

For the second time in minutes, Zoe didn't know what to say or think.

"Romeo's been talking my ear off about you ever since we left his office, and now that we've met, I can see why. You're stunning." Francesca flicked a finger in the air. "I love your outfit. Is it from Casa Di Moda?"

Zoe touched her chest. *You do?* Her long-sleeved plaid jumper was a gift from Jiovanni, and she loved how it fit her shape. "Yes, as a matter of fact it is. Jiovanni designed it," she said, proudly. "In fact, he's been dressing me ever since I arrived in Milan."

"I was stoked to hear about Casa Di Moda's plus-size line. How exciting!"

"Jiovanni is the creative force behind the line, and with him at the helm, it's going to be a runaway hit. He's talented and creative, and all of his designs are outstanding."

The owner appeared, carrying a tray filled with food, and put it down on the table.

"We'd love to hear more about the line," Romeo asked. "Can we join you?"

Zoe started to speak, but Jiovanni interrupted her.

"No, sorry, we were just leaving. Enjoy your lunch. Ciao!"

Zoe gave her best friend a funny look. He never missed an opportunity to flirt with an attractive woman or boast about his fresh, cutting-edge designs. She was surprised when he grabbed her hand and dragged her out of the ice cream shop. "What was that all about?" she asked, perplexed by his odd behavior. "You love meeting new people. Why didn't you want to hang out with Romeo and his sister?"

"Today you're mine, all mine, and I don't want the Morretti family interrupting our fun."

He draped an arm around her shoulder and gave her a wet, sloppy kiss on the cheek.

"You're crazy!" she said with a laugh.

They crossed the intersection arm in arm. Out of the corner of her eye, Zoe noticed Romeo watching them from the café window and hoped she hadn't blown her chance with the drop-dead gorgeous tycoon with the killer smile.

Chapter 13

"I think we should sever ties with Capone Costruzioni," Simona announced, clasping her hands together on the conference room table at Morretti Finance and Investments on Wednesday morning. "Mr. Capone blames the economic crisis for his company's financial woes, but his poor management and organization skills are to blame. Worse still, he treats people like crap."

Seated at the head of the mahogany table, reviewing the stack of business contracts his attorney had dropped off minutes earlier, Romeo listened as his chief operating officer complained about the owner of the beleaguered construction company. Morretti Finance and Investments had hundreds of clients around the world, and Romeo took great pride in connecting with his investors on a regular basis. There was nothing his employees could tell him that he didn't already know, but he enjoyed Simona's weekly updates and nodded his head as she spoke. He'd never met a more tenacious woman, and Romeo was thankful the Princeton graduate was an integral part of his executive team.

"All business isn't good business, and I think Mr. Capone is a liability. I'm worried he's going to do something to embarrass us, so it's imperative we act now…"

Tapping his diamond ink pen on his file folder, Romeo considered Simona's words. His gaze strayed to the wall clock hanging above the door, and he wondered what his favorite PR director was up to. Since running into Zoe at the gelato shop ten days ago, he'd seen her every night of the week. Without fail, he'd drop by Casa Di Moda at the end of her workday and convince her to have dinner with him. They'd talk and flirt for hours at a nearby pub. Romeo could always count on Zoe to make him laugh. Some nights they'd have dinner at a quaint, out-of-the-way bistro; other nights they'd check out a jazz bar or watch Christmas movies at her cozy studio apartment. Three weeks after meeting her, Romeo was ready to take himself off the market. "No ring, no rules," used to be his dating motto, but he didn't want Zoe unless he could have all of her—her heart, her mind and her body—and he didn't want to share her with anyone else. She was special to him, someone he could be himself around. There was nothing fake or pretentious about her. Zoe lived her life in an authentic way, and that appealed to him— "I know you rarely drop clients, but I hope you'll consider what I've said."

The sound of Simona's voice yanked Romeo out of his thoughts. "I take it your meeting last night with Mr. Capone at El Porteno didn't go well."

Her cheeks turned as red as an apple. Simona wore a troubled expression on her face, and Romeo felt guilty for not giving his COO his undivided attention. What had Zoe said yesterday? *You're a workaholic who's obsessed with making money, and you need to change your ways.* Then she'd plucked his cell phone out of his hands, dropped it into her snakeskin purse and dragged him out onto the dance floor at the Hollywood nightclub. Was it true? Had he fallen back into his old habits? And most importantly, was he putting his health at risk?

Romeo considered his furious work schedule. He did his best thinking on the treadmill, so he woke up every morning at the crack of dawn to jog eight miles. Exercising helped to clear his head, and three times a week he also took a tae kwon do class with his executive team. Building strong relationships with his employees was the key to his success, and he enjoyed getting to know his staff better. Romeo never forgot what it was like being a lowly associate at a successful financial institute in Milan, so he made a point to touch base with everyone who worked at Morretti Finance and Investments regularly.

Simona's cell phone pinged, and she picked it up off the table. "Oh, no, I just got an email from Mr. Capone. He's threatening to…to…" She trailed off. She dropped her cell on the table and glared at the device as if it were her mortal enemy.

"He's threatening to do what? Talk to me, Simona. I want to help." Last year, when he'd been away on three months' medical leave, she'd done an outstanding job running the office in his absence. Romeo wanted to support her now. "What happened last night?"

Simona picked up her mug and sipped her coffee.

"Should I call Mr. Capone and ask him, or are you going to tell me?"

"It was nothing. He had too much to drink and crossed the line, but I handled it."

Setting aside his contracts, Romeo took off his reading glasses and stared at his COO. Slender with curly black hair, the Venice native looked more like a preschool teacher than a brilliant investment banker with decades of experience. "He made a pass at you during your meeting and you shot him down, didn't you?"

"No," she said, a smirk twisting her peach lips. "He grabbed my ass in the parking lot. I slapped him so hard his glasses flew off his face and landed in a mud puddle!"

Romeo cracked up. Picturing the scene in his mind's eye—his soft-spoken COO, slapping the crap out of the burly construction worker—made him chuckle so hard his body shook. "Damn, Simona. That's the funniest thing I've heard in a long time," he said, shaking his head in disbelief. "Thanks for the laugh."

Her eyes widened. "You're not mad at me for losing my cool?"

"Why would I be mad at you? You handled the situation perfectly."

"Mr. Capone says he has a black eye. He's threatening to file a police report."

Romeo scoffed. "I'd like to see him try. Ignore him. He's bluffing."

"What about his contract? Do we have to honor it?"

"Not if he put his hands on you. I'm behind you one hundred percent, Simona, so prepare the necessary paperwork and have the legal team review it."

Simona sighed. "Great. I'll get right on it and follow up with you at Blue Bar tonight."

"I have plans, so let's touch base tomorrow morning."

"You're skipping out on drinks with the executive team again? How come? You used to encourage everyone to go, and lately you're a no-show."

Romeo wanted to tell Simona about Zoe, but thought better of it and shrugged. Thirsty, he reached for his mug. Realizing it was empty, he decided to go to the staff room for more. He'd been in the conference room from for hours—returning phone calls, proofreading contracts, rewriting mistake-ridden proposals—and he wanted to stretch his legs before the eleven o'clock board meeting. "Let's go make some fresh coffee," he proposed as he stood up and opened the door. "It's going to be a long day, and we're going to need some caffeine."

"Speak for yourself. I did yoga this morning and I feel great. *You* should try it sometime."

Laughing, they exited the conference room and walked down the corridor. The scents of peppermint and cinnamon overwhelmed his senses. To please Simona and the rest of his Christmas-loving staff, he'd agreed to let them decorate the office, but they'd gone overboard. Strings of miniature lights lined the windowsill, velvet stockings were displayed on the walls, and candy canes, colored ornaments and gingerbread men hung from the Santa-themed tree. It had a belt and a red tutu. Every time Romeo looked at it he chuckled.

The office was quiet except for the sound of the ringing telephones, but Romeo knew his staff was hard at work. He spotted two men in dark suits enter the reception area and suspected they were cops. The man in the sunglasses had a gruff demeanor, and his partner wore a terse expression on his fleshy face. Romeo's gut was telling him something was wrong, so instead of ducking into the staff room to feed his caffeine addiction, he stalked into the waiting area.

"Good morning, Officers."

Romeo put his empty coffee mug on the glass desk and slid his hands into the pockets of his gray pin-striped suit. It was a gift from Davide, but every time he wore it he thought about Zoe. She meant a lot to him. He was so excited about their relationship, he wanted to spend all of his free time with her. He'd cleared his schedule for the weekend so they could hang out at his villa, but he still had to convince her to be his guest.

"I'm Romeo Morretti, and this is my chief operating officer, Simona Vitti," he explained, nodding his head in greeting. "What can we do for you today?"

Double Chin flashed his badge, then introduced his short balding partner with the chipped front tooth. "We have a sensitive matter to discuss with you," he said in a quiet tone of voice. "Is there somewhere we can speak in private?"

"Yes, of course, right this way, Officers. We can talk in my office."

Leading the group through the corridor, Romeo tried to figure out why the police were at his company. His thoughts ran wild, jumping from one theory to the next. Maybe they wanted to discuss his speeding tickets. But why would they waste their time? It was only a few thousand euros, and the late penalty was minimal. Besides, he'd racked up speeding tickets numerous times before and never received a visit from Milan's finest.

Entering his office, Romeo was temporary blinded by the intensity of the sun and closed the window blinds. He offered the detectives something to drink from the bar, but they declined and sat down in the padded armchairs in front of his desk.

"To what do we owe this pleasure?" he asked, anxious to get down to business. He had an executive board meeting in forty-five minutes and wanted the officers long gone before it started. "Is this about my speeding tickets? If it is, I can pay them today."

Double Chin reached into his suit jacket, took out a photograph and dropped it on the desk. Romeo picked it up and a cold chill flooded his body.

"Do you know who the man in that mug shot is?"

Simona took the picture from Romeo's hand and

dropped it on the table. "Yes, of course. It's Julio Mario Domínguez. I signed him to Morretti Investments last year, and we have a great business relationship. In fact, he's one of our most successful investors."

"Were you aware of his ties to organized crime when you took him on as a client?"

Romeo was taken aback by the question, but he wore a blank expression on his face. "Every investment we've done on his behalf in the past year has been legal, by the book."

Chipped Tooth snarled like a pit bull. "You knew full well about his shady business practices and criminal endeavors. *You* handled his money."

It was a statement, not a question, but Romeo wasn't afraid to set him straight. "As with most of our clients, we only handled a small fraction of his income. Fifteen percent to be exact."

"Fifteen percent of a billion dollars is a substantial amount of money, Mr. Morretti."

Double Chin leveled a finger at him. "That's chump change to a man like you, but regular folks like me think a hundred and fifty million euros is a ton of money. If we find out you're lying we'll prosecute you and everyone at this company to the full extent of the law."

"Do you have proof that a crime has been committed?" Simona asked, pursing her lips.

"Julio Mario Domínguez was arrested in Paris this morning and charged with money laundering for a notorious Colombian drug dealer with a lengthy criminal record."

Romeo glanced at Simona. She didn't even bat an eyelash. Detectives had revealed pertinent information about the criminal case against Julio Mario Domínguez, but his COO maintained her calm disposition. As always, he could count on her to have his back.

"With all due respect, Detectives, I don't understand

why you're here," Romeo said, projecting confidence, even though sweat was dribbling down the back of his dress shirt. "If Mr. Domínguez was arrested, then there must be a strong case against him. Why are you here, interrupting our busy workday?"

Leaning forward in his seat, Double Chin wore a twisted smile on his mouth. "Because Julio Mario Domínguez named *you* as his co-conspirator."

The hair on the back of his neck shot up, but Romeo remained perfectly still.

"My guess? Domínguez is probably cutting a deal with French authorities as we speak."

"That's ludicrous," Simona said. "He's lying to save his neck."

"I don't think so. I think Mr. Domínguez has a very compelling story."

Simona pointed a finger at her chest. "I'm the one who handled Mr. Domínguez's personal investments, not Romeo. Furthermore, neither one of us has anything to hide."

"The way I see it, you have two choices. Cooperate with authorities or face jail time."

Chipped Tooth glanced around the office. "We need to see your financial records."

"And I'll need to see a warrant."

The detectives shared a look, and Romeo knew they didn't have one. Thanks to Markos, he knew his legal rights, and once Tweedledee and Tweedledum left his office, he would be calling his brother. His family was coming to Milan for the Christmas Wonderland Ball, but this was an emergency, and Romeo needed to speak to Markos as soon as possible. Before he was arrested for a crime he didn't commit.

"You have seventy-two hours to decide."

"But we're swamped with work right now," Simona argued. "Surely this can wait until the New Year."

"Justice waits for no man." Chipped Tooth stood and buttoned his wrinkled gray suit. "It would be in your best interest not to repeat the details of this conversation with anyone. It could compromise the investigation. I'd hate to see you charged with obstruction of justice."

Stretching, as if he'd just taken a power nap, Double Chin rose from his chair.

"We'll be back," Chipped Tooth said, with a curt nod. "Don't forget your warrant next time."

Simona offered to walk the detectives out, and Romeo was so glad to see them leave his office he sighed in relief. He needed a moment to catch his breath. To think things through. To regain control before he called Markos.

The detectives' threats loomed in his mind. Was it true? Had one of his richest clients been arrested for money laundering? Did Mr. Domínguez have ties to criminal organizations, or had the police made a grave mistake?

Taking his cell out of his pocket, Romeo accessed the internet. Every morning, he read the local newspapers and his favorite business magazines, but there'd been no mention of Julio Mario Domínguez being arrested in Paris. Still, his heart raced.

How could this happen? Every month, he contacted his clients to ensure they had no major issues and concerns... Romeo bolted upright in his chair. Is that why the Colombian businessman had been dodging his calls? Because he was busy cutting deals with the authorities? He shuddered to think what would happen if the story got out. If his esteemed clients discovered he'd been accused of money laundering.

Romeo gulped. It would destroy him, cripple his financial empire and ruin his reputation. To clear his head, he stood and moved to the window. Staring out at the bright blue sky, he feared his first Christmas with Zoe was going to be memorable for all the wrong reasons.

Chapter 14

"Wrong, wrong, wrong," Zoe complained, pitching clothes over her shoulder and onto the bedroom floor. Standing in front of her closet on Friday night searching for an outfit to wear to the Il Divo concert—when Romeo was due at her apartment in an hour—was stressful, but Zoe was determined to find the perfect dress for their five o'clock date. It was a miracle she'd made it home from work on time. All afternoon she'd been promoting the Christmas holiday line and the Men of Milan calendar. If she didn't have plans with Romeo, she'd still be at the office tweeting and blogging on Casa Di Moda's social media pages.

Heat flushed her cheeks, warming her body all over. Just the thought of seeing Romeo again made her pulse race. What a difference a few weeks make, Zoe thought, as treasured memories filled her heart. Last night, after the Christmas tree lighting ceremony, they'd strolled the streets hand in hand. Romeo had been quiet and withdrawn, seemed to be in another world. It was obvious his mind was still at work, but when she'd asked him what was wrong, he'd apologized for ignoring her and kissed her passionately on the lips.

Surprised by Romeo's public display of affection, she'd pressed herself flat against him and wrapped her arms around his waist. Days earlier, while they were cooking dinner together in the gourmet kitchen at his penthouse, they'd agreed to keep their relationship quiet. Every day, her colleagues grilled her about her love life, but she skillfully evaded their questions. She knew Jiovanni was upset with her for not confiding in him, but Zoe wanted to honor Romeo's request. After everything his ex-fiancée had put him through, he was leery about dating in the public eye, and Zoe didn't blame him.

Reflecting on their marathon date, Zoe couldn't recall ever having so much fun. The area was a popular hangout spot among millennials, and they'd spent the evening sampling popular Christmas desserts, mulled wine and roasted chestnuts. The Navigli district was known for its canals, and when Romeo suggested a boat ride, she'd agreed. Zoe would remember their trip to Lake Maggiore as long as she lived. Nestled in Romeo's arms, staring at the star-filled sky, she'd felt as if she were in another era. Zoe didn't know how it happened, but one minute they were snapping selfies together and the next Romeo was kissing her passionately. When Romeo drove her home at the end of the night, she invited him inside for a cup of coffee, and they'd wasted no time picking up where they'd left off on the boat.

Zoe ran her hands along the bodice of the snug-fitting, deep red gown she'd found in the back of her closet, then yanked it off the velvet hanger. *If this doesn't knock Ro-*

meo's socks off, I don't know what will! she thought, laughing to herself.

Chucking her satin bathrobe on the canopy bed, Zoe slipped on the dress and scrutinized her appearance. Feeling chic and sophisticated in the gown Jiovanni had made for her months earlier, she admired her profile in the floor-length mirror. The capped sleeves and cinched waist flattered her hourglass figure, but she worried about tripping on the long ruffled train. Romeo made her nervous, on edge, and when he touched her anything could happen.

Zoe wet her lips with her tongue. Last night in her living room, one sensuous kiss had led to another, and in the blink of an eye they were moaning and groaning, desperately pawing at each other's clothes. Overcome with need, they'd made out on the couch for hours.

Her cell phone rang. Remembering the last place she'd seen it, she raced inside the bathroom and scooped it off the counter. Zoe read the name and number on the screen. It was her mom calling from New York. Even though she had a date to get ready for, she wanted to check in with her family. Wanting to "see" her mother, she pressed the Video button and laughed as her mom waved and blew kisses.

"Hi, baby girl. How are you doing?"

"Great. I'm just getting ready to go out for dinner."

"With Jiovanni? Again? You spend *way* too much time with that boy."

Laughing, Zoe picked up her favorite bottle of perfume off the counter and sprayed her neck and wrist. "Mom, I've told you a million times, we're just friends."

"Good, I don't want Khalil to think he has any competition."

Zoe was annoyed with her mom, but she spoke in a calm voice, didn't let her frustration show. "Mom, you have to move on. Khalil and I are not getting back together—"

"He's still crazy about you, you know."

"Mom, we haven't spoken to each other in months," she pointed out.

"Together forever, never apart. Sometimes in distance, but never in heart."

Zoe hated when her mother quoted inspirational sayings and wished her dad were around to help her talk some sense into her. Noticing the time on her cell phone, she propped it against the tissue box so she could finish getting ready for her date.

"When will you be home? Have you booked your flight? Are you staying for a month?"

Her body tensed. All week, she'd been dreading this moment. The last thing Zoe wanted to do was disappoint her parents, and she knew they'd be crushed when she told them the bad news, but she couldn't keep putting it off. "Mom, I won't be coming home for the holidays."

The smile slid off her face. "Why not? Didn't you get your Christmas bonus?"

"No, and my credit cards are all maxed out," she explained. "I just can't afford it."

"I'm not surprised. Milan is one of the most expensive cities in the world. Even though your dad and I told you it was a bad idea, you just had to take a job there."

Her dad peered over her mom's shoulder, wearing a broad grin, and Zoe smiled. Her parents couldn't be more different. Statuesque with burgundy locks, Collette Smith loved to socialize and make new friends. Not her husband of thirty-five years, whom she'd met in grade school in Trinidad. Slender with dark brown skin, Reuben Smith was a soft-spoken man who'd rather watch CNN than party. But their personalities complemented each other perfectly.

"Zoe, is that you, baby girl?" he asked. "How is life treating you in Milan?"

Before Zoe could respond to her dad's question, her mom spoke up.

"It's terrible. Our daughter can't come home for Christmas because she's flat broke."

"Baby girl, don't worry," Reuben said in a soothing voice. "I'll buy your ticket."

"Dad, don't. I have to work. There's no way I'll get the time off this late in the game."

Her mom snapped her fingers. "Fine, then we'll come see you."

"Good idea, honey. We're retired. Why not go see our hardworking daughter in Milan for a few weeks? Shelby is thinking of volunteering in Peru again this Christmas, so we might as well visit you, Zoe." Reuben nodded so hard his eyeglasses slid down his thin nose. "I'll call the travel agent first thing tomorrow to see what flights are available."

Zoe missed her parents, but she didn't want them flying to Milan during the holidays. The plane tickets would be ridiculously expensive; the airports would be a jam-packed. Zoe didn't want her parents flying during the busiest time of the year. "No. Don't. I'll be home in February," she explained, speaking in a cheery voice, though her heart was sad. "We can hang out then."

"Christmas won't be the same without you."

The doorbell rang, and Zoe groaned. "Oh, no, Romeo's early, and I'm not ready!"

"Who's Romeo?" Reuben asked, furrowing his brow. "Is he one of your colleagues?"

No, Dad, he's the guy I've fallen hard for, Zoe thought, but didn't dare say. She had strong feelings for Romeo and wanted to tell her parents about him, but it was too soon. They'd only been seeing each other for a few weeks; there was no guarantee their red-hot relationship would last. "Mom, Dad, I have to go, but I'll call you on the weekend."

"Be safe, honey, and remember what I said about Jiovanni. He seems like a nice guy, but he's not the right man for you so don't let him charm you."

Zoe laughed. "Okay, Mom, I won't, and you remember what I said about Khalil."

"Don't be silly. Of course you're going to get back together. You're soul mates."

The doorbell rang again, but Zoe couldn't end the call until she set her mother straight.

"Mom, Khalil and I are over. He's moved on with his life, and so have I."

Her dad nodded his head in understanding, and Zoe was grateful for his support.

"Baby girl, as long as you're happy we're happy."

"Like hell we are!" her mom said, puckering her thin lips. "Khalil's practically family, and his mother and I have been dear friends for many years. You *have* to marry him."

"No, I don't, Mom. It's my choice, not yours."

"You've been in Milan for two years, but you still haven't met anyone who lights your fire." Collette wore a triumphant smile. "Face it. No one will ever be able to measure up to Khalil. He's your first love and your only love. No one can take his place in your heart."

"I'm crazy about Romeo, and I want to have a future with him."

Zoe cupped a hand over her mouth. She couldn't believe she'd revealed her innermost thoughts and wished she could stuff the words back down her throat.

"Y-Y-You're what?" Collette stammered. "Where did you meet this guy? Who is he? What does he do for a living?"

Her cell phone buzzed, cueing her that she had an incoming call, but Zoe didn't answer it.

"Romeo is a successful businessman with real estate properties all over the world," Zoe boasted. She tried to temper her excitement, but it seeped into her tone. "We haven't know each other long, but he's a good man, and I enjoy his company."

"That's wonderful, baby girl. We look forward to meeting him in the near future."

Collette scoffed. "Speak for yourself. Khalil will always be my first and *only* choice."

Zoe almost rolled her eyes, but since she didn't want to do anything to set her mother off again, she said goodbye to her parents. "Bye, Mom. Bye, Dad. I love you."

"We love you, too. Have fun tonight, and give Romeo Morretti my regards," her dad said cheerfully.

"You know who he is?" she asked, raising an eyebrow. "How?"

"I just Googled him. His cousin Demetri is one of the greatest baseball players of all time, so be a good daughter and get an autograph for your old man. I'm a huge fan."

"I'll see what I can do."

Her dad pumped his fist in the air. "That's my girl!"

Shocked to see the time on her cell, Zoe ended the call and exited the bathroom. She hoped Romeo wasn't mad at her for making him wait outside, and sent him a text message explaining why she was running behind schedule.

"There you are, bellissima. How are your parents?"

Zoe stopped. Glancing up from her cell, her eyes widened. Confused, she couldn't make sense of what was going on. *What is Romeo doing in my living room? How did he get in? The doors locked!*

"I rang the buzzer several times, but you didn't answer," he explained, sliding his hands into the pockets of his slacks. "I tried the door and it opened, so I decided to wait for you in here. I hope that's okay."

Thinking back to the afternoon, Zoe slowly nodded her head. "I got home late from work, and I was in such a rush to get ready, I must have forgotten to lock it when I came in."

"You have to be more careful. A stranger could waltz right in and catch you off guard."

"Don't worry about me. I kickbox, and I'm not afraid to use it."

"Thanks for the heads-up. I'll have to remember not to piss you off."

He reached for her hand, and her heart swooned. It happened every time Romeo touched her. He'd mastered the art of looking suave and sophisticated, and being in his presence did a number on her libido. Short of breath, her erect nipples strained against her lace push-up bra, dying for release. It took supreme effort, but Zoe tore her eyes away from his mouth and forced herself to quit fantasizing about ripping the clothes off his muscled body.

Romeo whistled. "Wow, Zoe, you're sensational."

"You say that every time you see me."

"That's because it's true. You never cease to amaze me. I love your elegant style."

"Thanks, Romeo. You look great, too." Admiring how handsome he was in his blue collared dress shirt and black pants.

"I'm almost ready. Just give me five minutes to do my makeup, and I'll be good to go."

"You don't need any. You're perfect just the way you are." Stepping forward, he captured her around the waist and held her close to his chest. "You're stunning, Zoe, and I'm in awe of your natural beauty."

"Then imagine how much better I'd look with mascara and lipstick."

"It's impossible to improve perfection," he whispered,

brushing his lips against the curve of her ear. "Did you pack an overnight bag like I asked?"

Pulling out of his arms, she stared up at him in disbelief. "Was I supposed to?"

"Last night during the boat ride, I told you I wanted to spend the weekend with you."

"I thought you were joking."

Romeo gestured to the bedroom door. "I wasn't. So go grab your stuff. I'll wait."

Zoe hesitated; she didn't know how to put her feelings into words without offending him and took a moment to process her thoughts. She loved the idea of hanging out with Romeo at his countryside villa for a few days, but she didn't want to give him the wrong idea. His past was a huge obstacle for her to overcome, and there were times she couldn't help feeling that she was fighting a losing battle. "I don't know if I'm ready for a sexual relationship."

"I understand. I'm okay with that," he said, tenderly rubbing her shoulders.

Zoe wondered if the word *sucker* was stamped on her forehead and shot him a you're-not-fooling-me look. "Really? You don't mind waiting a month? Or three? Or even six?"

"No. I don't, and furthermore I'd never pressure you to have sex. Contrary to what the media thinks, I'm not that kind of guy. It'll happen when we're both ready, and I'm prepared to wait as long as it takes."

Moved by his honesty, Zoe couldn't stop a smile from curling the corners of her mouth.

"You're special to me, and I don't want to lose you."

"Seriously? You're not just saying that to impress me?"

"I don't have to lie to impress you. I have adoring fans all over the city, remember?"

Romeo wiggled his eyebrows and Zoe cracked up, laughing long and hard.

"Okay, I'll come, but don't get any funny ideas. We're *not* knockin' boots this weekend."

A mischievous expression covered his face. "Why not? That's my favorite song!"

"Of course it is. You're the quintessential ladies' man."

"Not anymore. I'm a one-woman man." Romeo kissed her lips. "I'm your man."

His confession blew her mind, and seconds passed before she regained her voice. "You're serious?"

"Absolutely. And now that we're a couple, you'll have to make more room in your schedule for me. Ideally, I'd like to see you every day, but I know how busy you are at work, so I'm willing to compromise. Six dates a week sounds reasonable to me, don't you think?"

He tightened his hold around her waist and spoke in a silky, smooth voice.

"We have an incredible connection, and I'm excited to see what the future holds for us."

Her pulse was pounding out of control and it hurt to swallow, but Zoe pushed the question in her mind out of her dry mouth. "You want us to be exclusive? You're sure?"

"I'd love nothing more." Romeo brushed his nose against hers. "I have feelings for you, Zoe, and I don't want to compete with anyone else for your time and affection. It's time to change the status on your social media pages from 'single' to 'in a relationship.'"

Dumbstruck, Zoe couldn't believe what she was hearing. Was shocked by Romeo's candor, his openness.

"And one more thing," he continued, kissing the corners of her lips. "Tell Jiovanni and the other guys you work with who have the hots for you, you're spoken for..."

Romeo was way off base, dead wrong about her colleagues, but she didn't argue with him. Couldn't when he was playing in her hair and stroking her arms and hips. Zoe liked what he was doing with his hands, enjoyed feeling them against her flesh. No one had ever spoken to her in that tone before, and his bold attitude was a turn-on. Made her wet. They'd only known each other for a few weeks, but it felt like months had passed since their fateful meeting in November, and Zoe was moved—and aroused—by his words.

"I'll be back in a minute," she said, giving Romeo a peck on the lips. "Wait right here."

Feeling on top of the world, Zoe hurried down the hall and into her bedroom at the rear of the apartment. After putting on mascara and some red lipstick, she tossed toiletries, clothes and her journal into her overnight bag and zipped it up.

Zoe put on her stilettos and adjusted her dress. Catching sight of Romeo in her peripheral vision, she only hoped that when they arrived at his villa at the end of the night, her hormones wouldn't get her into any trouble. She desired him more than she'd ever wanted anyone, and liked the idea of breaking the rules with her dreamy crush.

Chapter 15

La Piastra Calda was known for its innovative cuisine, exceptional service and swank decor. Zoe knew from reading local newspapers that it routinely hosted diplomats, heads of state and British royalty. Like many of the best restaurants in the country, La Piastra Calda was family-owned with a devoted clientele and a six-month waiting list for reservations.

"I hope you brought your appetite, because I heard the dishes at La Piastra Calda are out of this world." Romeo helped Zoe out of the passenger seat of his Spada Vetture Sport and draped an arm around her waist. "I've never been here before, but if the food's even half as good as my brother Enrique says it is, then it's going to be a very delicious night."

The valet opened the front door and stepped aside to let them pass. *"Godere!"*

Zoe couldn't believe her eyes. The employees were

standing at attention in the waiting area and bowed in greeting as they entered the restaurant. Embarrassed that everyone in the room was staring at them, Zoe pretended to admire the colorful string art hanging on the walls.

A man with a bushy mustache stepped forward and introduced himself. "Welcome to La Piastra, Mr. Morretti," he bellowed. "I'm the owner and head chef of this fine establishment. It's an honor to have you here with us. If there is anything we can do to enhance your dining experience, please don't hesitate to ask."

The owner clasped his hands together, then gestured to the spiral staircase. "If you'll follow me, I'll show you to your private second-floor table."

Hearing noise and laughter coming from inside the restaurant, Zoe peered over the owner's shoulder and scanned the room. Saturated with ivory and various shades of blue, the dining area and adjoining lounge were packed with well-dressed diners. Zoe couldn't help gawking at the famous faces eating just an arm's length away from her.

The second floor was decked out in stone and glass. The elaborate chandeliers hanging from the vaulted ceiling beautified the space. The air smelled of pinecones and garland, and the refreshing scent reminded Zoe of how much fun she'd had in the summer with Jiovanni and their friends. They'd done it all: barbecued at neighborhood parks, fished and camped at Lake Garda, and danced at music festivals. Though Zoe couldn't imagine anything better than attending the Il Divo concert with Romeo later that evening.

"Since it's the holidays, I couldn't resist decorating the table in bright, festive colors," the owner said with a proud smile. "I trust that everything is to your liking…"

The round table in the middle the dining room had gleaming silverware, gold, silk linens and a bouquet filled with poinsettias. Hundreds of miniature candles twinkled, and the female pianist played "It's the Most Wonderful Time of Year" quietly in the background.

"This is one of our finest and most popular wines." Beaming, he picked up the gold-and-black bottle off the table, opened it, and filled their glasses to the brim. "Your server will be here shortly with your first course."

The owner nodded, then marched toward the staircase, his toothy smile still in place.

"That's odd," Zoe said, glancing around the room. "How come it's jam-packed downstairs, with dozens of people waiting for a table, but empty up here?"

Romeo pulled out her chair. "Because I rented out the second floor for our date. Every time we go out for dinner, you strike up a conversation with the people seated nearby, or end up making a new friend at the lounge or bar—"

"You have a problem with me being nice?" she said, taking a seat at the table. "Why?"

Romeo picked up his napkin, draped it across his legs and plucked a piece of toasted garlic bread out of the bread-basket. "No, of course not, but I'd like to spend a quiet evening with my girl without every Tom, Dick and Harry flirting with you. Is that too much to ask?"

Hearing Romeo call her his girl gave Zoe a rush, made her feel warm inside.

"Don't you think you're exaggerating a tad bit?" she asked, pinching two fingers together. "I'm a PR director, not a famous reality TV star with a billion Twitter followers."

"You might as well be. You attract attention wherever you go, and I'd be lying if I said I like it. I don't. The truth is, I want you all to myself tonight."

The waiter arrived with the first course, and while they ate their Tuscan chickpea soup, they discussed their busy workday, how talented the pianist was and the menu Romeo had created with the head chef for their date. "It has nine courses?" she repeated, bewildered by his words. "That's insane. I enjoy a good meal as much as the next girl, but I'll never be able to eat that much food. My waistline won't forgive me if I do!"

"As the popular Italian saying goes, 'the appetite comes from eating.' I suspect as the night wears on you'll care less about the calories and more about the next delicious course."

Wanting to know more about the acclaimed restaurant, Zoe picked up the menu, opened it and read the short paragraph about its forty-year history. Impressed with the owner's bio, she flipped to the second page and scanned the list of dishes.

Her eyes widened. Five hundred euros per person? Two thousand euros for their bottle of wine? Twenty-five percent gratuity? Fanning her face with the menu, she swallowed hard. Zoe didn't want to even think about how much Romeo had shelled out to rent out the second floor of the five-star restaurant, but her curiosity got the best of her. Zoe asked Romeo for details, but he changed the subject. He questioned her about Casa Di Moda, and she forgot about the restaurant's outrageous prices and chatted excitedly about her job and her colleagues. "I feel fortunate to be at Casa Di Moda," Zoe said, speaking from her heart. "Every company has its issues, and some days are better than others, but I'm happy at the fashion house and I wouldn't want to work anywhere else."

"What are your long-term plans? How much longer do you plan to live in Milan?"

"I don't know." Zoe took a piece of garlic bread from the basket, and tasted it. It was warm and moist, and she was so hungry she quickly finished it. "I miss my family. It's hard being away from them, especially during the holidays, but I've always dreamed of living and working abroad. I'm not ready to leave Milan just yet."

The waiter arrived with the second course, placed everything on the table, then left.

Zoe picked up her fork and tasted the squid Bolognese, savored the unique flavors tickling her taste buds. The appetizer was packed with so many spices Zoe pressed her eyes shut and moaned in appreciation.

"If you met the right guy, would you consider living in Milan permanently?"

"I don't know. It's hard to say. Italy's a long way from home."

Romeo shook his head. "Not if you have a private jet at your disposal."

"You're *so* right. What was I thinking? I'll tell Aurora and Davide to have their Boeing 727 ready for Monday." Zoe snapped her fingers. "Oh shucks, I forgot they don't have one."

"I do. Anytime you want to use it, just ask. *Il mio getto è vostro jet.*"

Zoe raised an eyebrow. *My jet is your jet? He can't be serious!* Convinced he was teasing her, she picked up her glass and took a sip. The fruity liquid took the edge off her nerves, helped her to relax even though Romeo was gazing at her intently.

"What about you?" she asked, deciding it was his turn to be in the hot seat. "Have you always wanted to be an investment banker, or did your parents encourage your career path?"

"When I was a kid my dream was to become a professional tap dancer, just like my idol, Gregory Hines. But my father threatened to disown me if I didn't get my MBA, so I gave it up."

"You can tap-dance? No way! Are you any good?"

Nodding, he wiped his mouth with his napkin, then dropped it on his empty salad bowl. "Of course I was good. I studied tap for several years. My instructor said I had raw, natural talent. I wanted to move to the States to study at the University of the Arts in the City of Brotherly Love. It's one of the most prestigious dance schools in the world..."

"I don't believe you. You're pulling my leg."

Romeo stood. "Normally, I don't tap-dance to slow songs, but what the heck. There's a first time for everything, so here goes."

Intrigued, Zoe put down her fork and stared at him intently. *What is he doing?*

Tapping his feet in rhythm to the music, he lifted his leg high in the air and tapped the ball of his foot against the floor. Romeo rocked back and forth, bouncing from one leg to the next, swinging and shuffling his long limbs. He swung his arms in time to the beat, and watching him make music with his feet excited her. He moved with such ease and confidence, Zoe was mesmerized, couldn't take her eyes off him. The pianist finished playing "The Little Drummer Boy," and Romeo struck a pose—head cocked, arms crossed, eyebrows raised. Forgetting she was at an upscale restaurant and not a sporting event, Zoe surged to her feet, cheering at the top of her lungs. "Romeo, that was incredible!" she praised, blown away by his impromptu performance. "You come alive when you tap-dance. It's amazing to see."

Returning to the table, Romeo took his seat, grabbed his glass and took a sip of his ice water. "I haven't danced in years, but that was a lot of fun. It brought back good memories."

"How did you learn to dance like that?"

"Fred Astaire. My mom used to watch his movies when I was a kid, and to make her laugh, I'd try to imitate his moves." He wore a twisted smile. "My mom thought I had talent and enrolled me in dance classes. Everything was great until my dad found out."

Zoe leaned forward in her seat, eager to hear more.

"He told me I needed to be 'a man,' and that I'd never make it as a tap dancer, so I got my business degree at the University of Milan, and my MBA in international business a couple years later."

"Do you regret not pursuing your dream of being a tap dancer?"

His jaw clenched, but he spoke in a calm voice. "Life's too short for regrets."

"I know, I know, life's about closing deals, making money and wooing clients," she quipped, quoting him verbatim. "But do you wish you had done things differently? Do you regret not following in the footsteps of your childhood idol, Gregory Hines?"

Silence fell across the table. It lasted so long, Zoe feared Romeo was upset with her.

"Honestly, I don't know. I love what I do, and I'm good at it. Most importantly, my dad is proud of me and my success. In the Italian culture, pleasing your parents is everything, and even though my old man was hard on me, I never wanted to disappoint him."

A grim expression covered his face as he spoke about his tense relationship with his father and his tumultuous childhood. Zoe's heart ached for him. She'd been raised in a loving, supportive home with parents who praised her accomplishments. Thanks to her mom and dad, she was living her dreams. Listening to Romeo talk about his background and the stress of growing up in a high-profile family, Zoe was more convinced than ever that Lizabeth had lied to the tabloids about him. She felt guilty for giving Romeo a hard time when they first met.

Zoe's thoughts returned to that fateful November morning, and she cringed. She of all people should have known better than to judge a book by its cover. Because of her dark skin and kinky hair, people assumed she was an uneducated African immigrant, often treating her with disdain. But once she spoke Italian, they sang another tune. Meeting Romeo had taught her a valuable lesson. Everyone deserved a fair shake—even dangerously handsome playboys.

Every few minutes, the waitstaff would arrive with another expertly prepared dish and their conversation would be put on hold. Dining at La Piastra Calda wasn't about the food, it was about the ambience, and Zoe enjoyed it all. Eating at the celebrity hot spot was a thrilling, exciting event, and Zoe couldn't wait to tell her sister all about her dream date with Romeo.

"Have you ever been engaged?" Romeo asked, leaning back comfortably in his chair.

Heat burned her cheeks, and her throat closed up, but she spoke in a calm voice.

"Once, but it didn't work out. He threatened to dump me if I traveled to Europe for the summer, so I broke things off." Zoe confided in him about her past relationships, was open and honest about the mistakes she'd made with her first love and her burning desire to get married and have children. She tried to gauge Romeo's mood, to figure out if her confession had turned him off, but he was a hard man to read and wore a blank expression on his face.

"I don't know if I'll ever get married or have kids," he said, shrugging his shoulder.

"But you were engaged for over a year. What happened to change your mind?"

"I proposed because it seemed like the right thing to do at the time, but my heart wasn't in it." Sadness filled his eyes, and he spoke in a somber tone. "I don't think Lizabeth was ready for marriage, either. The only thing she seemed committed to was spending my money."

They sat in silence for several seconds.

"From the moment we met, I was completely and utterly captivated by you…"

Moved by the sincerity of his voice, Zoe leaned forward in her chair, desperate to hear more.

"The more time we spend together, the more I desire you," Romeo confessed, intertwining his fingers with hers. "To be honest, these days I can't think of anything *but* you…"

Zoe's mouth dried. It was hard to breathe, to think straight when Romeo was gazing deep in her eyes and caressing her hands. Questions about the future rose in her mind, but it felt like her lips were glued together, and she couldn't pry them apart.

The waitress arrived with the final course, and Zoe had never been more relieved to see anyone in her life. The tension in the air made her temperature climb, her palms sweat, and when the lights dimmed Zoe wondered what other surprises Romeo had up his sleeve. Their conversation was getting intense, his hands too close for comfort, and if he licked his lips one more time, *he* was going to be dessert.

"We'll need to leave in the next thirty minutes to be on time for the concert."

Zoe snatched her purse off the table and rose to her feet. "Why wait? Let's go now."

"*Someone's* anxious to see Il Divo," Romeo teased.

"Damn skippy! I've been looking forward to tonight for weeks."

"Is that why you agreed to be my date? Because you have the hots for the male quartet?"

Zoe flashed an innocent smile. "I'll never tell."

Zoe sat beside Romeo in the Teatro degli Arcimboldi staring at Il Divo as they sang the last song of their three-hour concert. Mesmerized by the sound of their melodic voices, she closed her eyes and settled back comfortably in her cushy seat. The quartet was so talented, and their voices were so soulful, Zoe got goose bumps. It was an outstanding show, hands down the best concert she'd ever been to, and their heartfelt rendition of the classic Christmas song moved her to tears. Seasoned performers who'd traveled all over the world thrilling fans for years, they sang in Spanish, English and Italian, and wowed the audience with their stellar vocals and dance moves.

Applause erupted across the auditorium. Dumping her shawl on her seat, Zoe stood and cupped her hands around her mouth. She shouted louder than anyone, whistled and cheered as the quartet waved to their fans, then marched off the stage in single file.

"What do you think?" Romeo asked with a lopsided grin, hugging her to his side. "Did I get ripped off, or were our front-row seats worth every penny?"

Overcome with happiness, Zoe rested her head on his shoulder and snuggled against him. Her heart was full, bursting with joy, and she reveled in the moment and how incredible it felt being wrapped up in his arms. "Romeo, thank you for an incredible evening…"

His aftershave washed over her, derailing her thoughts, and seconds passed before she regained the use of her tongue. The oh-so-sexy tycoon was her weakness, the only man she'd ever met who made her want her to break all of the rules. It was a challenge to keep her wits about her when all she could think about was making love to him.

"This is going to go down as one of the best dates I've ever had."

"There's still more to come."

Her body tensed, and the smile slid off her face.

"Zoe, baby, relax. It's not what you think. I have a surprise for you."

Relief flooded her body, and Zoe moved toward Romeo instead of away from him. "Another one? Don't you think you've done enough? You've been spoiling me since you picked me up from my apartment. I don't think my heart can handle any more surprises tonight."

Fans streamed up the aisles to the marked exits, chatting and giggling, and Zoe wondered if she looked as exuberant as they did. Vibrating with excitement, she couldn't wait to upload her pictures of the concert on her social media sites. She knew her girlfriends in the States would be green with envy when she told them about her wonderful, magical night with Romeo.

"I've arranged for you to meet Il Divo."

"Sure you did, and I'm twenty-one!" Zoe joked.

"Baby, I'm serious. My publicist knows their manager, and she arranged everything."

Zoe stopped laughing. "Come again?"

"You'll meet Il Divo, take pictures with them and receive a swag bag filled with supercool autographed merchandise."

Before Zoe could respond, a redhead in a shapeless black gown appeared in the aisle, clutching a metal clipboard to her chest. "You must be Romeo."

"Guilty as charged," he said with a boyish smile.

"It's a pleasure to finally meet you. Giuseppe talks

about you all the time, but don't worry, I never believe anything he says."

Chuckling, he draped an arm around Zoe's waist and hugged her to his side. "Thank you so much for the meet-and-greet passes, Anna-Marie. My girlfriend is a huge Il Divo fan, and she's so excited to meet them, her hands are shaking."

Not just my hands. I'm shaking all over! Perspiration wet Zoe's forehead and trickled down the back of her designer dress. She'd never fainted before and didn't know what the signs and symptoms were, but her skin was clammy, and her head was spinning so fast Zoe feared she'd drop to the floor. Thankfully, Romeo was at her side. He gave her a reassuring smile, and the butterflies in her stomach vanished.

"Right this way. The guys are excited to meet you, so follow me to their greenroom."

The tour manager took them onstage, past the black velvet curtains and down a long, narrow corridor swarming with lighting technicians, sound engineers, service staff and suit-clad men in designer sunglasses who looked important. The air held the faint scent of roses and cigar smoke, and Zoe could hear jazz music playing in the distance. They followed the redhead into a spacious room filled with scrumptious sofas and armchairs, stained-glass windows, and the largest fish tank Zoe had ever seen. And there, standing at the bar, was her favorite group of all time. Blown away, in such a state of shock she couldn't speak, all Zoe could do was smile and nod. One by one, they hugged her and kissed her on each cheek. She felt like a ninny for clamming up and was grateful Romeo talked and cracked jokes with the group. The meet and greet was a blur, and although Zoe only said a few words, it was one of the coolest things that had happened to her since moving to Milan. They took pictures with the group, and Zoe beamed when the leader sing gave her an autographed gift bag filled with Il Divo merchandise.

"How was that?" Romeo asked as they exited the auditorium through the staff entrance. "Was the meet and greet with Il Divo everything you'd thought it would be?"

Zoe wore a sheepish smile. "Yes, but I wish I hadn't clammed up in the greenroom."

"You met your all-time favorite group. It could happen to anyone."

Taking his car keys out of his pocket, he disabled the alarm and unlocked the doors.

"I feel like such a tool," Zoe confessed, dropping her face in her hands. Pressing her eyes shut, she relived her ten-minute visit to the greenroom over and over again in her mind. "It was my chance to tell Il Divo how much I love their music, and I blew it."

Romeo opened the passenger-side door, then rubbed her bent shoulders. "You're wrong. It was obvious to everyone in the room how much you admire them, so quit beating yourself up."

Raising her head, she looked him straight in the eye, a girlish smile curling her lips.

"Is it obvious how much I appreciate you and everything you did tonight?"

Zoe draped her arms around his neck. To show Romeo how she felt about him, she closed her eyes and brushed her lips against his mouth. In that moment, standing in the middle of the Teatro degli Arcimboldi parking lot kissing her gorgeous date, Zoe had a change of heart. She wasn't going to sleep in the guest cottage at Romeo's villa. They were going to make love in his master suite, and Zoe could hardly wait.

Chapter 16

On Saturday morning, Zoe emerged from the en suite bathroom in the guest bedroom of the lavish Morretti villa feeling relaxed and carefree, even though she'd screwed up last night. *So much for a passionate night of lovemaking*, she thought, plopping down on the canopy bed to lotion her body with shea butter. She'd fallen asleep during the forty-five-minute drive to the Morretti estate. Zoe was so tired when they'd finally arrived, Romeo had to help her inside to the guest bedroom.

All wasn't lost, Zoe decided, glancing at the bronze clock on the marble end table. If she hurried, she could have everything ready by the time Romeo finished working out. A creature of habit who never skipped his morning workout, she'd bet he was already running on the treadmill or lifting weights in his home gym.

Standing, Zoe pulled on a mauve off-the-shoulder sweater and denim jeans. To make it up to Romeo for dozing off, she was going down to the kitchen to make him a breakfast fit for a king. She'd woken up an hour earlier thinking about Romeo and the Il Divo concert. Eager to tell her friends about their romantic date, she'd found her cell phone in her purse and switched it on. But it didn't work. In her haste to leave the apartment yesterday, Zoe had forgotten to pack her cell phone charger, but decided not to fret about it. She was always preaching to Romeo to take a break from his electronic devices, and it was time she took her own advice.

To clear her head, she'd treated herself to a long, luxurious bubble bath, but now that Zoe was dressed and her hair and makeup were done, she was anxious to start cooking. She put on her wedge sandals, threw open the bedroom door and hurried down the hall.

Sunlight spilled through arched windows, brightening the villa. It was surrounded by leafy trees, a vibrant landscaped garden and rolling hills, and as Zoe admired her elegant surroundings, her eyes widened. Decorated in marble and glass, with designer furniture, bejeweled chandeliers and hardwood floors so shiny she could see her reflection, she noted the twelve-bedroom villa had an Italian Renaissance ambience and more amenities than a five-star hotel.

Frowning, Zoe stopped and slanted her head to the right. She heard voices. Laughter. Someone speaking in rapid-fire Italian. She glanced around the second floor, but she didn't see anyone. Realizing the noise was coming from the end of the hall, she moved to the closed door, gripped the handle and creaked it open.

A smile warmed her mouth. Entering the lavish bedroom, which was decorated with plush carpet, scrumptious leather furniture, decorative floor lamps and an entertainment unit filled with every electronic known to man, Zoe spotted Romeo standing on the balcony talking on his cell through his earpiece and swallowed a moan. Holy heavens! What a sinfully sexy profile! Bare-chested, in nothing but a pair of black boxer briefs that fit his physique like a second skin, he reminded her of a swimsuit model. He had broad shoulders, a great butt and a pair of long, toned legs. Desire rippled across her skin.

Romeo ended his call, but as he turned away from the balcony, Zoe noticed he had a pill bottle in his right hand and a miniature needle in the other. A gasp rose in her throat, and she cupped a hand over her mouth. Zoe wanted to leave, but her legs were frozen, and her feet glued to the floor. She wanted to speak, to ask him what was going on, but her mouth didn't work.

Romeo looked up, noticed her standing beside the closet door and turned white. Guilt covered his face. He dumped the needle on the bed, but it was too late.

He reached for her, but she moved backward. For the first time, she noticed the scar on his chest that stretched from his collarbone to the top of his abs.

"Zoe, wait, it's not what you think!"

"I know what I saw. I'm not stupid."

His jaw tensed, but he spoke in a soft, quiet voice. "I have a prescription."

Wanting to be alone, she turned toward the door, anxious to return to the spare bedroom.

Moving fast, Romeo beat her to it, and slid in front of the door. "Zoe, I'm telling the truth. I swear," he said, raising his hand in the air. "Look at the vial. My doctor's name, the address of his clinic and his office number is on the label. Check it out."

The prescription was in Italian, and although Zoe could read it she didn't know what papaverine hydrochloride was, or how to pronounce it. His explanation was plausible, but she still had her doubts. "If what you're telling me is true, then why do you look so guilty?"

"I don't feel guilty." He rubbed a hand along the back of his neck. "I'm embarrassed."

"About what?"

"I wasn't trying to deceive you. I was waiting for the right time to tell you."

"Waiting for the right time to tell me what?"

Romeo looked pale, sounded breathless, unlike his cool, debonair self. "I was going to tell you before things got serious with us…" He trailed off speaking.

"Tell me what? You're talking in circles, Romeo, and I don't understand."

He gestured to the king-size bed draped in black satin, but Zoe didn't move. Couldn't. She was so upset and confused she couldn't think, let alone move, and still wanted to make a break for the door. Taking her hand, Romeo led her over to the love seat in the corner of the spacious room and sat down beside her.

Zoe had a million questions racing through her mind. Romeo owed her an explanation, and although her inner voice was screaming at her to leave, she clasped her hands in her lap and waited for him to explain what the hell was going on.

The air was charged with tension, and nervous energy filled the sun-drenched room.

Zoe didn't know how long they sat there in silence, but her anxiety increased with each passing second. How could something like this happen? Had she missed the signs? Been so smitten with Romeo and flattered by his attention that she'd ignored the obvious? Panic seized her heart. What else was he hiding from her?

"Romeo, talk to me," she pleaded. "Help me understand what's going on."

"I had a heart attack last year."

His words didn't make sense, didn't register in her brain. "But you're only thirty-two and you're healthy, fit and strong. How is that possible?"

"I've been asking myself the same thing for the past sixteen months, but I still don't have the answers, and neither does my medical team…"

Her stomach growled for food, but Zoe ignored her hunger pangs and listened to Romeo's shocking story. They were sitting side by side on the couch, but he spoke in such a quiet voice, Zoe had to strain to hear him. A muscle flickered in his jaw, and anger seeped from his pores as he opened up to her about collapsing in his home office one morning in August. He was angry at his body for failing him, for letting him down, and Zoe didn't know what to say to comfort him. Romeo praised his publicist Giuseppe Del Piero not only for saving his life, but for keeping his medical condition out of the media.

"If Giuseppe hadn't stopped by my penthouse to check on me, I wouldn't be here."

"Thank God he did," Zoe whispered, resting a hand on his leg. Romeo was a survivor, a fighter, and she'd never respected him more. He shared details about the weeks he'd spent at the private hospital and the exceptional care and support he'd received from the doctors and nurses there, but what impressed Zoe most was how his family had rallied around him. They'd dropped everything to be at his side, had flown in from all around the world to nurse him back to health, and he appreciated the sacrifices they'd made.

"How do you feel now? Have the doctors given you a clean bill of health?"

For the first time since she'd entered his room, Romeo smiled. "Yes, they have."

Perspiration dotted her forehead and clung to her sweater, but she sighed in relief.

"I take a blood thinner three times a day and give myself an injection to help lower my blood pressure so my heart and arteries can function," he explained, rubbing his eyes with the back of his hand. "I've been taking the medication since I was discharged from the hospital. I hate giving myself injections, but if I want to prevent another trip to the emergency room, I have no choice. I'll need to be on the medication for the rest of my life."

"Romeo, your story is so moving, it gave me chills," Zoe confessed. "You should share it with others. In doing so, you could save a lot of lives."

He shook his head. "I change lives by donating to charity, and that's more than enough. I'm a private person, and I don't want the whole world knowing my business."

"I know a clinical physiologist who runs a support group for people who've survived—"

"No." His voice was firm. "It's not for me. I don't want my clients or my staff to know I had a heart attack. It's humiliating, and I don't want them to think less of me."

"No one will think less of you. You're a brave and courageous man who beat the odds."

His cell phone rang, and his gaze darted around the room. Zoe wanted to keep talking, to hear more about Romeo's fears, and hoped he'd let the call go to voice mail. He did, and she smiled her thanks. Resting her head on his shoulder, she snuggled against him. She enjoyed the warmth of his touch, and his scent relaxed her.

"Thanks for sharing your story with me. It means a lot to me."

Romeo cleared his throat, then coughed into his fist. "I have one more thing to tell you."

Zoe sat up. Her body tensed, and her stomach curled into a knot.

"The doctors did a battery of tests on me, and they discovered that I'm genetically predisposed to having high blood pressure and heart failure," he explained, a pained expression on his face. "If I had children there's a fifty percent chance I could pass it on to them."

Filled with sympathy, she wore a sad smile. "Is that why you don't want to get married or have kids? Because you had a heart attack?"

"It wouldn't be fair to pass my genetic condition on to an innocent child." Exhaling deeply, he raked a hand through his short, tousled hair. "What if it happens again? What if I collapse on my wedding day? Or drop dead at my son's or daughter's youth football game?"

She cupped his face in her palms, forcing him to look right at her. "Romeo, you can't live your life in fear," she said in a soothing voice, desperate to reach him with her words. "Try not to dwell on your condition or worry about the future. Make the most of each day, and enjoy the beauty of every single moment."

Romeo covered her hand with his own and kissed her palm. "You're only thirty-two," he teased, cocking an eyebrow. "How did you become so wise at such a young age?"

"My grandmother was hospitalized in life-threatening condition a few days after I graduated from Long Island University, and one of the last things I remember her telling me was to live each day as if it were my last, because tomorrow wasn't guaranteed."

"Is that why you traveled abroad? Because you wanted an adventure?"

"Yes, and to gain some self-confidence and independence. Leaving home and everything that was familiar to me was a tough decision to make, and it cost me my college sweetheart, but if I had to do it all over again I'd make the same choice."

"One man's failure is another man's success," Romeo said with a lopsided grin.

"You are *so* wise. Do you have any other pearls of wisdom, oh smart one?"

"Obey all traffic laws. If you don't, you could get hurt."

Outraged by his joke, Zoe snatched a throw cushion off the sofa and hit him in the shoulder. "You're terrible!" she shouted, striking him again. "You should be in prison for reckless driving instead of sitting here making fun of me—"

Standing, Romeo scooped Zoe up in his arms, spun her around the room, then dropped her on the bed. It happened fast, catching her off guard, and she never saw it coming. He jumped on top of her, and Zoe burst out laughing. "You're a madman!"

"I've had enough of your mouth for one day," he growled, pinning her arms above her head, mischief glimmering in his eyes. "What am I going to do with you?"

Aroused by the huskiness of his voice and the feel of his erection against her thigh, Zoe pressed her lips to his chin, his collarbone, then along the faint scar on his chest. "I could think of a couple things, Diavolo Sexy, but you'd have to strip first."

"Last night when I picked you up from your apartment you said you weren't ready for a sexual relationship. What happened to change your mind?"

Zoe inhaled sharply. Romeo had serious baggage, and if Casa Di Moda folded in the new year, she'd be leaving Milan for good, but none of that mattered. The truth was she desired him, wanted him and was tired of fighting their attraction. Couldn't do it any longer. Zoe loved to be touched, and kissed, and held, and Romeo wasn't shy about showing his feelings. Didn't care who was around or who was watching. Zoe felt beautiful and desirable in his arms.

"Yesterday, I was scared of you hurting me by hooking up with your ex, but I'm not afraid anymore. I'm going to take my grandmother's advice and live life to the fullest, without fear."

Romeo spoke to her in Italian.

His words made her heart soft. *Beautiful, wise and sexy? Damn, you are the total package, and I'm glad you're mine, all mine.* Encouraged, Zoe nibbled his bottom lip. "We're going to make love, and it's going to be sexy and passionate and freaky."

A deep, throaty chuckle erupted from his mouth. "You are *such* a nasty woman."

Zoe winked. "Thanks, I'll take that as a compliment."

"As you should."

He slipped a hand under her bottom, cupped and massaged her ass through her jeans.

"It's obvious you're a woman of many talents, and I want to experience them all."

Draping her arms around his neck, she licked the rim of his ear with her tongue and rubbed her hips against his crotch. "Do you have protection?"

Sitting up, Romeo yanked open the top drawer of the end table beside the bed. He rummaged around for several seconds, mumbling to himself in Italian. Grinning from ear to ear, he raised his fist triumphantly in the air. "I found one!" he shouted, diving on top of her. "Buckle up, baby. I'm going to rock your world."

Laughing and kissing, they rolled around on the bed, holding each other close. Zoe was floating on air, so giddy with excitement as thoughts of making love to Romeo consumed her mind. His touch was exhilarating and thrilled every inch of her body. His hands were her downfall, her undoing. As he caressed and stroked her skin, she tingled all over.

The strangest thing happened. An intense flood of pleasure inundated every inch of her body, and a moan fell from her lips. Zoe knew it couldn't be the alcohol she'd had last night at dinner that made her feel bold but the intoxicating pleasure of his kiss. Shedding her clothes, she climbed onto Romeo's lap, and shoved him down on the bed. Eager to please, she trailed kisses along his neck. Sucked a nipple into her mouth. Rubbed his shoulders. Whispered dirty words into his ear. Took off his boxer briefs and tossed them on the floor. Seized his shaft in her hands. Watched with wide eyes and a dry mouth as it doubled in size. It was long and thick, and stroking his package excited her. Aroused her. Made her want to suck it, lick it.

Embarrassed, Zoe closed her gaping mouth. She grabbed the gold packet off the bed, opened it and rolled the condom onto Romeo's erection. Turning around so she was facing his feet, Zoe lowered her head to his lap and kissed the tip of his erection. In that moment, pleasing Romeo was all that mattered, all she cared about, and she wanted nothing more than to make him smile. Last night, he'd spent thousands of dollars on her, had spoiled her silly from the moment he'd picked her up from her apartment, and now it was her opportunity to return the favor. She wanted to show Romeo how much she desired him, craved him, and used her tongue as an instrument of pleasure.

"Zoe, you're amazing," he said in a drowsy voice, burying his hands in her hair. "Baby, keep doing what you're doing... Don't stop... Your technique is incredible..."

Encouraged by his praise, she sucked his shaft, pressed kisses along his inner thigh and licked the trail between his legs. Romeo buried his face in her butt cheeks, surprising

her, and feeling his tongue against her fleshy lips caused
Zoe to moan. To grip the designer bedsheets.

Her breathing was shallow and her mouth was dry, but
Zoe was ready for the main event. Was desperate to feel
him inside her. Sunlight shone through the windows and
the balcony doors were wide open, but Zoe didn't care,
refused to let her doubts and insecurities ruin the mood.
It didn't matter that she didn't have the perfect body or
that she wasn't a size four. Romeo was staring at her, and
love shone bright in his eyes. His desire to please her was
evident in his kiss, his caress, and the heartfelt words he
whispered against her lips.

Careful not to lose her balance, Zoe spun around and
positioned herself on his erection, but this time she had
the confidence of a burlesque dancer on a Las Vegas stage.

In perfect sync, as if they'd known each other years,
rather than a few weeks, they moved together as one body.
His fingers were in her hair, playing with her braids, then
tweaking her nipples and stroking her hips. Zoe pressed
her eyes shut, tried to savor every feeling, every emotion,
every sensation flowing through her.

Kissing her lips, Romeo praised her in Italian.

Tossing her head back, Zoe erupted in laughter as his
words played in her mind. *I love everything about you…
your inner strength, your zest for life, your keen mind,
and most importantly, how fantastic your ass looks in a
pair of tight blue jeans!* Their lovemaking was wild and
intense, filled with playful and intimate moments, and Zoe
loved everything about it. Mostly the deliciously sexy man
thrusting his hips energetically beneath her.

Fireworks exploded inside her, one after another, with
no end in sight. She rocked against Romeo, hard and fast,
rode him like a prizewinning Thoroughbred. Couldn't stop
even if she wanted to. Clutching his shoulders, she moved

faster, pumped her legs harder, swiveled her hips in tight circles. He traced his tongue around her nipples, nipping with his teeth, and an orgasm with the force of a category three hurricane knocked her over and flat on her back.

"Now it's my turn." Stretching out over her, Romeo showered her face with kisses. He didn't stop there. A wicked grin worked its way onto his mouth as he thrust his erection between her legs. He pressed his lips against her neck, mashed her breasts together, squeezed her bottom, eagerly licking and sucking her earlobe. Zoe felt high, on top of the world, and wanted to experience the mind-blowing rush of having another orgasm. To make it happen, she clamped her legs around his waist and dug her nails into his butt cheeks, urging him deep inside her. Pumping his hips, he moved his body in an erotic way.

"Baby, I'm coming," she panted, bucking against him. *"Più forte! Più veloce! Sì!"*

He obliged. His thrust becoming faster, harder, he gripped her hips, then hiked her legs in the air and kissed her inner thigh. Her orgasm must have triggered his own, because his head fell forward and he released a deep, guttural groan.

Sweat coursed down his forehead and dripped from his muscled body. His breathing was so shallow, Zoe feared he'd overexerted himself and worried about his heart condition. "Baby, are you okay? I don't want you to overdo it or push yourself too hard. We have the rest of the weekend to make love," she pointed out. "Maybe we should stop and take a break."

"Hell no." He wore a lopsided grin. "I'm great. Couldn't be better. Isn't it obvious?"

Giggling, she brushed her lips against the hollow of his throat. To please him, Zoe flicked his nipple with her tongue, then sucked it into her mouth. His body tensed, going rigid and stiff. Zoe wanted to tell Romeo she loved him and wanted a future together, but her tongue was stuck to the roof of her mouth.

Rolling onto his side, he gathered her in his arms and blew out a deep breath. "You're incredible, you know that?" Romeo kissed her forehead. "If I'd known you were a sex goddess, I would have invited you to spend the weekend at my family villa the day we met!"

Zoe screamed with laughter. His toothy smile and playful banter made her crack up, and discussing what they enjoyed most about their lovemaking helped to strengthen their bond.

"Baby, sorry about this morning. I was going to get up early and make you breakfast, but Giuseppe called and I got sidetracked," he explained, holding her close to his chest. "You must be starving. What do you want for breakfast?"

"You *are* my breakfast, and if you think you can hang, I'd like some more."

In a blink, Romeo maneuvered Zoe onto her stomach, straddled her back and slapped her ass. Once, twice, three mind-blowing times. Unable to control herself, she moaned beneath him, salivating as she envisioned his erection between her legs.

"Keep talking smack, and I'll take you over my knee."

"Please do." Wearing a cheeky smile, she glanced over her shoulder and poked her butt in the air. "I told you things were going to get freaky, and I meant it, so show me what you got."

Romeo brushed his lips against her ear. "With pleasure."

Chapter 17

"We're here," the taxi driver announced. "Casa Di Moda fashion house, right, Miss?"

Zoe wanted to finish journaling about her romantic weekend with Romeo, but she dropped her notebook in her workbag, took out her wallet and paid the driver. "Yes. Thanks."

The cab was parked in front of Casa Di Moda, but there were so many people gathered on the sidewalk that Zoe couldn't open the passenger-side door. *What in the world?* she thought, peering out the window at the young, well-dressed crowd camped out at the fashion house bright and early on Monday morning. Women were waving at her and shouting in Italian, but Zoe didn't understand what they were saying. Couldn't make sense of what was going on. *Are we doing a Christmas promotion someone forgot to tell me about? A free giveaway, perhaps?*

The noise was deafening, so loud, Zoe could feel a

headache forming in her temples. If she'd known Casa Di Moda was a zoo she never would have left the comfort of Romeo's arms, and wondered if it was too late to return to the Morretti family villa. He was working from home today, and although he'd asked her to stay and keep him company, she'd kissed him goodbye and hurried to the waiting taxicab parked outside the villa. She had no choice. The Christmas Wonderland Ball was in six days, and there was so much to do before the black-tie event that Zoe had three to-do lists on her office desk. Aurora was counting on her to not only promote the holiday collection, but to also persuade her contacts in the fashion world to do a feature cover story on Casa Di Moda. Zoe didn't want to let her boss down.

Mumbling under his breath, the heavyset cab driver jumped out of driver's seat and marched around the hood of the white compact car. Waving his hands in the air, as if he were swatting a bee, he shouted at the crowd to get out of his way, then yanked open the back door.

Grateful for his help, Zoe tipped the driver and shouldered her way through the crowd. Snowflakes fell from the sky, and the crisp wind whipped her hair around her face.

"It's her! Zoe Smith! Romeo Morretti's new lady love!"

"How does it feel to be dating the most eligible bachelor in Milan?"

"Did you have fun at the Morretti family villa this weekend?"

Paralyzed with shock, Zoe froze. She could feel the blood drain from her body. Cameras flashed in her eyes, temporarily blinding her, as reporters hurled personal questions at her. *What the hell? How do they know I spent the weekend with Romeo? I never told anyone our plans, not even Jiovanni, and he's my best friend!* Willing her legs to move, she shielded her face with her hands and dashed toward the front doors.

"Welcome to Casa Di Moda, everyone! Please feel free to come inside for a tour. You can take as many pictures as you want, and interview Zoe Smith as well..."

Like hell they can! Brushing past Aurora, who looked thrilled to see the crowd of entertainment reporters and paparazzi jostling for position on the cobblestoned sidewalk, Zoe marched into the lobby, panting like a marathon runner. Decorated with tinsel, garland and Christmas-themed lanterns, the space looked festive and bright. Glass jars of different heights and shapes were filled with colorful ornaments, and the unique window display was eye-catching. The air smelled of gingerbread cookies and apple cider, but Zoe was too upset to eat and didn't want to hang out with her colleagues in the staff room.

Entering the reception area, Zoe glanced nervously around the room. There were boxes and garment bags everywhere, interns were running in every direction clutching pink invoices in their hands, deliverymen were loading their carts, and telephones rang off the hook.

"Good morning, Zoe," greeted the receptionist. "Looking great as usual. Cute dress."

"Thanks. What's going on? There's stuff everywhere," she said, gesturing to the clothes and shoes piled high on the velvet couch. "Are we doing another an online sale?"

Beaming, Aurora marched into the room chatting a mile a minute. "You don't know?"

"Don't know what?"

"Have you been living under a rock the past forty-eight hours?"

"No, my cell's dead, and I forgot my tablet in my office on Friday night," she explained. "Now, could someone tell me what's going on, because I'm clueless."

"Zoe, you broke the internet!" Aurora shrieked. "I'm so happy I could scream!"

Could scream, Zoe thought, rubbing her ears to soothe the pain. *You* just *did.*

"MilanoFashionista.com posted pictures of you and Romeo at the Il Divo concert on their social media pages on Friday night, and an hour later the Casa Di Moda website crashed."

There was no music playing, but Aurora danced around the decorative, glass table.

Zoe's cheeks burned. "There are pictures of me and Romeo online?" she croaked, a burning sensation spreading through her chest. "*Please* tell me you're joking."

Aurora took her cell out of the back pocket of her plaid high-waisted pants, swiped her finger across the screen and raised her iPhone in the air. "See for yourself."

Feeling as if her eyes were bugging out of her head, Zoe cupped a hand over her gaping mouth. There were pictures of her and Romeo eating dinner at La Piastra Calda, slow dancing at the Il Divo concert and French kissing in front of his sports car. Why didn't she realize they were being followed? How come she didn't notice paparazzi snapping pictures?

That's because you were too busy playing tonsil hockey with Romeo! teased her inner voice. *If you had kept things PG instead of pouncing on him, you wouldn't be in this mess now.*

Zoe plucked Aurora's cell out of her hand and accessed the Internet. To her surprise, the pictures were everywhere—on gossip blogs, the local newspapers, social media outlets—and seeing them filled her with shame. Not because she regretted kissing Romeo, but because she knew when he saw the photographs he'd be pissed. The last thing Zoe wanted to do was upset him. He had enough on his plate with the problems he was having at work, and she didn't want to add to his stress. Last night in bed, after making love, he'd opened up to her about his meeting with police detectives, and even though Zoe knew nothing about investment banking or money laundering, she'd encouraged him to do the right thing, no matter what. Moved by his honesty, she'd confided in him about things she'd never shared with anyone, not even her closest friends. Romeo asked her to spend Christmas Day with him, and tears had filled her eyes. Zoe was nervous about meeting his loved ones, especially since they'd only been dating for a few weeks, but since spending the day with the Morretti family beat eating a frozen dinner alone in her apartment, she'd enthusiastically agreed.

"We sold out of everything from the holiday Christmas line, and all of our boutiques reported increased sales and foot traffic. Isn't that great? We're *finally* on top where we belong!"

Zoe swallowed hard. On one hand, she was thrilled that the holiday line was a hit with consumers, but on the other hand, she was upset that someone had taken pictures of her and Romeo and posted them online. A lump formed in her throat. What would he think when he saw the photographs? Would he be disappointed that their secret was out? Would he blame her?

"I haven't told you the best part," Aurora said, her eyes wild with excitement.

Zoe braced herself for more bad news, but she couldn't think of anything worse than being secretly photographed. Burning up, she took off her green military-style jacket and draped it over her forearm. All she could think about was Romeo. Zoe wanted to call him, but since she didn't want her colleagues listening in on their conversation, she decided to wait until she got to her office to ring his cell.

"According to *Celebrity Patella* you and Romeo are Milan's newest 'it' couple, and they've nicknamed you RoZo. Cute, huh?" Aurora threw her hands around Zoe and rocked her vigorously from side to side. "I'm so happy for me! I mean, you. I'm so happy for *you*."

It was time to leave. If she didn't, Aurora would squeeze her for the rest of the morning, and she didn't want to miss her ten o'clock phone interview with *Haute Couture*. The editor was a good friend, and Zoe was looking forward to promoting Casa Di Moda's holiday line on the popular blog. Add to that, she had calls to return, press releases to write, emails to answer and a website to update. Desperate to escape her boss's clutches, she broke free of Aurora's tight, suffocating hold and moved as fast as her suede booties could take her. "I'll see you later."

On top of the world, Aurora continued speaking, chatting excitedly in Italian.

A scowl curled her lips. *Seize the moment?* Zoe repeated. *But I don't want to date Romeo in the public eye. It could ruin our relationship, and we have the most amazing bond!* Increasing her pace, she shot across the lobby, could feel her heart racing as she ran for her life.

Entering her office, Zoe dumped her handbag on her armchair, then plugged her cell into the charger. It had been one hell of a morning, and she was grateful for a few minutes of peace and quiet, but the moment Zoe sat down at her mesh armchair, her desk phone rang. She considered letting the call go to voice mail, but she was waiting to hear back from the regional manager of the Casa Di Moda boutiques in Venice about running a New Year's Eve makeover contest and snatched the receiver off the cradle. "Good morning, Zoe Smith."

"How do you do it?"

Her heart leaped inside her chest. "Do what, Romeo?"

"Make me feel better just by hearing your beautiful voice."

Coiling the phone cord around her index finger, Zoe tried to calm her nerves by taking a deep breath and slowly pushing it out her mouth. "I'm glad you're still in a good mood. I was worried you'd be mad at me when you saw the photographs of us online."

"At first I was pissed, because those sneaky paparazzi spied on us, but when my cousins and brothers called to congratulate me on dating a Caribbean bombshell, I got over it."

"Are all the men in your family charming and suave? It sure sounds like it."

"Naw, they've got nothing on me," he bragged. "Just call me Mr. Smooth."

Zoe laughed. Relieved that he wasn't upset with her, she sat back comfortably in her chair, crossed her legs and listened as he talked about his eventful morning and his phone conversation with his brother Enrique. "I'm nervous, but also really excited about meeting Enrique and his fiancée, Isabelle, tonight at Dolce Vita. What time should I be ready for dinner?"

"That's why I'm calling. We have to reschedule for next week."

Suddenly his tone was somber, and Zoe feared something was wrong.

"Baby, what is it?" she asked, straightening in her seat. "You sound worried."

"I am. I just heard back from my lawyers, and they strongly advised me to meet with French authorities. To be honest, it was an easy decision to make."

"I'm proud of you for doing the right thing." Zoe wished they were face-to-face instead of chatting on the phone, but she didn't let the distance stop her from speaking from the heart. "Once you meet with French authorities and tell them your story you'll be exonerated. I believe it with every ounce of my being, and Romeo, you should, too."

"Thanks, babe. Your support means everything to me."

Zoe stared at her desk calendar. "When are you leaving? When will you be back?"

"I'm leaving tonight after work, but I'll be back on Saturday afternoon. Just in time to escort you to the Christmas Wonderland Ball," he explained.

"Do you want me to come with you? I want to be there to support you."

"Baby, thanks for the offer, but I know you're busy getting ready for the ball, and I don't want to take you away from work. Besides, Simona's going to be interviewed as well, so we'll fly there together with my lawyers in my private jet."

Nodding, Zoe coiled the phone cord around her index finger. She'd met Simona last week when she'd dropped by Morretti Finance and Investments with lunch for Romeo, and they'd spent a few minutes talking about the weather, their plans for the holidays and their favorite Christmas foods. Simona mentioned that her boyfriend was a trained chef, and Zoe had cheered inwardly. Now she didn't have to worry about the chief operating officer putting the moves on her man.

An intern with dyed red hair appeared in the doorway holding a garment bag in one hand and a coffee mug in the other. "Can I talk to you for a minute?" she whispered, a troubled expression on her face. "It's important, and I don't know who else to ask."

Zoe nodded, then faced the window so the intern couldn't hear what she was saying on the phone. "Romeo, I have to go, but text me when you land in Paris. It doesn't matter how late. I just need to know that you arrived safely."

"Zoe, don't worry. It's a ninety-minute flight from Milan to Paris. I'll be fine."

"I know, humor me, okay?" she said with a laugh. "Have a safe trip."

"Will do. Be good while I'm away."

"I should be telling you the same thing, Mr. Smooth!"

The sound of his throaty chuckle filled the line, tickling her ear and warming her heart. Zoe dropped the receiver in the cradle and marched around her desk to find out what the intern wanted, but she couldn't wipe the smile off her face. Romeo brought out the best in her, made her feel alive, and she adored everything about him, especially his fun-loving personality. It was a challenge, because her thoughts were on Romeo and his upcoming trip to Paris, but Zoe focused intently on what the intern was saying.

"The editor from *Bellezza Moderna* magazine just called," she explained, shifting and shuffling her feet. "She wants us to send over three distinct outfits complete with accessories and shoes for their Valentine's Day issue. I just need someone to look it over before I have everything delivered to her office."

Zoe unzipped the garment bag, noticed the intern had crammed three outfits inside, and spoke in a calm but firm voice. "This is unacceptable. If you send things out haphazardly, the editor of *Bellezza Moderna* will think we don't value the dresses or this company."

The color drained from the intern's face. "I'm sorry. I didn't know. What should I do?"

"Take everything out of the bag and carefully steam each dress," she instructed, pointing to the creases on the strapless burgundy gown. "When you're finished, hang each outfit on a velvet hanger, then spray it with perfume. One outfit per bag, no exceptions."

"Can you help me?" she squeaked. "I'm scared I'm going to make another mistake."

Zoe hesitated, struggled with what to do. She had a lot on her plate, and if she helped the intern she'd be even further behind. In the two years she'd been at Casa Di Moda, she'd done it all: fetched coffee, set up props for photo shoots, grabbed lunch for her boss, and even cleaned up after office parties and industry events. Zoe loved her job and her colleagues, and since she wanted to see the intern succeed, she nodded. "Let's go. I'll teach you."

Walking down the corridor with the intern nipping at her heels, Zoe heard Christmas music playing in the distance, boisterous laughter, smelled coffee and flowers in the air. Spotting Jiovanni at the end of the hallway, she smiled and waved. Swamped at work and busy with Romeo in the evenings, Zoe hadn't seen him in days, but noticed he had a pep in his step as he swaggered toward her and assumed things were going well with his new girlfriend. The intern promised to meet Zoe in the conference room and ducked into the staff washroom.

"Hey, beautiful! How the heck have you been?" he asked, kissing her on each cheek.

"Don't ask. Things have been crazy this week, and with Christmas right around the corner they're only going to get crazier." Zoe blew out a deep breath. Just thinking about everything she had to accomplish in the next six days made her head pound, but she was determined to complete each and every task on her list. "How have you been?"

"Fantastic. I'm one step closer to launching my own clothing line, Designs by Jiovanni, and if everything goes according to plan, I'll be leaving this dump in the new year." A broad smile filled his lips. "Let's do lunch. You can tell me all about your whirlwind romance with Romeo Morretti and your romantic weekend at his villa. You *did* see something besides the inside of his bedroom, right?"

Zoe didn't like him teasing her and punched him in the arm. "That's not funny."

"It is to me!"

"Bye, Jiovanni," she said, stepping past him.

"Lunch is on me. I'll even throw in a cup of pistachio ice cream."

Zoe stopped and glanced over her shoulder. "*Now* you're talking my language. I'm in."

"Cool. I'll meet you in the lobby at noon." Jiovanni took his cell out of the back pocket of his blue jeans, and groaned. "My phone's dead, and I need to snap some pictures of the models in the outfits I'm working on for the spring collection."

"You can use my camera," she said. "It's in my office in my workbag. Go grab it."

"Thanks, Zoe, you're the best."

"I know. I'm the best thing that's ever happened to you!"

"Damn right," Jiovanni said with a laugh. "See you at lunch, Zoe. Don't be late."

Chapter 18

Hundreds of famous names from the world of fashion, entertainment, politics and business descended on one of the oldest castles in Italy on Saturday night for the fifteenth annual Christmas Wonderland Ball. Built in the thirteenth century, the stately brick building with arched windows and picturesque views had a magical, ethereal ambience. Known as the Oscars of Milan, the black-tie event was the most talked-about party of the year, and as Romeo exited the white Rolls-Royce limousine, lights flashed, paparazzi shouted his name, and reporters clutching microphones jockeyed for position on the red carpet.

Celebrities were everywhere, but when Zoe stepped out of the luxury vehicle, the crowd pressed against the metal barricades, cheering uncontrollably. Romeo didn't blame them. Stunning in a feathered burgundy gown with a dramatic train, his girlfriend seized the attention of everyone around them, even the pop stars and Hollywood actors signing autographs. Only Zoe could wear a designer gown and look relaxed and carefree. The press couldn't get enough of her. The more she smiled and waved at the crowd, the louder they chanted her name.

Hearing snickers, Romeo glanced over his shoulder to see what was making the crowd laugh. A British supermodel in a cutout dress, platform shoes and a Mohawk struck a pose. The Christmas Wonderland Ball was by invitation only, but some of the outfits on the red carpet were so outrageous, Romeo felt as if he were at a Comic-Con convention.

"I'm not trying to brag," he whispered, gazing into her eyes. "But you're the best dressed woman here tonight, bellissima, and after the party wraps up, you're mine all mine."

"Not me, *we*," Zoe corrected. "You're so handsome I can't stop staring at you…"

Her words made his chest inflate with pride. To complement Zoe's one-of-a-kind gown, he'd paired his custommade Casa Di Moda tuxedo with a burgundy bow tie, handkerchief and leather shoes. In the limousine during the thirty-minute drive from his villa to the castle, they'd flirted and kissed. Romeo was so hot for Zoe, all he could think about was making love to her. She was the perfect distraction, just what he needed after being interrogated by authorities for three days.

Romeo considered the past seventy-two hours. Initially, he'd been reluctant to hand over his financial records or fly to the City of Lights to meet with authorities, but after talking things over with his attorney, his brothers and Zoe, he'd agreed to the interview. Markos told him not to worry, assured him that everything would be okay, but his gut feeling was that French authorities were out to get him. Through a translator, he'd vehemently defended his name. He told them the truth about his relationship with Julio Mario Domínguez, but they'd accused him of breaking the law for profit. Shocked by the crimes his client had been charged with, Romeo realized he'd never really known the Colombian businessman. He thanked his lucky stars they'd never traveled in the same social circles. The interview was a nightmare, and once authorities told him he was free to go he'd headed straight for the airport. Last night he'd returned to Milan and the first thing he'd done once his jet landed was call Zoe. On his way to his villa, he'd picked her up, and he'd been so happy to see her he'd wrapped her up in his arms, and held her tight.

"When we get back to your place it's on, so don't overdo it on the dance floor tonight." Winking, Zoe reached out and adjusted his silk bow tie. "I have something special planned for you, and you're going to need all your strength."

"RoZo, this way!"

"Smile, RoZo, the camera loves you!"

"How about a kiss? Lay one on her, Morretti. Show the world how it's done!"

Amused by the paparazzi, Romeo shook his head. Discreetly tugging his arm, Zoe raised an eyebrow, as if to ask, "What are you waiting for?" and slowly licked her lips. That was all the encouragement Romeo needed. The air crackled with energy, and adrenaline shot through his veins as their eyes bored into each other. Romeo couldn't stop staring at her lips, could almost taste them, feel them against his. "You asked for it," he warned with a knowing smile.

Tipping his head toward her, he lowered his mouth and devoured her lips. Warm and soft, they were intoxicating, and one kiss wasn't enough. Didn't satisfy him. Left him feeling horny, not satiated. Forgetting they were on the red carpet and not in the privacy of his home, he enjoyed the pleasure of her kiss, her touch, her sweet, feminine scent. His heart swelled, overflowing with love. If Zoe hadn't broken off the kiss and climbed the steps, they never would have made it inside for cocktail hour.

Entering the main floor of the castle, Romeo heard music playing and was surprised to see the Milan Children's Choir singing in front of the ten-foot Christmas tree. They sounded like angels, and seeing their adorable faces warmed his heart. The event was for a worthy cause. Romeo hoped millions of dollars was raised for the money-strapped hospital.

"Wow, I've never seen anything like this. This must be what heaven looks like…"

Over the years, Romeo had attended many Christmas Wonderland Balls, but he'd never paid attention to the decor, so listening to Zoe ooh and aah about the extravagant decorations throughout the castle made him appreciate the beauty of the venue. Satin ribbons and silver ornaments dangled from antique chandeliers. Floral arrangements were filled with amaryllis flowers, pine branches and leaves. The room was full of tea lights, fairy lights and more candles than a Catholic cathedral.

Celebrities streamed into the venue, but Romeo only had eyes for Zoe. Intertwining his fingers with hers, he led her around the room, introducing her to notable and influential guests. Servers wearing top hats and red bow ties held trays filled with champagne, cocktails and hors d'oeuvres. Romeo enjoyed sampling everything they had to offer. Anxious to hear from his attorneys, he'd hadn't eaten anything for lunch, and his stomach was groaning and growling so loud it drowned out the children's choir.

"Do you care for some Basilicata?" a waiter asked in a thick Italian accent.

Zoe frowned, and Romeo nodded to assure her the appetizer was delicious.

"Cod with fried bell peppers," he explained. "Try one. You'll love it."

As he fed Zoe appetizers from off his plate, Romeo spotted his family members sitting at the round table directly in front of the stage. He wiped his mouth with a napkin, put his empty plate on a passing server's tray and led Zoe through the jam-packed reception hall. Intent on reaching his family, Romeo marched briskly toward the stage, but stopped abruptly when Aurora threw her arms around him, hugging him as if she were stranded at sea and he was a flotation device. "Merry Christmas to you, too," he said, staring down at the exuberant designer.

"Event coordinators just told me what you did." Aurora had tears in her eyes and spoke with awe in her voice. "On behalf of everyone at Casa Di Moda, thank you for your incredible generosity. You're a modern-day saint, a dapper one, too!"

Romeo chuckled. Wanting to do something special for Zoe, he'd purchased three dinner tables in her name, and when she saw her colleagues decked out in fancy gowns and shiny tuxedos, she screamed. Romeo loved surprising her and laughed out loud when Zoe jumped into his arms and kissed him hard on the mouth. Photographers swarmed them, capturing every moment with their cameras. But Romeo didn't mind. It was a festive occasion, a night he hoped Zoe would never forget. As long as his girlfriend was happy, he was happy.

"How did you pull this off without me knowing, and why didn't you say anything?"

Romeo kissed her forehead. "Because it wouldn't be a surprise if I told you."

Staring at him for a long moment, Zoe clasped his hand and squeezed it. "You're a good man, Romeo, and meeting you last month has been one of the best things that's ever happened to me."

"Baby, I feel the same way. You're in a class all by

yourself, Zoe. A humble, beautiful soul, and if I thought you'd say yes, I'd pop the question right here, right now."

Her eyes doubled in size, and her lips parted wordlessly. His confession had taken her by surprise, but Romeo meant every word. He hated being apart from Zoe, and kept a close eye on her whenever other men were around. But he'd never felt more secure in a relationship, and loved the idea of living with Zoe in holy matrimony. Now he understood why his cousins and brothers had proposed within weeks of meeting their girlfriends. He'd found the woman of his dreams and wanted to spend his days and nights loving her, spoiling her, treating her the way she deserved. In February, Zoe was going home to visit her family for two weeks, and he was going with her. He'd sit down with Reuben Smith and ask for his daughter's hand in marriage. Once her father gave him his blessing, he was going to plan a romantic proposal for his ladylove.

Out of the corner of his eye, he noticed his sisters-in-law Jariah and Tatiyana waving frantically at him. He also saw Francesca beckoning him over, and gestured to table one. "We better go check in with my family. As you can see, they're really excited to meet you."

Releasing his hand, Zoe fluffed her hair and adjusted the bodice of her designer gown. "I'm so nervous my heart is racing. Gosh, I hope they like me."

"What's not to like?" To make her laugh and to calm her nerves, he wiggled his eyebrows made a funny face. "You're gregarious, witty, and you have great taste in men. Baby, you've got this, so let's go wow my family!"

As they approached table one, Romeo sent Zoe a reassuring smile. She looked tense, as if she were at the dentist's office rather than a black-tie party. Placing a hand on her lower back, he gently caressed her skin. Diamonds were draped from her ears, neck and wrists, and her jewelry twinkled in the candlelight. Awed by her beauty, he was shocked that his girlfriend suddenly lacked self-confidence.

"Are you going to stand there like a well-dressed mime for the rest of the night, or are you going to introduce us to your lovely date?"

The sound of Dante's voice jolted Romeo back to the present, and he broke free of his thoughts. Pleased to see everyone, he glanced around the table. The newlyweds, Markos and Tatiyana, were busy kissing, Enrique and Isabelle were feeding each other olives, Francesca and her blonde, blue-eyed boyfriend were arguing in Italian, and Dante and his wife, Jariah, who was six months pregnant, were whispering to each other.

Thrilled to have Zoe on his arm, he proudly introduced her to his family members. To make her feel more comfortable, he shared funny stories about each couple, and soon everyone was laughing. Romeo pulled out her chair, then sat down beside her.

"Oh my goodness," Zoe shrieked, touching a hand to her mouth. "You're all wearing something from Casa Di Moda's holiday line. How cool is that!"

Enrique wore a wry smile. "We had no choice. Francesca and our sister-in-law Paris both decided to invest in the fashion house. They said if we didn't buy something they'd kill us. Needless to say, it was an easy decision to make."

"I had no idea," Zoe said with a laugh, giving Francesca a one-arm hug. "Why didn't you say anything when we met for sushi the other night?"

"Because I wanted it to be a surprise. Aurora and Davide asked if I'd be interested in being the face of the line, and I said hell yes! Thanks to you, Zoe, my life has meaning and purpose again. I'm going to make the most of this incredible opportunity…"

Romeo watched his sister and his girlfriend embrace.

He hadn't seen Francesca this excited in years, and he hoped resurrecting her modeling career and working for Casa Di Moda would help ease the pain of Lucca's death. Since losing her only child, she'd been angry at the world, but if anyone could turn their life around it was his sister. To stand out among the crowd, she'd styled her silky shoulder-length hair in a bouffant and donned a shimmery gold gown that clung to her skin like Saran Wrap. Romeo wouldn't be surprised if he woke up tomorrow morning to find Francesca on the cover of every online fashion magazine and blog in the country.

The mood at table one was cheerful and festive, the conversation lively. Romeo could tell by the way Zoe interacted with his family members that she was having a good time. The celebrity hosts entertained diners throughout the five-course meal. Soon Romeo's jaw ached from laughing, and his stomach was filled to the brim. Spending time with his family helped him momentarily forget the relentless questioning he'd endured in Paris hours earlier and his fears of being charged with a crime he didn't commit.

"RoZo, how did you meet?" Tatiyana asked, with a smile. "Was it love at first sight?"

A grin dimpled his cheek. "Absolutely. Zoe wanted to meet me so bad she drove her mountain bike into the side of my Lambo."

Zoe kicked him under the table, but Romeo was determined to finish his story.

"The police wanted to charge her with reckless driving, but I convinced them not to," he said, popping his collar to earn a laugh. "An amazing first kiss, and the rest is history."

Everyone at the table cracked up except Zoe, and Romeo wondered if he'd gone too far.

"You forgot the part about trying to pay me off and

begging me relentlessly for a date," Zoe quipped, wearing a cheeky grin. "No worries, I'll save that titillating story for dessert."

His brothers chuckled, the women gave one another high fives, and Zoe winked at him. Romeo couldn't contain his laughter. He loved her wit, and he enjoyed listening to her joke around with his family.

Francesca cupped a hand around her ear. "Anyone else *hear* wedding bells?"

"Come on, you guys." Zoe wore a shy smile. "We've only been dating for a few weeks. Hardly long enough to be thinking about marriage—"

Interrupting, the women all spoke at once. By the time they were finished telling Zoe about their whirlwind romances and lightning-fast engagements she looked stunned, as if she'd never heard anything more shocking in all her life.

"Wow," fell from her lips for the umpteenth time, and everyone laughed.

"Zoe, are you spending Christmas Day with us?" Jariah asked, rubbing her baby bump.

"Yes, and I'm really looking forward to it. My family's in New York, so it'll be nice to celebrate the holidays with you guys." Zoe picked up her flute. "Romeo promised to make me homemade ravioli with garlic focaccia, and I can't wait to try it. It's my favorite dish."

"Great!" Isabelle said with a cheer, her auburn curls tumbling around her forehead. "We're going to have so much fun. We'll open gifts, eat brunch, sing Christmas carols around the piano, then eat some more!"

Feeling his cell phone vibrate inside his jacket, he took it out of his pocket and saw Simona's number on the screen. He wondered if his COO had an update about the money laundering investigation. She'd remained in Paris, but had promised to touch base with him before she left for her family ski trip in the morning. "I need to take this," he said, wearing an apologetic smile. "I'll be right back."

Standing, Romeo pressed his cell to his ear and marched out of the reception hall. Noisy and crowded, the lobby was filled with so many people he couldn't hear himself think. Needing privacy, Romeo breezed past the fashionable group and ducked inside the men's washroom. "Have you heard from our attorneys? Are the French authorities going to press charges?"

"No, thank God," Simona said, releasing a sigh. "I found out from our attorneys that Markos called the lead investigator this afternoon, and had a lengthy conversation with him…"

Filled with relief and gratitude, Romeo nodded his head as she spoke. Markos never told him about his conversation with French authorities, but he wasn't surprised by what his brother had done. That was the Morretti way. Like the rest of his family, he had his back. Romeo could always count on Markos.

"I don't know what your brother said to get French authorities off our backs, but Markos came through for us big time. The next time I see him I'm going to give him a big fat kiss!"

"Please don't. His wife will go ballistic, and I don't want you to get hurt."

"Thanks for the heads-up. I'll just send him a Christmas fruit basket and call it a day."

They laughed, and for the first time since he'd learned about the arrest of Julio Mario Domínguez, he felt calm; he could finally breathe.

"Simona, I have to go. I'm at the Wonderland Ball with my family. They'll kill me if I spend the rest of the night on my cell," he explained, checking his reflection in the mirror.

"No worries. I understand. Merry Christmas, Romeo. Take care."

"Thanks, Simona," he said, adjusting his crooked bow tie. "Happy holidays. Have fun skiing with your sisters in Val Thorens tomorrow. Be careful. Don't break anything."

Simona giggled. "I'll try not to. See you in the New Year."

A man of African descent with lifeless eyes and pock-marked skin emerged from the handicapped stall and approached the sink.

Eager to share his good news with his family, and thank Markos for his help, Romeo turned to the door.

"For two hundred million euros, no one ever has to know about your massive heart attack last year or your weekly papaverine hydrochloride injections…"

Romeo stopped. The room spun around him at a hundred miles an hour, then flipped upside down on its head. His knees buckled, but he faced his tormentor. Took a good look at the creep who was blackmailing him. Over six feet tall, with a lanky frame hidden under a weathered, black trench coat, Romeo knew the stranger was no match for him. One punch and he'd be flat on his back, sleeping like a baby. Filled with anger, he struggled to control his temper. He was at an A-list party, crawling with reporters and paparazzi, and since Romeo didn't want to do anything to embarrass himself or his family, he kept his cool.

The stranger moved toward him wearing a menacing expression on his face, and Romeo curled his hands into fists. His tuxedo felt tighter than a straitjacket, and his bow tie was cutting off his air supply. But he was ready for war. If the man touched him it was on. He'd kick his ass like he stole something, then worry about the consequences later.

"Take this," the stranger instructed, holding up a white business card. It had a row of numbers written in black ink.

The man gestured to it with a flick of his head. "Deposit the money into this account by midnight."

Romeo spoke through clenched teeth. "And if I don't?"

"Your secrets will be published online for the whole world to read." He wore a smug smile. "I wonder what your celebrity clients will think when they find out about your ties to organized crime?"

Rage boiled inside him, causing his entire body to quiver. A minute ago he was relieved that French authorities weren't going to charge him with money laundering, and now he was stuck in the men's room, face-to-face with the devil. When was he ever going to catch a break? Refusing to feel sorry for himself, he shrugged. "I'm not giving you shit."

The man rocked on his heels, as if he'd been slugged in the stomach. "S-S-She said you'd pay. That you'd do anything to keep the story out of the papers."

"Publish whatever you want. I don't negotiate with criminals, and I don't give a—"

A British pop band, their bodyguards, and a wave of cigarette smoke filled the room. Thinking fast, Romeo slipped through the open door and out into the lobby. His heart was racing, pounding out of control. Romeo didn't know why he thought he could have a successful relationship. He'd had bad luck with the opposite sex all his life, but he'd hoped things would be different with Zoe. But like all the women in his past she'd played him, and he hadn't even seen it coming. Had never guessed in a million years she'd break his heart.

Questions bombarded his mind. Played in his ear like a bullhorn. Was Zoe dating the man in the trench coat behind his back? Had they plotted together to ruin him? He couldn't quiet his thoughts, didn't know what to believe or think, and feared the woman he'd fallen hard for had plotted his demise. *Why?* he wondered. *Why would Zoe hurt me like this?*

Desperate to reach his family, Romeo marched through the reception hall, oblivious to the world around him. Ignored the partiers smiling, waving and shouting his name. Spotting Zoe standing at the dessert table with Isabelle and Francesca, conflicting emotions flooded his body. Sadness, confusion, hurt and love. His tongue felt heavy, his throat tight. Grabbing her arm, he led her to a quiet corner of the room, away from the crowd and demanded answers. The music was loud, and Romeo had to shout to be heard over the R&B singer crooning onstage.

"What did you do?" he asked, glaring at her. "Who's the guy in the trench coat? Are you guys lovers? Why did you tell him about my heart attack?"

Frowning, Zoe reached for him, but he pushed her hands away. "Romeo, calm down. What are you talking about? You're not making any sense."

"Someone just threatened to post my health problems online if I don't pay him millions of dollars."

Her eyes widened, and her mouth fell open.

"Answer me, Zoe. What did you do?"

"I didn't do anything. I swear. I never told anyone about our conversation. I wouldn't."

"Did you hear what I just said?" he shouted, pointing at the doors. "A guy just tried to shake me down in the men's room. He knew about my heart attack, the medication I'm on, and the money laundering case."

Blinking rapidly, Zoe fervently shook her head, her earrings swishing back and forth as she denied the accusations. "I never said a word. Baby, you have to believe me. I'd never betray you like that. Not for any amount of money."

Francesca tried to talk to him, but Romeo ignored her. He was so riled up about his conversation with the man in the trench coat, he was shouting. "You did it. You screwed me over. I know you did. You betrayed me for two hundred million dollars—"

"I-I-It wasn't me," she stammered, her voice low and strained, as if it were painful for her to talk. "It could have been Lizabeth, or Giuseppe or someone who's jealous of you…"

"Lizabeth and I weren't together at the time I was hospitalized, and Giuseppe would never sell me out. Not for any amount of money. He's my mentor, and I trust him explicitly."

"And you don't trust me?"

Her gaze bored into him. His tongue stuck to the roof of his mouth, and his feet were glued to the floor. He couldn't escape even if he wanted to. And he did. Desperately. He wanted to get far away from the man in the trench coat and the partygoers dancing around them. "No. I don't. Not anymore," he said, burying his hands in his pockets to avoid reaching out to wipe the tears from her eyes. She'd betrayed him, but it hurt Romeo to see the woman he loved cry, made him feel like the scum of the earth even though he'd done nothing wrong. As much as he didn't want to believe it he couldn't ignore the facts: he and Zoe were over.

Needing to be alone and anxious to leave the party, he searched for his brothers. Zoe touched his forearm, warming his chilled body, but he hardened his heart. Told himself she was no longer worthy of his love. That she was his past, not his future, and she never would be.

"Romeo, *non farlo*," she pleaded, wiping at her eyes with the back of her hands. Zoe spoke in Italian, but he didn't believe her, couldn't look at her.

Her words blew his mind. *Don't do this? We can fix this. We can work things out.*

"Work what out? There is no us. You ruined us when you betrayed me."

"Stop saying that! I never told anyone about your health issues. Not even my sister."

"Then how the hell does that scumbag know about the worst day of my life?"

Zoe hugged her arms to her chest. Tears dribbled down her cheeks, running the expensive makeup she'd spent an hour putting on in his master bathroom as he'd gotten dressed for the Wonderland Ball. She was shaking so violently, Isabelle had to come to her aid. He didn't know how much of his argument with Zoe family members had heard, and didn't want to put them in the middle of his relationship dispute, but he needed their help.

"Francesca, see to it that Zoe gets home safe," he whispered in her ear. "Please? As a favor to me? I need to be alone right now. I can't be here. I need to go."

"I understand. I will." Francesca kissed his cheek. "I love you, bro. Take it easy."

Romeo turned and walked out of the room, but as he pushed open the glass door he noticed he wasn't alone. His brothers were beside him, shoulder to shoulder. For as long as Romeo lived, he'd never forget the night they'd sacrificed time with their wives to comfort him.

The air was crisp and cold; the wind was howling, the ground now covered in snow. Ducking inside the limousine parked at the front entrance of the castle, Romeo collapsed into the backseat and yanked off his bow tie. Tossing it on the floor, he stretched his legs out in front of him. He tried to block out the noises in his head, the memory of his argument with Zoe, but he couldn't do it. Pressing his eyes shut, he prayed when he woke up he'd discover that the Christmas Wonderland Ball had been nothing more than a bad dream, and the vivacious Long Island beauty he adored in every way was still his ladylove.

Chapter 19

Zoe yanked open the front door of Casa Di Moda so hard she was surprised it was still on its hinges. The burly security guard with the thick beard must have seen the peeved expression on her face, because he moved out of her way and took cover behind a leafy, potted tree.

Stomping through the darkened reception area, her suede over-the-knee boots slapping against the floor, she struggled to control her emotions, the sadness and anger pulsing through her veins. Zoe had never experienced such pain in all her life, and every time she remembered what happened at the Christmas Wonderland Ball on Saturday night she'd break down. Couldn't help it. Couldn't stop the tears from falling once they started. She'd tell herself to toughen up, but she didn't have the strength it required.

Each day without Romeo was unbearable. It had only been four days since he'd dumped her, but it felt like months had passed since she'd seen the man she loved.

Stuck in her apartment, listening to sad love songs only made her feel worse, but Zoe didn't know what to do to get out of her funk.

For days, she'd mentally reviewed their argument, analyzing everything he'd said and done at the party. That morning, while Zoe was curled up in bed looking at pictures of Romeo on her cell phone, she'd realized she'd overlooked something important. Something she should have told Romeo before he stormed off. She never told anyone what he'd told her about his health issues, but she'd journaled about it in the taxicab after their first weekend together at the villa on her way to work.

A light bulb had gone off in her head. Scrambling to her feet, she'd jumped out of bed, grabbed her leather tote bag from the closet and opened it. To her surprise, her journal was inside. Flipping through it, she noticed all of the pages were intact, and her owl-shaped bookmark was right where she'd left it.

Disappointed, she'd slumped to the floor, striking the carpet with her fists. She'd thought her journal was stolen, was convinced someone had taken it from her purse when she'd gone Christmas shopping with Francesca or to the movies with Jiovanni, just days before the Wonderland Ball. Finding it meant she was back to square one.

Another thought had come to her. Had one of her colleagues read her journal, then hired someone to blackmail Romeo? It was hard to believe, but the more Zoe considered it, the more plausible it was. She had great relationships with her colleagues and couldn't imagine any of them snooping through her things, but she couldn't rule it out, either.

Who would do something so sinister? So cruel, she'd wondered, racking her brain. Who had motive? Opportunity? A desire for fame and fortune that rivaled a reality

TV star? A chilling thought rocked her mind. Conversations she'd had with Aurora in recent weeks blared in her ears. *Romeo Morretti's a smart, influential businessman with friends in high places, and we could use someone like him in our corner... Hooking up with a Morretti is a once-in-a-lifetime opportunity, so don't blow it... Do whatever it takes to persuade him to invest in Casa Di Moda... I'll do anything to save Casa Di Moda. It's my life, and I won't lose it.*

Convinced she finally knew who the guilty party was, Zoe had tossed her journal aside, surged to her feet and marched into the bathroom to shower and change. An hour later, a taxicab had dropped her in front of Casa Di Moda. The office was closed for the holidays, but Zoe knew Aurora was hard at work on the spring collection. Zoe wasn't leaving the fashion house until the cold and callous designer answered her questions.

Heading toward her boss's large corner office, her anger intensified. Obsessed with fame and fortune, Aurora would do anything to achieve her goals—including stabbing her in the back and destroying the best relationship Zoe had ever had. Hell, she'd probably fake her own death and collect the insurance money if she thought she could get away with it, Zoe thought. *I can't believe I ever considered Aurora a friend!*

Seeing the Christmas wreath hanging on the staff room door reminded Zoe of the plans she'd made with Romeo and his family for the holidays. Plans she was now excluded from. Zoe never imagined she'd be at Casa Di Moda on Christmas Eve, instead wishing she was with Romeo and his family at the Milan Christmas parade. Last night she'd reached out to Francesca, and to her surprise and relief, she agreed to talk to Romeo on her behalf. It was the best news she'd received all week, and even though Francesca told her not to get her hopes up, Zoe was praying for a Christmas miracle.

"Davide, what should I do? Should we tell Zoe the truth or wait…"

Zoe stopped. Hearing voices coming from the end of the hall, she spun around and peeked inside the staff room. And there, sitting at the round table sipping coffee and eating cookies, were Aurora and Davide. Sketchbooks, file folders, fashion magazines and vibrant silk fabric were spread out in front of them. But it was obvious they were relaxing not working. Italian music was playing on the stereo, and the festive up-tempo song only made Zoe feel worse about being alone on Christmas Eve.

Something snapped in Zoe, and as she stormed over to the table she shouted her words. "Aurora, how could you do this to me? To Romeo? Don't you have a heart? Don't you care about anybody but yourself?"

The couple stared at her, their mouths ajar.

"I helped you, supported you, did everything in my power to promote Casa Di Moda, and how do you repay me? By betraying me. How could you?"

Aurora dropped her utensils on her plate, wiped her mouth with a red star-shaped napkin and rose to her feet. "I saw the articles online about Romeo's health crisis, but I had nothing to do with it. I didn't even know he was sick," she said quietly, meeting her gaze. "You're important to me, Zoe, and I'd never do anything to hurt you. Neither would Davide."

Biting the bottom of her lip, Zoe stared down at her boots. For some strange reason, she believed her. Knew in her gut that Aurora was telling the truth. That her boss didn't sell the story to the press her.

"You helped us save Casa Di Moda, and we're forever in your debt. You're our family, Zoe, and we'd never do the things you're accusing us of. How could we? If not for you and the rest of our amazing staff, we would have lost everything." Standing, his arms outstretched, Davide crossed the room toward her. "We'll get through this together. I promise."

The couple wrapped their arms around her. Zoe's throat closed up and water filled her eyes, blurring her vision. She felt guilty for yelling at her boss, ashamed of herself for ever thinking that Aurora and Davide would screw her over. She quickly apologized for her assumptions.

Davide wore a sympathetic smile. "Don't sweat it. We all make mistakes."

"Romeo dumped me," she croaked, wiping her eyes with the sleeve of her beige cardigan. "He thinks I released information about his health...but I didn't...now he hates me."

Aurora cupped Zoe's face in her hands. "Don't talk like that. Romeo's just upset. Give him time. Once the media storm dies down, he'll realize breaking up with you was a mistake."

"When? He won't take my calls or respond to my texts. It's killing me inside."

"Don't worry, Zoe. He'll come to his senses. Romeo loves you, and he wants a future with you," Davide said with assurance. "I know it's hard, but be patient with him. He's going through a lot right now. I bet he's just as upset as you are."

Zoe considered Davide's words and smiled through her tears. "Look at me, I'm a mess."

"You sure are!" Aurora said, making a face. "You better hurry up and get yourself together because time is of the essence. Your goddaughter will be here in five months, and I'm going to need your help."

Davide sighed, as if he had the weight of the world on

his shoulders, then wore a sheepish smile. "Me, too. I know zilch about babies, and even less about changing diapers!"

A feeling of elation came over Zoe, and she let out a scream. "You guys are pregnant?"

"No, not me. Just Aurora," Davide joked, touching his wife's stomach. "Our little bundle of joy should be here by May. Just in time for my fortieth birthday. Pretty cool, huh?"

"Congratulations, you guys! I'm so happy for you." Hugging them both, she decided it was cause for celebration and offered to buy them lunch at the bistro across the street.

"We should be the ones spoiling you. You saved Casa Di Moda from financial ruin."

I did? Zoe thought, bewildered by Aurora's words.

"Thanks to you, the Chic and Curvy line is our bestseller," Davide explained.

"The fashion blogs can't get enough of your effortless style, and we've seen a three hundred percent surge in online sales since you were photographed with Romeo at the Il Divo concert," Aurora said, putting on her belted tweed jacket. "I call it the Zoe Effect, and our increased popularity and staggering profits are making our new investors very happy."

"I'm glad that everything worked out. You're an incredible talent, Aurora, and you deserve every bit of success," Zoe said. "I just know you're going to be an amazing mom."

"Damn right. My daughter's going to be the best-dressed kid in preschool!"

Laughing, the trio left the staff room, their exuberant voices carrying down the hall. It had been days since Zoe smiled or joked around. She missed Romeo desperately and longed to see him again, but she was glad she could spend some quality time with her boss.

Remembering she'd bought Christmas presents for Romeo's family and stashed them under her office desk, Zoe asked Davide to help her carry them to the reception area and opened the door. Her purse fell from her hands, and everything inside spilled onto the carpet. *Is this really happening?* she wondered, giving her head a shake to clear the terrifying image before her eyes. *Is my best friend stealing from me? Is Jiovanni the one who stabbed me in the back?*

Zoe forced herself not to cry. He'd always had a word of encouragement for her, had always been her biggest cheerleader. His betrayal cut deep. It felt as if there were a hole in her chest where her heart should have been, but she didn't succumb to her pain. For the first time since the Christmas Wonderland Ball, her mind was clear. In that moment, Zoe realized everything her colleagues had said about Jiovanni over the last few months was true. He was angry and bitter, and if he was her friend he wouldn't be standing behind her desk, snooping through the gifts she'd bought for Romeo's family. "Looking for something? My journal perhaps?"

His head snapped up, and he dropped the diamond earrings he was holding on the desk.

"It was you," she hissed, pointing a finger at his face.

"Z-Z-Zoe, what's up? I just came by to grab the issue of *Vogue* I lent you."

"Liar! You read my journal, then arranged to have some low-life criminal blackmail Romeo at the Wonderland Ball, knowing full well he'd blame me."

"Don't make it sound so sinister," he said with a shrug. "It wasn't like that."

"I thought we were friends. I thought you cared about me—"

"I do," he said, interrupting her. "It wasn't personal. Alessandra and I saw an opportunity to make some easy cash and we took it. You of all people know how much I want to launch my own fashion label."

Feeling woozy, as if she was about to be sick, Zoe took a deep breath, willed herself not to lose it.

"Alessandra and I sold the story to our favorite celebrity blog, and now I finally have enough money to fulfill my lifelong dream."

"Get out before I throw you out," Aurora warned, stepping forward. "People like you make me sick. You'll do anything for money, but what you fail to realize is when you hurt people in your quest for success, you'll never get ahead."

"Bullshit. It's the survival of the fittest in the fashion world, and only the strongest survive."

Davide gestured with his thumb to the open door. "Jiovanni, you're fired. Leave now or the security guards will escort you out. It's your choice."

"With pleasure. I was going to quit after the holidays, so thanks for saving me the trouble of having to write a formal resignation letter." Wearing a confident smile, he swaggered through the office. "I'm debuting my collection, Designs by Jiovanni, during Milan Fashion Week and it's going to mop the floor with Casa Di Moda. You just wait and see."

"Boy, bye!" Flapping her hands in the air as if she were a queen on her throne, Aurora narrowed her gaze. "You're not welcome here anymore, so please leave."

Jiovanni stopped in front of Zoe, but she stepped back. She couldn't stand to be near him.

"I know you're upset, and you have every right to be, but I hope one day you'll find it in your heart to forgive me," he said in a sincere tone of voice.

Zoe scoffed, couldn't believe his nerve. "Don't hold your breath."

"I messed up. I'm man enough to admit it. Doesn't that count for something?"

"Stay away from me. Don't call me, don't text me, don't come by my apartment. In fact, lose my number permanently."

"Zoe, you don't mean that. We're best friends. I love you. You know that."

Jiovanni reached out to touch her face, and Zoe slapped his arm so hard a sharp pain shot through her wrist. "Don't touch me. Don't you dare touch me," she hissed through clenched teeth. "Stay. The. Hell. Away. From. Me. Or. You'll. Be. Sorry."

His cheeks paled. He started to speak, but Zoe gave him her back, keeping her gaze fixed on the picture of her family hanging on the wall. What bothered her more than anything was his cocky, self-righteous attitude. Had he ever cared about her? Had he been screwing her over from day one? Filled with a profound sense of sadness, as if she were all alone in the world, Zoe bit the inside of her cheek to keep the tears at bay.

Jiovanni mumbled an apology, but Zoe refused to acknowledge him.

Out of the corner of her eye, she saw her ex-best friend leave her office, his shoulders bent, his head down, and wondered if his outward show of remorse was genuine or just an act. Deciding it was the latter, she stared out the window. She needed a moment to collect her thoughts. Zoe couldn't believe she'd lost her boyfriend and her best friend in the same week. She dropped into her favorite chair, and tears flowed fast and furious down her cheeks. It didn't matter how hard she tried, she couldn't make them stop.

Chapter 20

"Uncle Romeo, wake up, wake up, it's Christmas Day!" Matteo wailed in a high-pitched voice. "You have to come downstairs, uncle. Everyone's waiting. Santa came, and it's time to open presents!"

Groaning, Romeo buried his head under a pillow. Warm and cozy in his king-size bed, he didn't want to leave the comfort of his master suite. He silently wished Dante would come and collect his loud, hyper son. The tantalizing aromas of sausage, mozzarella cheese and sautéed mushrooms filled the air. Even though Romeo was starving, he still didn't budge. Exhausted and desperate for more sleep, he closed his eyes.

"Please, Uncle Romeo?" Matteo begged, vigorously shaking Romeo's shoulders.

"I'll be up in an hour, li'l man. I promise."

"No, get up now. I'm tired of waiting. You've been sleeping forever."

Rolling onto his side, he peered at the alarm clock on the side table. Six forty-seven a.m.? Oh, hell no! Yesterday, his nonna had arrived from the States with his cousins Demetri, and Rafael, and their wives and children. After the kids went to bed, the adults had stayed up late into the night, drinking homemade wine, eating savory snacks and sharing their favorite Christmas memories. Unfortunately, conversation had turned to Romeo's love life, and to his shock and dismay, his sisters-in-law didn't like how he'd treated Zoe. The women were disappointed in him for yelling at her at the Christmas Wonderland Ball. Francesca was convinced Zoe had nothing to do with the blackmail scheme and encouraged him to reach out to her. On the fence about what to do, he'd promised to give some thought to what his sister said, and he had. In fact, he'd thought about Zoe all night. That's why he didn't have the energy to get out of bed now.

"I'm going to tell Auntie Cesca you're being mean to me," Matteo said in a wobbly voice, jumping to his feet. "You're going to get it!"

Feeling guilty for upsetting his nephew, Romeo decided to take the first grader for a ride in his red Ferarri after breakfast. Images from his dream played in his mind, and a lump formed inside his throat. Zoe was goofing around with him at his estate in Lake Como, frolicking and laughing in the turquoise-blue water. Memories of all the good times they had over the past few weeks made his heart sad.

Romeo couldn't quiet his thoughts, couldn't change the channel in his mind. Since the Wonderland Ball, her words had haunted him. *I didn't do anything. I swear...I never told anyone about our conversation. I wouldn't...I'd never betray you...* Did he make a mistake? Had he lashed out at the wrong person? Had someone else in his inner circle sold him out? Did it even matter now that everyone knew about his health problems?

Remembering the headlines splashed across every magazine in the country gave him pause. Romeo Morretti Health Crisis! one paper had written. Morretti Millionaire Found Unresponsive at Lavish Penthouse! claimed another one. On the Brink of Death, reported his favorite newspaper.

Considering everything that had happened since the story broke five days earlier, Romeo realized he'd been worried for nothing. The response from his clients, friends and business associates had been overwhelmingly supportive. All week, he'd been bombarded with phone calls, text messages and emails. Everyone told him how brave he was, called him an inspiration, a survivor. He'd been wrong. No one thought less of him or made him feel weak. Giuseppe persuaded him to share his story with the world. Now Romeo had so many speaking engagements lined up in the new year, he'd have to reschedule his birthday trip with his brothers and cousins to Monte Carlo in January. The Heart Disease Foundation of Milan had reached out to him about filming a public service announcement. After discussing it with his family, he'd agreed. He'd taped it yesterday in his home office, and within hours of the PSA being posted on the foundation's website, it had over two million views. Filming the commercial, speaking openly and honestly about his heart attack last year, had been cathartic. The weight he'd been carrying on his shoulders disappeared. For the first time since Romeo had been discharged from the hospital, he felt at peace with his body.

Romeo heard laughter, lively Christmas music and animated voices echoing throughout his estate. There were so many people at his house it was noisier than an amusement park, but Romeo was glad his relatives were with him. He cherished the time they spent together, loved hanging out with his cousins and brothers, and was thrilled they'd be in Milan until the new year, especially now that he didn't have Zoe by his side. The unthinkable had happened: he'd found the woman of his dreams and lost her in the blink of an eye, through no fault of his own.

Yawning, he stretched his tired muscles. It had been a year of extreme highs and lows, but despite everything that had happened with Zoe at the Wonderland Ball, she was still the woman he wanted. The object of his affection. His heart. His everything, and he couldn't help wondering who she was spending Christmas Day with. Was she with Aurora and Davide? Hanging out with Jiovanni and his family? Or relaxing at home watching her favorite Christmas movie for the hundredth time?

High heels slapped against the marble floor, echoing throughout the second story, ruining the peaceful mood. Romeo cursed under his breath. Sensing what was coming next, he threw the blanket over his face and pretended to snore.

"Get up, sleepyhead!" Francesca trilled in a singsong voice. "Everyone's waiting for you downstairs, and they're starting to get restless, so shake a leg."

Romeo grunted, blew deeply through his nose to sell his performance.

"I told you, Auntie Cesca. He's not listening," Matteo whined.

"We'll see about that."

Romeo held his breath, prayed his sister wouldn't do anything crazy like jump on his bed or worse, toss a bucket of ice water on him. Someone yanked off his blanket, stole his pillow, and whacked him upside the head with it. Squinting, he propped himself on his elbow to see who the culprit was. The blinds were drawn, the balcony doors were open, and the crisp morning air made his body cold.

Francesca stood at the foot of the bed, licking a candy cane, a hand stuck to her hip. "Are you going to come willingly, or do we have to drag you out of the bed?"

"Merry Christmas to you, too, sis," Romeo drawled in a sleepy voice, patting back a yawn. "Go ahead and start without me. I don't mind."

"Nice try, Scrooge, but that's not a Morretti family tradition. On Christmas Day, we open presents together, eat brunch, then sing Christmas carols around the piano."

Deciding to have a little fun with his sister and nephew, he shook his head and faked a scowl. Stretching out, Romeo clasped his hands behind his head and crossed his legs at the ankles. "My house, my rules, so bounce. I'll be down in an hour, and if you don't like it that's too bad."

"Come on, Matteo. Let's get him. I'll grab one leg, you grab the other!"

Before Romeo knew what was happening, Francesca and Matteo had dragged him off the bed. He fell flat on his back and let out a groan. Giggling, his nephew pointed at him with one hand and cupped his mouth with the other. Caught off guard by the surprise attack, Romeo didn't know whether to laugh or to cry.

"I'm going to get even when you least expect it, so you better watch your back!" he warned, hurling a pillow across the room. It hit the wall with a thud, and Matteo laughed even harder.

"You can't catch us. You can't catch us," the first grader chanted, wiggling his hips.

Crossing her arms, Francesca tapped her red-heeled pumps impatiently on the floor, her gaze dark and narrow. "I'd like to see you try. Now get up, get dressed and come downstairs pronto or we'll be back. The next time we won't go easy on you."

"Yeah," Matteo shouted, his curls tumbling around his face as he nodded his head. "I got a Super Soaker water gun from Nonna yesterday, and I'm not afraid to use it."

Giggling uncontrollably, Francesca and Matteo fled the room. Romeo wore a wry smile. Worried they'd return and make good on their threat, he dragged himself to his feet, shuffled into the bathroom and locked the door. A quick shower and shave, and Romeo was ready.

Jogging down the staircase, whistling "I'll Be Home for Christmas," he decided to call Zoe after breakfast. Romeo didn't know if they'd ever get back together, but he wanted to clear the air and apologize for the way he'd behaved at the Wonderland Ball. He'd been hurt and confused, but that was no excuse for his behavior. Romeo considered phoning her now, but since he didn't want Matteo to drench him with his water gun, he changed his mind.

"I'm here," Romeo announced, entering the living room. "Happy now?"

Matteo jumped into his arms, waving a square wooden box in the air. "Uncle Romeo, look what Ms. Zoe got me! It's an edible chemistry set," he said proudly, wearing a toothy smile. "I'm going to make rocks and fossils for everyone to eat for brunch!"

His family members laughed, then one by one turned toward the fireplace. That's when Romeo saw her. Zoe. For a moment, he thought he was dreaming, but as she crossed the room toward him, her floral perfume filled his nostrils and Romeo realized she wasn't a figment of his imagination. Beautiful in a sparkly tunic, black dress pants and ankle-tie pumps, he admired her effortless style. He wanted to kiss her, to wrap her up in his arms, but resisted the urge.

"Merry Christmas," she said, stopping in front of him. "It's good to see you."

His tongue was tied, but he managed to speak. "Zoe, what are you doing here?"

"You invited me to spend the holidays with you and your family, remember?"

"That was before we broke up. We're not together anymore. You shouldn't be here."

Francesca raised a hand in the air. "I picked her up an hour ago, and I'm glad I did. Zoe did nothing wrong."

Glancing around the living room, Romeo saw the sympathetic expressions on the faces of his family members and sighed heavily. Was he missing something? Why weren't his relatives on his side? Was he the only one who had a problem with what Zoe had done?

Shrieks, giggles and cheers erupted around the room as his nieces and nephews ripped wrapping paper to shreds, tossed it in the air as if it were confetti, then ran around in circles.

"Romeo, can we go somewhere quiet to talk?"

He shook his head, refused to consider her request. "Whatever you have to say to me you can say right here. What you did not only affected me, it affected my entire family, and they deserve to know the truth just as much as I do."

"Baby, I didn't do it. I swear. I love you, and I would never do anything to hurt you," she said, meeting his gaze. "You mean the world to me, and all I want is for you to be healthy and happy. I would never, ever do anything to jeopardize the incredible bond we have."

Romeo stared into her eyes. She'd said those words before, when they were arguing at the Wonderland Ball, but this time was different. Her voice was strong, convincing, the expression on her face one of fierce determination.

Romeo believed her. Sensed in his gut that she was telling the truth. But if she didn't betray him, then who did?

"I went to Casa Di Moda yesterday to resign, because I thought Aurora and Davide were behind the story, but I found Jiovanni in my office snooping through my things. I quickly put two and two together." Water filled her eyes, and her lips trembled.

"Go on. I'm listening."

"Jiovanni must have read my journal, photocopied the entries I wrote about our weekend at your villa, then gave them to his girlfriend, Alessandra. They paid someone to blackmail you, and when that didn't work they sold the information to the media. I never had anything to do with it…"

Joy, sadness and anger flooded his heart in equal measures. Disgusted by what Jiovanni had done, Romeo felt his eyes narrow and his hands curls into fists. Wasn't he supposed to be Zoe's best friend? How could he betray someone he claimed to love and respect? Romeo had never liked the associate designer and suspected he'd been plotting to break them up from day one. Thankfully, his evil scheme didn't work. "Jiovanni must have also tipped off the paparazzi about the Il Divo concert and the location of my villa as well," he said, thinking out loud. "That's how they knew where to find us."

"He must have, because I didn't tell a soul. We agreed to keep our relationship quiet, and since I was determined to keep my promise to you I had stopped confiding in Jiovanni about my personal life. I never imagined he'd snoop through my things though."

Hope surged through his body, filling his heart to the brim. A feeling of elation came over him, but Romeo didn't sweep Zoe into his arms and dance around the living room.

He wanted to hear everything, though, didn't want to miss anything she said.

"Baby, I'm so sorry about what Jiovanni did. I wish I could have stopped him, but—"

He interrupted her, couldn't stand to hear her apologize on Jiovanni's behalf, and pressed a finger to her mouth to stop her from saying another word. "Don't apologize for him. What happened is not your fault, it's his."

"I know, but I still feel horrible about it."

Romeo wore a sad smile. "And, I feel like an ass for the way I treated you."

"You do?" she asked, her eyes wide.

"Yes, I do. I jumped to conclusions instead of listening to your side of the story. I'm sorry. I was angry and upset after my run-in with that scumbag in the men's room and I lost my temper. I hope you can find it in your heart to forgive me."

"Of course, I forgive you. You're the man I love."

Zoe threw her arms around his neck and held him tight. Closing her eyes, she pressed her lips to his mouth. She kissed him slowly, tenderly, as if they had all the time in the world to please each other, and they did. Romeo wasn't going anywhere, would gladly spend the rest of the day making out with the woman he loved.

"I love you so much, and I can't live another day without you."

"Bellissima, you won't have to. I'm man enough to admit I made a mistake. I promise I'll never hurt you again or doubt your love. You have my word."

His family cheered as if they were watching a football game on TV, and Romeo laughed. "I missed you."

"I missed you, too," Zoe whispered, caressing the back of his head. "The last five days have been torture without you, and if not for Francesca, I never would have survived."

Romeo kissed the tip of her nose. "Bellissima, it sounds like you could use some R and R. How do you feel about spending New Year's Eve in Trinidad?"

"Trinidad? Really? Baby, that would be amazing!"

"You can say that again. We're going to have a blast on the island."

"I can see it now. Eating juicy mangoes, strolling along Mayaro Beach hand in hand, dirty dancing to calypso and soca music."

"Don't forget making love," Romeo added, caressing her cheeks with his thumb.

Closing her eyes, she gave him a sweet, soft kiss on the lips. "Can we leave tonight?"

"No," he whispered, against her mouth, "but when the coast is clear we can tiptoe upstairs for a Christmas Day quickie."

"Diavolo Sexy strikes again!" she joked. "Romeo, your family's here, and they have tons of activities planned this afternoon. We can't spend the rest of the day in bed—"

"Like hell we can't! My house, my rules, and *all* I want for Christmas is you."

Chuckling, Romeo sat down on his favorite chair, pulled Zoe down onto his lap, kissed her lips. The living room was crowded and noisy, filled with excitement as his family members sipped champagne and opened their presents. Romeo had everything he needed in Zoe, and didn't care what was under the tree. She was the center of his world, his one true love, and he'd never get tired of being with her. They shared the same hobbies and interests, and were a hundred percent committed to each other. Zoe understood him, appreciated him, and more than anything, made him feel loved and accepted. And it had nothing to do with his net worth.

Romeo took her hand to his, raised it to his mouth and

kissed her palm. In a playful mood, he couldn't resist teasing her and flashed a toothy smile. "I've lived a lot and experienced the best of everything, but you are the greatest thing that has ever happened to me, bellissima. Thanks for crashing your bike into my Lambo that fateful November morning."

"No, thank you," she insisted. An amused expression covered her face. "I can't take all of the credit. After all, *you* caused the accident, not me!"

Romeo gave an unrestrained laugh. His heart was full of love and happiness, and his smart, beautiful girlfriend was the reason why. Holding the woman he loved in his arms, surrounded by his relatives, was the best Christmas gift Romeo had ever received. He was in such a good mood he knew he'd never be able to wipe the smile off his face.

* * * * *

HOT CHRISTMAS KISSES

JOSS WOOD

Prologue

Christmas, the year before

In a rural part of Devon, three thousand miles from her home in Boston, Massachusetts, DJ Winston smoothed her hands over the maroon-and-silver dress and turned to face her computer screen.

Her two best friends, twins Darby and Jules Brogan, lounged on Jules's couch in her office back in Massachusetts, coffee cups on the table in front of them. As was their custom, they'd shortly be closing their business for the Christmas break, ending the year by treating their staff to lunch.

"Send everybody my love and tell them I hope they have a lovely minivacation."

DJ ignored Darby rolling her eyes at DJ's inability to wish anyone a merry Christmas. She tried, she really did, but the words always got stuck in her throat.

*Merry Christmas! Happy holidays! Ho, ho, ho…*nope, she couldn't do it. She could talk interest rates and contract terms, equity and cash flow, but she stuttered and stammered her way through December. The festive—hah!—season made her feel like she was eight again, alone, frightened and wondering why neither of her parents loved her.

DJ knew the twins would like to discuss her antipathy toward Christmas, but it was, like so many other subjects, off-limits.

DJ adored the twins, but she believed in keeping some distance between her and the people she loved. Distance was her safety net, her belay rope, her life vest. Distance was how she'd always protected herself. And since it had worked for her as a child and as a teen, what was the point of changing her strategy now?

Darby cocked her head to one side. "That dress looks fantastic with your dark hair and eyes, DJ."

Jules nodded her agreement. "Vibrant colors suit you. But with your height and build, anything looks good on you, you know that."

She didn't, though.

While the twins saw her as attractive, she still saw herself as the gangly, dark-haired teenager who embarrassed her blond, blue-eyed mother. DJ was smart enough, Fenella reluctantly admitted, but she was too tall, too lanky, with not enough charm. So Fenella said when she was in a good mood.

DJ tried not to remember the words Fenella let fly when she was angry.

"What shoes are you wearing?" Darby asked.

"My Jimmy Choos, the ones you made me buy last week." DJ nodded to the sexy silver shoes on the bed.

"So…" Darby drawled. "When is Matt arriving?"

DJ released an irritated sigh. "He's not."

"He stood you up? Nice Christmas present." Jules was sarcasm personified.

DJ sighed. Darby and Jules didn't understand that her and Matt Edwards's ad hoc arrangement worked for them, as it had for the past six years. Depending on their schedules, she and Matt met for a night or a weekend. That was when DJ stepped out of her life, pushing aside numbers and profit margins, cash-flow issues and cost projections. When she was with Matt, she allowed herself the freedom to be another version of herself—fun-loving, exuberant and sensuous.

Neither she nor Matt had any expectations, and DJ was very conscious of the fact that, despite making this unusual situation last for many years, their arrangement was a temporary thing.

They had no ties to each other, nothing to bind them except for the expectation of good sex, a few laughs and a relaxing time spent in undemanding company. She didn't need more. A partner, boyfriend or permanent lover wasn't something she wanted for herself; after being abandoned by her father and rejected by Fenella, DJ wasn't prepared to hand over her battered heart to another human to kick around. She was keeping possession of that fragile organ.

Spontaneous weekends spent with Matt worked well for her, but yesterday he'd blown her off, saying that he, despite it being Christmas, needed to stay in the Netherlands, to consult with a client who was in a world of hurt. Because Matt was a fantastically successful human-rights lawyer, *hurt* could mean his client was a political refugee ducking prison time, or a tribe of aboriginal people who'd been kicked off their ancestral land and were facing the imminent loss of their culture and way of life.

The fact that his on-and-off lover needed to escape Christmas and was horny as hell didn't nudge the needle of his what-international-laws-did-this-violate? scale.

DJ had considered missing her friend's wedding but that meant *doing* Christmas in Boston. Ugh. Attending this Christmas Eve wedding was the lesser of two evils.

Her friends on the screen were still waiting for her response. Right, they'd been discussing Matt's non-arrival. "We have an understanding that work always comes first. He's tied up doing something terribly important."

What he wasn't doing was her.

DJ pulled a face, glanced at the corner clock on her laptop screen and sighed. "I'd better slap on some makeup or else I'm going to be late for the church service."

Darby frowned and waved at DJ's dress. "Take that off first. You do not want to get makeup on that dress."

Good point. Friends since kindergarten, she was superbly comfortable disrobing in front of them. Allowing them to see her messed-up inner world was what she found difficult. DJ gently pulled the dress over her head and laid it on the bed.

Jules whistled. "Push-up bra, tiny thong, heels. Edwards has no idea what he's missing out on."

"I agree."

That voice.

DJ whipped her head up and looked toward the doorway. Her heart, stupid thing, did cartwheels in her chest.

Matt, a shoulder pressed to the doorframe, looked as effortlessly sexy as he always did. A tall blond with deep green eyes and a surfer's tan, he had the face and body to advertise sun, sea and sex. He didn't look like what he was: a brilliant international lawyer with a steel-trap mind.

The moisture in DJ's mouth disappeared and it took all her willpower not to run to him and start removing his clothes. She desperately wanted to slide the cream linen jacket down his arms and rip apart his navy button-down shirt. The leather belt would be next, and she'd soon have the buttons of his designer jeans undone. In her hand he'd be hot and hard...

It had always been this way. Matt just had to look at her with those incredibly green eyes and she went from cool and collected to crazy in ten seconds flat. She didn't love him—hell, she barely knew him—but, damn, she craved his mouth, his hands on all her long neglected and secret places.

Okay, try to hold it together. For God's sake, be cool.

"I thought you couldn't make it," DJ said, wincing at the happy note in her voice. *Yeah, opposite of cool, Winston.*

She glanced at her dress lying on the bed, considered slipping it on and then shrugged. Why bother? Matt had seen everything she had, more than once.

Matt stepped into the room, walking with a grace not many big men possessed. "My client was delayed."

Matt crossed the room to her and his hand lifted to cradle her face, his thumb brushing across her lower lip. He looked down, and she felt the heat of his gaze on the tiny triangle low on her hips and her equally frivolous bra. She was, in turn, both entranced and brutally turned on by the passion flaring in his eyes. Being wanted by this sexy man always shot a ray of enhanced sunshine through her veins.

"Nice outfit, Dylan-Jane," Matt said when their eyes locked again, his voice extra growly.

He was the only person, apart from her mother, who'd ever called her by her full name, and on Matt's lips it was a caress rather than a curse.

"Hi."

The single-syllable greeting was all her tangled tongue could manage.

"Hi back." Matt lowered his mouth to hers and as their lips touched they both hesitated, as they always did. DJ had no idea why Matt waited but she enjoyed stretching out the moment, ramping up the anticipation. Yes, she was desperate for his touch, but she also wanted to make the moment last. The first kiss, after so long apart, was always exceptional.

Finally, Matt's clever mouth touched hers and it was, as always, sweet and sexy—a little rediscovery and a whole bunch of familiarity. The kisses they'd exchange later would be out of control, like a wildfire, but this one was tender and, in its way, as soul-deep sexy as what would come later.

Talking about later…

It took everything DJ had to pull her mouth off his, to drop her hands from that wide, warm chest. "If we don't get dressed we're going to be late for the wedding."

"Yeah, you have about fifteen minutes to get out of that room to beat the bride to the church."

DJ yelped at Darby's dry voice. DJ took a step to the side to look past Matt's arm to the computer screen. Her friends were still there, both looking worried. DJ was thankful that they'd only had a view of Matt's broad back and truly excellent butt during that kiss.

"Hey, Matt," Darby said.

Matt pinched the bridge of his nose, shook his head

and rolled his eyes at DJ. With a rueful smile he turned around and looked at the screen. "Ladies."

"Well done for arriving in the nick of time," Jules said, her voice tart.

Matt just raised one sandy, arrogant eyebrow. Then he stepped up to the desk, looked down at the screen and smiled. "'Bye, ladies." He closed the lid to the laptop and turned back to face DJ.

"I've missed you."

DJ tipped back her head to look into his eyes, her cynical side wondering if he said that as a way to talk her into bed. But the look on his face was sincere, his eyes radiating honesty. Besides, Matt didn't use coercion. She was either fully on board or he backed off; Matt did not whine or beg or force.

Besides, they both knew she was going to slide into bed with him the moment she saw him standing in the doorway. She was putty in his hands.

"You, half-naked in sexy lingerie, is my early Christmas present." Matt lifted a curl off her forehead and tucked it behind her ear. His mouth curled up into a deprecating half smile. "But I'm embarrassed to tell you that I hightailed it out of my office to make my flight and I've been rushing ever since. I didn't want to be late, so I didn't stop to buy condoms. You wouldn't happen to have any, would you?"

DJ shook her head. Well, crap. Matt never, ever made love to her without one.

"So, damn. No condoms. Maybe we should go to the church and pick this up later."

Oh, hell, no.

"Or we could just carry on…" DJ ran her finger down his hard erection before fumbling with the snap on his pants.

Matt groaned. "Dylan-Jane, oral isn't enough. I need to be inside you. I'll go pick up some condoms and come back. We'll miss the service, but we could still make the reception."

Hearing his rough, growly, frustrated voice, DJ melted. "I'm on the pill, Matt. I'm clean, there hasn't been anyone since we last hooked up, and if you can tell me you are…"

Matt nodded. "Yeah, I am." He kissed her lips before pulling back again. "Can I trust you with this, Dylan-Jane? There won't be any unexpected surprises?"

If he knew her better, he wouldn't have to ask. Sure, the time they spent together was a fantasy, hot and wild, but that wasn't the person she was in real life. In Boston, she didn't do the unexpected and she hated surprises. Her life was planned, regulated, controlled.

And a baby was Darby's dream, not DJ's.

"I've got this, Matt." DJ pushed his pants and boxers down his hips, wound her arms around his strong neck and lowered her mouth onto his, whispering her words against his lips. "Come inside me, Matt, it's been too damn long."

Matt didn't hesitate, quickly pushing her panties to the side. He slid inside her, held her there and then lowered her to the bed. Gathering her to him, DJ knew that he'd try to be a gentleman—he always tried to make their first encounter together slow and reverential. She didn't need either—she needed hot and hard and fast.

"Matt, I need to burn," DJ told him in a tortured whisper.

Matt pushed himself up and slowly rolled his hips. When she released a low moan, he smiled.

He had a repertoire of smiles, from distracted to

dozy, but this one was her favorite: part pirate, part choirboy, all wicked.

"Well, then, let's light a match, Dylan-Jane."

Matt slid his hands under her hips, lifted her up, slammed into her and catapulted her into that white-hot, delicious fire she'd longed for.

She was almost, but not quite, tempted to murmur "Merry Christmas to me."

One

Nearly a year later...

In the public area at Logan International Airport, Matt Edwards ignored the crowds and maneuvered his way around the flower bearers and card holders. He'd mastered the art of walking and working his smartphone: there were ten messages from his office and a few text messages. None, dammit, were from Dylan-Jane.

Despite reaching out over a week ago, she'd yet to give him a definitive answer about them getting together in Boston.

Maybe she was making him wait because he'd been out of touch for so long. But he'd been busy and it just happened that they'd had less contact this year than usual. A lot less. But he was here now, and he was hopeful they could recapture some of their old magic.

"Matt!"

Matt turned, saw the tall frame of his old friend Noah Lockwood striding toward him and smiled. Well, this was a pleasant surprise.

Matt pushed his phone into the inside pocket of his black jacket before shaking Noah's hand. "It's great to see you, but what are you doing here?"

Noah fell into step beside him. "I've just dropped Jules off. She's flying to New York to meet a client. I knew you were coming in today, saw the flight times and thought I'd buy you a beer."

An excellent plan. It had been months, maybe even more than a year, since he and Noah had exchanged anything other than a brief phone call or a catch-up email. At college, they'd been tight, and despite their busy lives, he still considered Noah a friend.

Noah had also introduced Matt to DJ, and for that he'd always be grateful.

"I'd love a beer."

They walked to the nearest bar and Matt headed to two empty seats at the far end of the joint, tucking his suitcase between him and the wall before he slid onto the barstool. Within minutes he had a glass of an expensive microbrew in front of him.

Noah raised his glass and an enquiring eyebrow. "What brings you back to Boston?"

How to answer? Matt ignored the ache in that triangle where his ribs met. This visit, unlike those quick visits to see his grandfather, was going to be...difficult.

Emotional. Draining. Challenging.

All the things he most tried to avoid.

"I'm moving my grandfather into an assisted-living facility." Stock answer.

Noah looked surprised. "The judge is moving out of his home? Why?"

Matt took a sip of his beer before rubbing his eyes. "He's showing signs of dementia and Alzheimer's. He can't live on his own anymore."

"I'm sorry to hear that," Noah said. "How long are you going to be in town for?"

Matt tapped his finger against his glass. "I'm not sure, but since I don't have any court appearances scheduled until the New Year, probably until after Christmas. So, for the next three weeks at least."

Noah's eyes were steady on his face and Matt felt the vague urge to tell his friend the other reason he was in Boston. But talking wasn't something he found easy to do.

Noah didn't push, but changed the subject by asking another question. "So, are you going to contact DJ while you're in town?"

Matt sent Noah a sour look. "Who's asking, you or your fiancée?"

Noah grinned. "Jules's last words to me weren't 'I love you, you're such a stud,' but 'get Matt to tell you why he and DJ haven't spoken for nearly a year.'"

Matt shook his head. "You are so whipped, man."

Noah just grinned.

"I thought Jules and Darby would be happy to hear that DJ and I drifted apart. They aren't my biggest fans."

Noah rubbed the back of his neck. "Look, I'm in the middle here. I introduced you to DJ but I never expected your no-strings affair to last for years. I've told the twins to leave you two alone. You are adults and you both know what you are doing.

"But they love her and they are worried about her," Noah added.

Matt's head shot up. "Why are they worried about her?"

Noah released a soft curse. "You've got to know how much I love Jules, because if I didn't, I wouldn't ever consider broaching this subject."

Yep, whipped. If Matt wasn't the subject of the conversation, he'd find Noah's dilemma amusing. "The twins are worried because she hasn't been the same this past year. She's been quieter, more reserved, less... happy," Noah told him.

Matt filled in the blanks. "And they are blaming me for that?"

"Not so much blaming as looking for an explanation. DJ isn't talking, so my fiancée, damn her, asked me to ask you. Man, I sound like a teenager."

"So you didn't just accost me to have a beer?"

"The beer was an added incentive," Noah said, obviously uncomfortable. "Look, forget it, Matt. It's not my or Jules's business and I feel like a dick raising the subject."

Matt wanted to be annoyed but he wasn't. He'd always envied the friendship Dylan-Jane and the twins shared. They were a tight unit and would go to war for each other. He'd been self-sufficient for as long as he could remember, and his busy career didn't allow time for close friendships. It certainly didn't allow time for a relationship.

Matt carefully picked his words. "DJ and I have an understanding. Neither of us are looking for something permanent. I'm sorry if she's had a tough year but I don't think it's related to me. We were very clear about our expectations and we agreed there would be no hard feelings if life, or other people, got in the way of us seeing each other."

"Other people? Are you seeing someone else?"

Was Noah kidding? It had been a hell of a year and

he hadn't needed the added aggravation of dating someone new. He'd had a slew of tough cases and he'd been sideswiped by explosive news and saddened by an ex's untimely death. And he was now required to make life-changing decisions for his once brilliant grandfather.

Starting something new with someone new when he was feeling emotionally battered wasn't the solution to anything. As a teenager he'd learned the hard lesson that emotion and need were a dangerous combination.

He'd fallen in love at sixteen and he'd walked around drunk on emotion. His ex, Gemma, and he had made their plans: they'd graduate, go to college, get married, have kids…and they'd feel like this forever. She was the one, his everything…

At seventeen she'd informed him she was pregnant. A part of him had been ecstatic at the news of them having a baby—this would be the family he'd never really had, his to protect, his to love. *His*. All his…

After ten days of secret planning, and heart-to-heart discussions, Gemma flipped on him, telling him she'd miscarried and was moving across town and changing schools.

She didn't love him, she never really had…

He'd vowed then that love was a myth, that it was a manipulative tactic, that it didn't really exist. His parents, his grandparents, Gemma—they all proved his point. At seventeen, he'd dismissed love and forever as a fabrication and nothing since had changed his mind.

He now believed in sex, and having lots of it safely, but love? Not a chance.

And sex, in his mind, meant DJ.

DJ didn't want anything permanent, either. Just like him, she was allergic to commitment. They spent just enough time together to enjoy each other but not enough to become close. It was the perfect setup...

Or it had been.

He was back in Boston, in her city, and he saw no reason not to meet. It had been too long since he'd held her, since he'd tasted her skin, inhaled her fruity scent, heard her laugh. DJ, fun-loving, exuberant and sensuous, was exactly the medicine he needed. She'd be a distraction from thinking about how to handle the bombshell news he still hadn't wrapped his head around.

Matt looked at Noah. "I really don't know what's going on in DJ's life, but I doubt it has anything to do with me."

Noah drained his beer. "Are you going to see her while you're in Boston?"

Of course he was. "Yeah."

"Then I've been told to tell you that if you hurt her, they'll stab you with a broken beer bottle."

Matt rolled his eyes. DJ's friends were fierce. "Understood. But, as I said, we have a solid understanding."

Noah lifted his hands. "Just the messenger here." He pulled some cash out of his wallet and ignored Matt's offer to contribute. "If you don't want to spend the next month or so in a hotel, you're welcome to use the carriage house at Lockwood House. When we are home, Jules and I live in the main house."

Noah's property was, if Matt remembered correctly, the cornerstone of a very upmarket, expensive golfing community north of Boston. It was a generous offer and Matt appreciated it. "Thank you. That would be great."

"It was Jules's idea. That way she can keep an eye on you." Noah smiled. "And you do know that our house is directly opposite where Darby, DJ and Levi Brogan live? The same Levi Brogan who is superprotective and has no idea that you've been sleeping with the woman he loves like a sister for the last five-plus years?"

Oh, crap.

"It's going to be fun watching you tap-dance around him," Noah said before he clapped Matt on the shoulder and walked out of the bar.

Matt looked down at his phone and automatically stabbed his finger on the gallery icon. He flicked through the images of Dylan-Jane, memories sliding over him, and stopped when he came to a topless photo he'd snapped of her lying on the sand on a private beach in St. Barts. She was facing the sea but had turned her head back to look at him and the camera, her sable hair skimming the sand. She was all golden gorgeousness—flashing dark eyes, flushed cheeks, rosy nipples on her perky, tanned breasts.

Unable to resist her, he'd picked her up and carried her to the water, where they'd had amazing sea sex.

He had lots of great memories of DJ but, hell, making love to her in the sea and later on the sand was one of his favorites.

He desperately wanted to make more memories…

Shaking his head, Matt pulled up his last chat with DJ and quickly skimmed over the words they'd exchanged over the past week. He'd told her that he'd be in Boston the following week and asked if they could meet. DJ had sent him a surprised-face emoji as a reply…

Matt frowned. A surprised face wasn't a yes…

Neither was it a no…

What it was, was a strange way for DJ to respond.

She'd always been up-front and honest about telling him her plans, whether she could meet him or not. They didn't play games, didn't lie. They either wanted to be together, for a day or three or four, or they didn't. They could either make time for each other, or they couldn't. This year they hadn't managed to meet and that was just the way life went. He presumed she was busy managing her rapidly expanding design firm and he'd had his all-consuming work and the additional personal dramas to deal with...

But could she be dating someone else?

Matt's stomach tightened and he told himself to get a grip. He had no right to be jealous. They'd both agreed they couldn't expect to be monogamous when they were so far apart. He had been for the past year but that was more through circumstances than choice. They'd agreed to be honest with each other, to tell each other if someone else was on the scene. He hadn't had a text or phone call or email from DJ saying that. In fact, since late March, she hadn't reached out to him once. Previously, he'd received the odd email from her, funny memes that made him laugh, silly selfies she took.

Matt frowned, remembering that her friends were worried about her, that they thought something was wrong. Was she sick? Busy? Annoyed?

Or, worse, done with him, with what they had?

His phone beeped again and this time it was a text message. The distinct tone told him who it was from.

Hi. I'm not ready. Can I take some more time?

Sure, he replied. No pressure. I'm in town until after Christmas, unless something urgent comes up.

Right, he had no choice now but to wait until the daughter Gemma had never told him about decided to contact him again. And he wasn't visiting his grandfather until tomorrow.

So, what could he do with the rest of his day?

Mmm, maybe he could drop in to see Dylan-Jane. See whether there was a chance of them taking up where they'd last left off…

And, he admitted, he could see for himself whether she was happy or not.

In the coffee shop on the Lockwood Estate, Mason James delivered an espresso to the student sitting at the table in the corner and glanced at the complex math equation the kid was solving.

Because math had once been his thing, Mason scanned the guy's rough notes and immediately saw where he'd gone wrong. Mason opened his mouth to point out the mistake before pulling back.

Three years ago, complex situations and equations, troubleshooting and problem-solving, was what he'd done for a living and he'd made a stupid amount of money from it. The responsibility of the problems he'd been given to solve—some of them with life-and-death outcomes—had generated enough stress to elevate his blood pressure to dangerous levels and burn a hole in his stomach. It had also ended his marriage and threatened his relationships with his sons.

So Mason got out of the think-tank business, buying a chic coffee shop to keep himself busy. He attended his boys' ice hockey and baseball games, played video games with them and helped them with their homework. He delivered coffee, muffins and pastries and told himself it was good to be bored.

Boredom didn't place a strain on his heart, or burn that hole deeper into his stomach.

Mason turned away and then heard the low curse. He looked around to see the student putting his head in his hands, tugging his hair in obvious frustration. It was, for him, simple math. What harm could it do to help?

Mason turned back, scanned the equation and tapped a line. "Rework this line."

Blue eyes flew up to meet his and Mason saw the doubt.

"With respect, I'm in the doctorate program at MIT…"

Mason shrugged and waited him out. He didn't bother to tell the guy that he'd been through that program and many more. He just tapped the line again until the kid finally turned his attention back to the equation. His brow furrowed and then he released a long sigh. Yep, the light had dawned.

"Hey, thanks so much."

Mason smiled briefly before retracing his steps back to his small kitchen. Before he reached his destination, he heard the muted ping that indicated he had a customer. He didn't need to see who was pulling the door open—his heart was way ahead of his eyes and it was already picking up speed.

Mason leaned his shoulder onto the nearest wall and watched his current obsession walk into his coffee shop, followed by a brunette clutching a stack of bridal magazines. The older of Callie's twin daughters, he remembered—Jules. Callie had her arm around Jules's waist and love for her child on her face.

Callie Brogan was a beautiful mom.

Mason ran his hand over his face. The last thing he was looking for when he opened Coffee Connection was to be attracted to a stunning, ebullient, charming widow. Yeah, she was older than him but who the hell cared? He could date younger woman, *had* dated many of them, and none of them captured his interest like Callie Brogan did. It was unexplainable and not something he could wish away.

God knew he'd tried.

Callie's head shot up and her eyes locked on his. Electricity arced between them and his pants, as they always did when she was in the room, tightened. Even though he was across the room, he could see her nipples respond—God, her breasts were fantastic. A flush appeared on her throat, down her chest. Despite her protests, Callie was as aware of him, as attracted to him, as he was to her...

Why hadn't they ended up in bed already?

Oh, because she wasn't ready and because she was still in love with her dead husband.

Mason looked up at the ceiling and shook his head. His was said to be one of the most brilliant minds of his generation, yet he was flummoxed by how to get this woman to sleep with him.

That's all he wanted, some fantastic sex with an attractive, interesting woman. He wasn't looking for love or forever—as a scientist, he didn't believe in either. The human species simply wasn't that evolved. But sex, a few hot nights? Yeah, he most certainly believed in man's most primal urge.

Mason started toward her—he couldn't stay away if he tried—but the infinitesimal shake of her head stopped him.

Right, he wasn't wanted. He should go and count stock or take out the trash or do his taxes.

Simple, stress-free jobs he could do with his eyes closed. But so blah and boring. Looking through the huge windows of his shop, he wished he could go caveman on Callie. He'd toss her over his shoulder and put her behind him on his Ducati—in his fantasy it was spring or summer—and ride away. When he reached the first isolated area, he'd stop.

He had this fantasy of stripping her down, bending her over his bike and taking her from behind, his hands on her amazing breasts, his lips on her neck, sliding into her wet, warm…

"Sorry, sir? I'm stuck again. Could you help me?"

Mason rubbed his face before squinting at the messy calculations.

Since bike sex, or even warm weather, wasn't in his immediate future, he could do math. And while he mathed, he could also keep an eye on Callie, which was his latest and greatest pleasure.

Two

Matt walked into Brogan and Winston's showroom on Charles Street and looked around.

A counter ran along an exposed brick wall and to the right of it was a waiting area with a striped green-and-white sofa and a white chair, both with perfectly placed orange cushions. Funky art hung on the walls and a vase brimming with fresh flowers sat on the coffee table. He liked what he saw, immediately understanding why Winston and Brogan had such an excellent reputation and were booked solid for months.

DJ, as the CFO, worked behind the scenes, but Matt knew how important her work was to the company's overall success. He couldn't do what he did without Greta, his office manager, who took care of the paperwork, the staff and the billing. Greta was as indispensable to him as DJ was to Winston and Brogan. Her name, after all, was on the door.

Matt heard footsteps on the iron staircase to the left and he turned to see a pair of knee-high boots and sexy knees coming down the stairs. He knew those legs, the shape of them. He'd tasted the backs of those knees, nibbled those pretty toes. The rest of DJ appeared: short skirt over black leggings, a white blouse, that gorgeous long neck. As she hit the bottom stair, he finally got to see her face for the first time in too many months and, as always, her beauty smacked him in the gut.

Her thick hair, as dark as a sable coat, was pulled back into a soft roll, tendrils falling down the sides of her face. Black-rimmed glasses covered her extraordinary brown-black eyes and her lips were covered in a soft pink gloss. She looked both beautiful and bossy, efficient and exciting.

Two steps and she could be in his arms—he'd duck his head and he'd be tasting her.

"Matt."

No excitement, no throwing herself into his arms, God, he didn't even rate a smile? What the hell had happened between last Christmas and now?

Matt took a closer look at her eyes and saw wariness, a healthy dose of I-don't-need-this-today. Well, tough. He didn't like unresolved situations. When he'd left DJ in the UK everything had been fine. Yeah, many months had passed but, unless she now had a boyfriend and had moved on, nothing should've changed. And if she had found someone—a thought that froze the blood in his veins—then why the hell hadn't she just said so? That was their deal, dammit.

"Got someone else, Dylan-Jane?"

It took her a little time to make sense of his words, but when she did, her eyes widened and she quickly shook her head. Yep, that was answer enough. So, no boyfriend. "Then what's the problem?"

DJ glared at him, sent the young receptionist a cool smile and jerked her head toward the stairway. "Can we discuss this in private?"

Matt jammed his hands into the pockets of his pants as he followed DJ up the stairs and down a short passageway to a corner office. He stepped inside the brutally neat room and watched her stride toward her wide desk.

She wanted to put a physical barrier between them but he had no intention of letting that happen. One long step allowed him to capture her wrist. He swung her around and pulled her to him so that her breasts touched his chest and the top of her head brushed his chin. He looked down at her, his mouth quirking at her shocked expression. "So, no new guy, then?"

"No."

Thank God. Matt dropped his gaze from her eyes to her mouth and after a couple of beats, looked her in the eyes again. She immediately understood what he wanted…and yeah, it was what she wanted, too. The attraction between them had always been a living, breathing thing. A year ago, he would've dived into the kiss and been sure of his welcome, but too much time and distance had created a barrier between them. It was hell to wait for her to make the first move, to wait for her to rise onto her toes and fit her mouth against his. It took a minute, maybe more, but then her lips were on his and the world suddenly made sense again.

Matt immediately took control of the kiss, covering her mouth with his, sliding his hands over her hips and bringing her flush against him. His pants immediately shrunk a size as he filled the empty places of his soul by kissing Dylan-Jane. Spice, sex, heat, heaven...

It took less than a heartbeat for Dylan-Jane to open her mouth up to his tongue, and a second later her arms were looped around his neck and her fingers were in his hair. Potent relief ran through him: she still, thank God, wanted him as much as he craved her.

Matt wound his tongue around hers, tasting her spiciness and sweetness, and sighed. Yeah, he'd missed this, missed her breathy moans and the purrs of appreciation she made in the back of her throat.

When DJ's fingers pushed into his hair, when she held his head to keep his mouth on hers, he knew she was fully, completely in the moment with him.

Matt pushed aside his urge to strip her, telling himself that he wasn't going to make love to her on her office couch in the middle of the day. But he could kiss her, let her fill up those hollow spaces in his soul. He needed nothing as much as he needed to hold her...

Soft, sweet and still sexy—Matt felt like he'd conquered the world when she quivered under his touch. He needed to taste more of her, kiss a place more intimate than her mouth, so he flipped open the top buttons of her designer silk shirt and pushed aside the fabric to reveal her lace-and-satin bra. Unable to wait, he pulled aside the cup and there she was, pretty and plump. Ducking his head, he touched his lips to her, swiping his tongue across her nipple, feeling the shudder run through her.

He loved that he could make her feel like this, that he could take her from mad and sad to pleasure, that he could put those purrs in her throat, make her arch her back in eagerness. Her fingers in his hair tightened as he blew air over her nipple and his name on her lips was both a plea and a demand for more.

He moved to her other breast, loving the taste and texture of her. His hand traveled down her hip. Matt slid his other hand over her ass, kneading her under the fabric of her skirt before inching the material up so his fingers brushed the back of her thighs. He wanted those legs around his hips, her breasts in his mouth. He needed to be inside her as soon as possible.

He wanted them naked; he needed *her*. Matt's hand slid between her legs, wishing away the fabric barriers between her secret places and his fingers…

Then Matt was touching air and DJ was…gone.

Matt looked at the empty space between them and shook his head. One minute she was in his arms and the next she was halfway across the room, staring at him, her mouth wet from his kisses and her eyes blurry with desire. She wanted him, so why the hell was she six feet away and he was here? Matt took a step toward her and DJ held up her hands.

"This is my office, Edwards. I'm not about to get naked with you here."

Fair point. How soon could they leave? It had been a hell of a long time since he'd seen her naked, kissed her senseless, heard her moan as she fell apart in his arms.

"I'm not about to get naked with you at all."

Matt blinked. What?

There wasn't anyone else. They'd just shared a kiss hot enough to melt glass. They'd been sleeping together for many years. He was going to be around for the foreseeable future and she was cutting him off?

What was happening here?

What was he missing?

DJ gestured to the sofa. "Take a seat, let's talk."

He'd rather be making love, but since that was out of the question Matt sat down, adjusting his still rock-hard erection and begging it to calm the hell down because it wasn't needed at this precise moment.

"Coffee?" DJ asked.

Matt nodded, stretched out his legs and ordered himself to get a grip. He watched DJ with narrowed eyes as she popped a pod into her fancy machine, powered it up and, when the mug was full, added a dash of milk. Ignoring the sugar dispenser, she walked over, placing the mug on the coffee table in front of him. Then she took the seat opposite him and draped one slim leg over her bouncing knee.

DJ was nervous. Now, that was interesting.

"What are you doing back in Boston, Matt, and how long do you intend to stay?"

"I have some personal business that necessitates me sticking around for a few weeks. One part of that personal business is persuading my grandfather to move into an assisted-living facility."

DJ's eyes turned warm with sympathy and his heart stuttered. He loved her expressive eyes, the way emotions swam through them, the way they resembled luxurious chocolate.

"Is he sick?"

Matt shook his head. "Alzheimer's."

"I'm so sorry, Matt." DJ tipped her head to the side, curiosity all over her face. "And your other personal business?"

He wasn't ready to talk to her, or anyone, about his daughter, Emily.

Besides, he wasn't here to *talk*. He wanted to *feel*. He wanted to touch the skin on the inside of DJ's thighs, pull her tasty nipples into his mouth, nibble her toes.

In her arms, while he loved her, he could forget about the complications of this past year.

Dylan-Jane was his escape, his fantasy woman, the perfect relationship because it was all surface. Because she didn't demand anything more than he was prepared to give.

But instead of falling into him and losing herself in the pleasure he could give her, she was retreating. Hell, if she had "back off, buster" tattooed across her forehead, her message couldn't be any clearer. DJ uncrossed her legs, leaned forward and rested her forearms on her bended knees. She stared at her hands for a long time before looking up at Matt. "Cards on the table, Matt?"

He didn't expect a good hand but nodded anyway.

"Your being back in Boston, even on a short-term basis, doesn't work for me."

Well, hell. Not what he wanted to hear. In his mind, reality crashed into fantasy and he felt a little sick. And a lot disappointed. He'd been relying on having some time with DJ as a way to step out of his head and regroup.

"I have a life here and that life doesn't have room for a hot lawyer who wants to share my bed." DJ glanced at her desk and lifted her eyebrows. "But maybe we can go somewhere in the New Year, see if the magic is still there."

Matt didn't know if she was being serious, and not knowing where he stood pissed him off. And there was something in her tone…something he couldn't put his finger on. Behind her tough-girl words, he could see vulnerability and…was that guilt?

"What aren't you telling me, DJ?"

DJ arched an eyebrow. "I don't know what you're referring to."

Damn if that prissy voice didn't make him harder than he already was, if that was possible. "Spill it, DJ."

Irritation flashed in her eyes and she shook her head, looking weary. "Lawyers. If you weren't so damn hot I wouldn't have hooked up with you." She sighed. "I don't have space in my life for an affair with you, Matt. I work long hours, I like my space. Also, I tend to get cranky around this time of year, so I prefer to be alone."

She didn't like Christmas? Why not? There was a story there. Another one. And why was he suddenly so curious? For seven years, he'd managed not to ask her questions, not to dig deeper, but now his first reaction to new information was to find a spade and start shoveling?

Get a grip, Edwards!

"Apart from a weekend of great sex with you here and there, I like being alone. Seeing you a couple of times a year is enough for me."

Matt leaned back, placed his ankle on his opposite knee and held DJ's gaze. She was trying so hard to remain calm, to persuade him that she was a cold woman who didn't feel anything, but she needed to become a lot better at lying before he bought into her BS. She wasn't cold, or sophisticated, or tough. What she was, was bone-deep scared of having him in Boston.

Why? Why could she easily handle a few days with him but seeing him regularly scared the pants off her?

And why did he care?

And why wasn't he saying to hell with this drama and walking out her door? He could leave, walk down the block and into a bar and, after a couple of cocktails and an hour or two of small talk, he was pretty sure he could score. But he didn't want sex with some random stranger.

There was only one woman he wanted…

Matt leaned forward and swiped his thumb across DJ's lower lip, his fingers lightly stroking her jaw. Desire burned in her eyes and under his fingers her skin heated. Glancing down, he noticed her nipples beading, pushing against the thin fabric of her silk shirt.

She'd never been able to hide her attraction to him, thank God. Because he saw her need for him, could feel her heat, could almost taste her…he pushed.

He kept his voice low, but his tone was resolute. "So here's what's going to happen, Dylan-Jane. I'm going to be living across the road from you and we're going to run into each other often. Your friends are mine and our paths *will* cross. And even if they don't, I'll make damn sure they do. It's been too damn long since I've had you and I want you under me as soon as possible. Yeah, this year has been unusual, I accept that. What I don't accept is this barrier you've flung up between us. But know this, I will pull it down and I will find out why you put it up in the first place."

"Matt—"

"Not done." He narrowed his eyes at her. "We've always been honest with each other and you're not being honest now. While I think part of what you said is true—you like being alone and Christmas sucks— that's not the whole truth."

"You haven't told me the whole truth about why you are back in Boston," DJ pointed out.

He hadn't, he had to give her that. "But that has nothing to do with you, nothing at all, and I know, don't ask me how, that your stay-away-from-me attitude is all about me, about us."

He saw agreement flash in her eyes and sighed. God, what was going on with her? And why couldn't she just spit it out? Matt closed his eyes and released a long breath.

"Jesus, DJ, just tell me already."

DJ stood up, walked over to the window and folded her arms across her stomach. She bowed her head and he could see her shoulders shaking. God, he hoped she wasn't crying. Tears were his Kryptonite. He stood up, went over to her and stood behind her, not touching her but silently offering his support. "You can tell me, Dylan-Jane."

DJ remained silent for a long time and when she finally turned, he saw the capitulation in her eyes. Finally!

"We made love on Christmas Eve and I got pregnant." Her words were a series of punches in his solar plexus. He battled to find air, to make sense of her words. Then DJ took another deep breath and spoke again. "I lost the baby in February."

It took a minute, an hour—a decade—for his brain to restart, his mouth to work. He thought he was calm but when the words flew out of his mouth, they emerged as a roar. "Why the hell didn't you tell me? As soon as you knew?"

DJ's face drained of color and she retreated a step so that her back was flush against the window.

"I tried—"

"Not that hard," Matt shouted, unable to control the volume of his voice. "I had a right to know, dammit! How dare you take that away from me? You lied to me! You let me believe one thing when the exact opposite was true. Jesus, Gemma!"

Gemma? Had he really said that?

Matt stared at DJ, noting her dark eyes dominating her face. She was edging her way to the door, needing to walk away from him. He didn't blame her. In his anger and shock, he'd overlapped Gemma's and DJ's actions and he wasn't sure which situation he was reacting to. He needed to leave, to get his head on straight, to think about what she'd said, what had happened.

To find distance and control.

Matt whirled around, walked to the door and yanked it open. Stepping into the hallway, he saw Jules and Darby jogging down the hallway toward him with Amazonian warrior-woman expressions on their faces. They blocked his path, momma bears protecting their cub.

"What happened?" Jules demanded, her expression fierce.

"Did you hurt her?" Darby asked, equally ferocious. "If you hurt her, we will make her press charges."

God, what did they take him for? "She's fine. We just had an argument," Matt wearily replied.

Air, he needed air.

"If she's hurt, Edwards, I swear to God we'll string you up," Darby told him before she and Jules pushed past him and rushed down the hallway to their friend's office.

Matt watched them rush away, his heart trying to claw its way out of his chest. He rubbed his hand over his breastbone, trying to ease the ache, a part of him still not believing DJ's declaration. For the second time in his life, he'd heard that a woman had miscarried his baby. Unlike the last time he'd experienced this news, the baby he'd briefly given DJ would not, like Emily had earlier this year, write him a letter and tell him that he, or she, was his biological child and ask if they could meet.

He didn't want a family, wasn't cut out to be a dad, but, *man*, that thought made him feel profoundly sad.